Thea Stilton
2 IN 1 #1

PAPERCUTZ ™

Thea Stilton

GRAPHIC NOVELS AVAILABLE FROM PAPERCUTZ

...ALSO AVAILABLE WHEREVER E-BOOKS ARE SOLD!

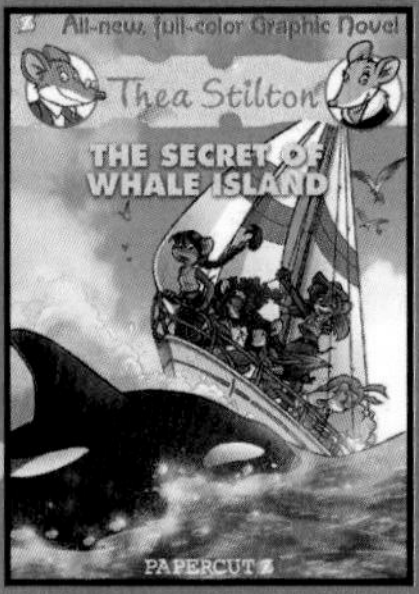
All-new, full-color Graphic Novel
Thea Stilton
THE SECRET OF WHALE ISLAND
PAPERCUTZ
#1
"The Secret of Whale Island"

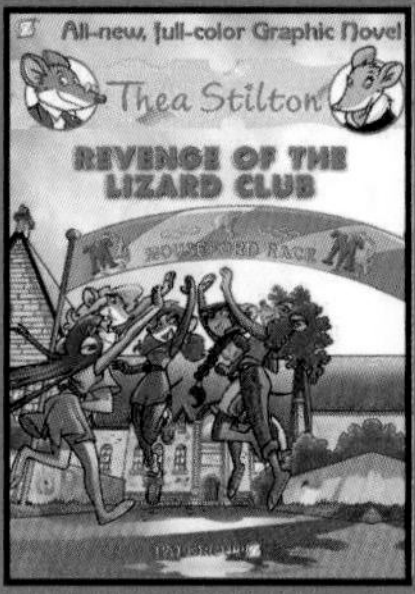
All-new, full-color Graphic Novel
Thea Stilton
REVENGE OF THE LIZARD CLUB
#2
"Revenge of the Lizard Club"

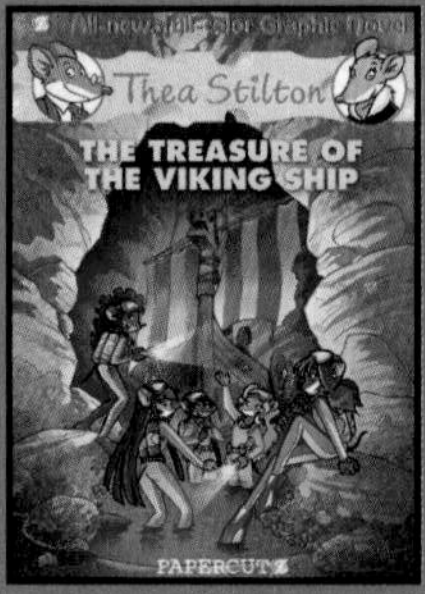
All-new, full-color Graphic Novel
Thea Stilton
THE TREASURE OF THE VIKING SHIP
PAPERCUTZ
#3
"The Treasure of the Viking Ship"

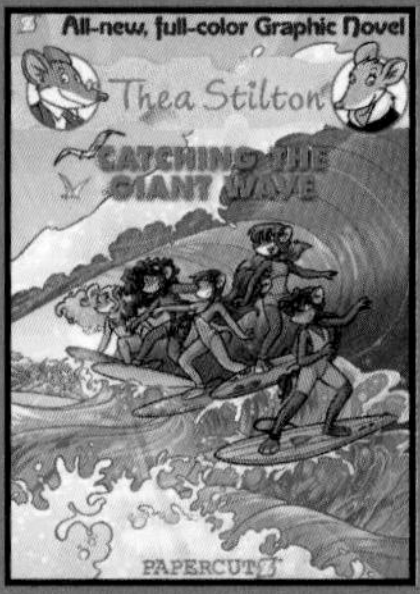
All-new, full-color Graphic Novel
Thea Stilton
CATCHING THE GIANT WAVE
PAPERCUTZ
#4
"Catching the Giant Wave"

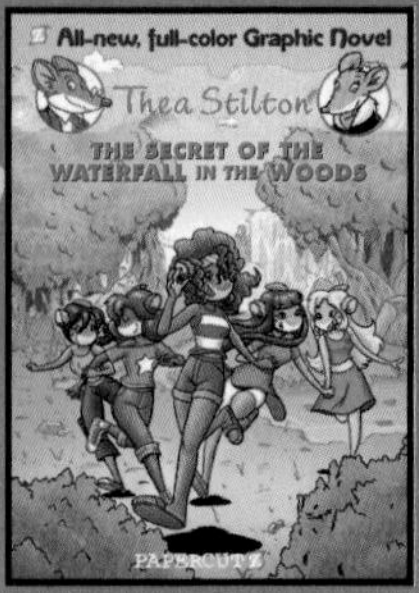
All-new, full-color Graphic Novel
Thea Stilton
THE SECRET OF THE WATERFALL IN THE WOODS
PAPERCUTZ
#5
"The Secret of the Waterfall in the Woods"

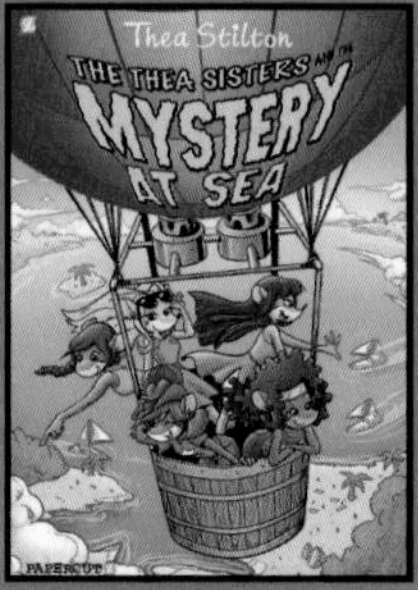
Thea Stilton
THE THEA SISTERS AND THE
MYSTERY AT SEA
PAPERCUTZ
#6
"The Thea Sisters and the Mystery at Sea"

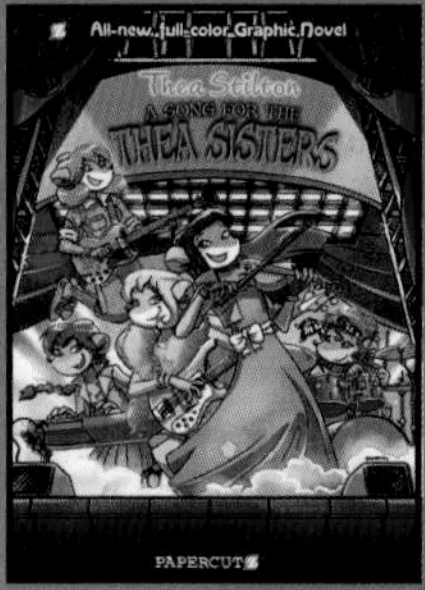
All-new, full-color Graphic Novel
Thea Stilton
A SONG FOR THE THEA SISTERS
PAPERCUTZ
#7
"A Song for the Thea Sisters"

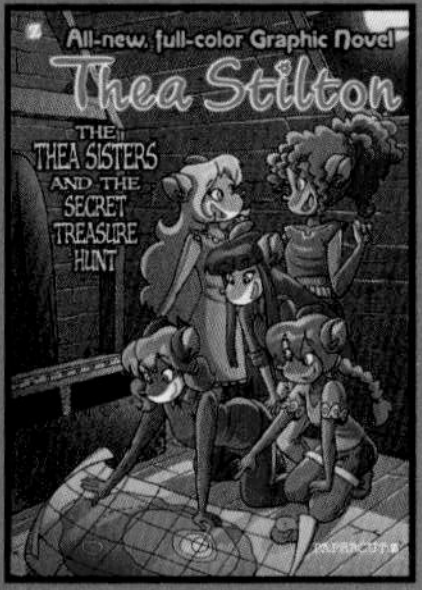
All-new, full-color Graphic Novel
Thea Stilton
THE THEA SISTERS AND THE SECRET TREASURE HUNT
PAPERCUTZ
#8
"The Thea Sisters and the Secret Treasure Hunt"

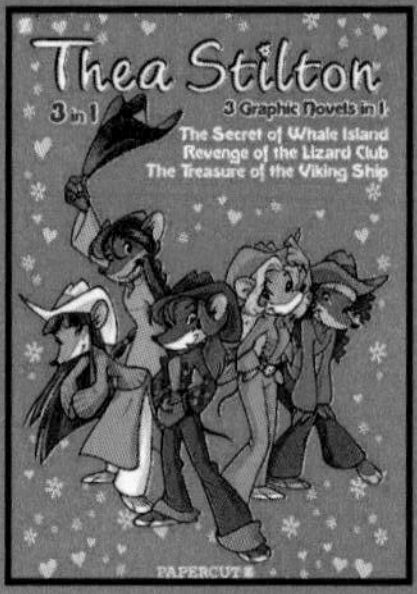
Thea Stilton
3 in 1
3 Graphic Novels in 1
The Secret of Whale Island
Revenge of the Lizard Club
The Treasure of the Viking Ship
PAPERCUTZ
#1
Thea Stilton 3 IN 1

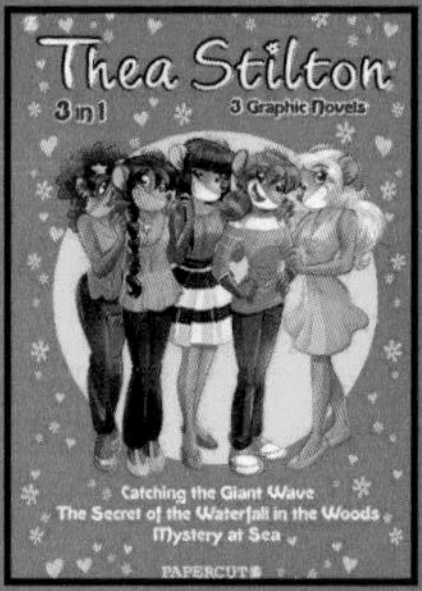
Thea Stilton
3 in 1
3 Graphic Novels
Catching the Giant Wave
The Secret of the Waterfall in the Woods
Mystery at Sea
PAPERCUTZ
#2
Thea Stilton 3 IN 1

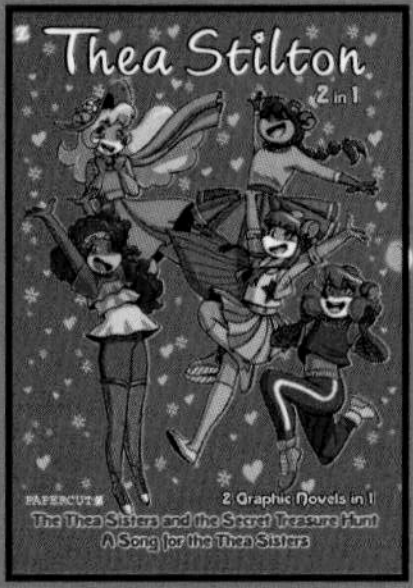
Thea Stilton
2 in 1
PAPERCUTZ
2 Graphic Novels in 1
The Thea Sisters and the Secret Treasure Hunt
A Song for the Thea Sisters
#1
Thea Stilton 2 IN 1

See more at papercutz.com

Thea Stilton
2 in 1 #1

"A Song for the Thea Sisters"
"The Thea Sisters and the Secret Treasure Hunt"

by Thea Stilton

New York

THEA STILTON 2 IN 1 #1

Based on an original idea by Elisabetta Dami

"A Song for the Thea Sisters"

Story by Thea Stilton
Original cover art by Ryan Jampole
Editorial supervision by Alessandra Berello and Chiara Richelmi (Atlantyca S.p.A.)
Script by Francesco Savino
Translation by Nanette McGuinness
Art by Ryan Jampole
Color by Laurie E. Smith
Lettering by Wilson Ramos Jr.

"The Thea Sisters and the Secret Treasure Hunt"

Story by Thea Stilton
Original cover art by Ryan Jampole
Editorial supervision by Alessandra Berello and Chiara Richelmi (Atlantyca S.p.A.)
Script by Francesco Savino
Translation by Nanette McGuinness
Art by Ryan Jampole
Color by Laurie E. Smith
Lettering by Wilson Ramos Jr.

Production – Big Bird Zatryb
Editorial Intern – Izzy Boyce-Blanchard
Managing Editor – Jeff Whitman
Jim Salicrup
Editor-in-Chief

ISBN: 978-1-5458-0417-9

Printed in India
January 2020

Papercutz books may be purchased for business or promotional use.
For information on bulk purchases, please contact Macmillan Corporate and Premium Sales Department at (800) 221-7945 x5442.

Distributed by Macmillan
First Printing

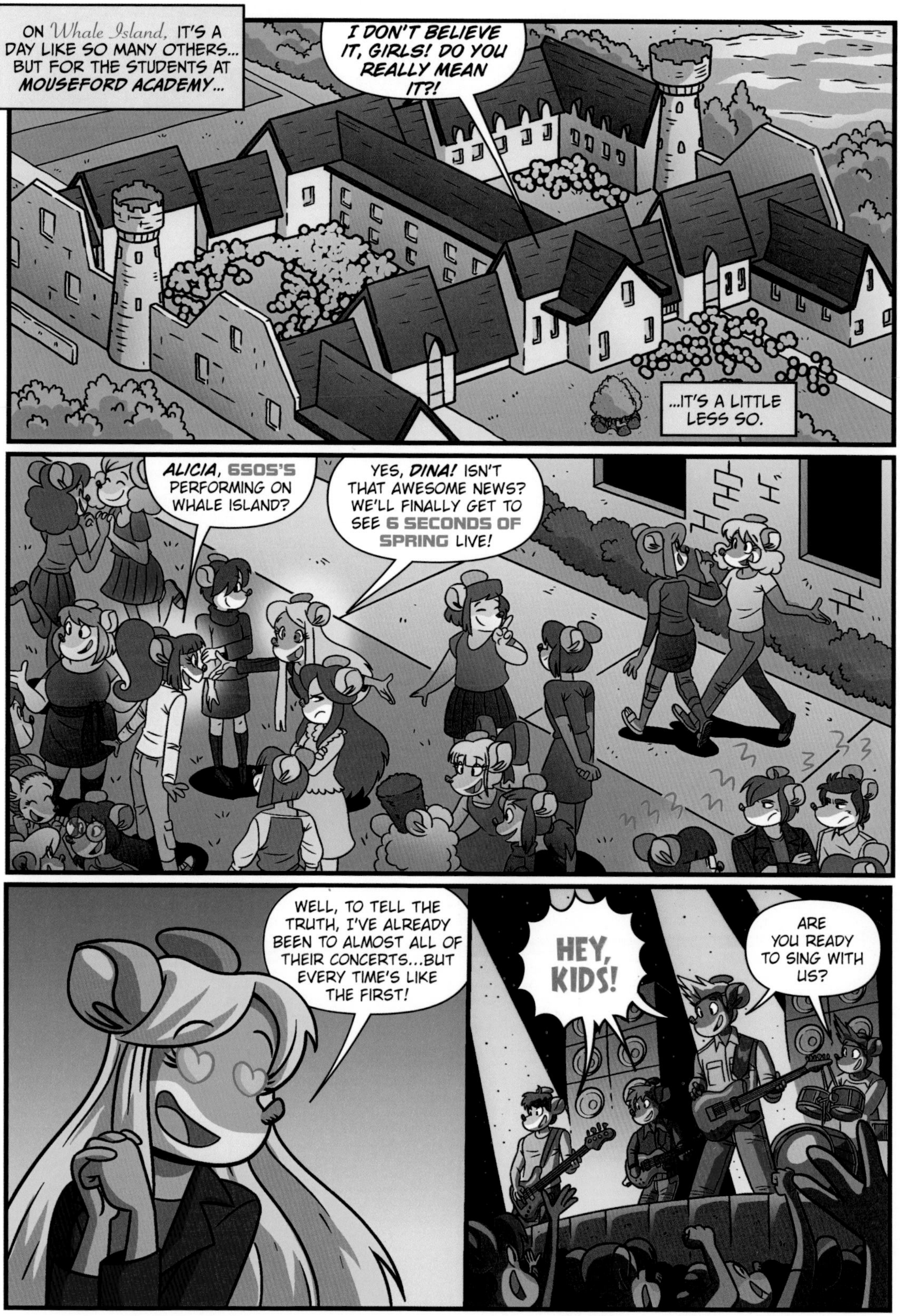
ON *Whale Island,* IT'S A DAY LIKE SO MANY OTHERS... BUT FOR THE STUDENTS AT MOUSEFORD ACADEMY...
I DON'T BELIEVE IT, GIRLS! DO YOU REALLY MEAN IT?!
...IT'S A LITTLE LESS SO.
ALICIA, 6SOS'S PERFORMING ON WHALE ISLAND?
YES, DINA! ISN'T THAT AWESOME NEWS? WE'LL FINALLY GET TO SEE 6 SECONDS OF SPRING LIVE!
WELL, TO TELL THE TRUTH, I'VE ALREADY BEEN TO ALMOST ALL OF THEIR CONCERTS...BUT EVERY TIME'S LIKE THE FIRST!
HEY, KIDS!
ARE YOU READY TO SING WITH US?

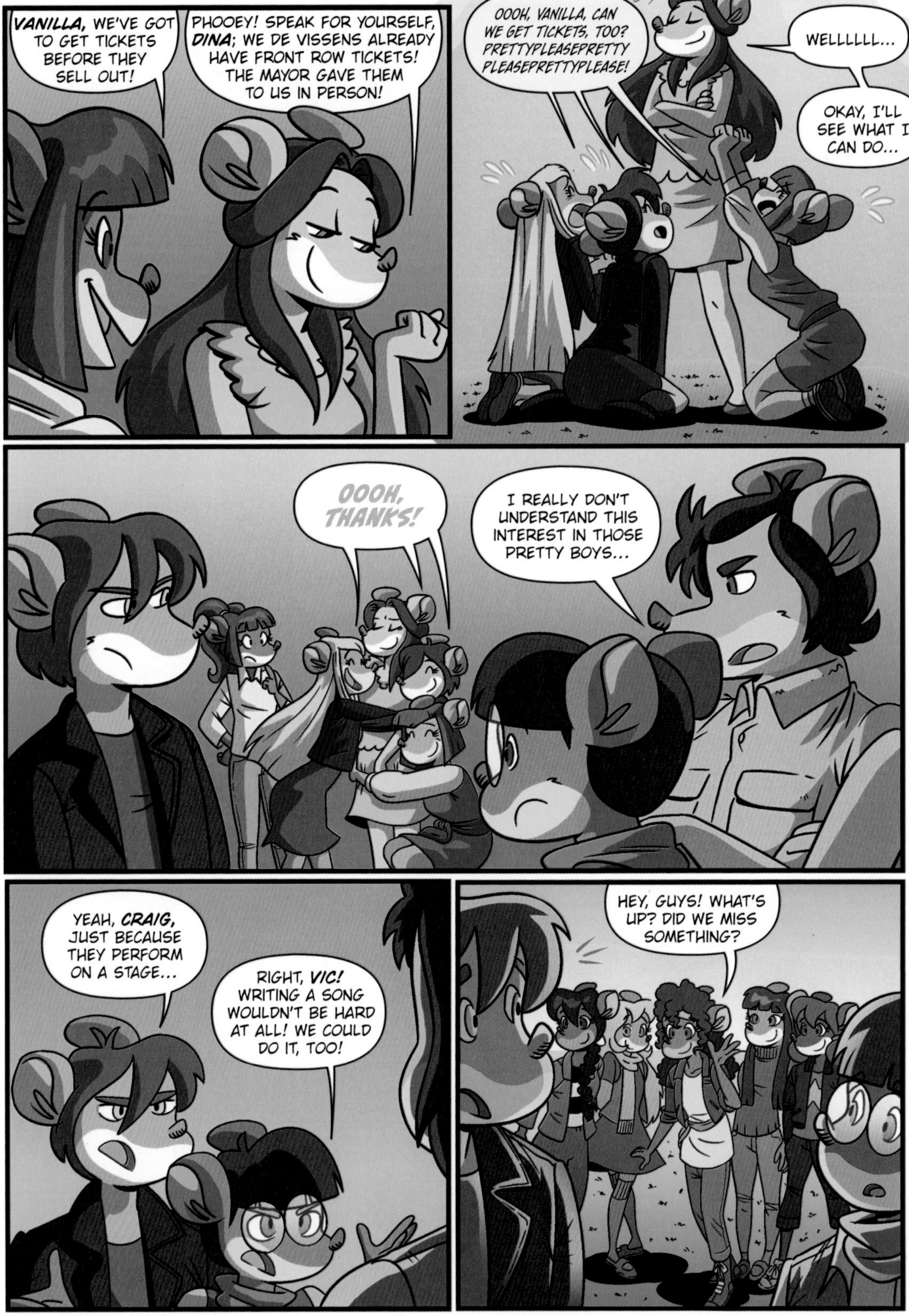
VANILLA, WE'VE GOT TO GET TICKETS BEFORE THEY SELL OUT!
PHOOEY! SPEAK FOR YOURSELF, DINA; WE DE VISSENS ALREADY HAVE FRONT ROW TICKETS! THE MAYOR GAVE THEM TO US IN PERSON!
OOOH, VANILLA, CAN WE GET TICKETS, TOO? PRETTYPLEASEPRETTY PLEASEPRETTYPLEASE!
WELLLLLL...
OKAY, I'LL SEE WHAT I CAN DO...
OOOH, THANKS!
I REALLY DON'T UNDERSTAND THIS INTEREST IN THOSE PRETTY BOYS...
YEAH, CRAIG, JUST BECAUSE THEY PERFORM ON A STAGE...
RIGHT, VIC! WRITING A SONG WOULDN'T BE HARD AT ALL! WE COULD DO IT, TOO!
HEY, GUYS! WHAT'S UP? DID WE MISS SOMETHING?

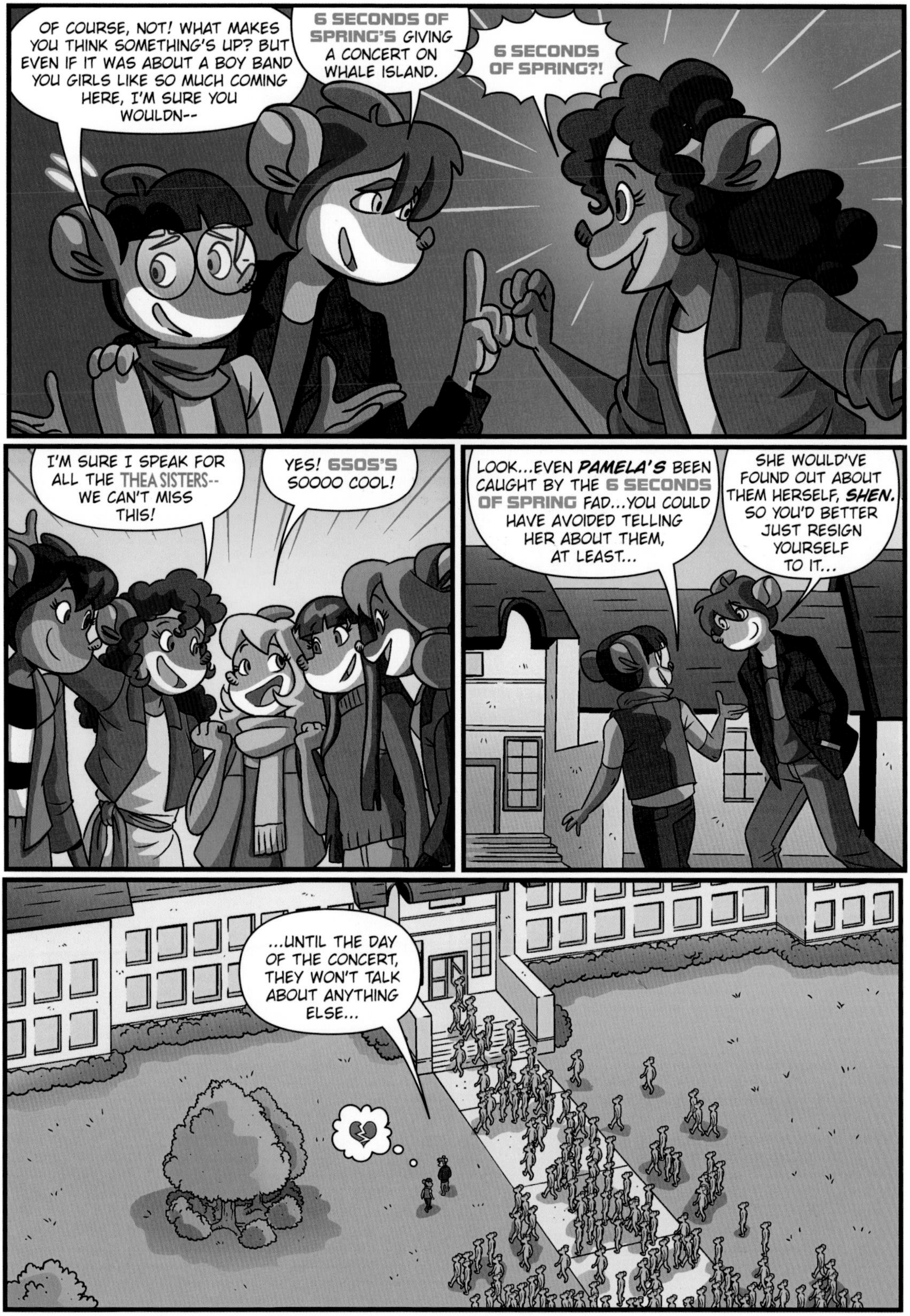

OF COURSE, NOT! WHAT MAKES YOU THINK SOMETHING'S UP? BUT EVEN IF IT WAS ABOUT A BOY BAND YOU GIRLS LIKE SO MUCH COMING HERE, I'M SURE YOU WOULDN--
6 SECONDS OF SPRING'S GIVING A CONCERT ON WHALE ISLAND.
6 SECONDS OF SPRING?!
I'M SURE I SPEAK FOR ALL THE THEA SISTERS-- WE CAN'T MISS THIS!
YES! 6SOS'S SOOOO COOL!
LOOK...EVEN PAMELA'S BEEN CAUGHT BY THE 6 SECONDS OF SPRING FAD...YOU COULD HAVE AVOIDED TELLING HER ABOUT THEM, AT LEAST...
SHE WOULD'VE FOUND OUT ABOUT THEM HERSELF, SHEN. SO YOU'D BETTER JUST RESIGN YOURSELF TO IT...
...UNTIL THE DAY OF THE CONCERT, THEY WON'T TALK ABOUT ANYTHING ELSE...

BEST NOT THINK ABOUT IT AND FOCUS ON CLASSES...

ATTENTION, ALL MOUSEFORD ACADEMY STUDENTS...

...PROCEED TO THE GYMNASIUM FOR A MEETING. THE HEADMASTER HAS AN ANNOUNCEMENT.

HUH?

WHAT'S THAT ABOUT?

WHO KNOWS...? MAYBE SOME EXTRA EXAMS?

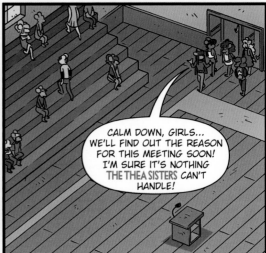

CALM DOWN, GIRLS... WE'LL FIND OUT THE REASON FOR THIS MEETING SOON! I'M SURE IT'S NOTHING THE THEA SISTERS CAN'T HANDLE!

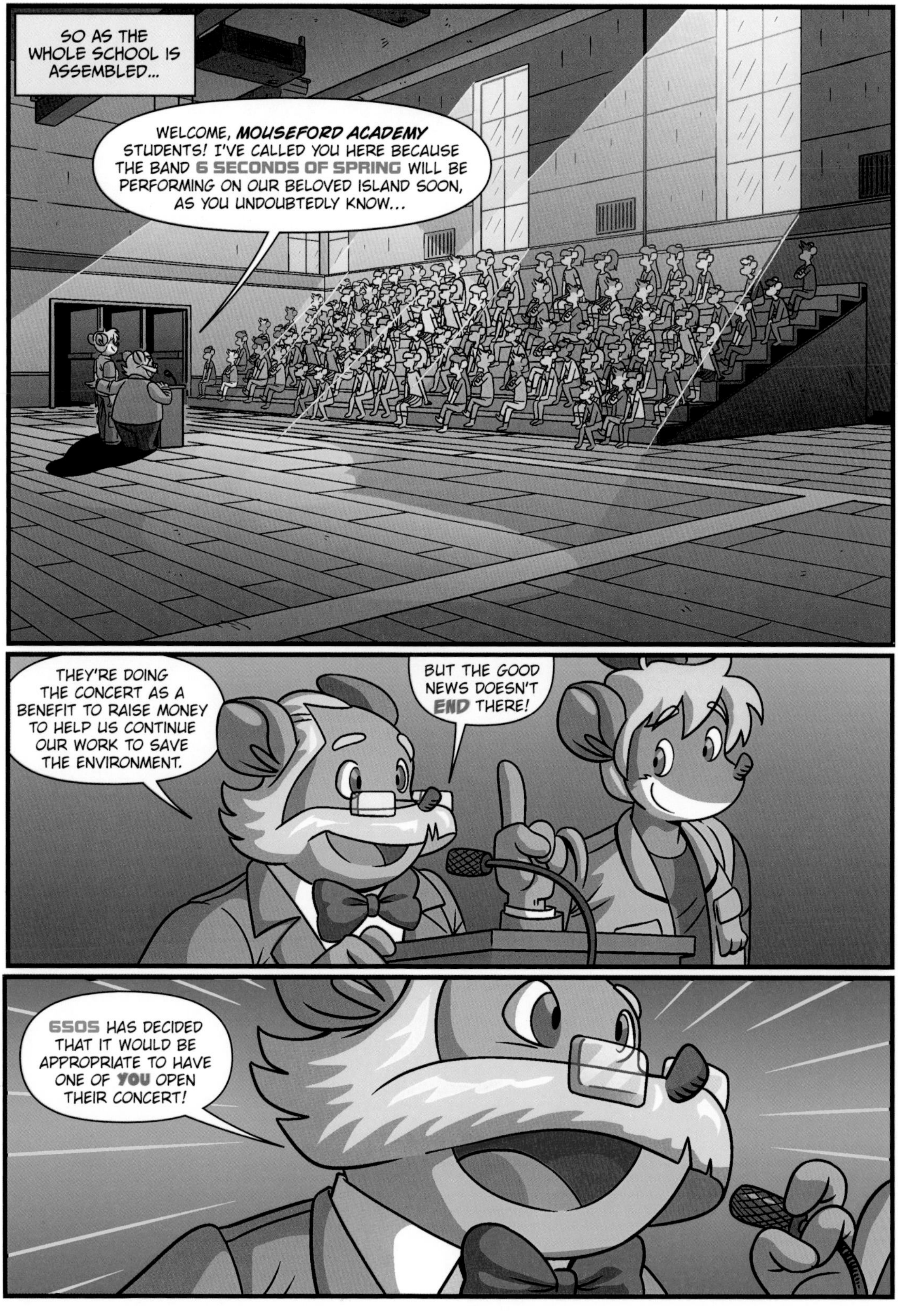
SO AS THE WHOLE SCHOOL IS ASSEMBLED...
WELCOME, ***MOUSEFORD ACADEMY*** STUDENTS! I'VE CALLED YOU HERE BECAUSE THE BAND **6 SECONDS OF SPRING** WILL BE PERFORMING ON OUR BELOVED ISLAND SOON, AS YOU UNDOUBTEDLY KNOW...
THEY'RE DOING THE CONCERT AS A BENEFIT TO RAISE MONEY TO HELP US CONTINUE OUR WORK TO SAVE THE ENVIRONMENT.
BUT THE GOOD NEWS DOESN'T **END** THERE!
6SOS HAS DECIDED THAT IT WOULD BE APPROPRIATE TO HAVE ONE OF **YOU** OPEN THEIR CONCERT!

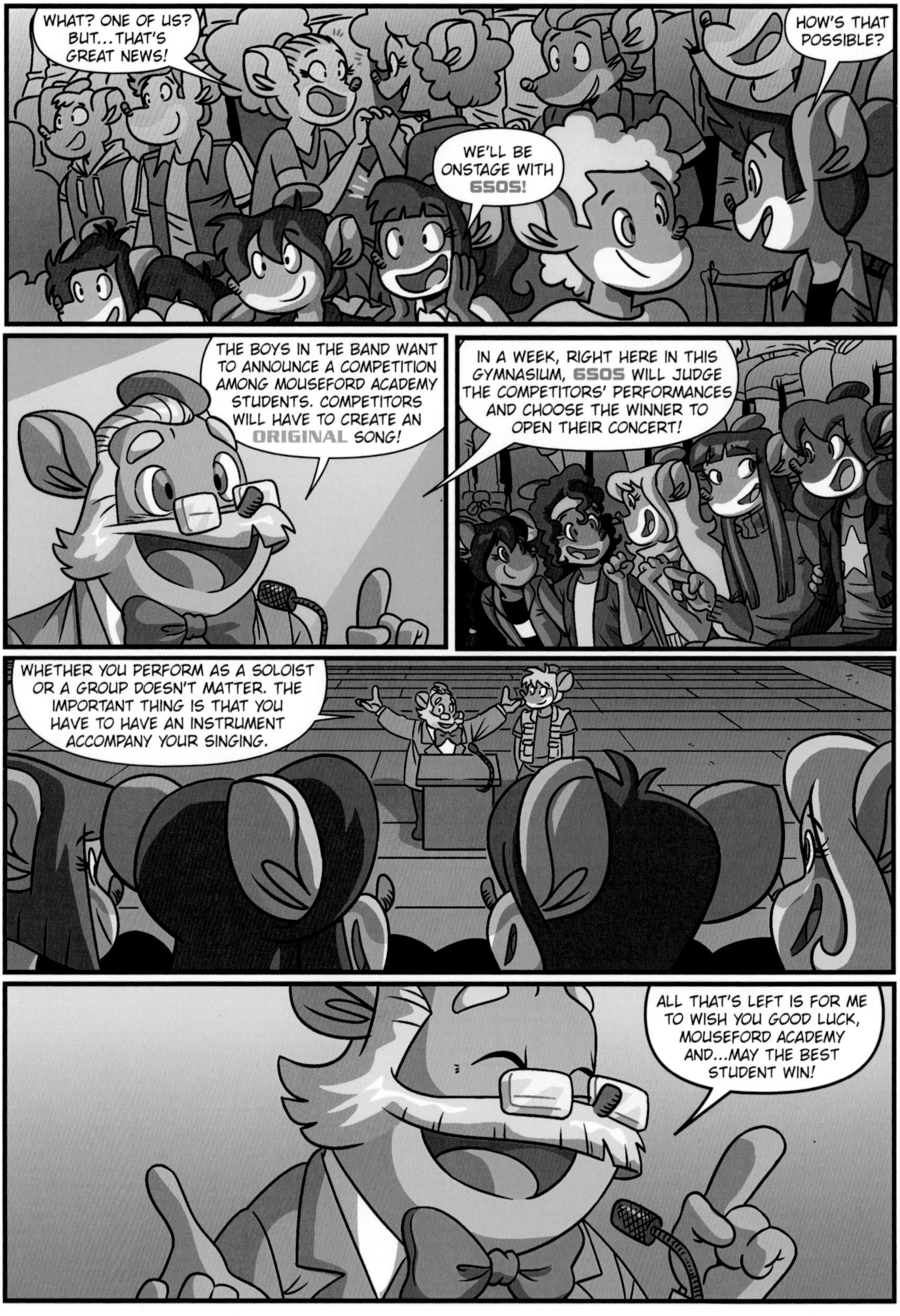
WHAT? ONE OF US? BUT...THAT'S GREAT NEWS!
HOW'S THAT POSSIBLE?
WE'LL BE ONSTAGE WITH 6SOS!
THE BOYS IN THE BAND WANT TO ANNOUNCE A COMPETITION AMONG MOUSEFORD ACADEMY STUDENTS. COMPETITORS WILL HAVE TO CREATE AN ORIGINAL SONG!
IN A WEEK, RIGHT HERE IN THIS GYMNASIUM, 6SOS WILL JUDGE THE COMPETITORS' PERFORMANCES AND CHOOSE THE WINNER TO OPEN THEIR CONCERT!
WHETHER YOU PERFORM AS A SOLOIST OR A GROUP DOESN'T MATTER. THE IMPORTANT THING IS THAT YOU HAVE TO HAVE AN INSTRUMENT ACCOMPANY YOUR SINGING.
ALL THAT'S LEFT IS FOR ME TO WISH YOU GOOD LUCK, MOUSEFORD ACADEMY AND...MAY THE BEST STUDENT WIN!

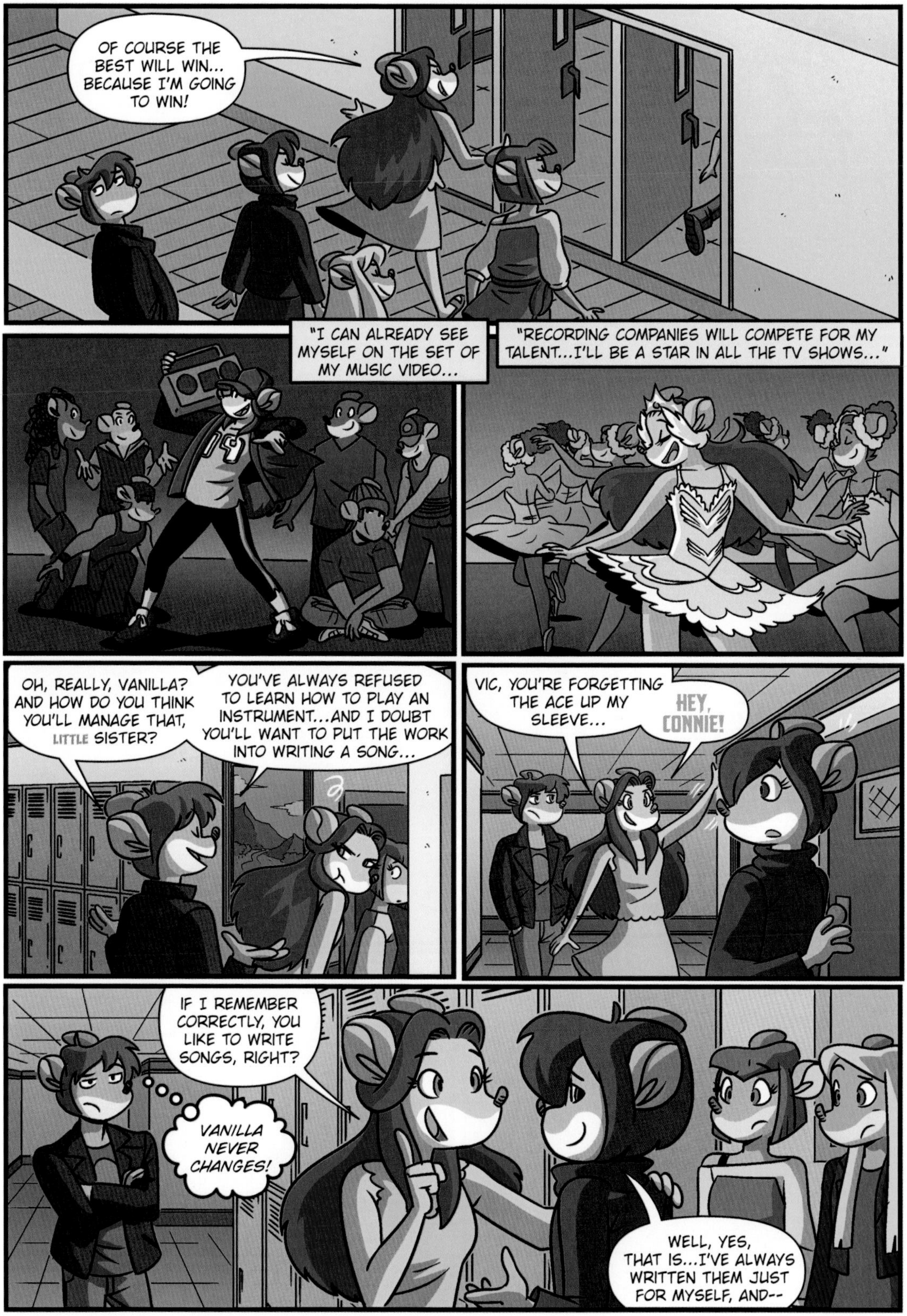
OF COURSE THE BEST WILL WIN... BECAUSE I'M GOING TO WIN!
"I CAN ALREADY SEE MYSELF ON THE SET OF MY MUSIC VIDEO...
"RECORDING COMPANIES WILL COMPETE FOR MY TALENT...I'LL BE A STAR IN ALL THE TV SHOWS..."
OH, REALLY, VANILLA? AND HOW DO YOU THINK YOU'LL MANAGE THAT, LITTLE SISTER?
YOU'VE ALWAYS REFUSED TO LEARN HOW TO PLAY AN INSTRUMENT...AND I DOUBT YOU'LL WANT TO PUT THE WORK INTO WRITING A SONG...
VIC, YOU'RE FORGETTING THE ACE UP MY SLEEVE...
HEY, CONNIE!
IF I REMEMBER CORRECTLY, YOU LIKE TO WRITE SONGS, RIGHT?
VANILLA NEVER CHANGES!
WELL, YES, THAT IS...I'VE ALWAYS WRITTEN THEM JUST FOR MYSELF, AND--

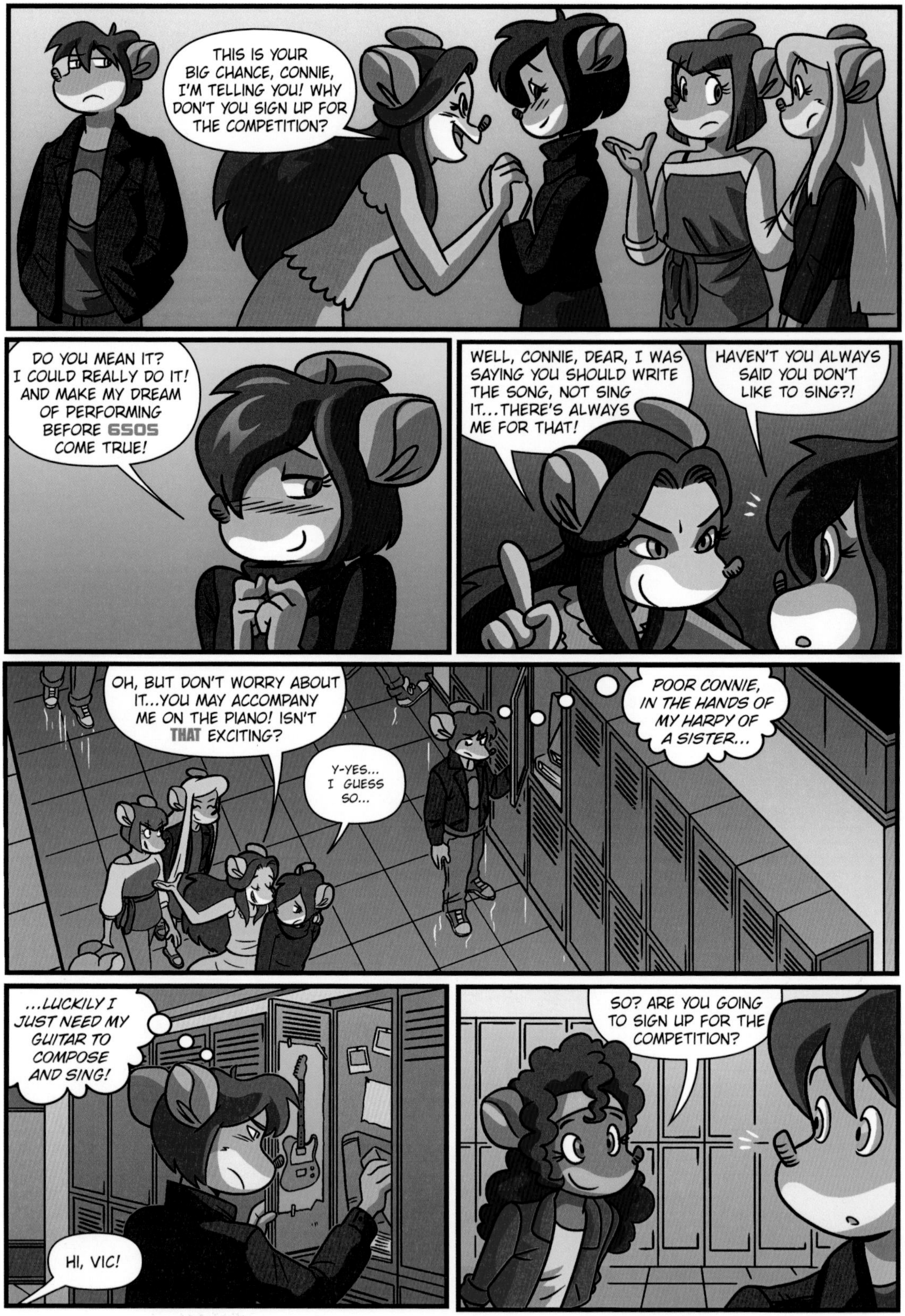
THIS IS YOUR BIG CHANCE, CONNIE, I'M TELLING YOU! WHY DON'T YOU SIGN UP FOR THE COMPETITION?
DO YOU MEAN IT? I COULD REALLY DO IT! AND MAKE MY DREAM OF PERFORMING BEFORE 6505 COME TRUE!
WELL, CONNIE, DEAR, I WAS SAYING YOU SHOULD WRITE THE SONG, NOT SING IT...THERE'S ALWAYS ME FOR THAT!
HAVEN'T YOU ALWAYS SAID YOU DON'T LIKE TO SING?!
OH, BUT DON'T WORRY ABOUT IT...YOU MAY ACCOMPANY ME ON THE PIANO! ISN'T THAT EXCITING?
POOR CONNIE, IN THE HANDS OF MY HARPY OF A SISTER...
Y-YES... I GUESS SO...
...LUCKILY I JUST NEED MY GUITAR TO COMPOSE AND SING!
HI, VIC!
SO? ARE YOU GOING TO SIGN UP FOR THE COMPETITION?

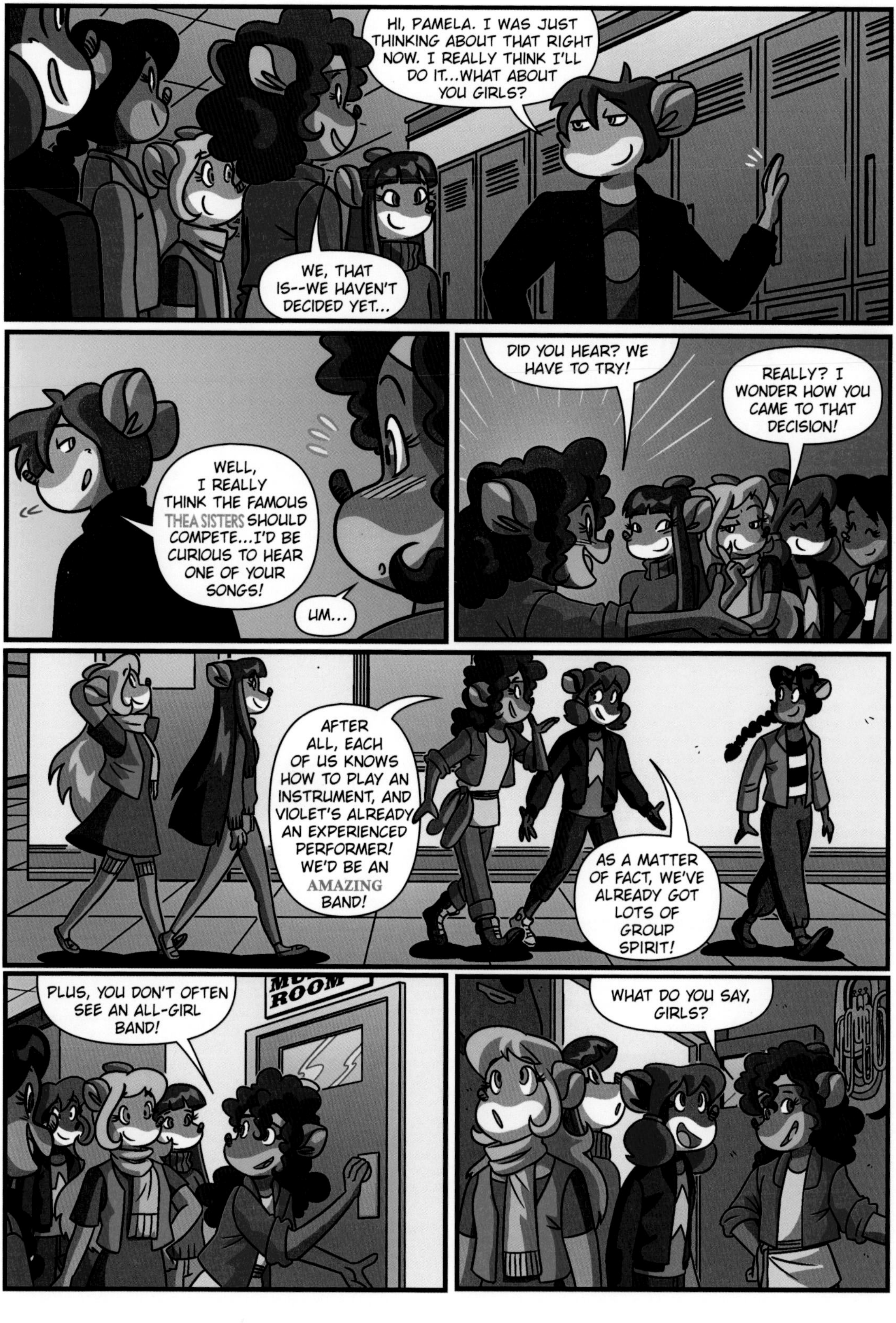
HI, PAMELA. I WAS JUST THINKING ABOUT THAT RIGHT NOW. I REALLY THINK I'LL DO IT...WHAT ABOUT YOU GIRLS?
WE, THAT IS--WE HAVEN'T DECIDED YET...
WELL, I REALLY THINK THE FAMOUS THEA SISTERS SHOULD COMPETE...I'D BE CURIOUS TO HEAR ONE OF YOUR SONGS!
UM...
DID YOU HEAR? WE HAVE TO TRY!
REALLY? I WONDER HOW YOU CAME TO THAT DECISION!
AFTER ALL, EACH OF US KNOWS HOW TO PLAY AN INSTRUMENT, AND VIOLET'S ALREADY AN EXPERIENCED PERFORMER! WE'D BE AN AMAZING BAND!
AS A MATTER OF FACT, WE'VE ALREADY GOT LOTS OF GROUP SPIRIT!
PLUS, YOU DON'T OFTEN SEE AN ALL-GIRL BAND!
WHAT DO YOU SAY, GIRLS?

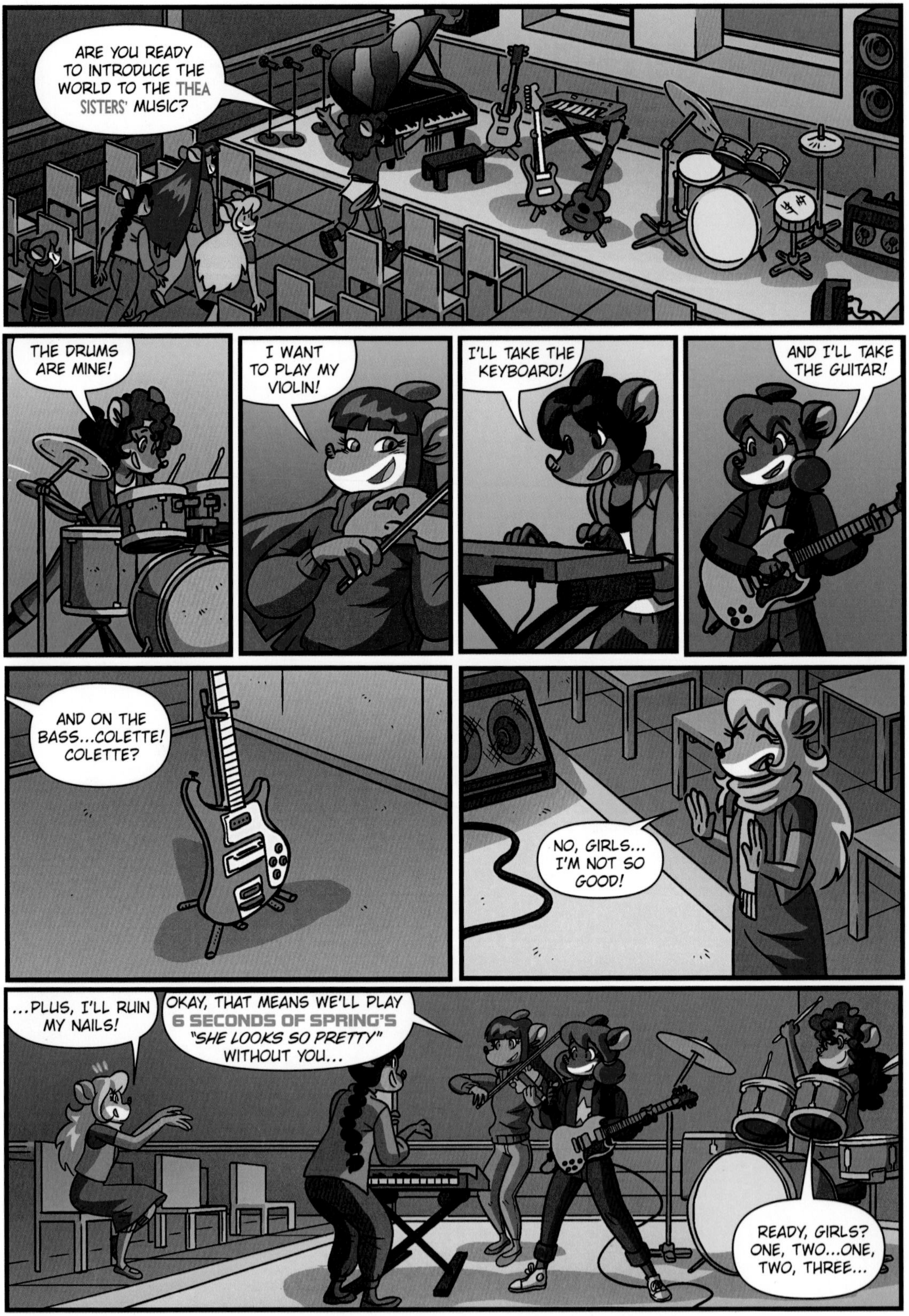
ARE YOU READY TO INTRODUCE THE WORLD TO THE THEA SISTERS' MUSIC?
THE DRUMS ARE MINE!
I WANT TO PLAY MY VIOLIN!
I'LL TAKE THE KEYBOARD!
AND I'LL TAKE THE GUITAR!
AND ON THE BASS...COLETTE! COLETTE?
NO, GIRLS... I'M NOT SO GOOD!
...PLUS, I'LL RUIN MY NAILS!
OKAY, THAT MEANS WE'LL PLAY 6 SECONDS OF SPRING'S "SHE LOOKS SO PRETTY" WITHOUT YOU...
READY, GIRLS? ONE, TWO...ONE, TWO, THREE...

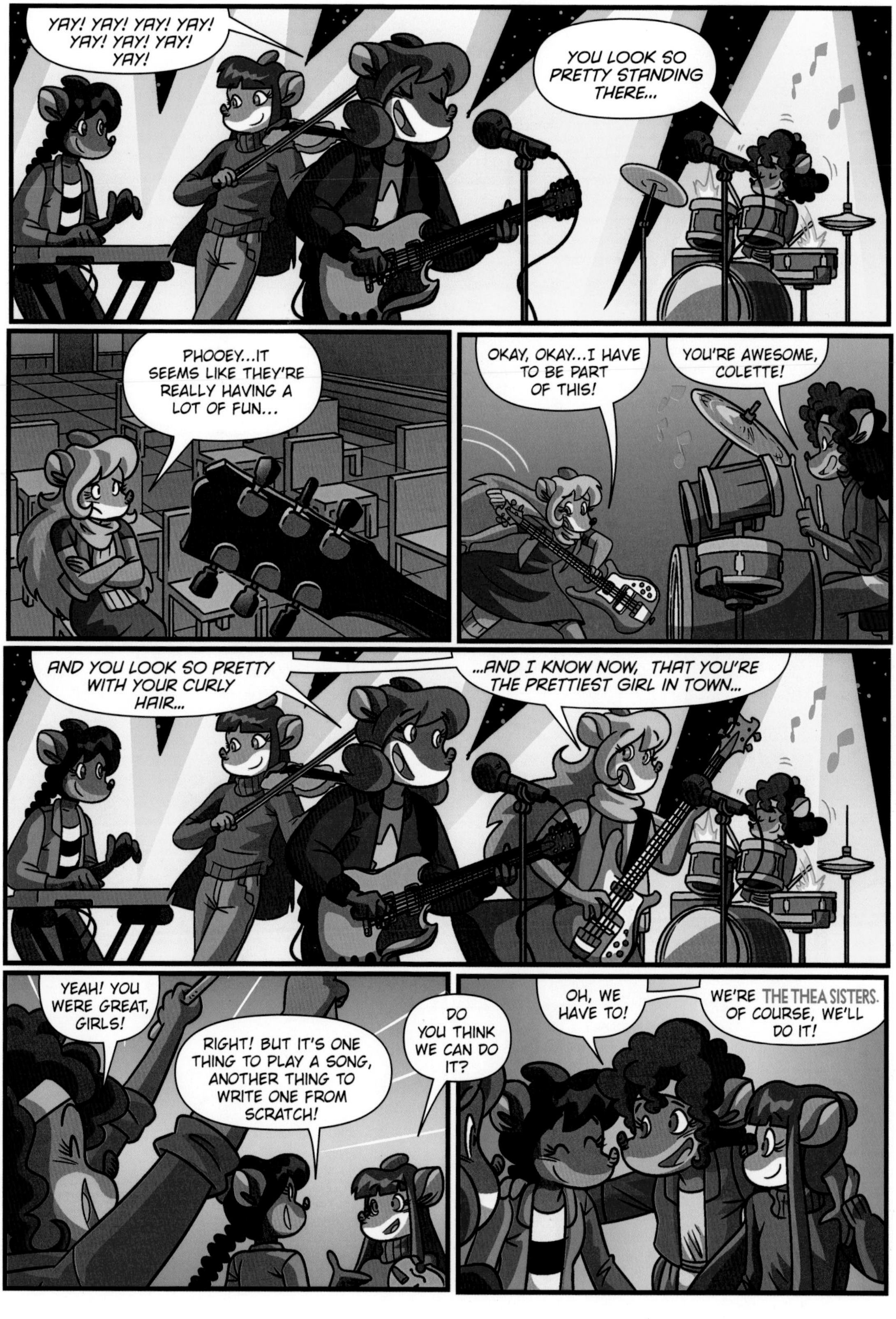
YAY! YAY! YAY! YAY! YAY! YAY! YAY! YAY!
YOU LOOK SO PRETTY STANDING THERE...
PHOOEY...IT SEEMS LIKE THEY'RE REALLY HAVING A LOT OF FUN...
OKAY, OKAY...I HAVE TO BE PART OF THIS!
YOU'RE AWESOME, COLETTE!
AND YOU LOOK SO PRETTY WITH YOUR CURLY HAIR...
...AND I KNOW NOW, THAT YOU'RE THE PRETTIEST GIRL IN TOWN...
YEAH! YOU WERE GREAT, GIRLS!
RIGHT! BUT IT'S ONE THING TO PLAY A SONG, ANOTHER THING TO WRITE ONE FROM SCRATCH!
DO YOU THINK WE CAN DO IT?
OH, WE HAVE TO!
WE'RE THE THEA SISTERS. OF COURSE, WE'LL DO IT!

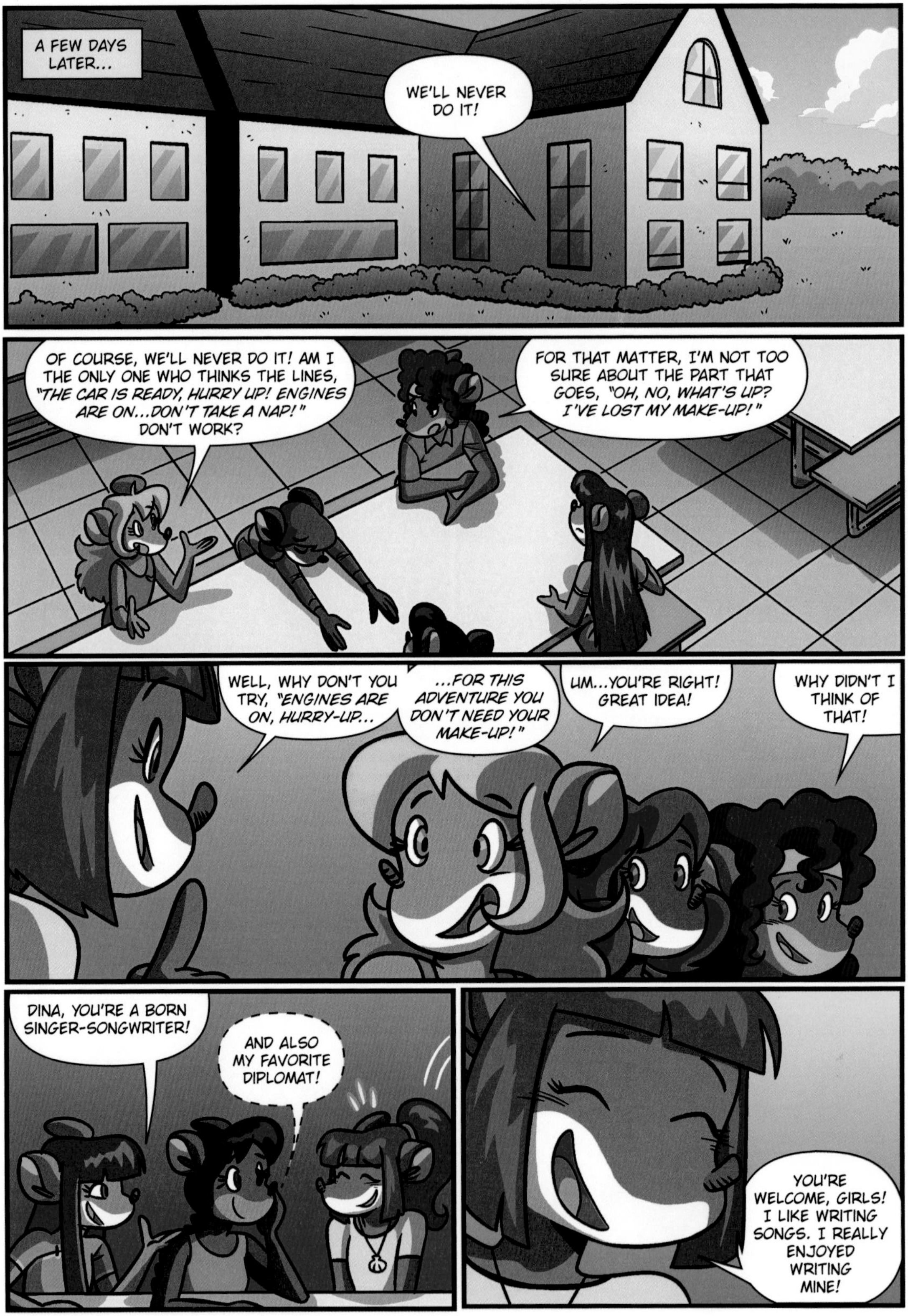
A FEW DAYS LATER...
WE'LL NEVER DO IT!
OF COURSE, WE'LL NEVER DO IT! AM I THE ONLY ONE WHO THINKS THE LINES, "THE CAR IS READY, HURRY UP! ENGINES ARE ON...DON'T TAKE A NAP!" DON'T WORK?
FOR THAT MATTER, I'M NOT TOO SURE ABOUT THE PART THAT GOES, "OH, NO, WHAT'S UP? I'VE LOST MY MAKE-UP!"
WELL, WHY DON'T YOU TRY, "ENGINES ARE ON, HURRY-UP...
...FOR THIS ADVENTURE YOU DON'T NEED YOUR MAKE-UP!"
UM...YOU'RE RIGHT! GREAT IDEA!
WHY DIDN'T I THINK OF THAT!
DINA, YOU'RE A BORN SINGER-SONGWRITER!
AND ALSO MY FAVORITE DIPLOMAT!
YOU'RE WELCOME, GIRLS! I LIKE WRITING SONGS. I REALLY ENJOYED WRITING MINE!

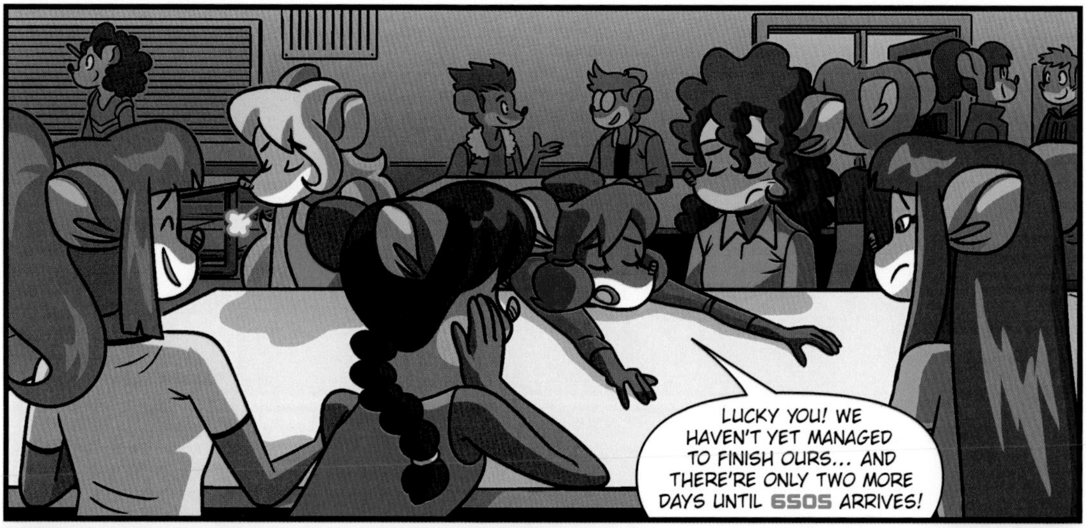
LUCKY YOU! WE HAVEN'T YET MANAGED TO FINISH OURS... AND THERE'RE ONLY TWO MORE DAYS UNTIL 6SOS ARRIVES!

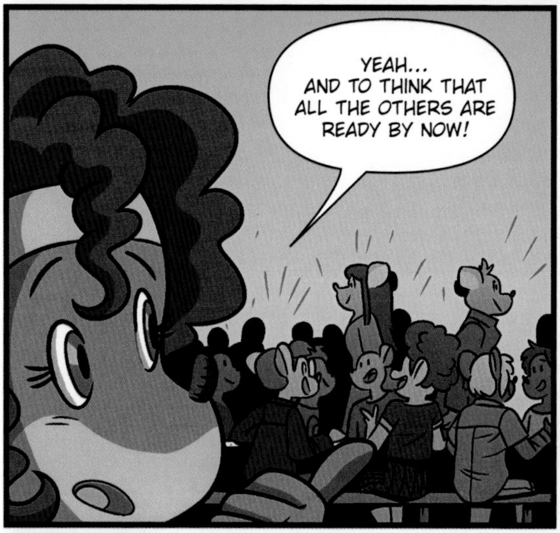
YEAH... AND TO THINK THAT ALL THE OTHERS ARE READY BY NOW!

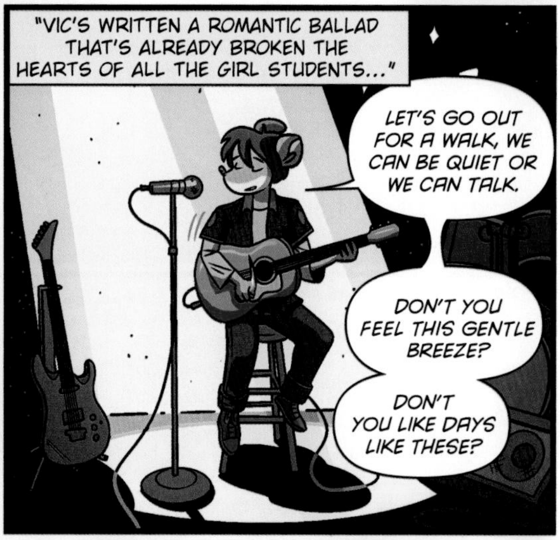
"VIC'S WRITTEN A ROMANTIC BALLAD THAT'S ALREADY BROKEN THE HEARTS OF ALL THE GIRL STUDENTS..."
LET'S GO OUT FOR A WALK, WE CAN BE QUIET OR WE CAN TALK.
DON'T YOU FEEL THIS GENTLE BREEZE?
DON'T YOU LIKE DAYS LIKE THESE?

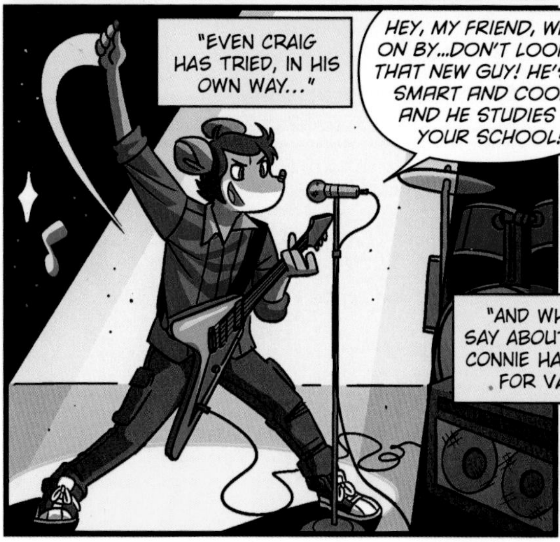
"EVEN CRAIG HAS TRIED, IN HIS OWN WAY..."
HEY, MY FRIEND, WALK ON BY...DON'T LOOK AT THAT NEW GUY! HE'S SO SMART AND COOL... AND HE STUDIES IN YOUR SCHOOL!

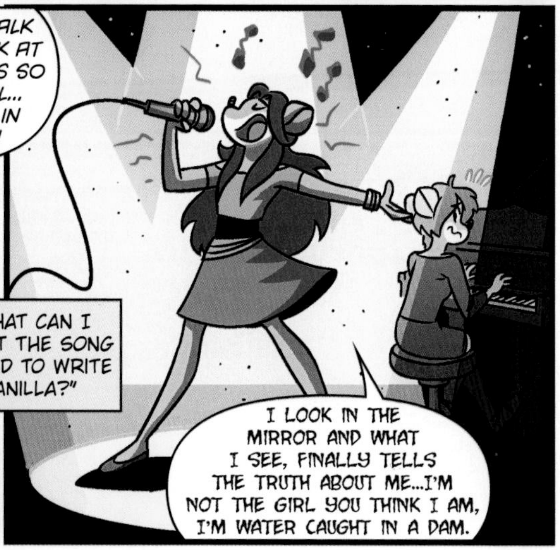
"AND WHAT CAN I SAY ABOUT THE SONG CONNIE HAD TO WRITE FOR VANILLA?"
I LOOK IN THE MIRROR AND WHAT I SEE, FINALLY TELLS THE TRUTH ABOUT ME...I'M NOT THE GIRL YOU THINK I AM, I'M WATER CAUGHT IN A DAM.

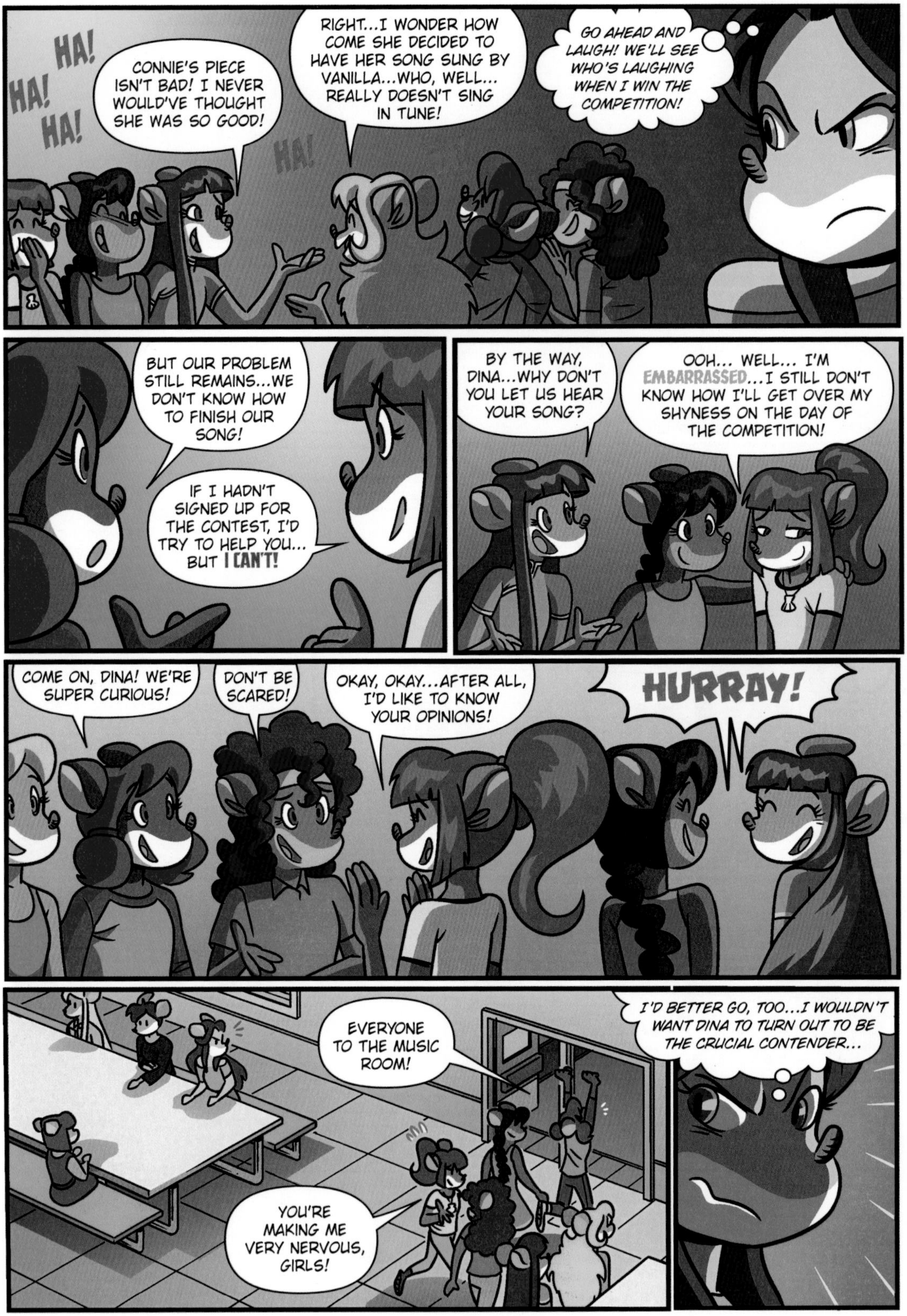
HA!
HA!
HA!
HA!
CONNIE'S PIECE ISN'T BAD! I NEVER WOULD'VE THOUGHT SHE WAS SO GOOD!
RIGHT...I WONDER HOW COME SHE DECIDED TO HAVE HER SONG SUNG BY VANILLA...WHO, WELL... REALLY DOESN'T SING IN TUNE!
GO AHEAD AND LAUGH! WE'LL SEE WHO'S LAUGHING WHEN I WIN THE COMPETITION!
BUT OUR PROBLEM STILL REMAINS...WE DON'T KNOW HOW TO FINISH OUR SONG!
IF I HADN'T SIGNED UP FOR THE CONTEST, I'D TRY TO HELP YOU... BUT I CAN'T!
BY THE WAY, DINA...WHY DON'T YOU LET US HEAR YOUR SONG?
OOH... WELL... I'M EMBARRASSED...I STILL DON'T KNOW HOW I'LL GET OVER MY SHYNESS ON THE DAY OF THE COMPETITION!
COME ON, DINA! WE'RE SUPER CURIOUS!
DON'T BE SCARED!
OKAY, OKAY...AFTER ALL, I'D LIKE TO KNOW YOUR OPINIONS!
HURRAY!
EVERYONE TO THE MUSIC ROOM!
YOU'RE MAKING ME VERY NERVOUS, GIRLS!
I'D BETTER GO, TOO...I WOULDN'T WANT DINA TO TURN OUT TO BE THE CRUCIAL CONTENDER...

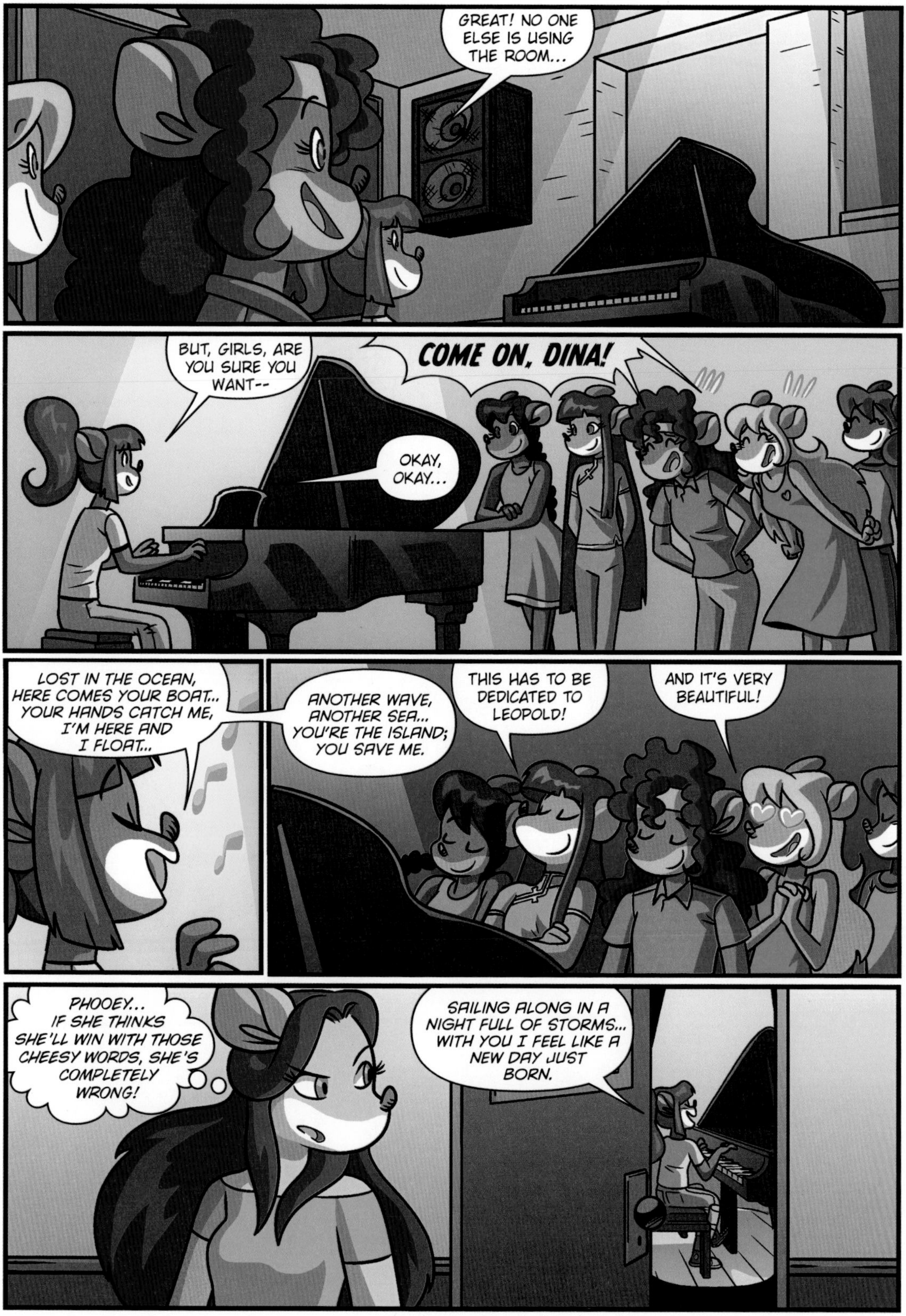
GREAT! NO ONE ELSE IS USING THE ROOM...
BUT, GIRLS, ARE YOU SURE YOU WANT--
COME ON, DINA!
OKAY, OKAY...
LOST IN THE OCEAN, HERE COMES YOUR BOAT... YOUR HANDS CATCH ME, I'M HERE AND I FLOAT...
ANOTHER WAVE, ANOTHER SEA... YOU'RE THE ISLAND; YOU SAVE ME.
THIS HAS TO BE DEDICATED TO LEOPOLD!
AND IT'S VERY BEAUTIFUL!
PHOOEY... IF SHE THINKS SHE'LL WIN WITH THOSE CHEESY WORDS, SHE'S COMPLETELY WRONG!
SAILING ALONG IN A NIGHT FULL OF STORMS... WITH YOU I FEEL LIKE A NEW DAY JUST BORN.

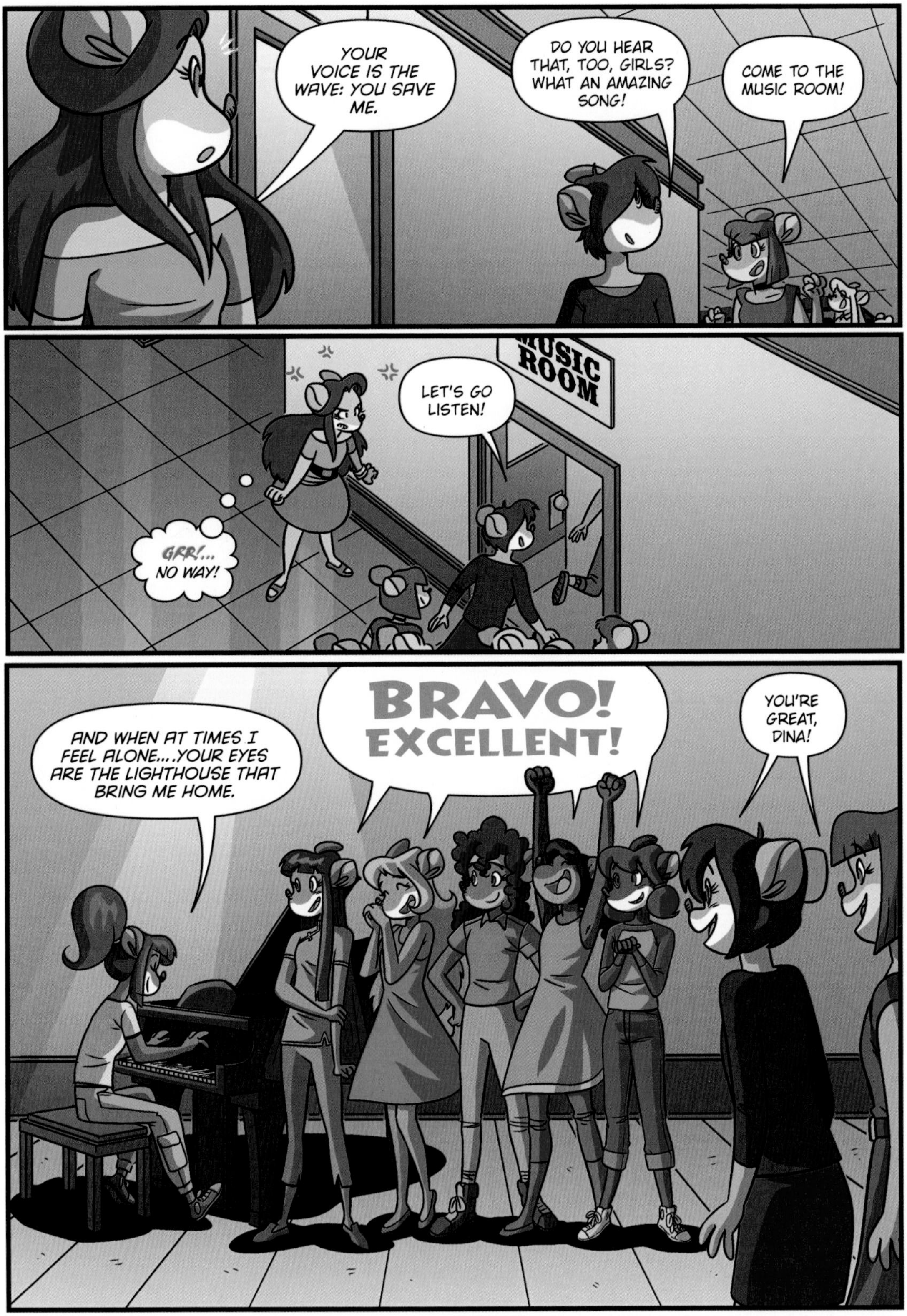
YOUR VOICE IS THE WAVE: YOU SAVE ME.
DO YOU HEAR THAT, TOO, GIRLS? WHAT AN AMAZING SONG!
COME TO THE MUSIC ROOM!
MUSIC ROOM
LET'S GO LISTEN!
GRR!... NO WAY!
AND WHEN AT TIMES I FEEL ALONE....YOUR EYES ARE THE LIGHTHOUSE THAT BRING ME HOME.
BRAVO! EXCELLENT!
YOU'RE GREAT, DINA!

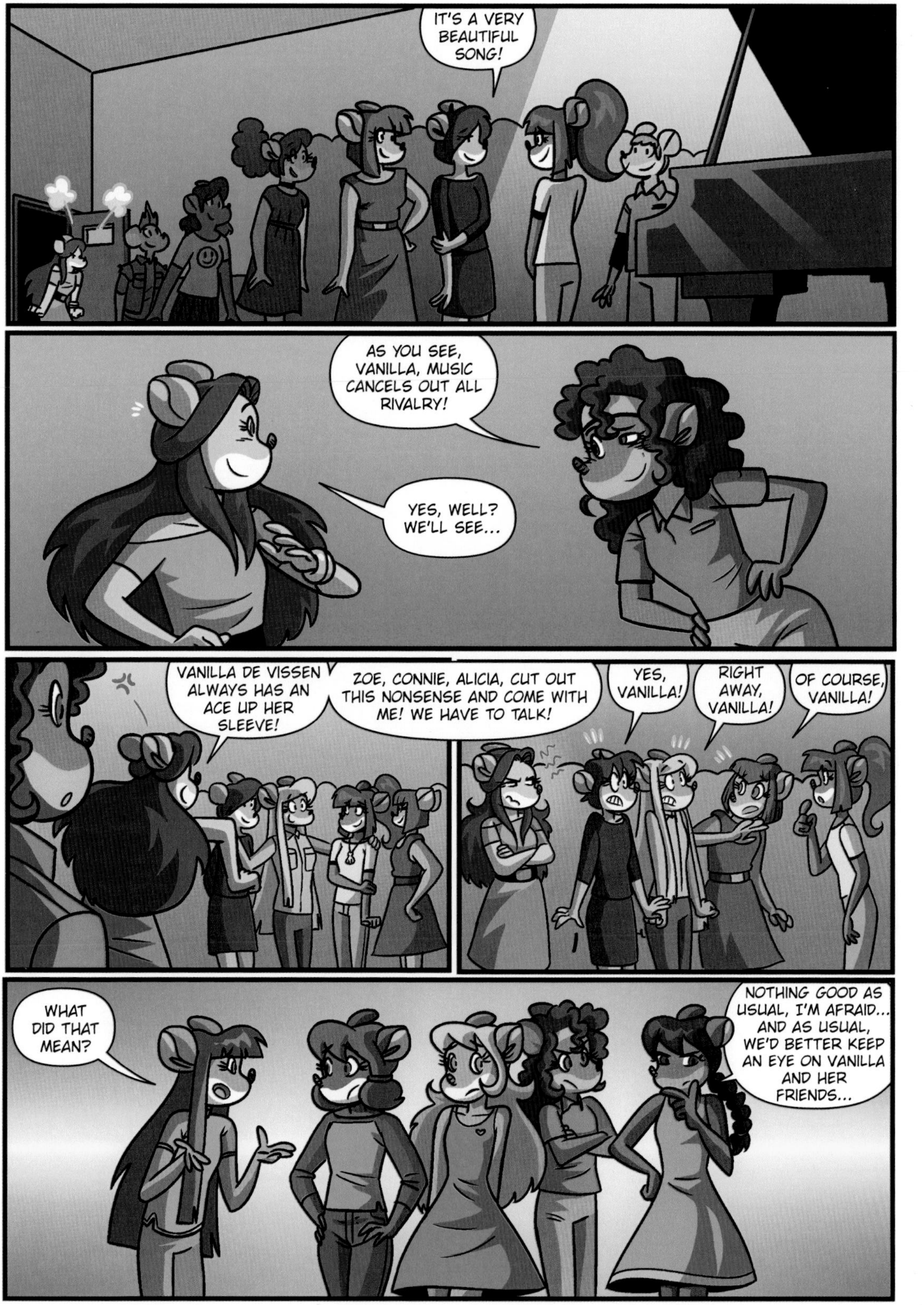

IT'S A VERY BEAUTIFUL SONG!
AS YOU SEE, VANILLA, MUSIC CANCELS OUT ALL RIVALRY!
YES, WELL? WE'LL SEE...
VANILLA DE VISSEN ALWAYS HAS AN ACE UP HER SLEEVE!
ZOE, CONNIE, ALICIA, CUT OUT THIS NONSENSE AND COME WITH ME! WE HAVE TO TALK!
YES, VANILLA!
RIGHT AWAY, VANILLA!
OF COURSE, VANILLA!
WHAT DID THAT MEAN?
NOTHING GOOD AS USUAL, I'M AFRAID... AND AS USUAL, WE'D BETTER KEEP AN EYE ON VANILLA AND HER FRIENDS...

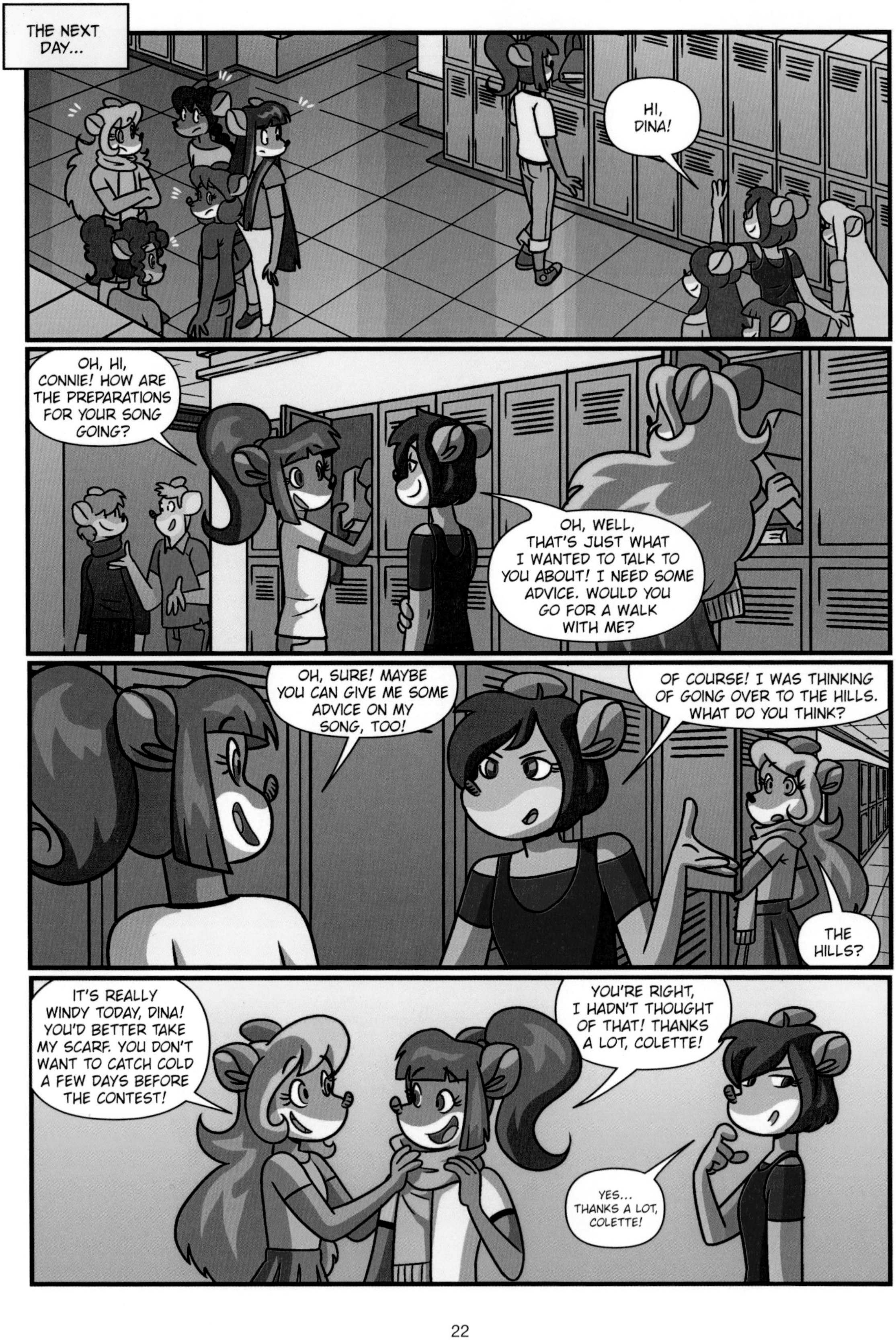
THE NEXT DAY...
HI, DINA!
OH, HI, CONNIE! HOW ARE THE PREPARATIONS FOR YOUR SONG GOING?
OH, WELL, THAT'S JUST WHAT I WANTED TO TALK TO YOU ABOUT! I NEED SOME ADVICE. WOULD YOU GO FOR A WALK WITH ME?
OH, SURE! MAYBE YOU CAN GIVE ME SOME ADVICE ON MY SONG, TOO!
OF COURSE! I WAS THINKING OF GOING OVER TO THE HILLS. WHAT DO YOU THINK?
THE HILLS?
IT'S REALLY WINDY TODAY, DINA! YOU'D BETTER TAKE MY SCARF. YOU DON'T WANT TO CATCH COLD A FEW DAYS BEFORE THE CONTEST!
YOU'RE RIGHT, I HADN'T THOUGHT OF THAT! THANKS A LOT, COLETTE!
YES... THANKS A LOT, COLETTE!

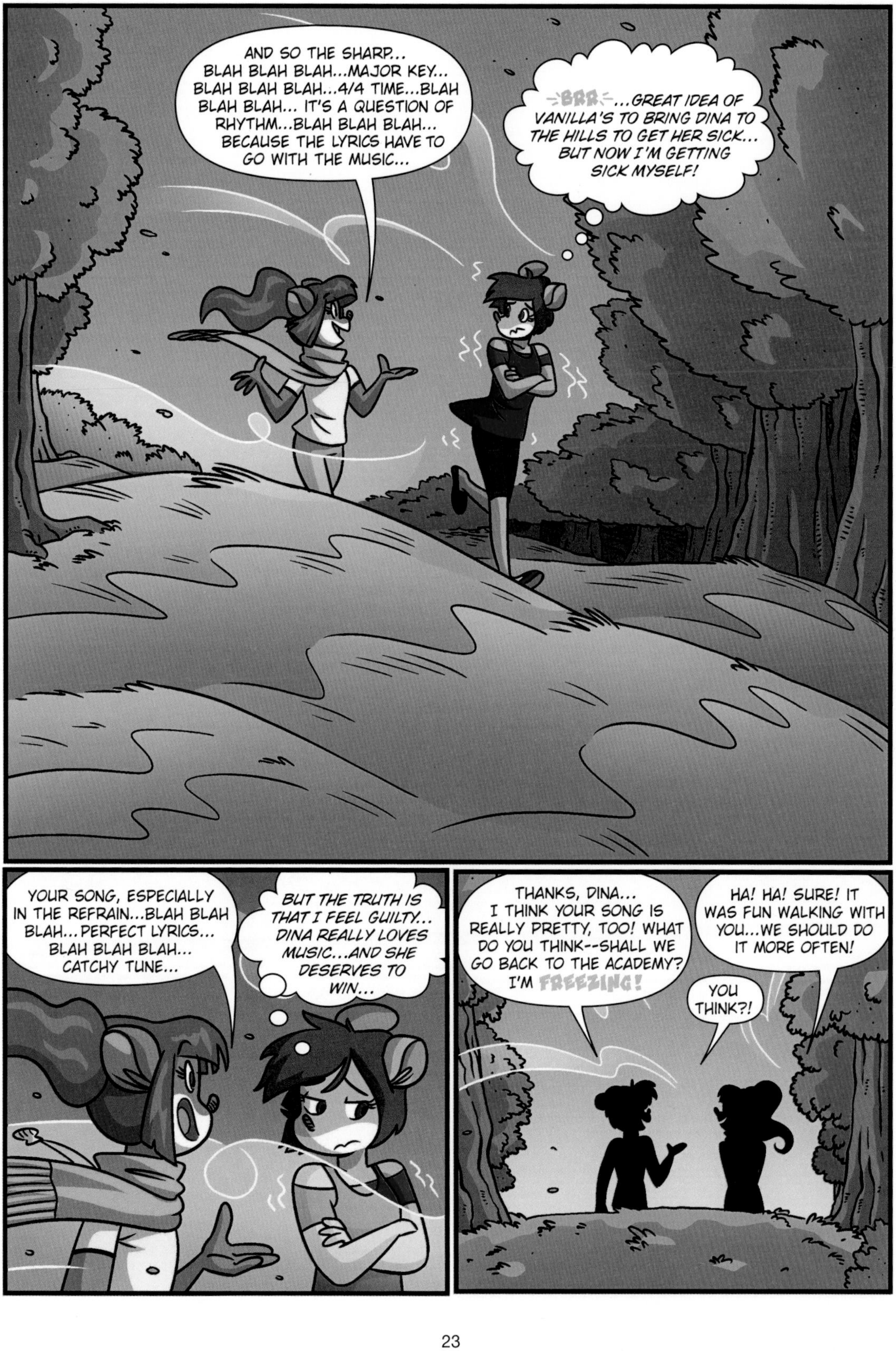
AND SO THE SHARP... BLAH BLAH BLAH...MAJOR KEY... BLAH BLAH BLAH...4/4 TIME...BLAH BLAH BLAH... IT'S A QUESTION OF RHYTHM...BLAH BLAH BLAH... BECAUSE THE LYRICS HAVE TO GO WITH THE MUSIC...
BRR ...GREAT IDEA OF VANILLA'S TO BRING DINA TO THE HILLS TO GET HER SICK... BUT NOW I'M GETTING SICK MYSELF!
YOUR SONG, ESPECIALLY IN THE REFRAIN...BLAH BLAH BLAH...PERFECT LYRICS... BLAH BLAH BLAH... CATCHY TUNE...
BUT THE TRUTH IS THAT I FEEL GUILTY... DINA REALLY LOVES MUSIC...AND SHE DESERVES TO WIN...
THANKS, DINA... I THINK YOUR SONG IS REALLY PRETTY, TOO! WHAT DO YOU THINK--SHALL WE GO BACK TO THE ACADEMY? I'M FREEZING!
HA! HA! SURE! IT WAS FUN WALKING WITH YOU...WE SHOULD DO IT MORE OFTEN!
YOU THINK?!

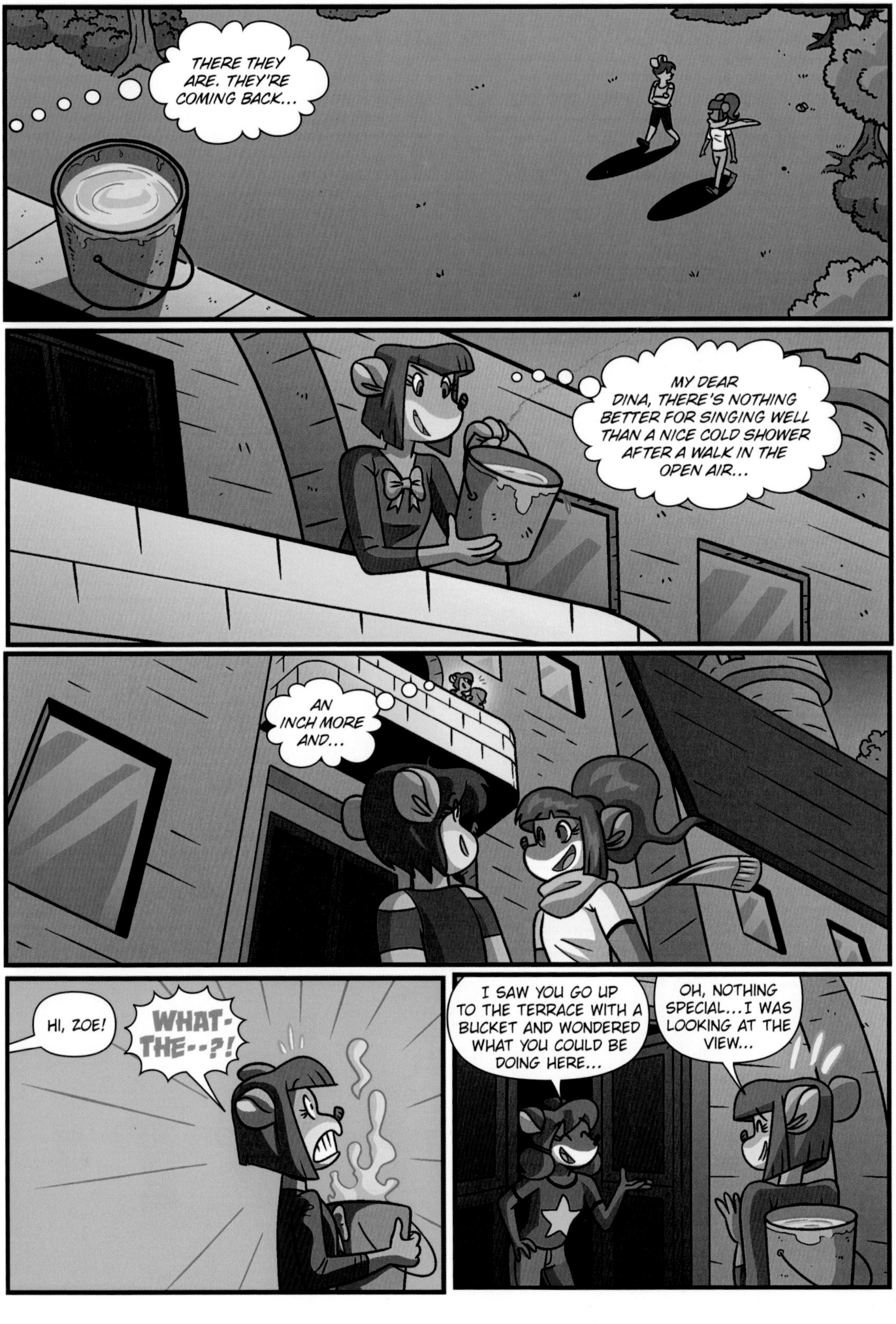
THERE THEY ARE. THEY'RE COMING BACK...
MY DEAR DINA, THERE'S NOTHING BETTER FOR SINGING WELL THAN A NICE COLD SHOWER AFTER A WALK IN THE OPEN AIR...
AN INCH MORE AND...
HI, ZOE!
WHAT-THE--?!
I SAW YOU GO UP TO THE TERRACE WITH A BUCKET AND WONDERED WHAT YOU COULD BE DOING HERE...
OH, NOTHING SPECIAL...I WAS LOOKING AT THE VIEW...

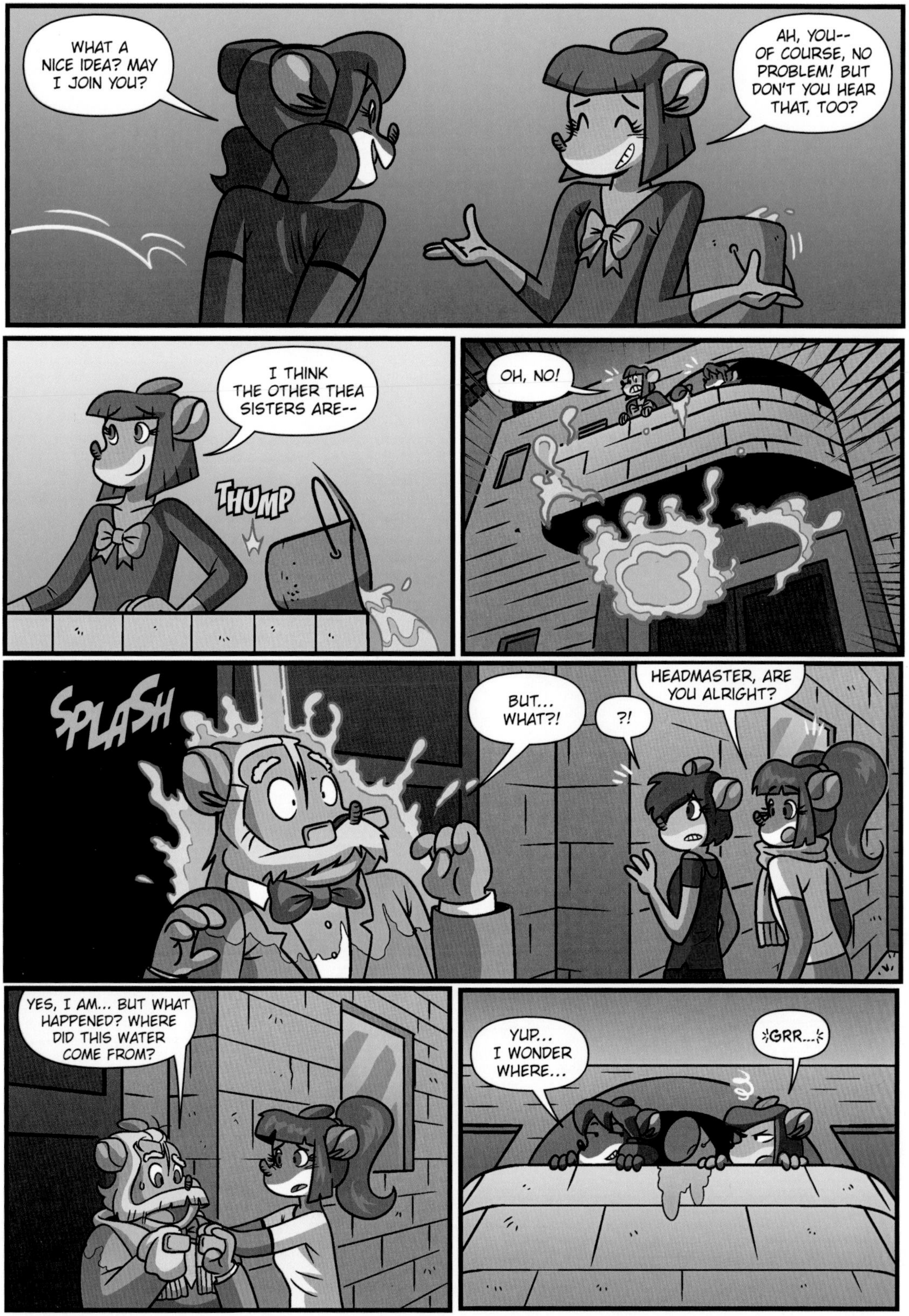
WHAT A NICE IDEA? MAY I JOIN YOU?
AH, YOU-- OF COURSE, NO PROBLEM! BUT DON'T YOU HEAR THAT, TOO?
I THINK THE OTHER THEA SISTERS ARE--
THUMP
OH, NO!
SPLASH
BUT... WHAT?!
?!
HEADMASTER, ARE YOU ALRIGHT?
YES, I AM... BUT WHAT HAPPENED? WHERE DID THIS WATER COME FROM?
YUP... I WONDER WHERE...
GRR...

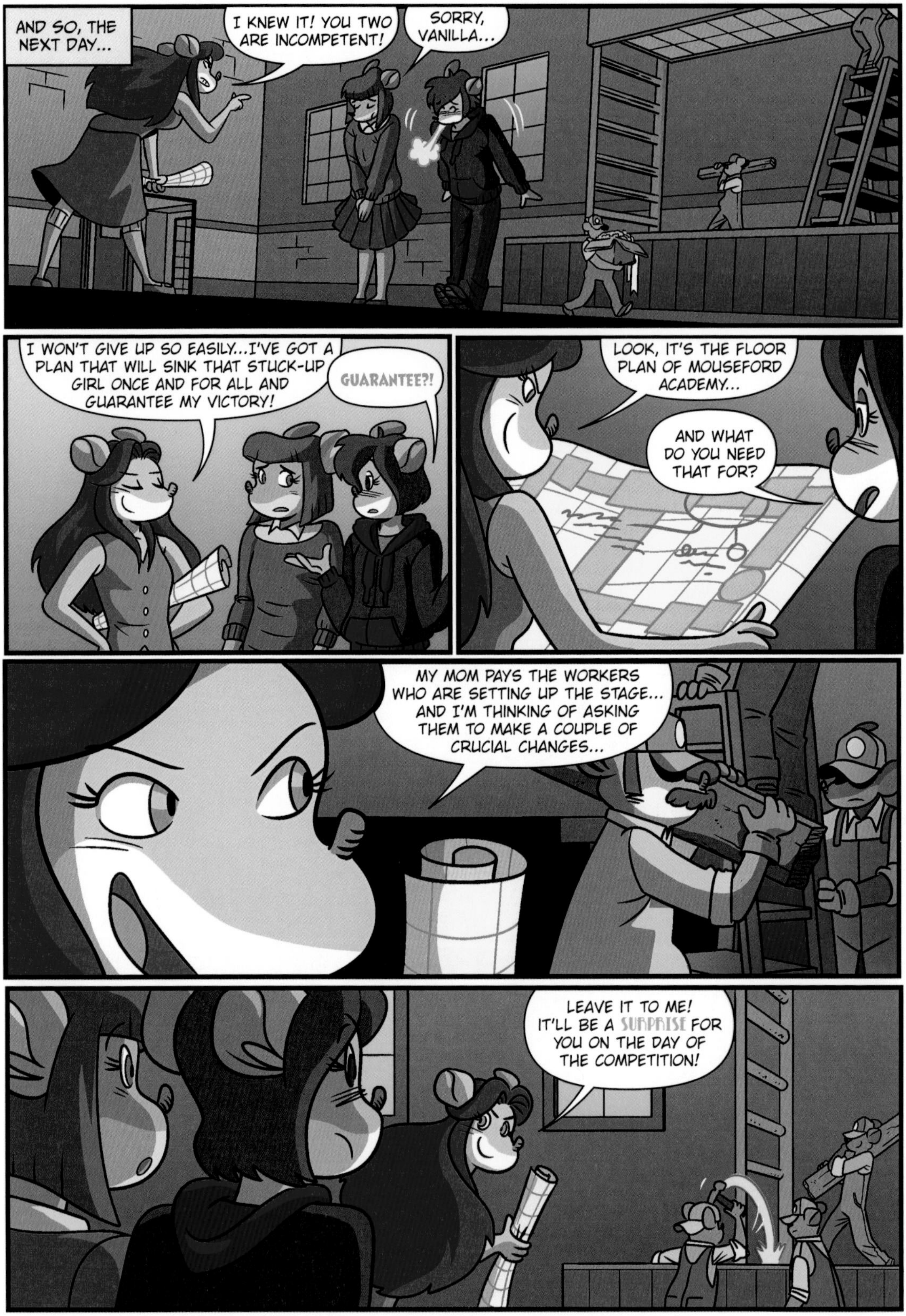
AND SO, THE NEXT DAY...
I KNEW IT! YOU TWO ARE INCOMPETENT!
SORRY, VANILLA...
I WON'T GIVE UP SO EASILY...I'VE GOT A PLAN THAT WILL SINK THAT STUCK-UP GIRL ONCE AND FOR ALL AND GUARANTEE MY VICTORY!
GUARANTEE?!
LOOK, IT'S THE FLOOR PLAN OF MOUSEFORD ACADEMY...
AND WHAT DO YOU NEED THAT FOR?
MY MOM PAYS THE WORKERS WHO ARE SETTING UP THE STAGE... AND I'M THINKING OF ASKING THEM TO MAKE A COUPLE OF CRUCIAL CHANGES...
LEAVE IT TO ME! IT'LL BE A SURPRISE FOR YOU ON THE DAY OF THE COMPETITION!

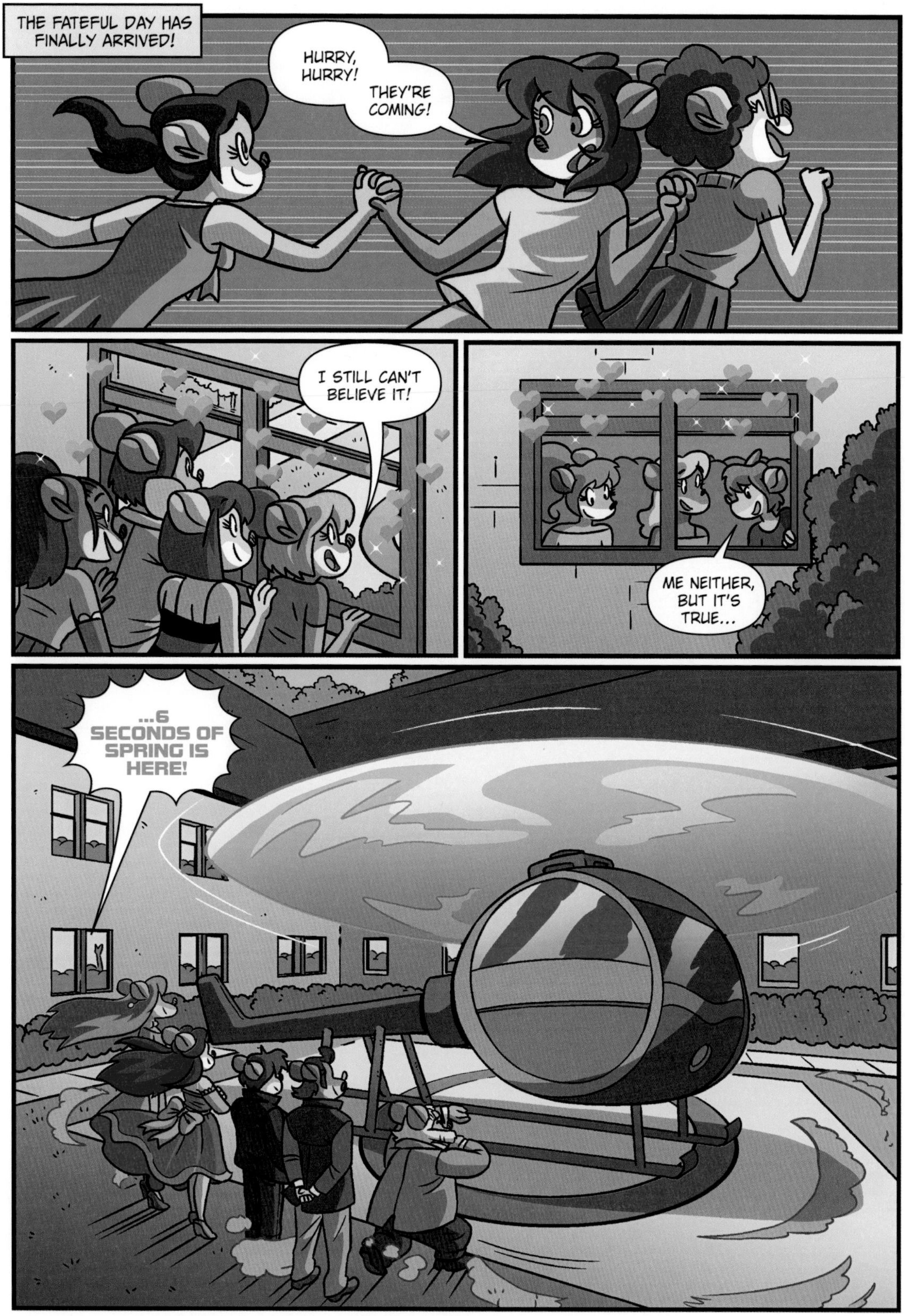
THE FATEFUL DAY HAS FINALLY ARRIVED!
HURRY, HURRY!
THEY'RE COMING!
I STILL CAN'T BELIEVE IT!
ME NEITHER, BUT IT'S TRUE...
...6 SECONDS OF SPRING IS HERE!

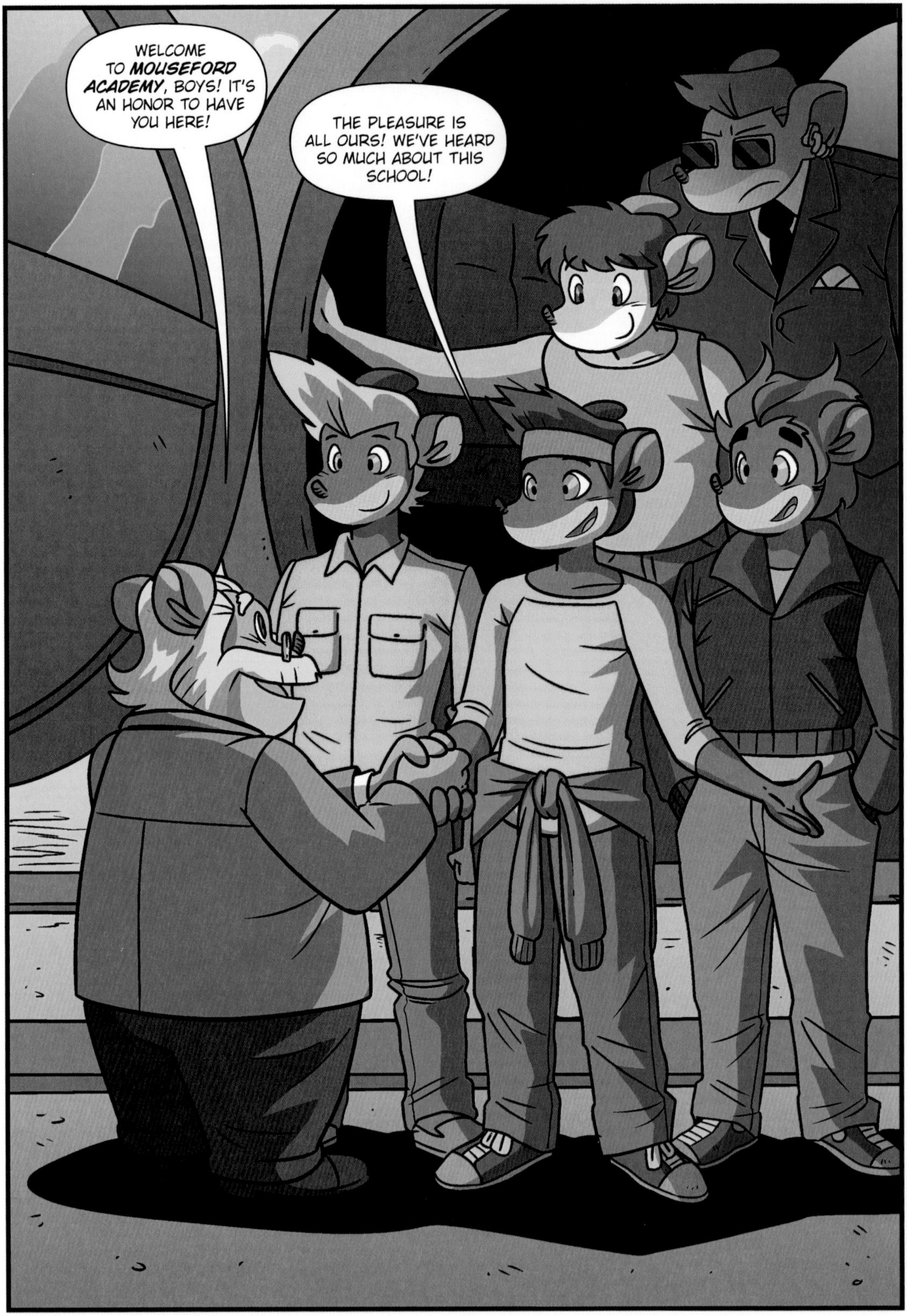
WELCOME TO MOUSEFORD ACADEMY, BOYS! IT'S AN HONOR TO HAVE YOU HERE!
THE PLEASURE IS ALL OURS! WE'VE HEARD SO MUCH ABOUT THIS SCHOOL!

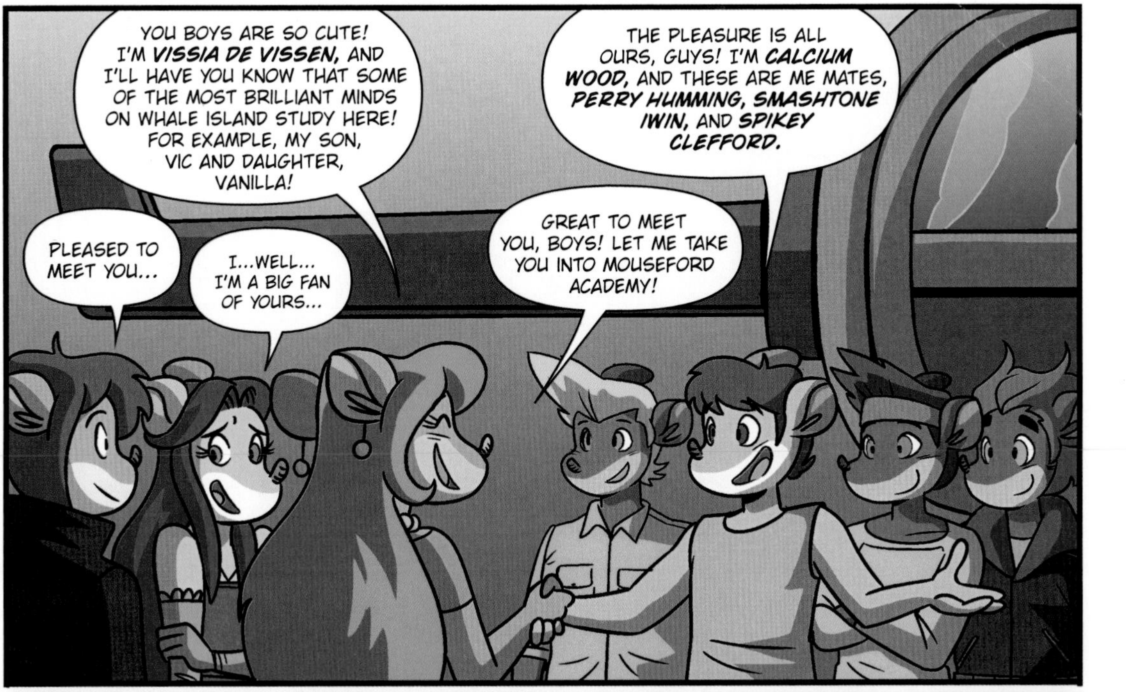
PLEASED TO MEET YOU...
I...WELL... I'M A BIG FAN OF YOURS...
YOU BOYS ARE SO CUTE! I'M VISSIA DE VISSEN, AND I'LL HAVE YOU KNOW THAT SOME OF THE MOST BRILLIANT MINDS ON WHALE ISLAND STUDY HERE! FOR EXAMPLE, MY SON, VIC AND DAUGHTER, VANILLA!
GREAT TO MEET YOU, BOYS! LET ME TAKE YOU INTO MOUSEFORD ACADEMY!
THE PLEASURE IS ALL OURS, GUYS! I'M CALCIUM WOOD, AND THESE ARE ME MATES, PERRY HUMMING, SMASHTONE IWIN, AND SPIKEY CLEFFORD.

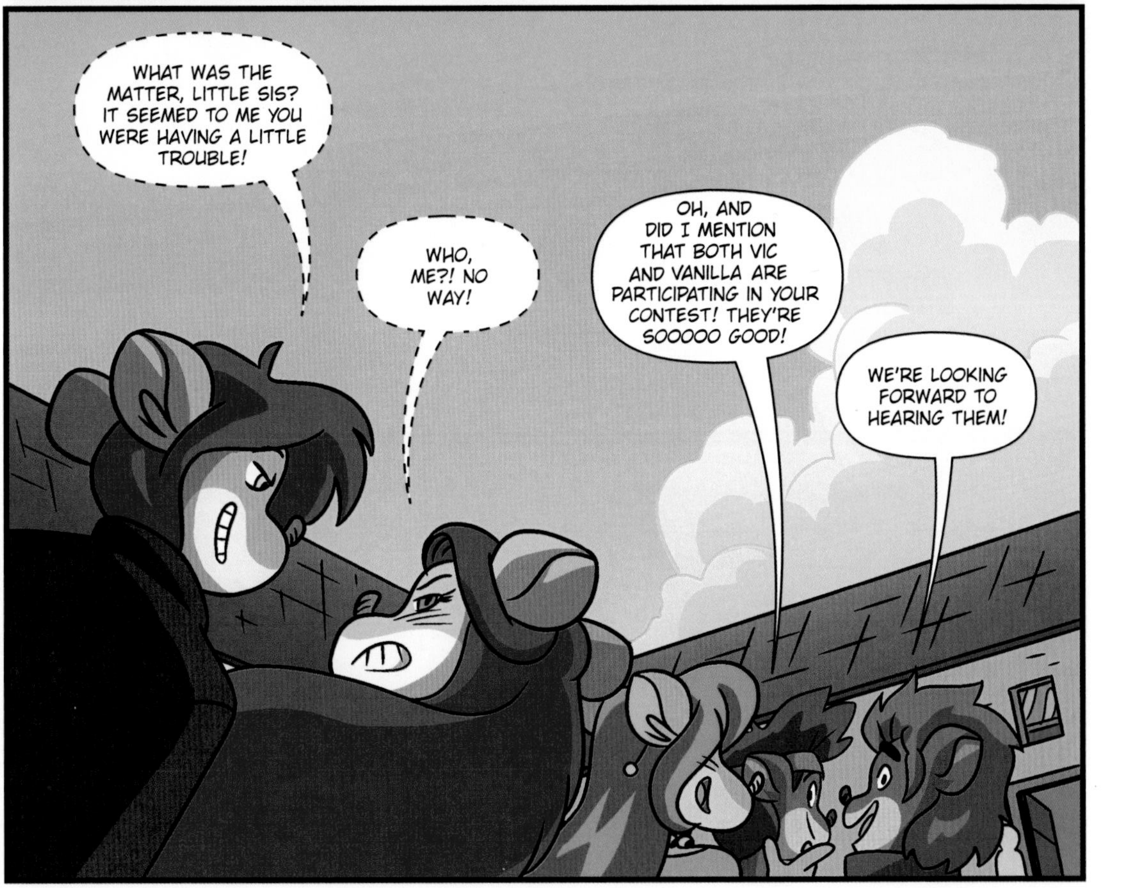
WHAT WAS THE MATTER, LITTLE SIS? IT SEEMED TO ME YOU WERE HAVING A LITTLE TROUBLE!
WHO, ME?! NO WAY!
OH, AND DID I MENTION THAT BOTH VIC AND VANILLA ARE PARTICIPATING IN YOUR CONTEST! THEY'RE SOOOOO GOOD!
WE'RE LOOKING FORWARD TO HEARING THEM!

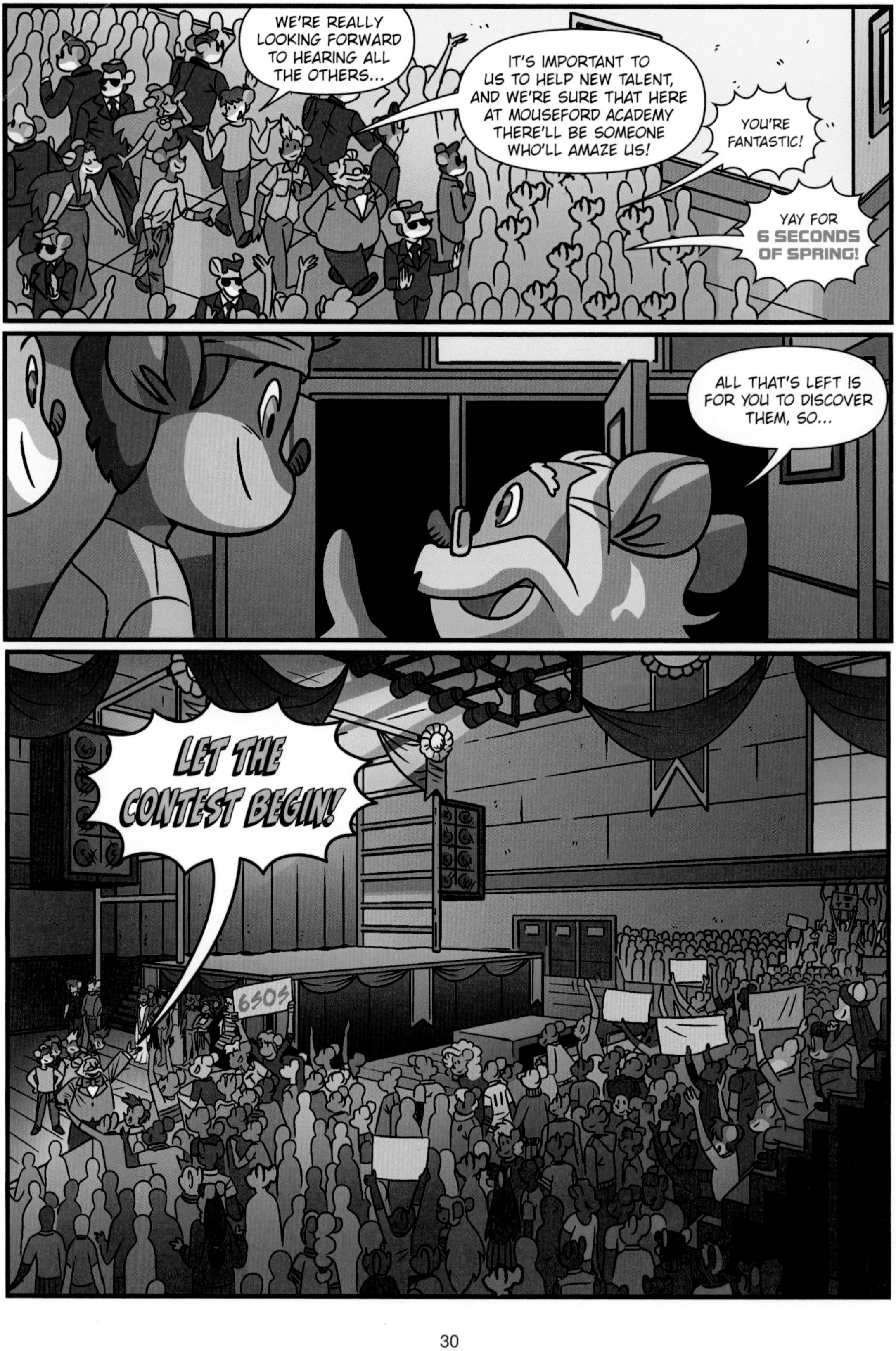
WE'RE REALLY LOOKING FORWARD TO HEARING ALL THE OTHERS...
IT'S IMPORTANT TO US TO HELP NEW TALENT, AND WE'RE SURE THAT HERE AT MOUSEFORD ACADEMY THERE'LL BE SOMEONE WHO'LL AMAZE US!
YOU'RE FANTASTIC!
YAY FOR 6 SECONDS OF SPRING!
ALL THAT'S LEFT IS FOR YOU TO DISCOVER THEM, SO...
LET THE CONTEST BEGIN!
6SOS

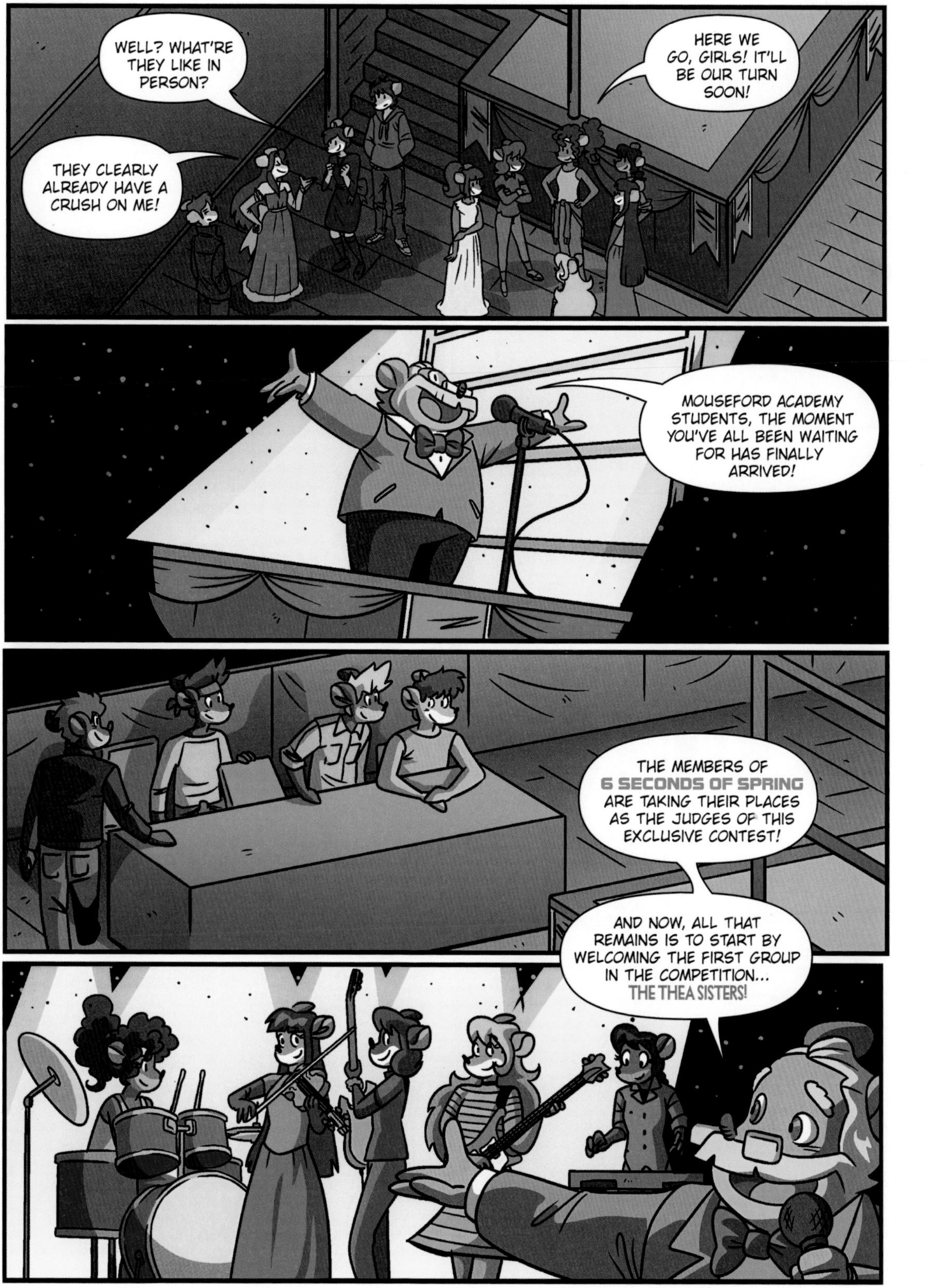
WELL? WHAT'RE THEY LIKE IN PERSON?
THEY CLEARLY ALREADY HAVE A CRUSH ON ME!
HERE WE GO, GIRLS! IT'LL BE OUR TURN SOON!
MOUSEFORD ACADEMY STUDENTS, THE MOMENT YOU'VE ALL BEEN WAITING FOR HAS FINALLY ARRIVED!
THE MEMBERS OF 6 SECONDS OF SPRING ARE TAKING THEIR PLACES AS THE JUDGES OF THIS EXCLUSIVE CONTEST!
AND NOW, ALL THAT REMAINS IS TO START BY WELCOMING THE FIRST GROUP IN THE COMPETITION... THE THEA SISTERS!

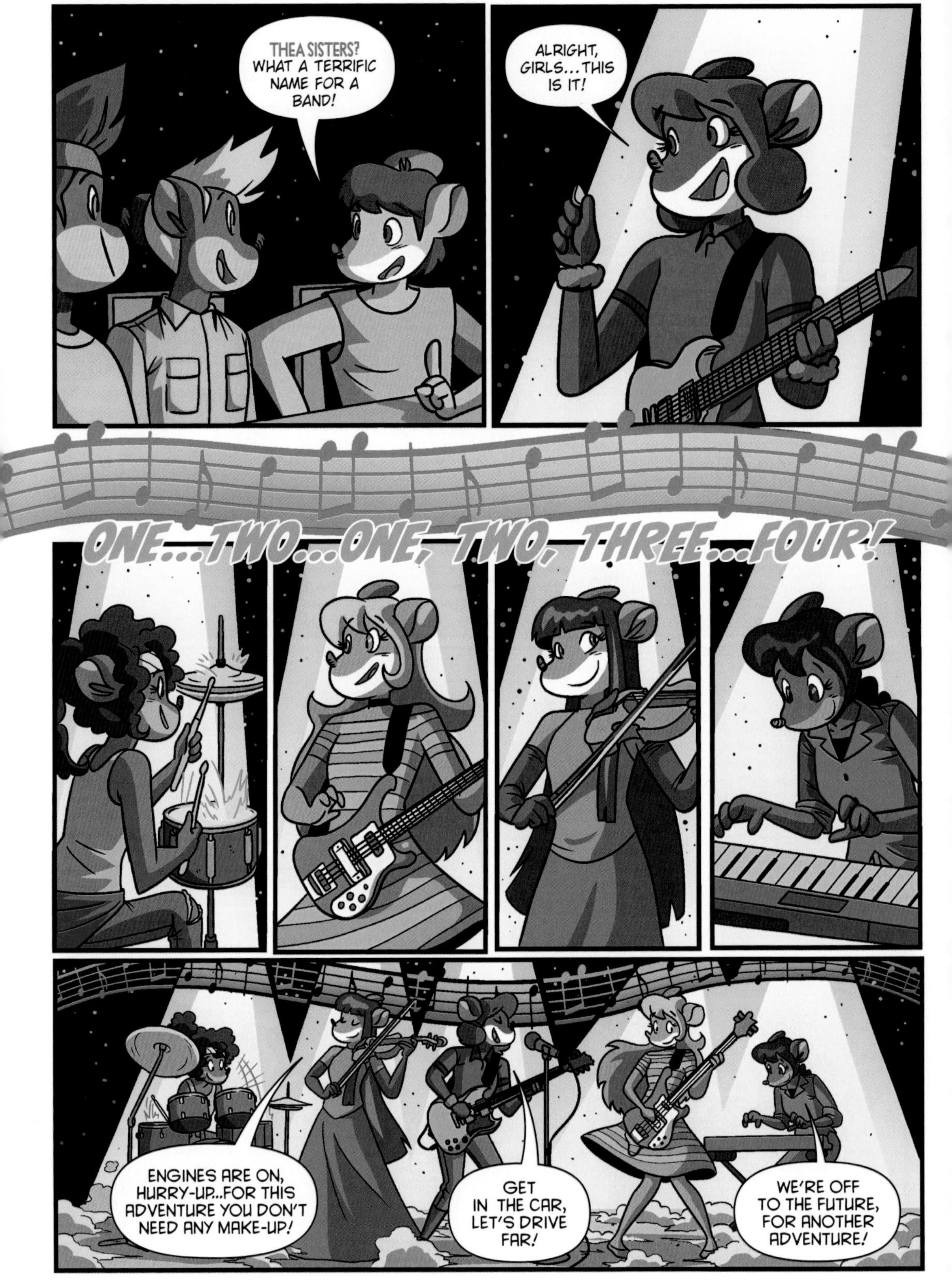
THEA SISTERS? WHAT A TERRIFIC NAME FOR A BAND!
ALRIGHT, GIRLS... THIS IS IT!
ONE...TWO...ONE, TWO, THREE...FOUR!
ENGINES ARE ON, HURRY-UP...FOR THIS ADVENTURE YOU DON'T NEED ANY MAKE-UP!
GET IN THE CAR, LET'S DRIVE FAR!
WE'RE OFF TO THE FUTURE, FOR ANOTHER ADVENTURE!

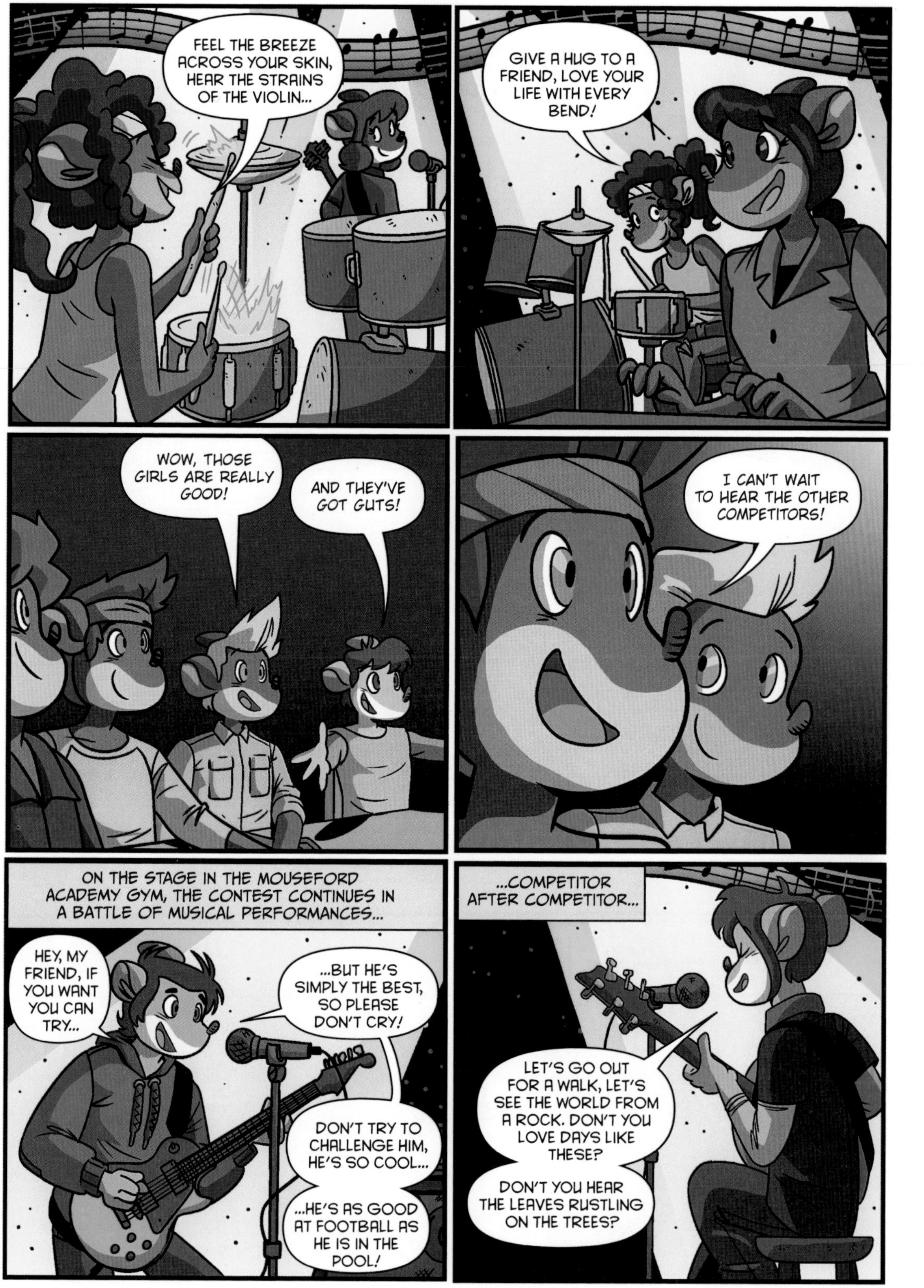

FEEL THE BREEZE ACROSS YOUR SKIN, HEAR THE STRAINS OF THE VIOLIN...
GIVE A HUG TO A FRIEND, LOVE YOUR LIFE WITH EVERY BEND!
WOW, THOSE GIRLS ARE REALLY GOOD!
AND THEY'VE GOT GUTS!
I CAN'T WAIT TO HEAR THE OTHER COMPETITORS!
ON THE STAGE IN THE MOUSEFORD ACADEMY GYM, THE CONTEST CONTINUES IN A BATTLE OF MUSICAL PERFORMANCES...
HEY, MY FRIEND, IF YOU WANT YOU CAN TRY...
...BUT HE'S SIMPLY THE BEST, SO PLEASE DON'T CRY!
DON'T TRY TO CHALLENGE HIM, HE'S SO COOL...
...HE'S AS GOOD AT FOOTBALL AS HE IS IN THE POOL!
...COMPETITOR AFTER COMPETITOR...
LET'S GO OUT FOR A WALK, LET'S SEE THE WORLD FROM A ROCK. DON'T YOU LOVE DAYS LIKE THESE?
DON'T YOU HEAR THE LEAVES RUSTLING ON THE TREES?

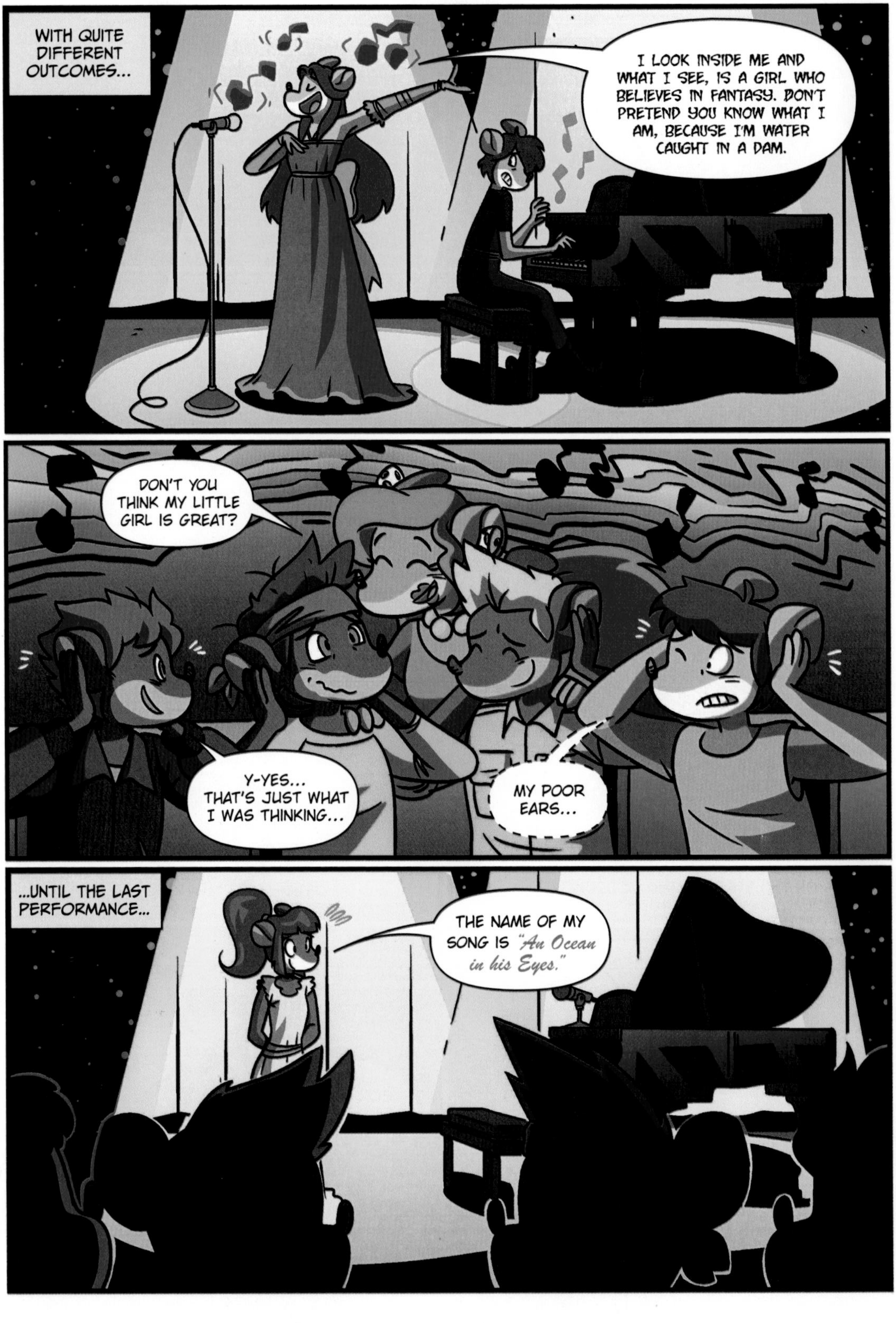
WITH QUITE DIFFERENT OUTCOMES...
I LOOK INSIDE ME AND WHAT I SEE, IS A GIRL WHO BELIEVES IN FANTASY. DON'T PRETEND YOU KNOW WHAT I AM, BECAUSE I'M WATER CAUGHT IN A DAM.
DON'T YOU THINK MY LITTLE GIRL IS GREAT?
Y-YES... THAT'S JUST WHAT I WAS THINKING...
MY POOR EARS...
...UNTIL THE LAST PERFORMANCE...
THE NAME OF MY SONG IS "An Ocean in his Eyes."

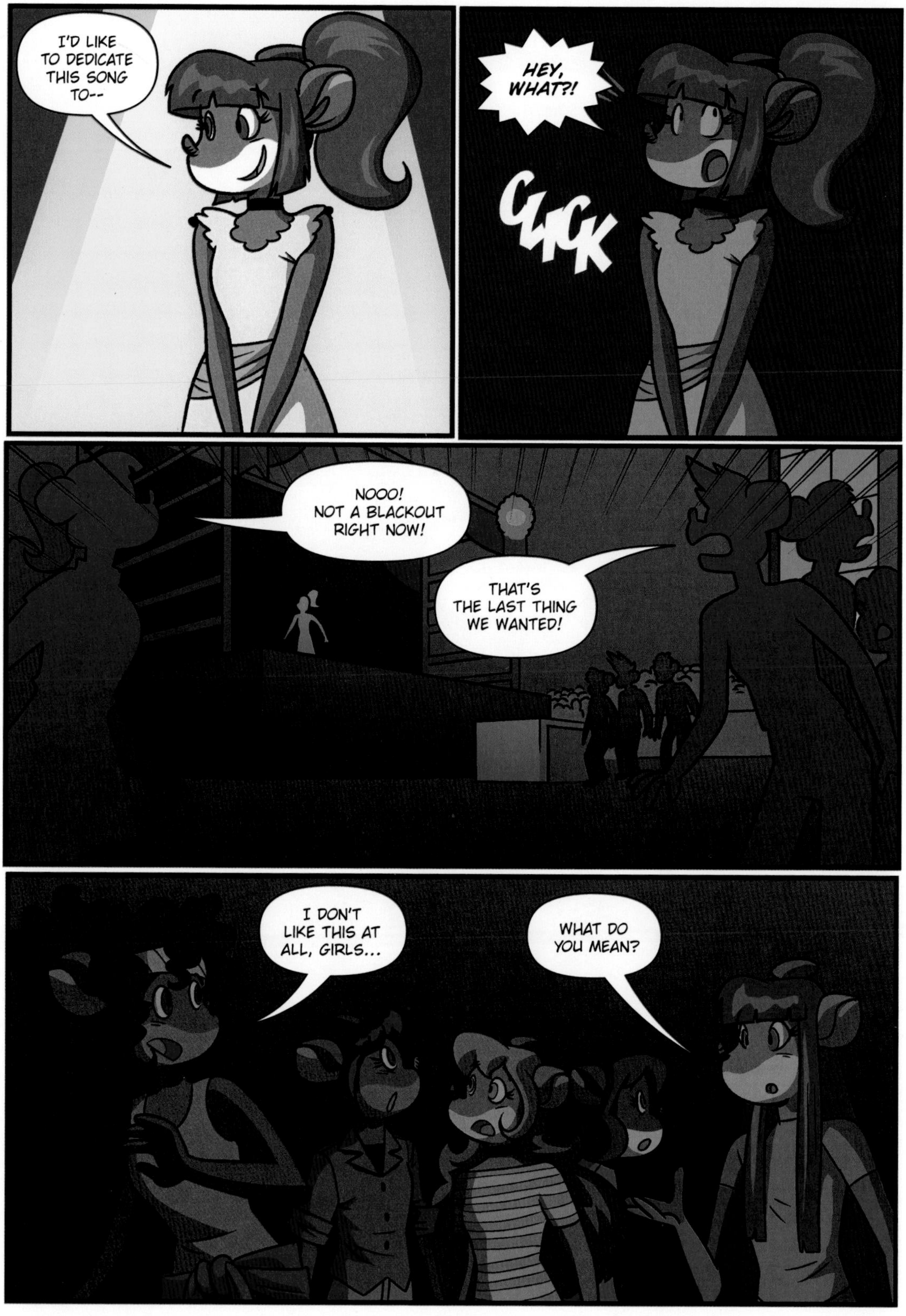
I'D LIKE TO DEDICATE THIS SONG TO--
HEY, WHAT?!
CLICK
NOOO! NOT A BLACKOUT RIGHT NOW!
THAT'S THE LAST THING WE WANTED!
I DON'T LIKE THIS AT ALL, GIRLS...
WHAT DO YOU MEAN?

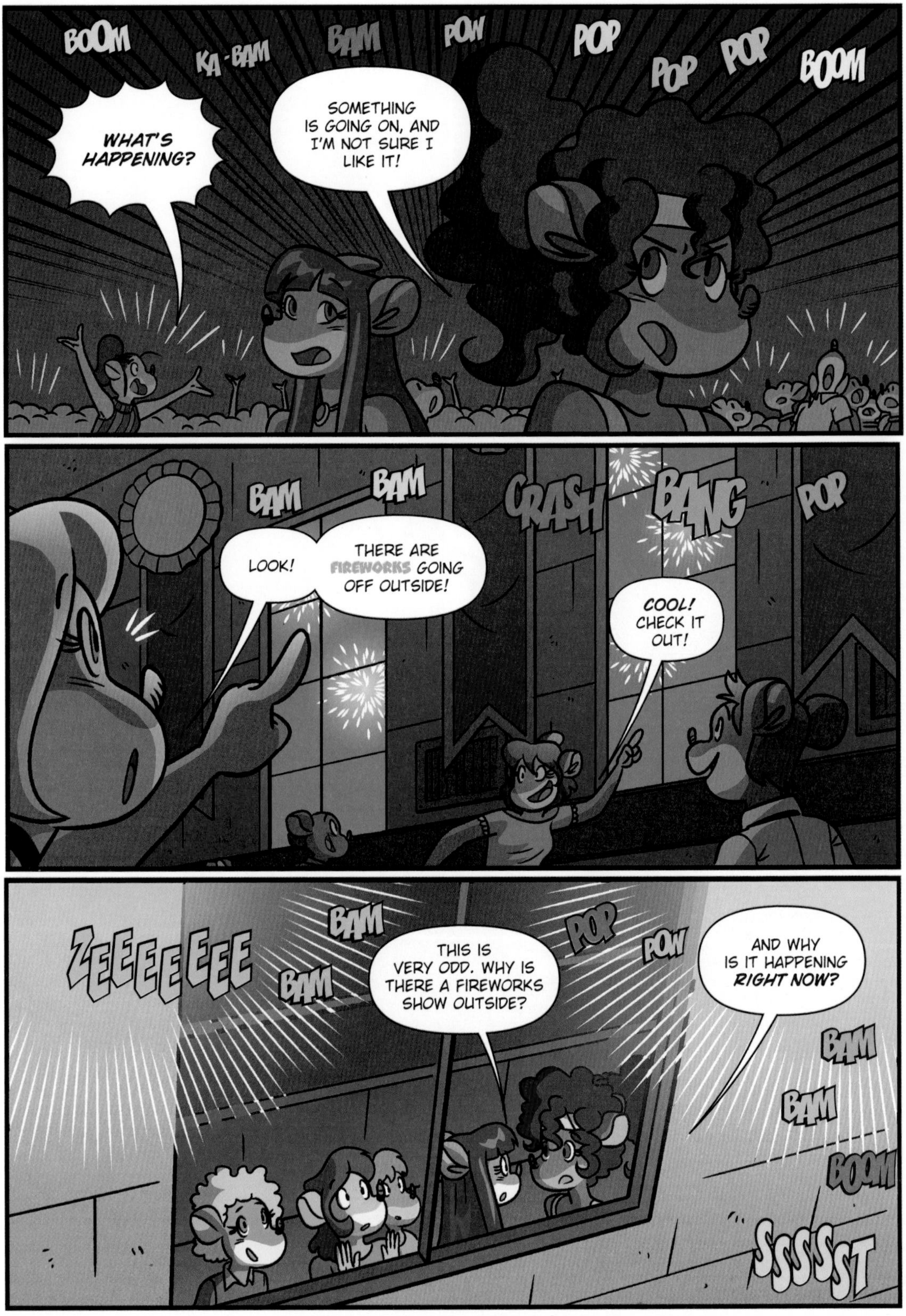
BOOM
KA-BAM
BAM
POW
POP
POP
POP
BOOM
WHAT'S HAPPENING?
SOMETHING IS GOING ON, AND I'M NOT SURE I LIKE IT!
BAM
BAM
CRASH
BANG
POP
LOOK!
THERE ARE FIREWORKS GOING OFF OUTSIDE!
COOL! CHECK IT OUT!
ZEEEEEEE
BAM
BAM
POP
POW
THIS IS VERY ODD. WHY IS THERE A FIREWORKS SHOW OUTSIDE?
AND WHY IS IT HAPPENING RIGHT NOW?
BAM
BAM
BOOM
SSSSST

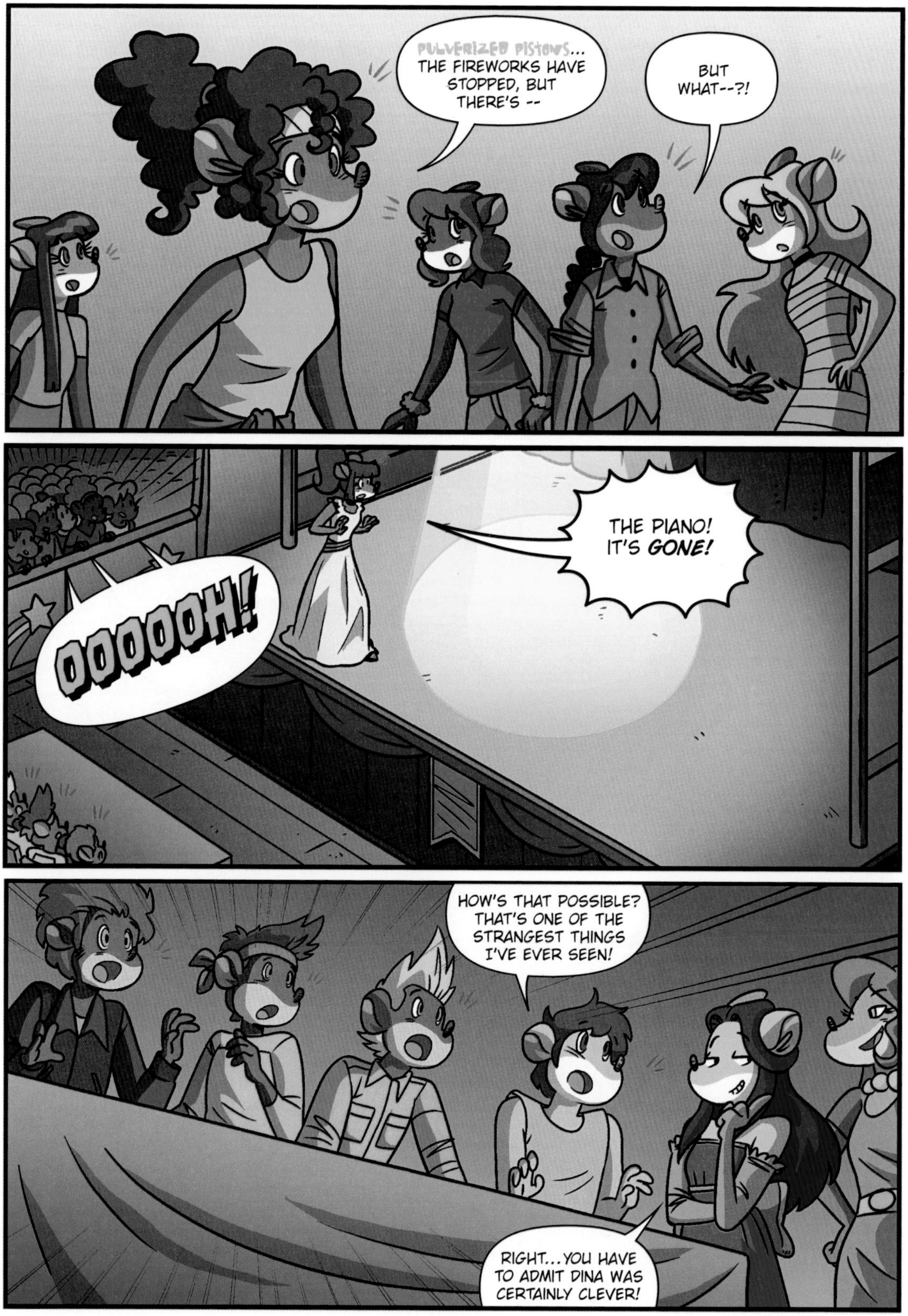
PULVERIZED PISTONS... THE FIREWORKS HAVE STOPPED, BUT THERE'S --
BUT WHAT--?!
THE PIANO! IT'S GONE!
OOOOOH!
HOW'S THAT POSSIBLE? THAT'S ONE OF THE STRANGEST THINGS I'VE EVER SEEN!
RIGHT... YOU HAVE TO ADMIT DINA WAS CERTAINLY CLEVER!

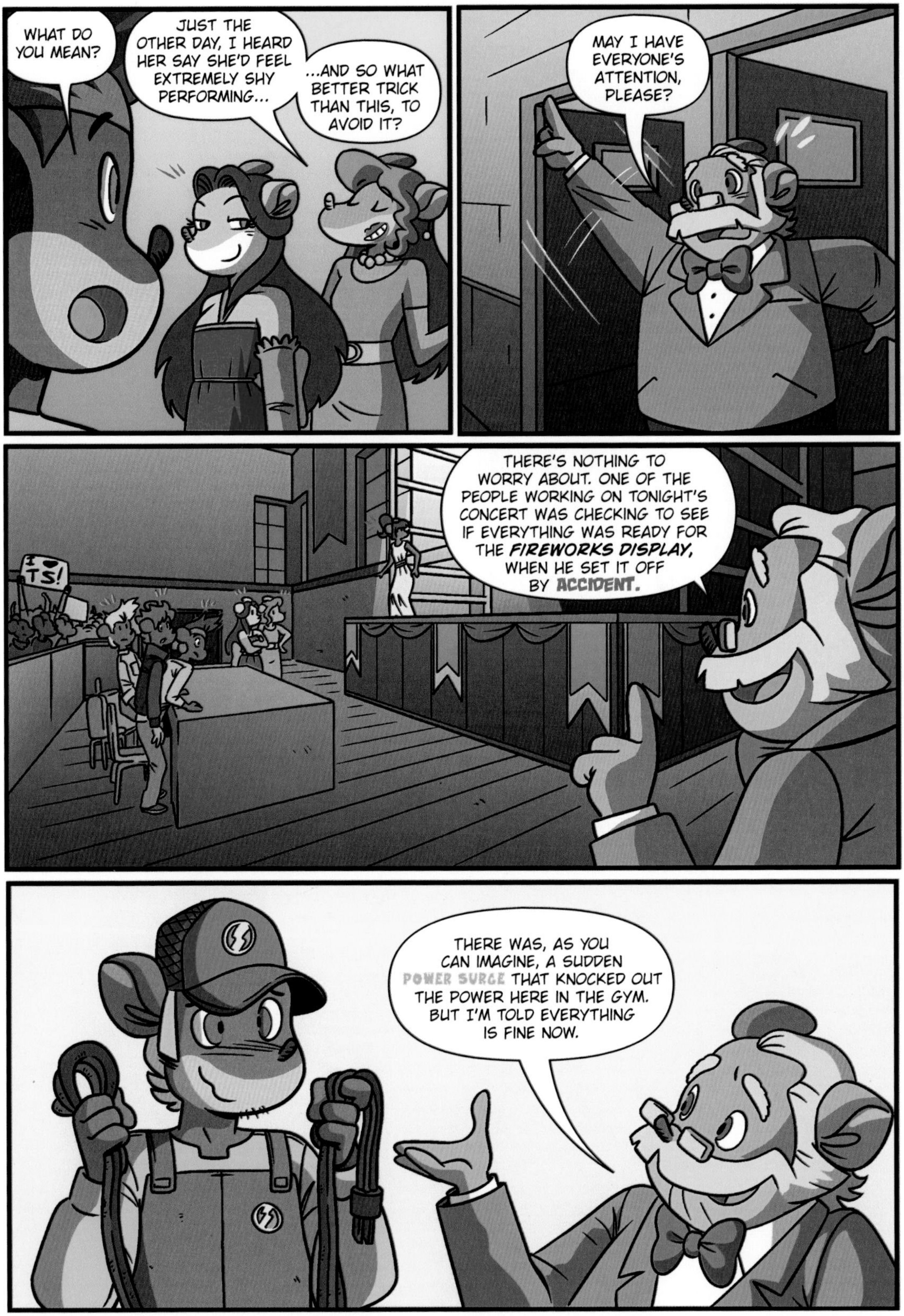
WHAT DO YOU MEAN?
JUST THE OTHER DAY, I HEARD HER SAY SHE'D FEEL EXTREMELY SHY PERFORMING...
...AND SO WHAT BETTER TRICK THAN THIS, TO AVOID IT?
MAY I HAVE EVERYONE'S ATTENTION, PLEASE?
I ♥ TS!
THERE'S NOTHING TO WORRY ABOUT. ONE OF THE PEOPLE WORKING ON TONIGHT'S CONCERT WAS CHECKING TO SEE IF EVERYTHING WAS READY FOR THE *FIREWORKS DISPLAY,* WHEN HE SET IT OFF BY ACCIDENT.
THERE WAS, AS YOU CAN IMAGINE, A SUDDEN POWER SURGE THAT KNOCKED OUT THE POWER HERE IN THE GYM. BUT I'M TOLD EVERYTHING IS FINE NOW.

BUT EVERYTHING'S *NOT* FINE! MY PIANO IS *MISSING!*

POOR DINA...SHE CAN'T PERFORM WITHOUT HER INSTRUMENT...DOES THAT MEAN SHE SHOULD BE DISQUALIFIED FROM THE CONTEST?

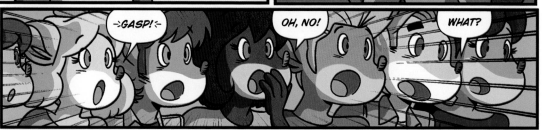

-:GASP!:-

OH, NO!

WHAT?

BUT I DIDN'T DO ANYTHING!

WE KNOW THAT, DINA...WE'LL FIGURE OUT THE TRUTH...

I DON'T WANT TO BE DISQUALIFIED!

IT WON'T HAPPEN, WE PROMISE YOU...

HEY, GIRLS!

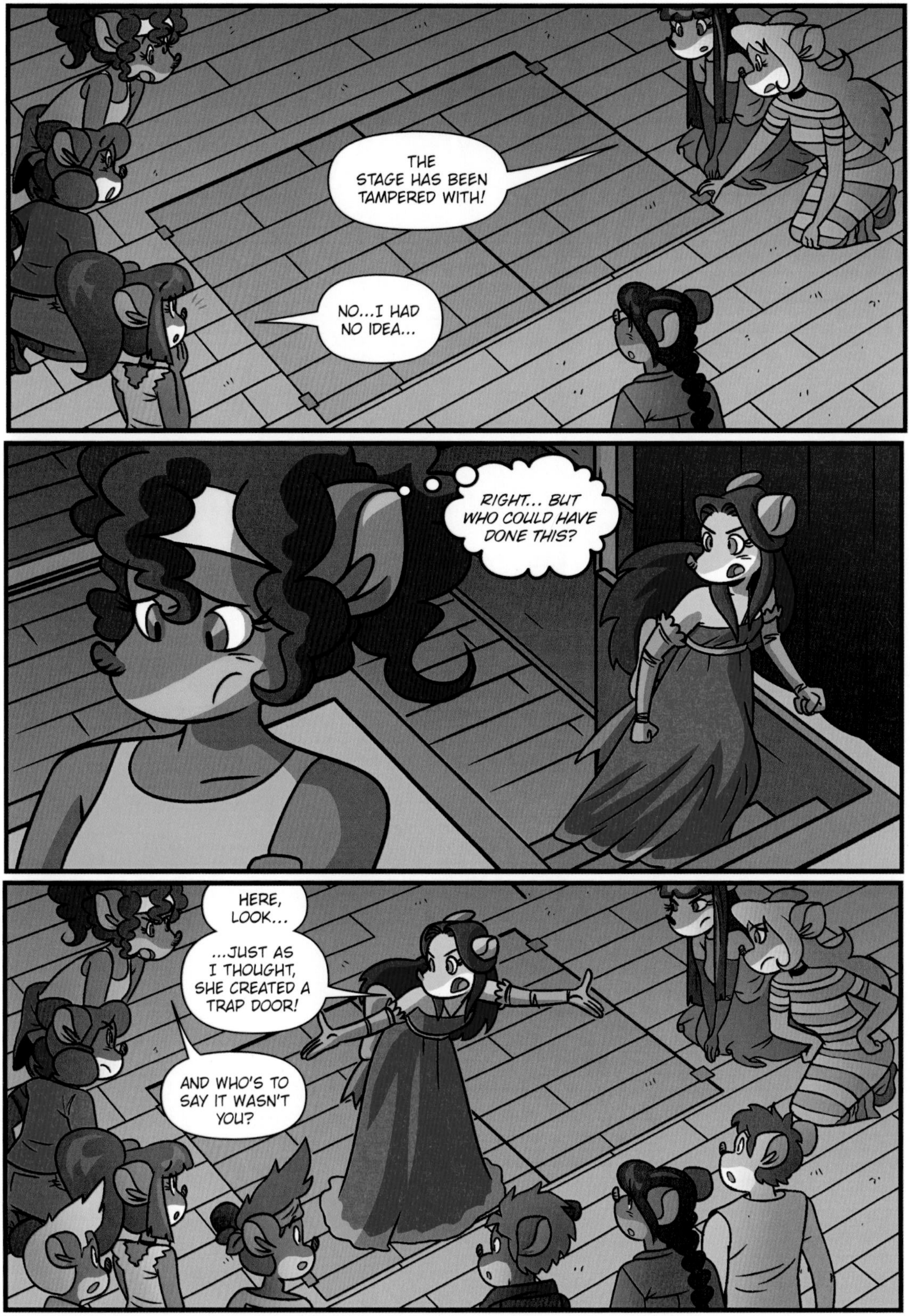
THE STAGE HAS BEEN TAMPERED WITH!
NO...I HAD NO IDEA...
RIGHT... BUT WHO COULD HAVE DONE THIS?
HERE, LOOK...
...JUST AS I THOUGHT, SHE CREATED A TRAP DOOR!
AND WHO'S TO SAY IT WASN'T YOU?

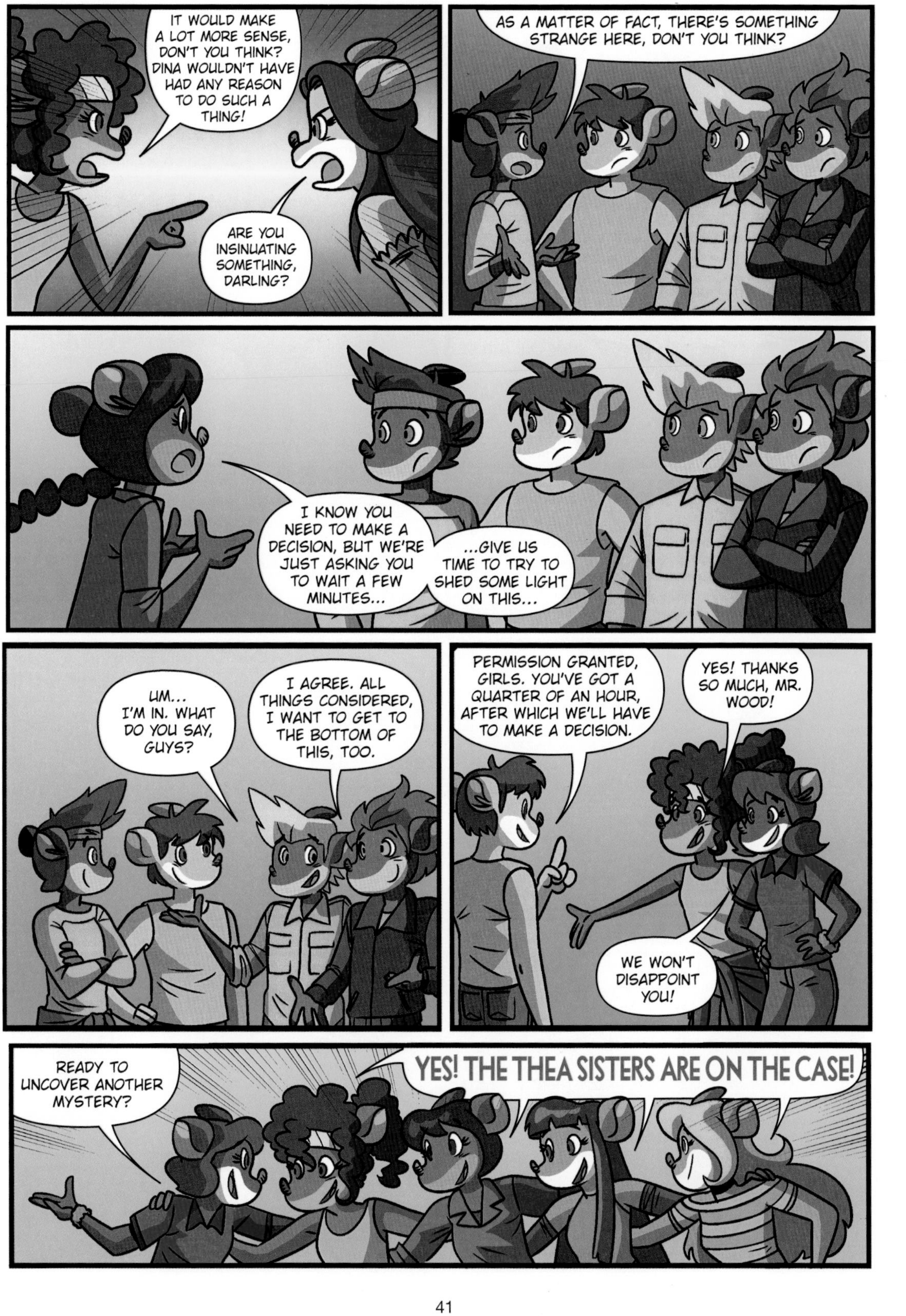
IT WOULD MAKE A LOT MORE SENSE, DON'T YOU THINK? DINA WOULDN'T HAVE HAD ANY REASON TO DO SUCH A THING!
ARE YOU INSINUATING SOMETHING, DARLING?
AS A MATTER OF FACT, THERE'S SOMETHING STRANGE HERE, DON'T YOU THINK?
I KNOW YOU NEED TO MAKE A DECISION, BUT WE'RE JUST ASKING YOU TO WAIT A FEW MINUTES...
...GIVE US TIME TO TRY TO SHED SOME LIGHT ON THIS...
UM... I'M IN. WHAT DO YOU SAY, GUYS?
I AGREE. ALL THINGS CONSIDERED, I WANT TO GET TO THE BOTTOM OF THIS, TOO.
PERMISSION GRANTED, GIRLS. YOU'VE GOT A QUARTER OF AN HOUR, AFTER WHICH WE'LL HAVE TO MAKE A DECISION.
YES! THANKS SO MUCH, MR. WOOD!
WE WON'T DISAPPOINT YOU!
READY TO UNCOVER ANOTHER MYSTERY?
YES! THE THEA SISTERS ARE ON THE CASE!

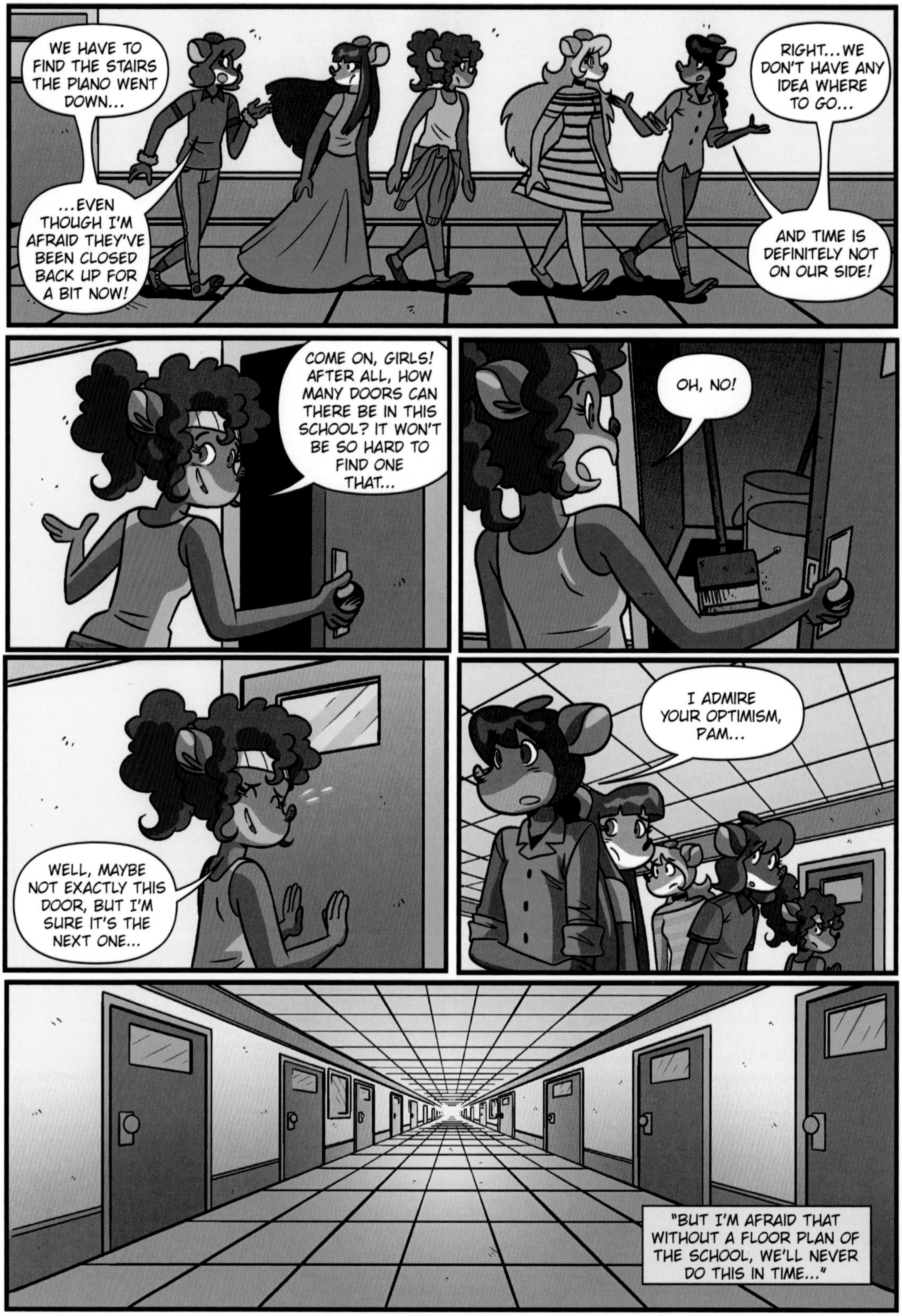
WE HAVE TO FIND THE STAIRS THE PIANO WENT DOWN...
...EVEN THOUGH I'M AFRAID THEY'VE BEEN CLOSED BACK UP FOR A BIT NOW!
RIGHT...WE DON'T HAVE ANY IDEA WHERE TO GO...
AND TIME IS DEFINITELY NOT ON OUR SIDE!
COME ON, GIRLS! AFTER ALL, HOW MANY DOORS CAN THERE BE IN THIS SCHOOL? IT WON'T BE SO HARD TO FIND ONE THAT...
OH, NO!
WELL, MAYBE NOT EXACTLY THIS DOOR, BUT I'M SURE IT'S THE NEXT ONE...
I ADMIRE YOUR OPTIMISM, PAM...
"BUT I'M AFRAID THAT WITHOUT A FLOOR PLAN OF THE SCHOOL, WE'LL NEVER DO THIS IN TIME..."

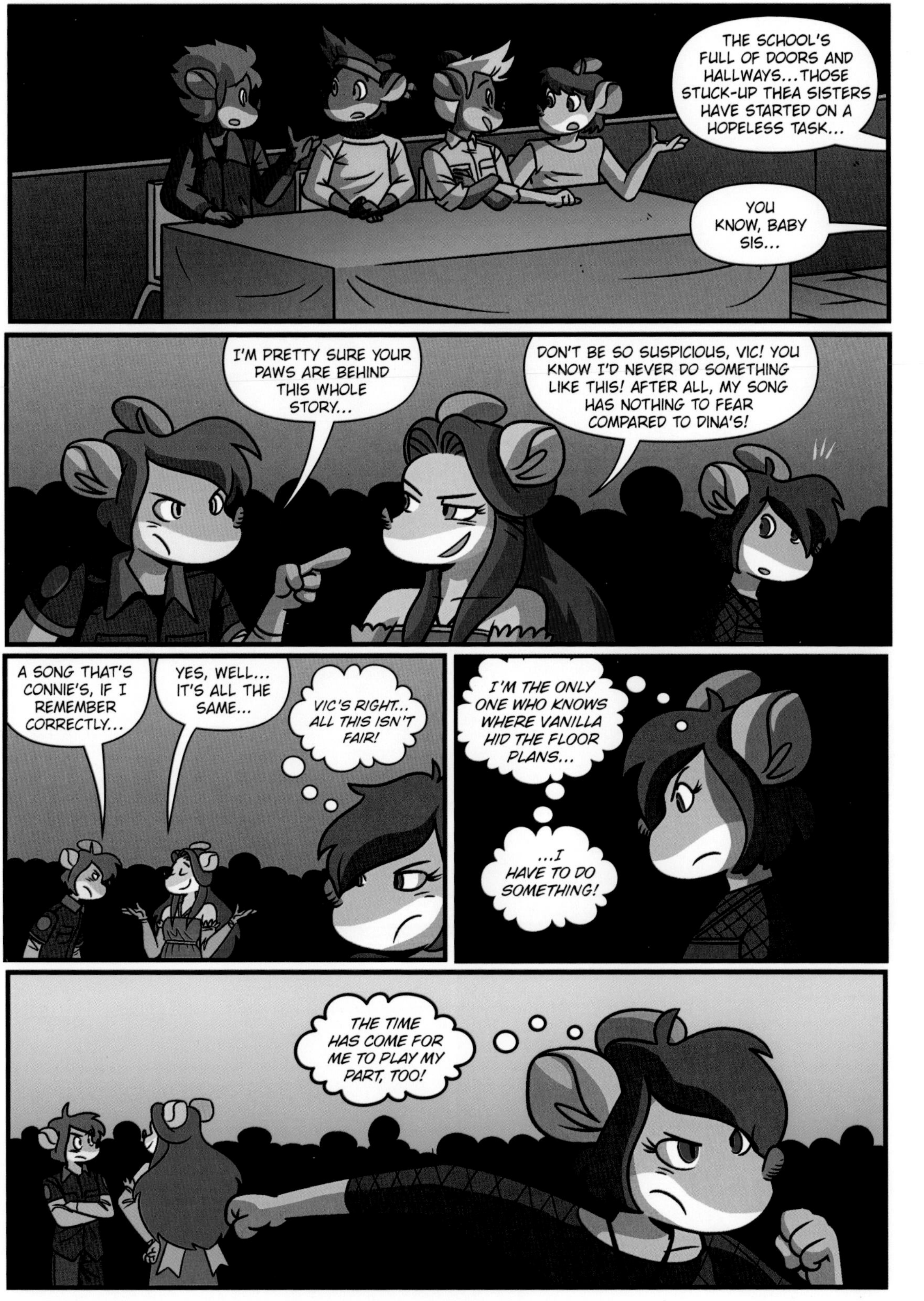
THE SCHOOL'S FULL OF DOORS AND HALLWAYS...THOSE STUCK-UP THEA SISTERS HAVE STARTED ON A HOPELESS TASK...
YOU KNOW, BABY SIS...
I'M PRETTY SURE YOUR PAWS ARE BEHIND THIS WHOLE STORY...
DON'T BE SO SUSPICIOUS, VIC! YOU KNOW I'D NEVER DO SOMETHING LIKE THIS! AFTER ALL, MY SONG HAS NOTHING TO FEAR COMPARED TO DINA'S!
A SONG THAT'S CONNIE'S, IF I REMEMBER CORRECTLY...
YES, WELL... IT'S ALL THE SAME...
VIC'S RIGHT... ALL THIS ISN'T FAIR!
I'M THE ONLY ONE WHO KNOWS WHERE VANILLA HID THE FLOOR PLANS...
...I HAVE TO DO SOMETHING!
THE TIME HAS COME FOR ME TO PLAY MY PART, TOO!

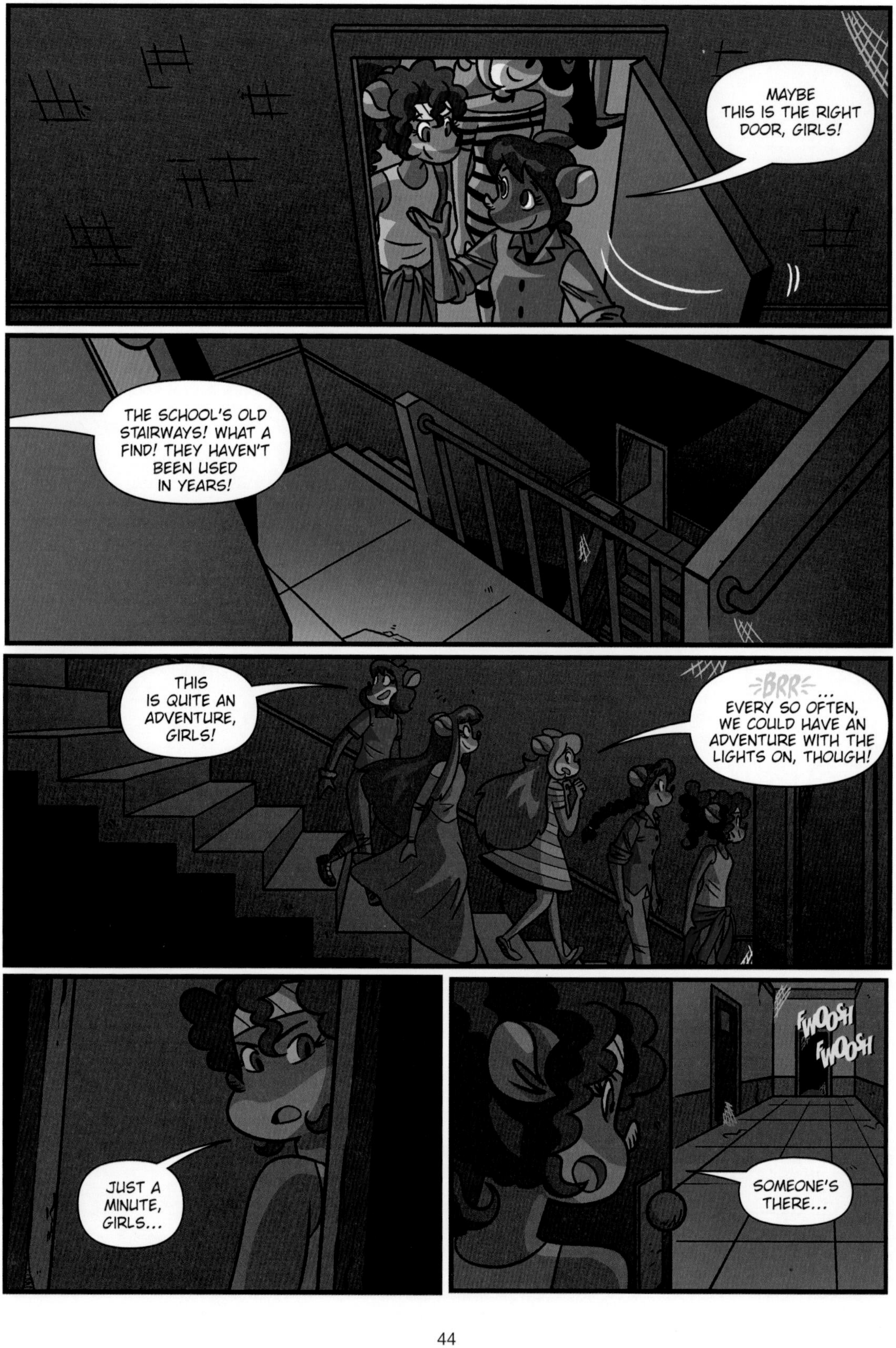
MAYBE THIS IS THE RIGHT DOOR, GIRLS!
THE SCHOOL'S OLD STAIRWAYS! WHAT A FIND! THEY HAVEN'T BEEN USED IN YEARS!
THIS IS QUITE AN ADVENTURE, GIRLS!
BRR... EVERY SO OFTEN, WE COULD HAVE AN ADVENTURE WITH THE LIGHTS ON, THOUGH!
JUST A MINUTE, GIRLS...
FWOOSH FWOOSH
SOMEONE'S THERE...

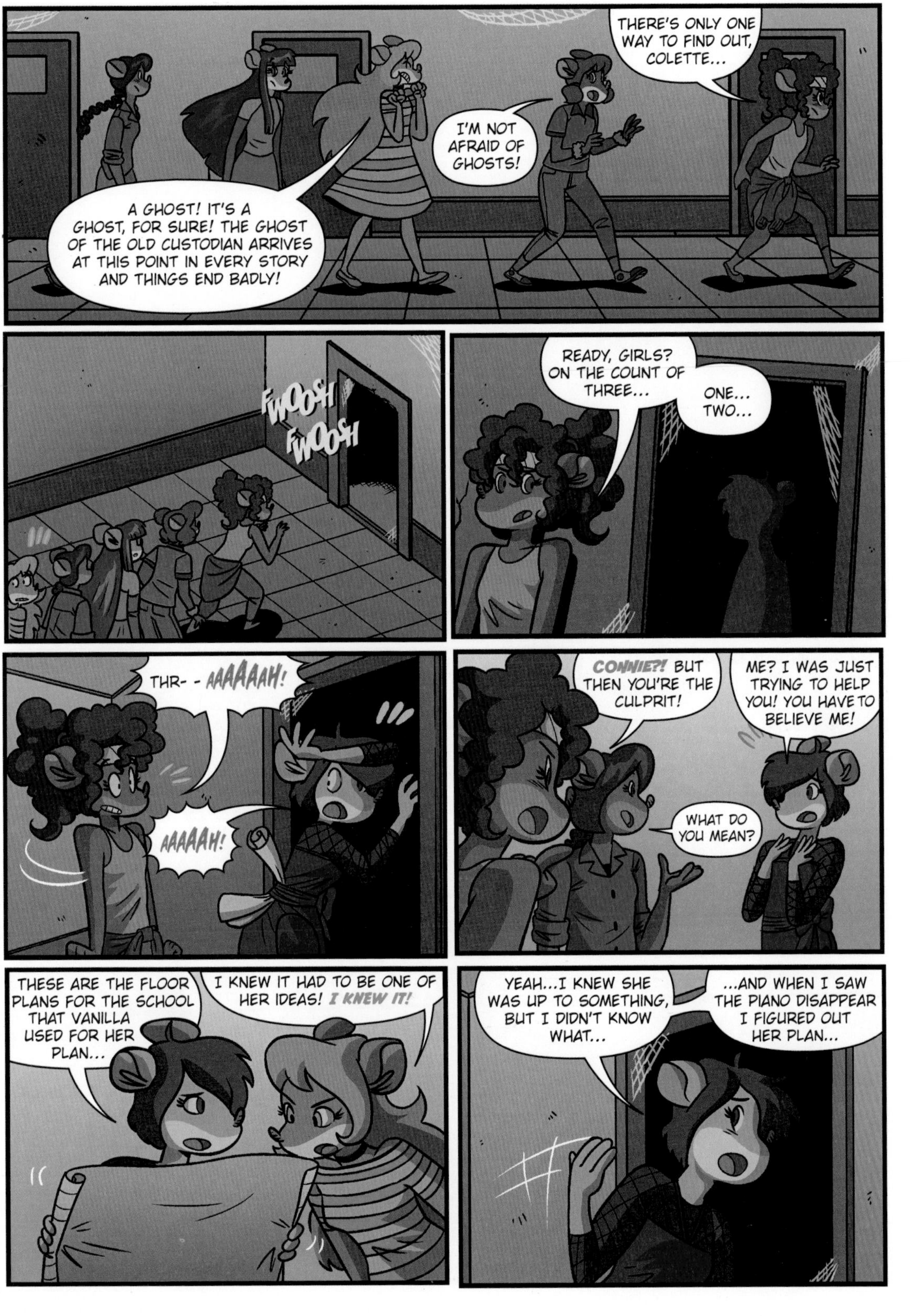
THERE'S ONLY ONE WAY TO FIND OUT, COLETTE...
I'M NOT AFRAID OF GHOSTS!
A GHOST! IT'S A GHOST, FOR SURE! THE GHOST OF THE OLD CUSTODIAN ARRIVES AT THIS POINT IN EVERY STORY AND THINGS END BADLY!
FWOOSH
FWOOSH
READY, GIRLS? ON THE COUNT OF THREE...
ONE... TWO...
THR- - AAAAAAH!
AAAAAH!
CONNIE?! BUT THEN YOU'RE THE CULPRIT!
ME? I WAS JUST TRYING TO HELP YOU! YOU HAVE TO BELIEVE ME!
WHAT DO YOU MEAN?
THESE ARE THE FLOOR PLANS FOR THE SCHOOL THAT VANILLA USED FOR HER PLAN...
I KNEW IT HAD TO BE ONE OF HER IDEAS! I KNEW IT!
YEAH...I KNEW SHE WAS UP TO SOMETHING, BUT I DIDN'T KNOW WHAT...
...AND WHEN I SAW THE PIANO DISAPPEAR I FIGURED OUT HER PLAN...

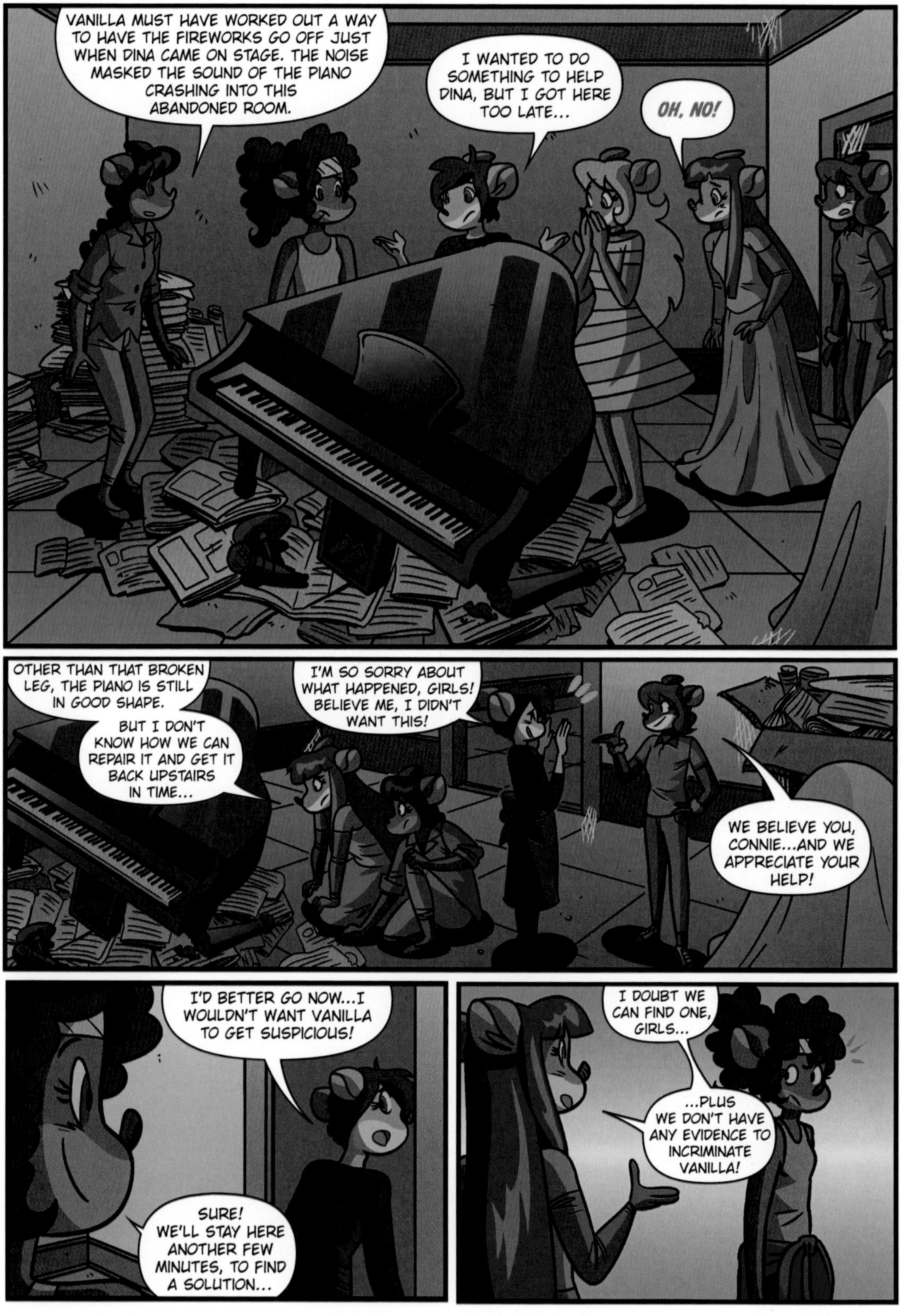
VANILLA MUST HAVE WORKED OUT A WAY TO HAVE THE FIREWORKS GO OFF JUST WHEN DINA CAME ON STAGE. THE NOISE MASKED THE SOUND OF THE PIANO CRASHING INTO THIS ABANDONED ROOM.
I WANTED TO DO SOMETHING TO HELP DINA, BUT I GOT HERE TOO LATE...
OH, NO!
OTHER THAN THAT BROKEN LEG, THE PIANO IS STILL IN GOOD SHAPE.
BUT I DON'T KNOW HOW WE CAN REPAIR IT AND GET IT BACK UPSTAIRS IN TIME...
I'M SO SORRY ABOUT WHAT HAPPENED, GIRLS! BELIEVE ME, I DIDN'T WANT THIS!
WE BELIEVE YOU, CONNIE...AND WE APPRECIATE YOUR HELP!
I'D BETTER GO NOW...I WOULDN'T WANT VANILLA TO GET SUSPICIOUS!
SURE! WE'LL STAY HERE ANOTHER FEW MINUTES, TO FIND A SOLUTION...
I DOUBT WE CAN FIND ONE, GIRLS...
...PLUS WE DON'T HAVE ANY EVIDENCE TO INCRIMINATE VANILLA!

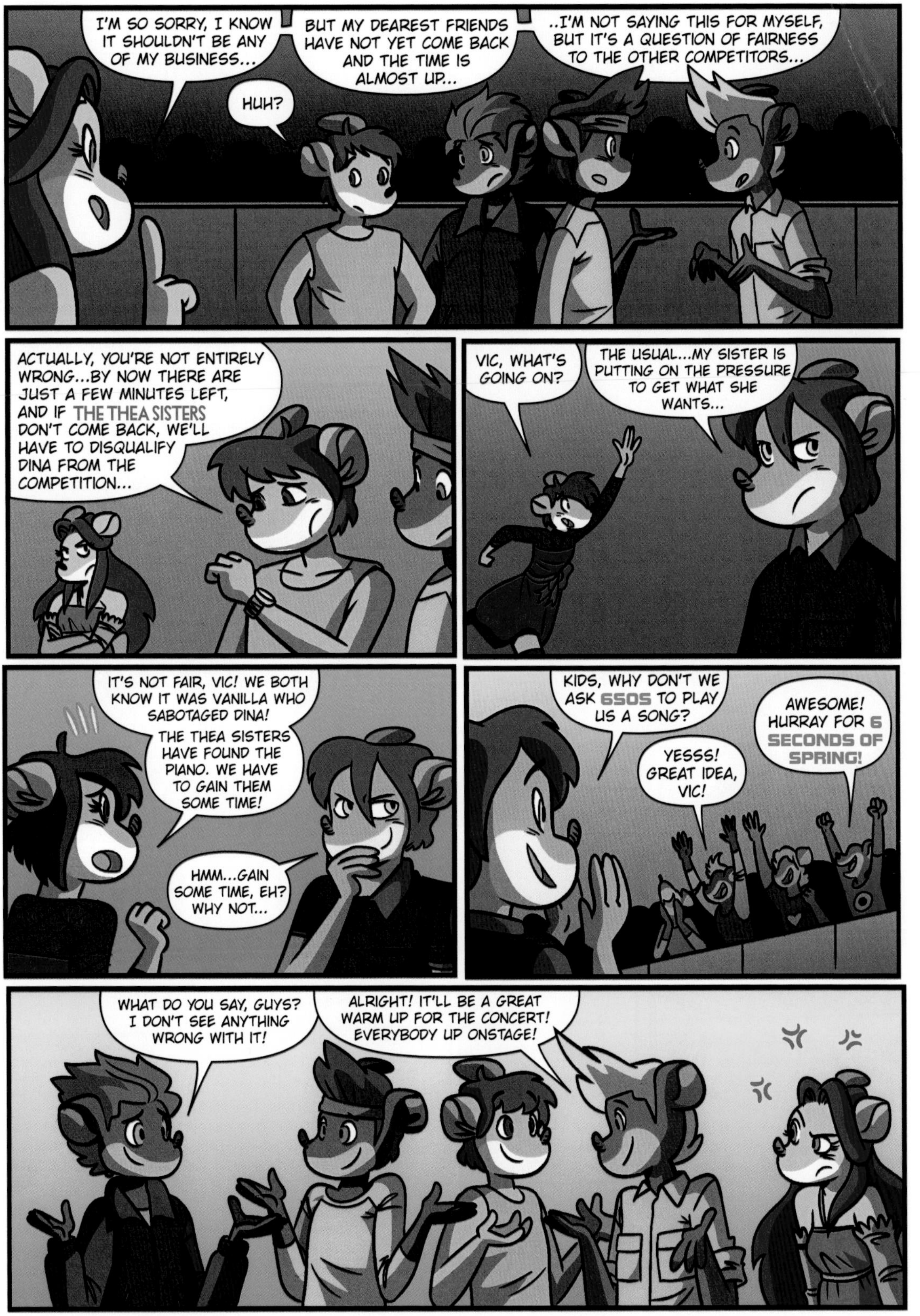
I'M SO SORRY, I KNOW IT SHOULDN'T BE ANY OF MY BUSINESS...
BUT MY DEAREST FRIENDS HAVE NOT YET COME BACK AND THE TIME IS ALMOST UP...
..I'M NOT SAYING THIS FOR MYSELF, BUT IT'S A QUESTION OF FAIRNESS TO THE OTHER COMPETITORS...
HUH?
ACTUALLY, YOU'RE NOT ENTIRELY WRONG...BY NOW THERE ARE JUST A FEW MINUTES LEFT, AND IF THE THEA SISTERS DON'T COME BACK, WE'LL HAVE TO DISQUALIFY DINA FROM THE COMPETITION...
VIC, WHAT'S GOING ON?
THE USUAL...MY SISTER IS PUTTING ON THE PRESSURE TO GET WHAT SHE WANTS...
IT'S NOT FAIR, VIC! WE BOTH KNOW IT WAS VANILLA WHO SABOTAGED DINA!
THE THEA SISTERS HAVE FOUND THE PIANO. WE HAVE TO GAIN THEM SOME TIME!
HMM...GAIN SOME TIME, EH? WHY NOT...
KIDS, WHY DON'T WE ASK 6SOS TO PLAY US A SONG?
YESSS! GREAT IDEA, VIC!
AWESOME! HURRAY FOR 6 SECONDS OF SPRING!
WHAT DO YOU SAY, GUYS? I DON'T SEE ANYTHING WRONG WITH IT!
ALRIGHT! IT'LL BE A GREAT WARM UP FOR THE CONCERT! EVERYBODY UP ONSTAGE!

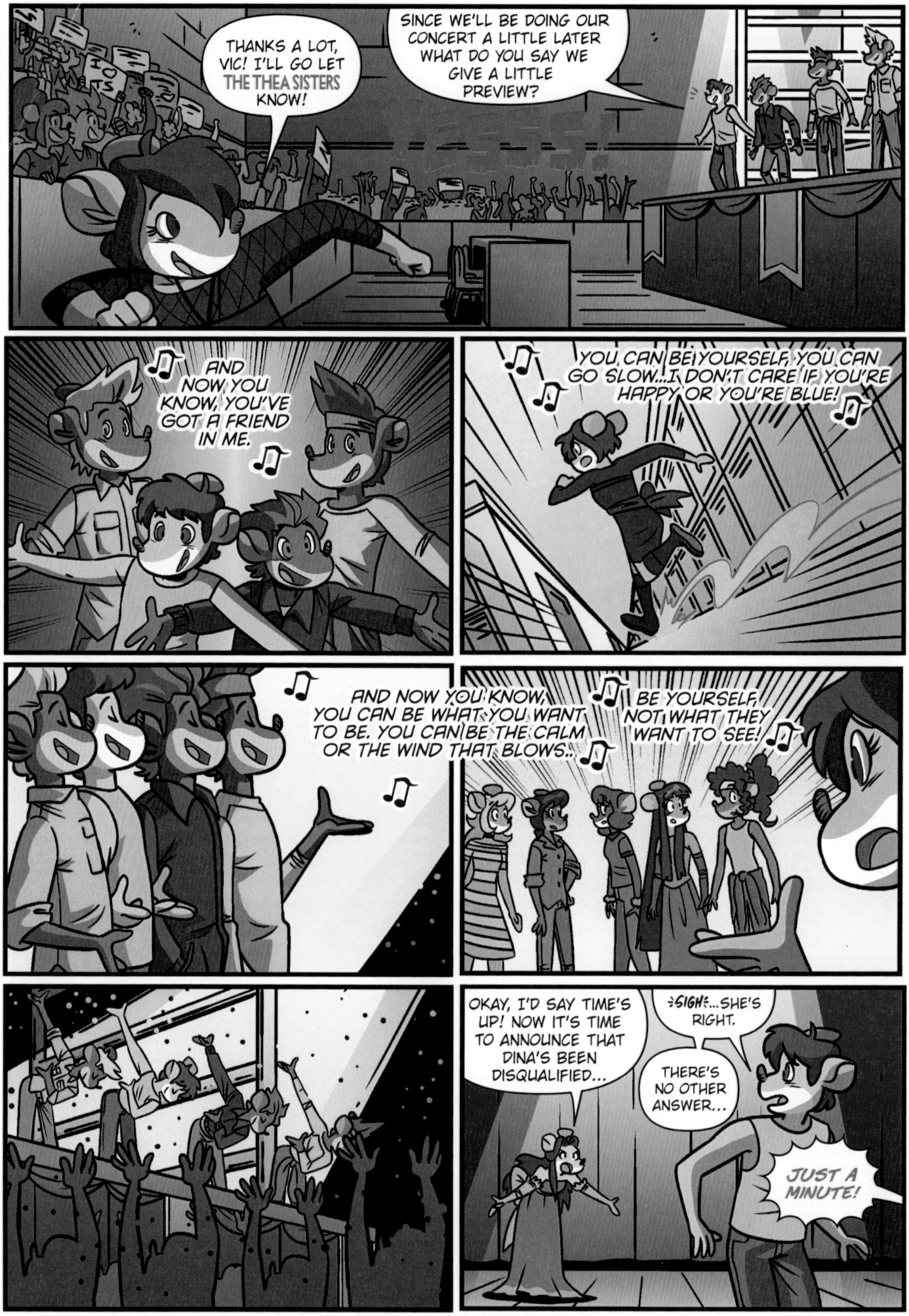

THANKS A LOT, VIC! I'LL GO LET THE THEA SISTERS KNOW!
SINCE WE'LL BE DOING OUR CONCERT A LITTLE LATER WHAT DO YOU SAY WE GIVE A LITTLE PREVIEW?
AND NOW YOU KNOW, YOU'VE GOT A FRIEND IN ME.
YOU CAN BE YOURSELF, YOU CAN GO SLOW... I DON'T CARE IF YOU'RE HAPPY OR YOU'RE BLUE!
AND NOW YOU KNOW, YOU CAN BE WHAT YOU WANT TO BE. YOU CAN BE THE CALM OR THE WIND THAT BLOWS...
BE YOURSELF, NOT WHAT THEY WANT TO SEE!
OKAY, I'D SAY TIME'S UP! NOW IT'S TIME TO ANNOUNCE THAT DINA'S BEEN DISQUALIFIED...
SIGH ...SHE'S RIGHT.
THERE'S NO OTHER ANSWER...
JUST A MINUTE!

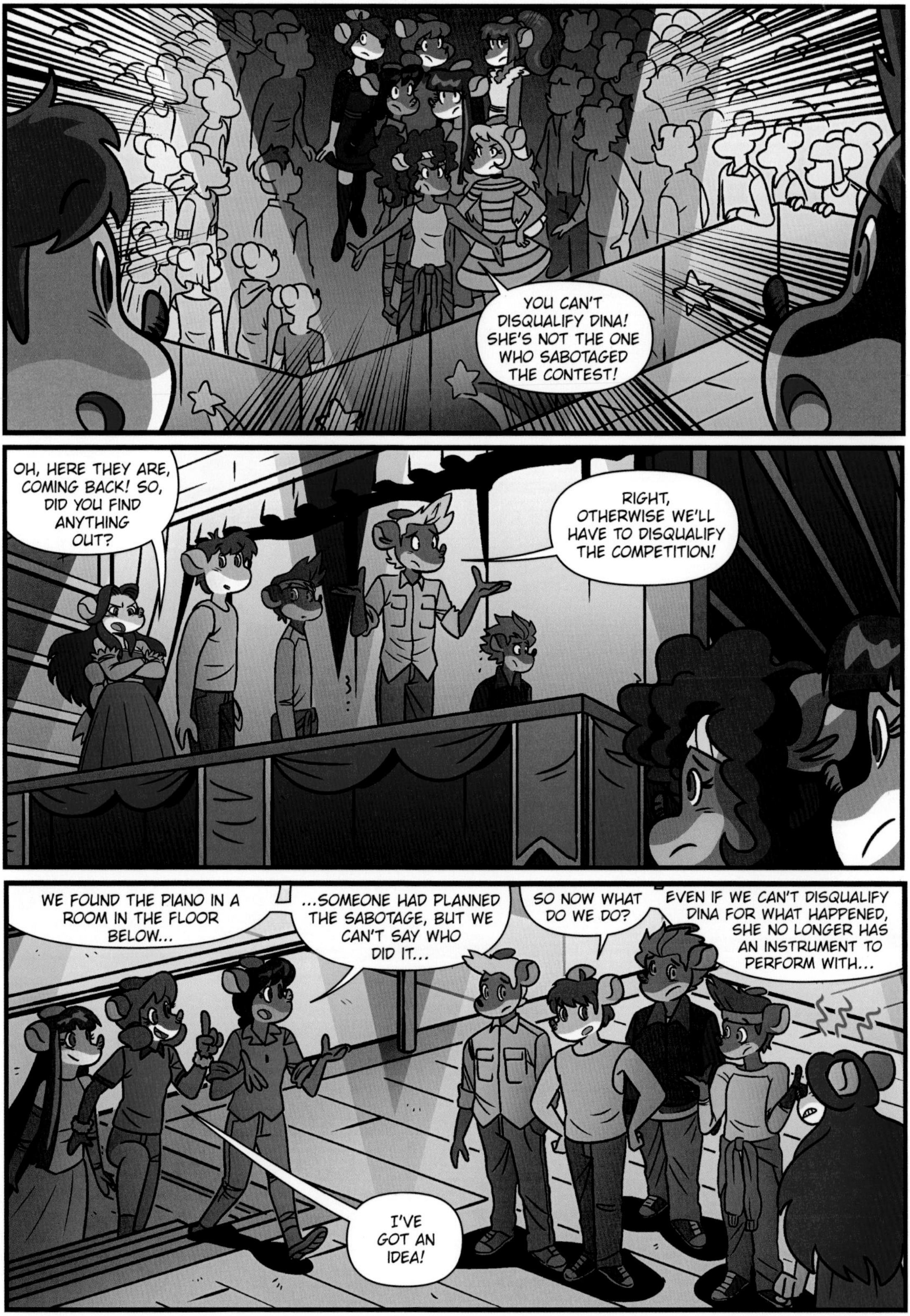
YOU CAN'T DISQUALIFY DINA! SHE'S NOT THE ONE WHO SABOTAGED THE CONTEST!
OH, HERE THEY ARE, COMING BACK! SO, DID YOU FIND ANYTHING OUT?
RIGHT, OTHERWISE WE'LL HAVE TO DISQUALIFY THE COMPETITION!
WE FOUND THE PIANO IN A ROOM IN THE FLOOR BELOW...
...SOMEONE HAD PLANNED THE SABOTAGE, BUT WE CAN'T SAY WHO DID IT...
SO NOW WHAT DO WE DO?
EVEN IF WE CAN'T DISQUALIFY DINA FOR WHAT HAPPENED, SHE NO LONGER HAS AN INSTRUMENT TO PERFORM WITH...
I'VE GOT AN IDEA!

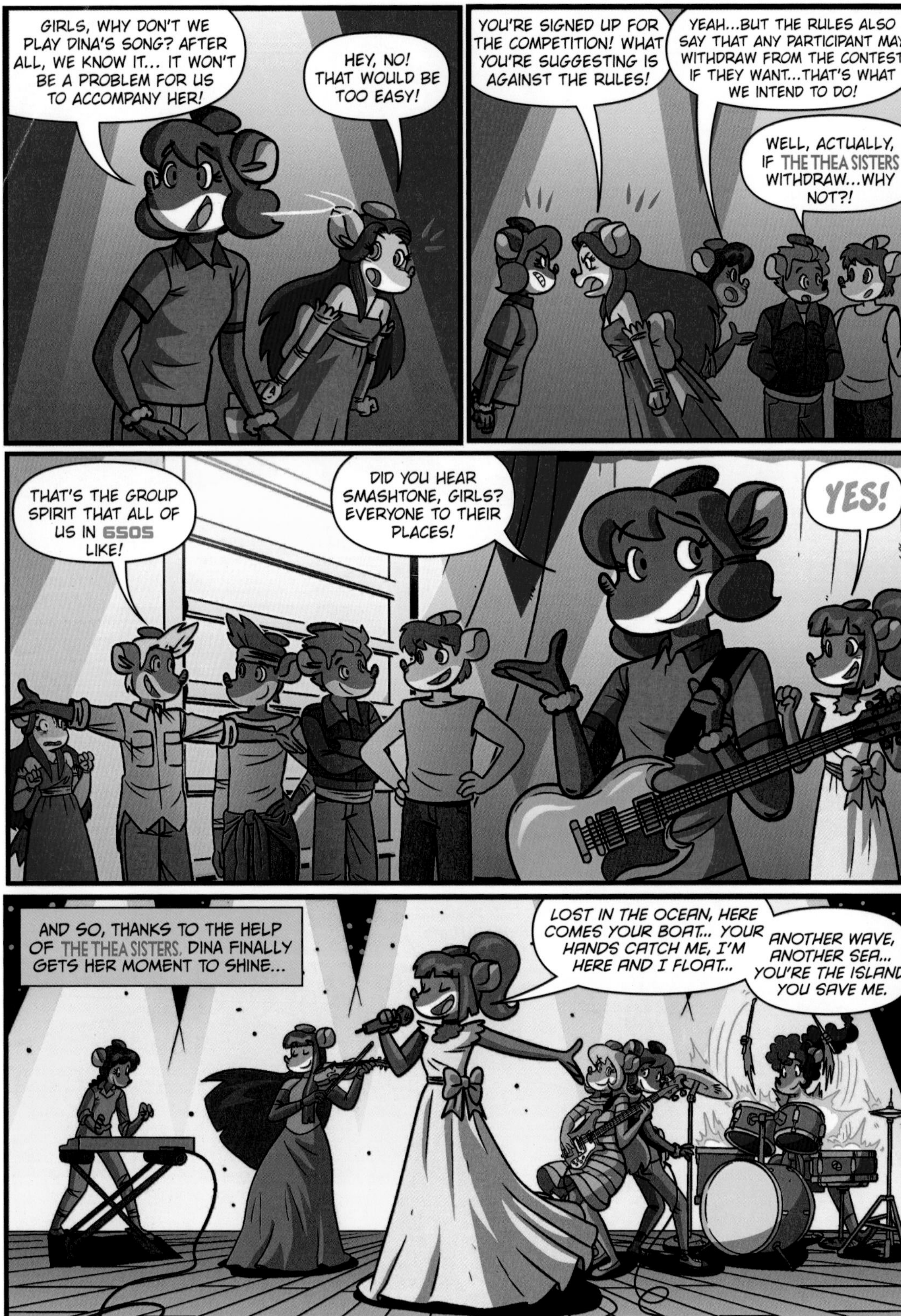
GIRLS, WHY DON'T WE PLAY DINA'S SONG? AFTER ALL, WE KNOW IT... IT WON'T BE A PROBLEM FOR US TO ACCOMPANY HER!
HEY, NO! THAT WOULD BE TOO EASY!
YOU'RE SIGNED UP FOR THE COMPETITION! WHAT YOU'RE SUGGESTING IS AGAINST THE RULES!
YEAH...BUT THE RULES ALSO SAY THAT ANY PARTICIPANT MAY WITHDRAW FROM THE CONTEST IF THEY WANT...THAT'S WHAT WE INTEND TO DO!
WELL, ACTUALLY, IF THE THEA SISTERS WITHDRAW...WHY NOT?!
THAT'S THE GROUP SPIRIT THAT ALL OF US IN 6SOS LIKE!
DID YOU HEAR SMASHTONE, GIRLS? EVERYONE TO THEIR PLACES!
YES!
AND SO, THANKS TO THE HELP OF THE THEA SISTERS, DINA FINALLY GETS HER MOMENT TO SHINE...
LOST IN THE OCEAN, HERE COMES YOUR BOAT... YOUR HANDS CATCH ME, I'M HERE AND I FLOAT...
ANOTHER WAVE, ANOTHER SEA... YOU'RE THE ISLAND, YOU SAVE ME.

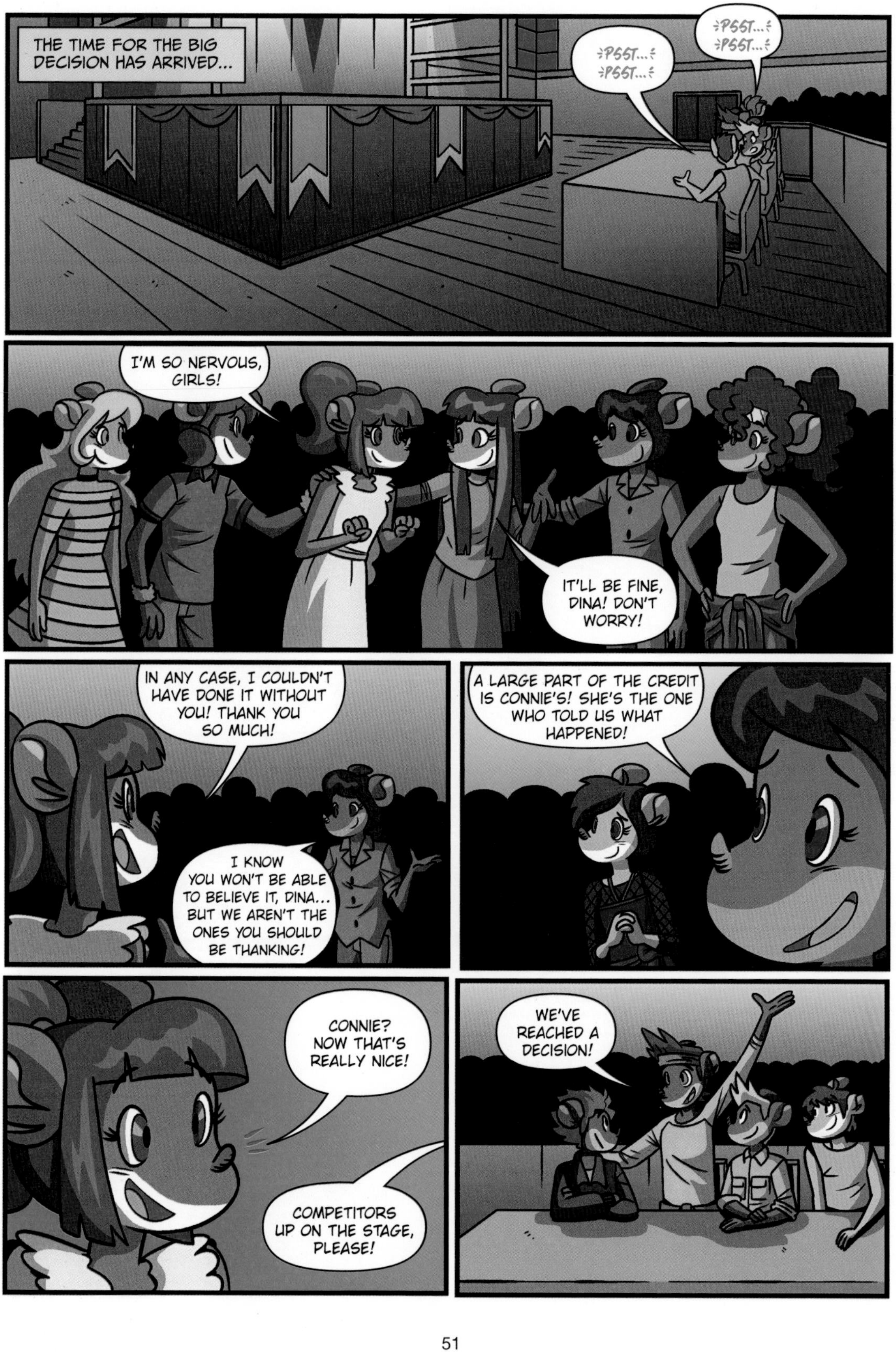
THE TIME FOR THE BIG DECISION HAS ARRIVED...
PSST... PSST...
PSST... PSST...
I'M SO NERVOUS, GIRLS!
IT'LL BE FINE, DINA! DON'T WORRY!
IN ANY CASE, I COULDN'T HAVE DONE IT WITHOUT YOU! THANK YOU SO MUCH!
I KNOW YOU WON'T BE ABLE TO BELIEVE IT, DINA... BUT WE AREN'T THE ONES YOU SHOULD BE THANKING!
A LARGE PART OF THE CREDIT IS CONNIE'S! SHE'S THE ONE WHO TOLD US WHAT HAPPENED!
CONNIE? NOW THAT'S REALLY NICE!
COMPETITORS UP ON THE STAGE, PLEASE!
WE'VE REACHED A DECISION!

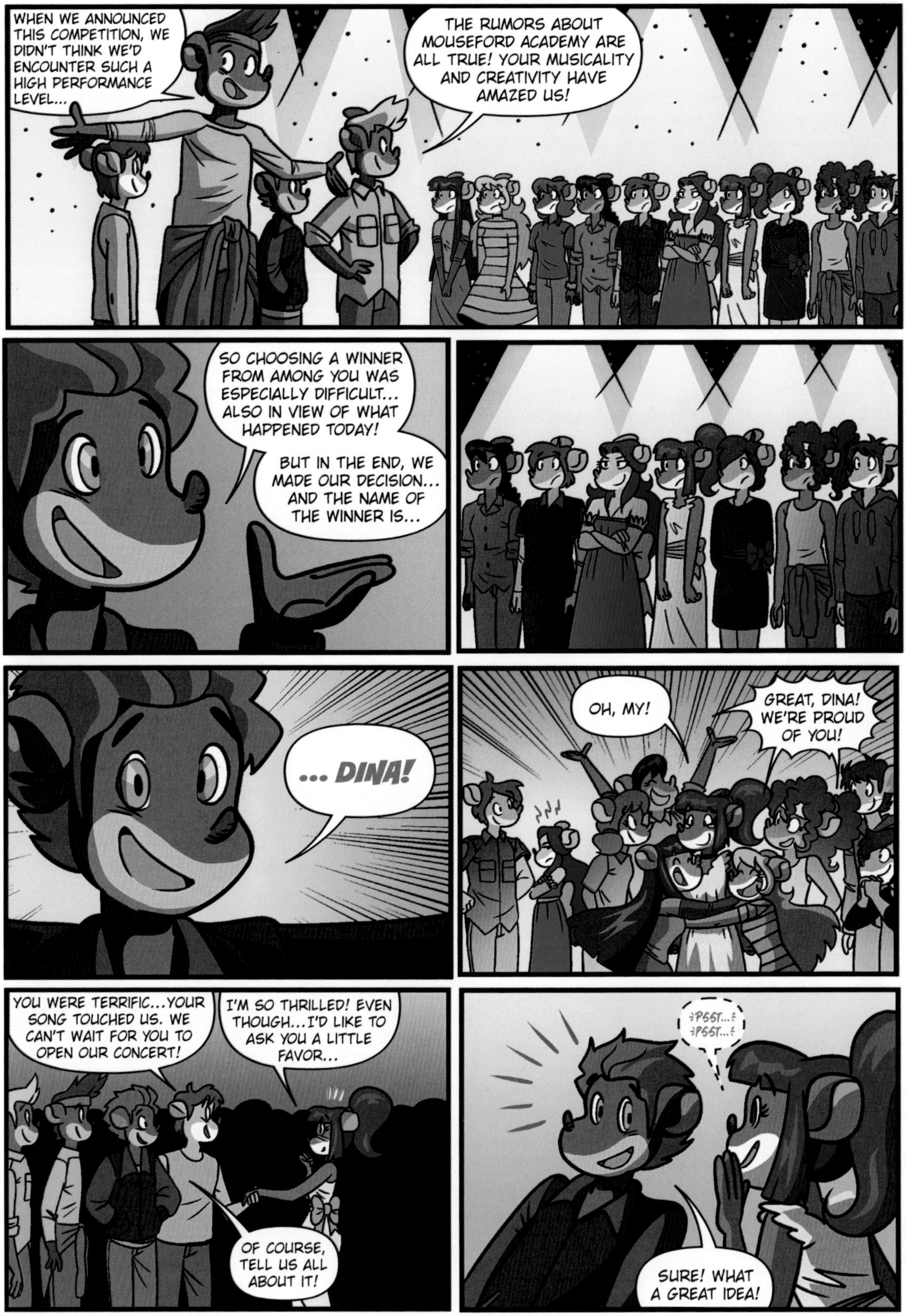
WHEN WE ANNOUNCED THIS COMPETITION, WE DIDN'T THINK WE'D ENCOUNTER SUCH A HIGH PERFORMANCE LEVEL...
THE RUMORS ABOUT MOUSEFORD ACADEMY ARE ALL TRUE! YOUR MUSICALITY AND CREATIVITY HAVE AMAZED US!
SO CHOOSING A WINNER FROM AMONG YOU WAS ESPECIALLY DIFFICULT... ALSO IN VIEW OF WHAT HAPPENED TODAY!
BUT IN THE END, WE MADE OUR DECISION... AND THE NAME OF THE WINNER IS...
... DINA!
OH, MY!
GREAT, DINA! WE'RE PROUD OF YOU!
YOU WERE TERRIFIC...YOUR SONG TOUCHED US. WE CAN'T WAIT FOR YOU TO OPEN OUR CONCERT!
I'M SO THRILLED! EVEN THOUGH...I'D LIKE TO ASK YOU A LITTLE FAVOR...
OF COURSE, TELL US ALL ABOUT IT!
PSST... PSST...
SURE! WHAT A GREAT IDEA!

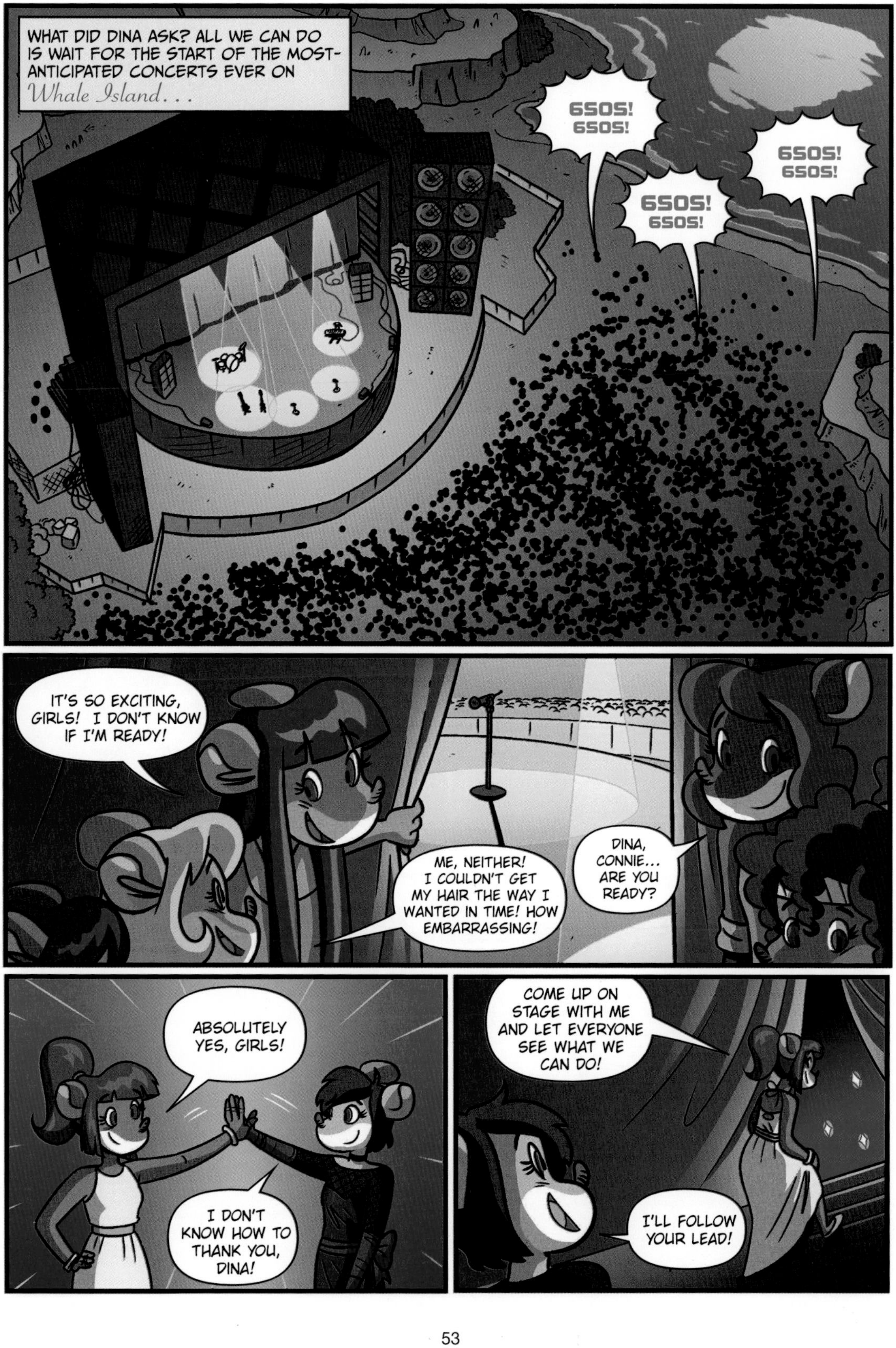
WHAT DID DINA ASK? ALL WE CAN DO IS WAIT FOR THE START OF THE MOST-ANTICIPATED CONCERTS EVER ON Whale Island...
6SOS! 6SOS!
6SOS! 6SOS!
6SOS! 6SOS!
IT'S SO EXCITING, GIRLS! I DON'T KNOW IF I'M READY!
ME, NEITHER! I COULDN'T GET MY HAIR THE WAY I WANTED IN TIME! HOW EMBARRASSING!
DINA, CONNIE... ARE YOU READY?
ABSOLUTELY YES, GIRLS!
I DON'T KNOW HOW TO THANK YOU, DINA!
COME UP ON STAGE WITH ME AND LET EVERYONE SEE WHAT WE CAN DO!
I'LL FOLLOW YOUR LEAD!

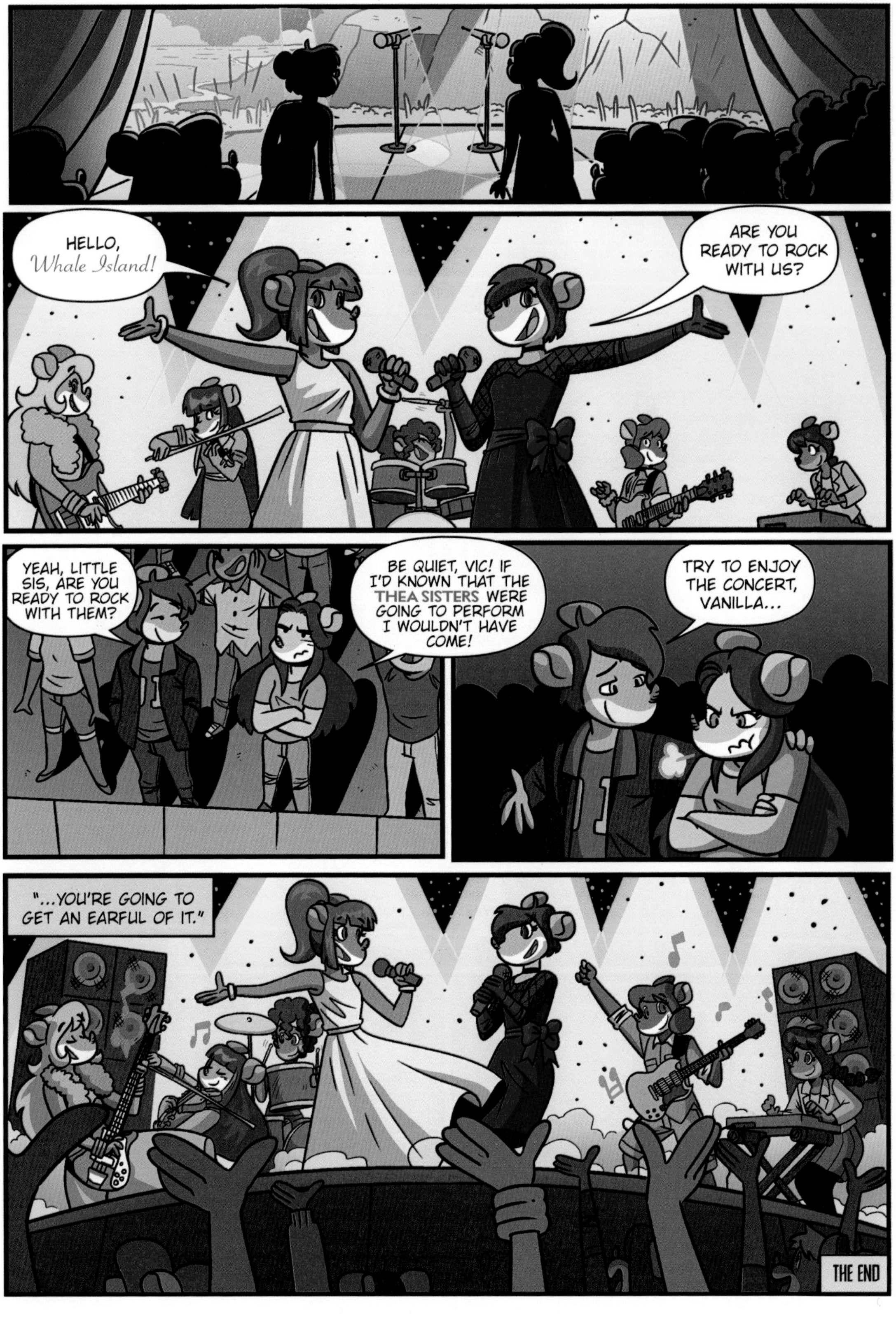
HELLO, Whale Island!
ARE YOU READY TO ROCK WITH US?
YEAH, LITTLE SIS, ARE YOU READY TO ROCK WITH THEM?
BE QUIET, VIC! IF I'D KNOWN THAT THE THEA SISTERS WERE GOING TO PERFORM I WOULDN'T HAVE COME!
TRY TO ENJOY THE CONCERT, VANILLA...
"...YOU'RE GOING TO GET AN EARFUL OF IT."
THE END

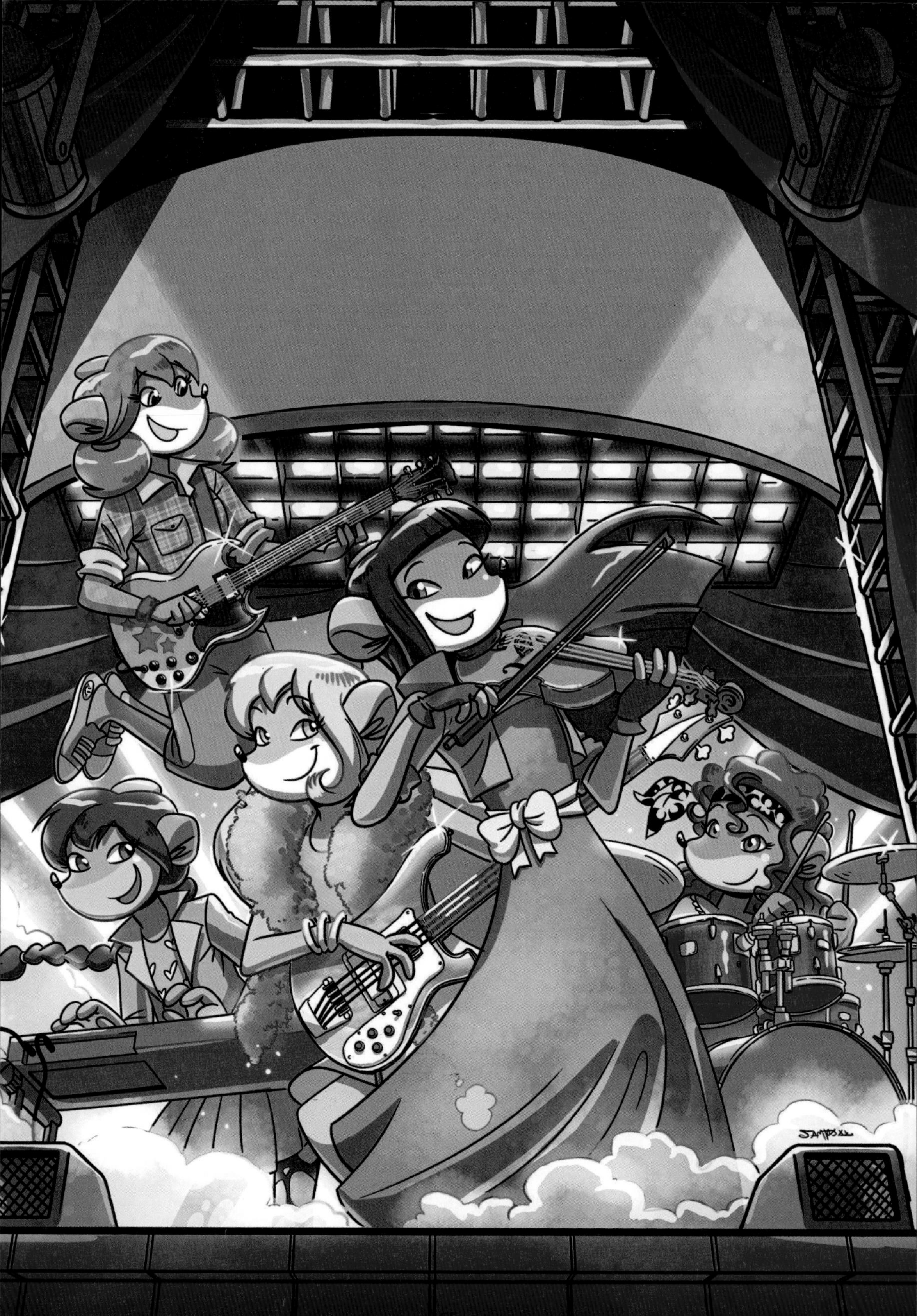

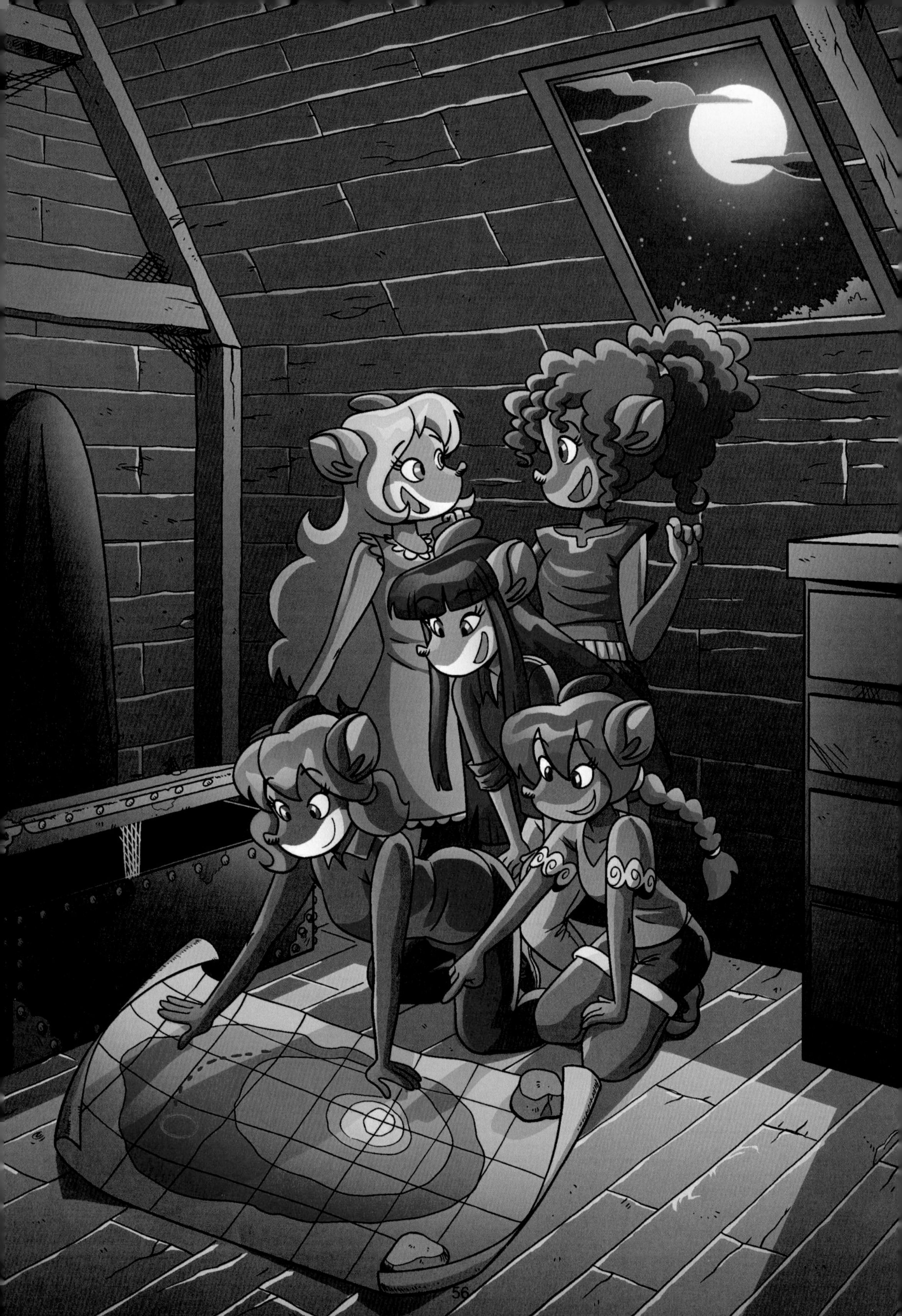

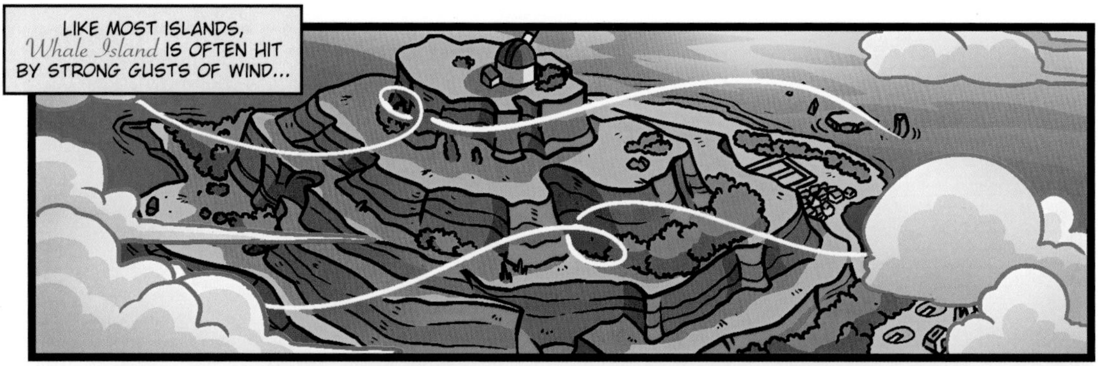
LIKE MOST ISLANDS, Whale Island IS OFTEN HIT BY STRONG GUSTS OF WIND...

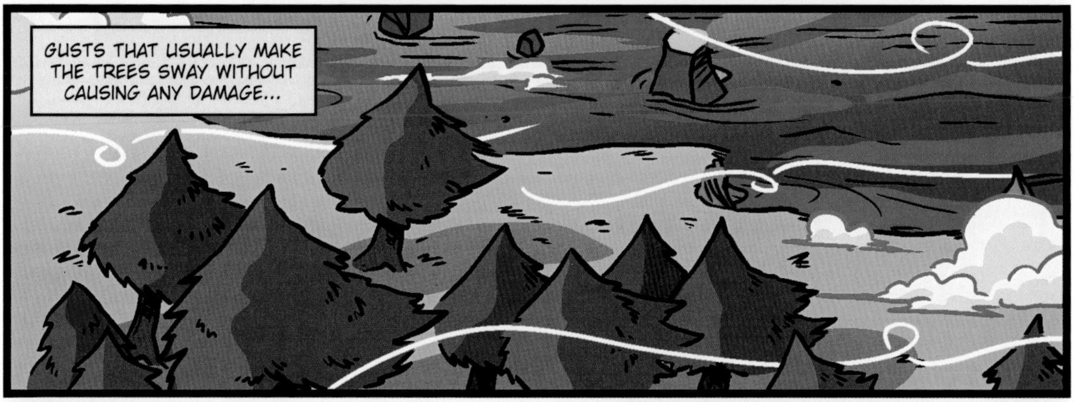
GUSTS THAT USUALLY MAKE THE TREES SWAY WITHOUT CAUSING ANY DAMAGE...

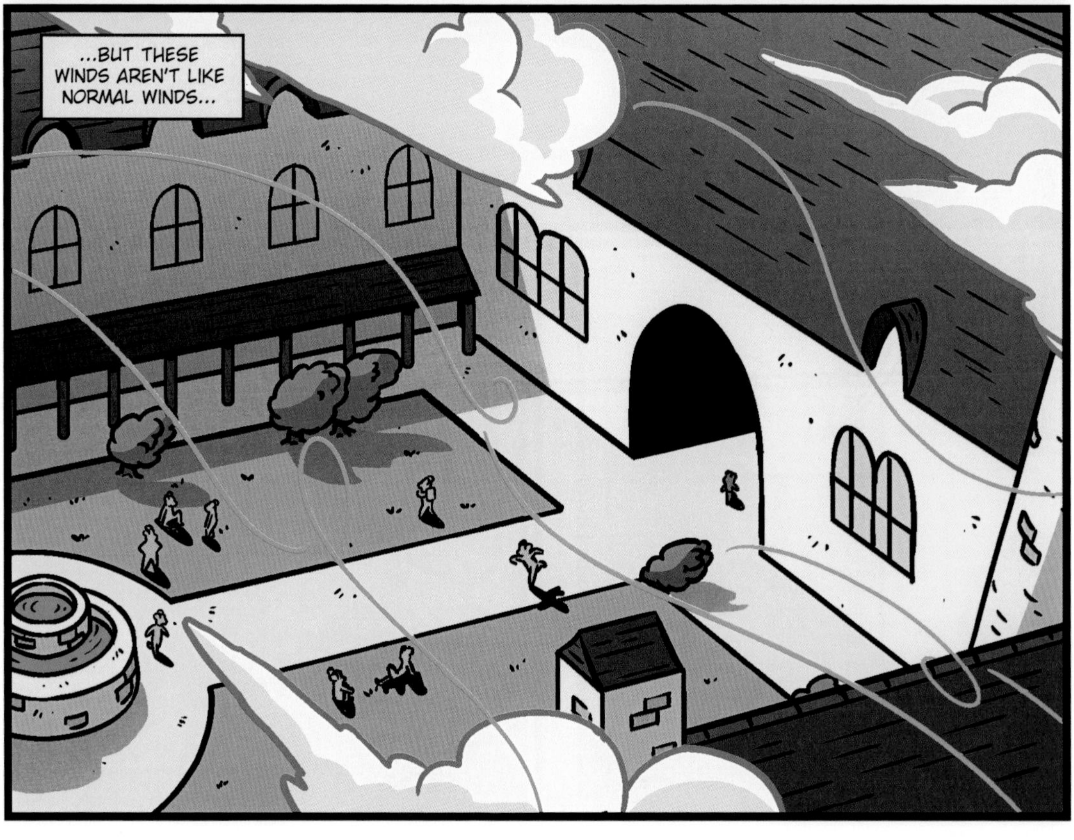
...BUT THESE WINDS AREN'T LIKE NORMAL WINDS...

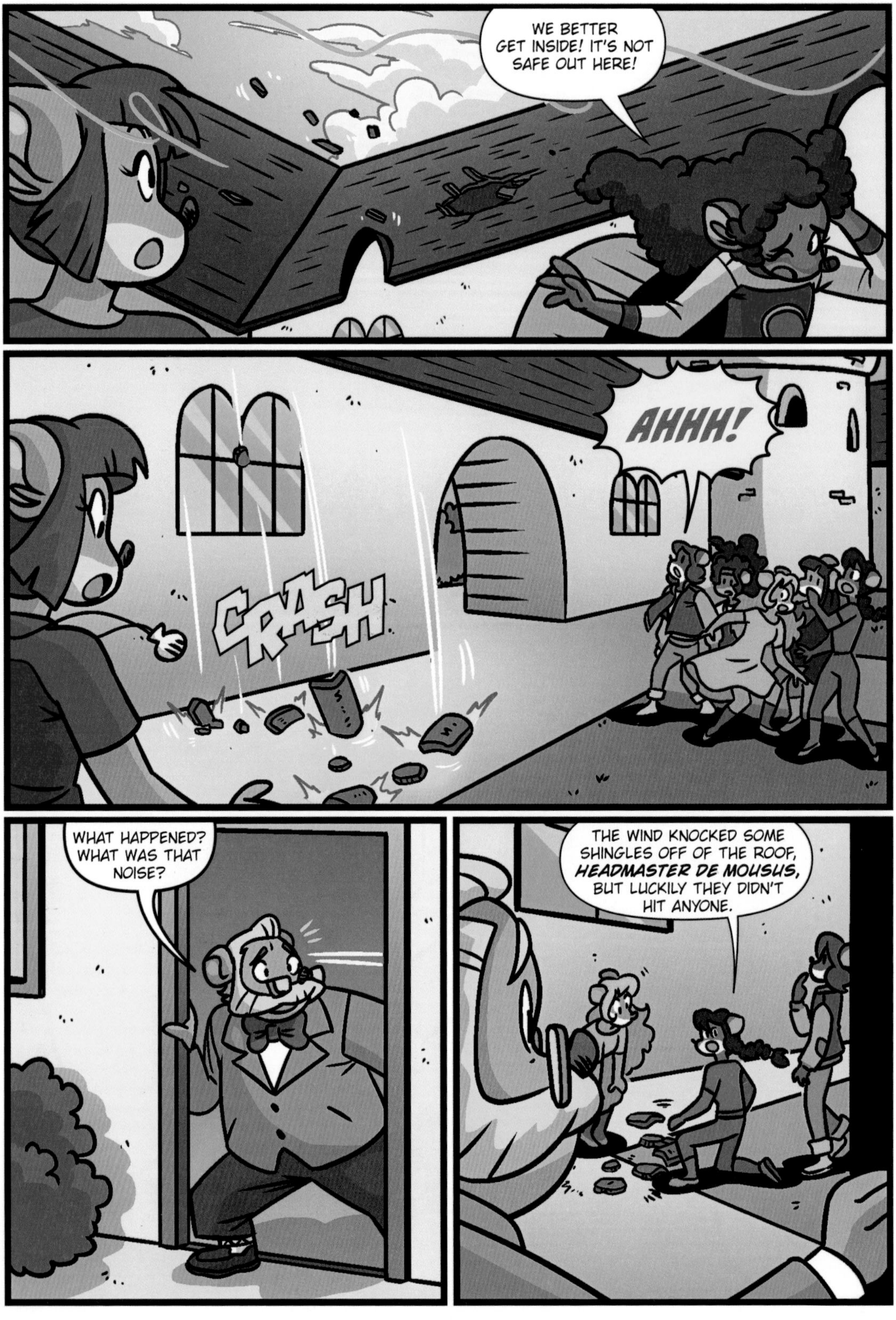

WE BETTER GET INSIDE! IT'S NOT SAFE OUT HERE!
AHHH!
CRASH
WHAT HAPPENED? WHAT WAS THAT NOISE?
THE WIND KNOCKED SOME SHINGLES OFF OF THE ROOF, **HEADMASTER DE MOUSUS,** BUT LUCKILY THEY DIDN'T HIT ANYONE.

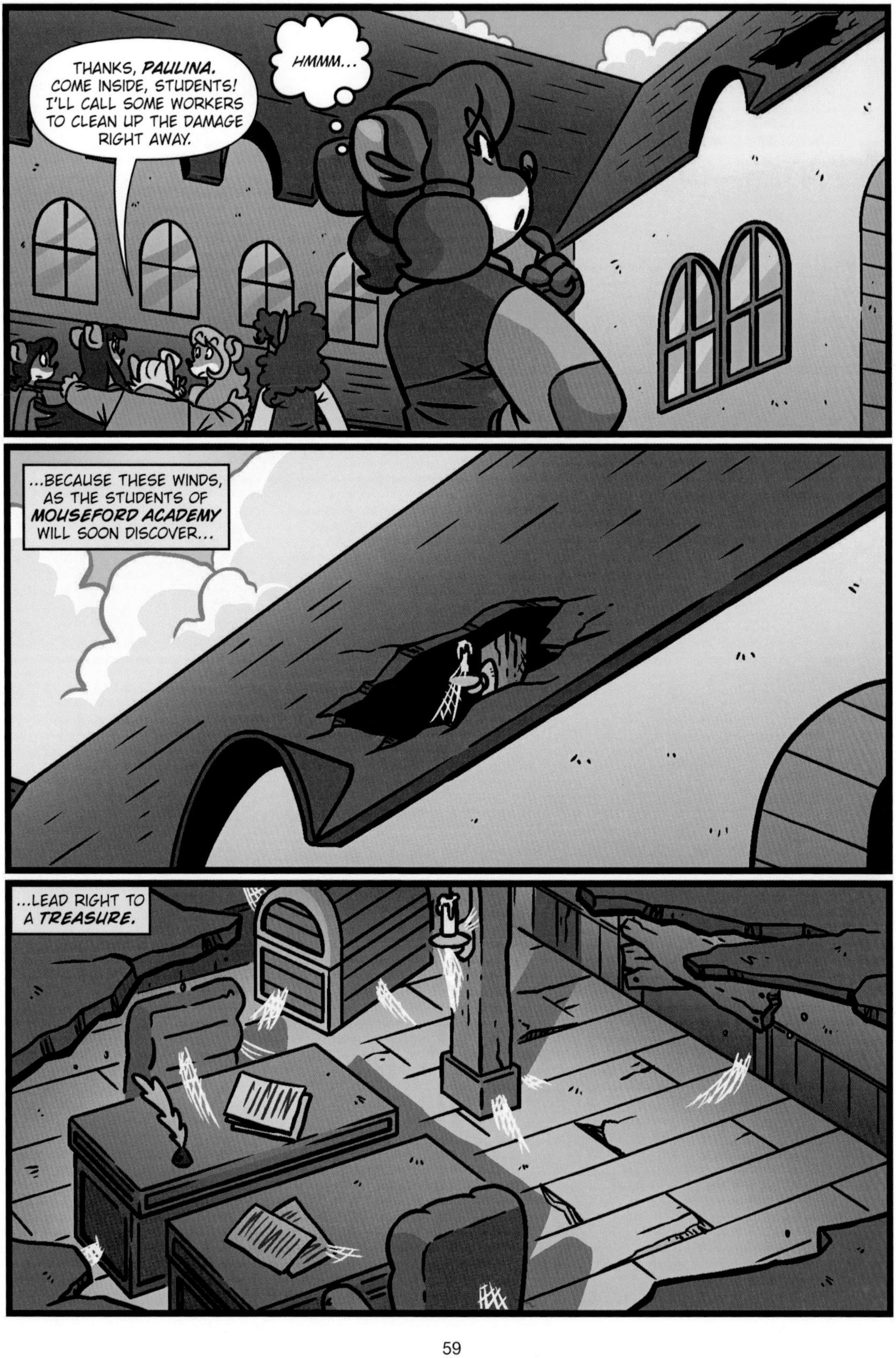
THANKS, PAULINA. COME INSIDE, STUDENTS! I'LL CALL SOME WORKERS TO CLEAN UP THE DAMAGE RIGHT AWAY.
HMMM...
...BECAUSE THESE WINDS, AS THE STUDENTS OF MOUSEFORD ACADEMY WILL SOON DISCOVER...
...LEAD RIGHT TO A TREASURE.

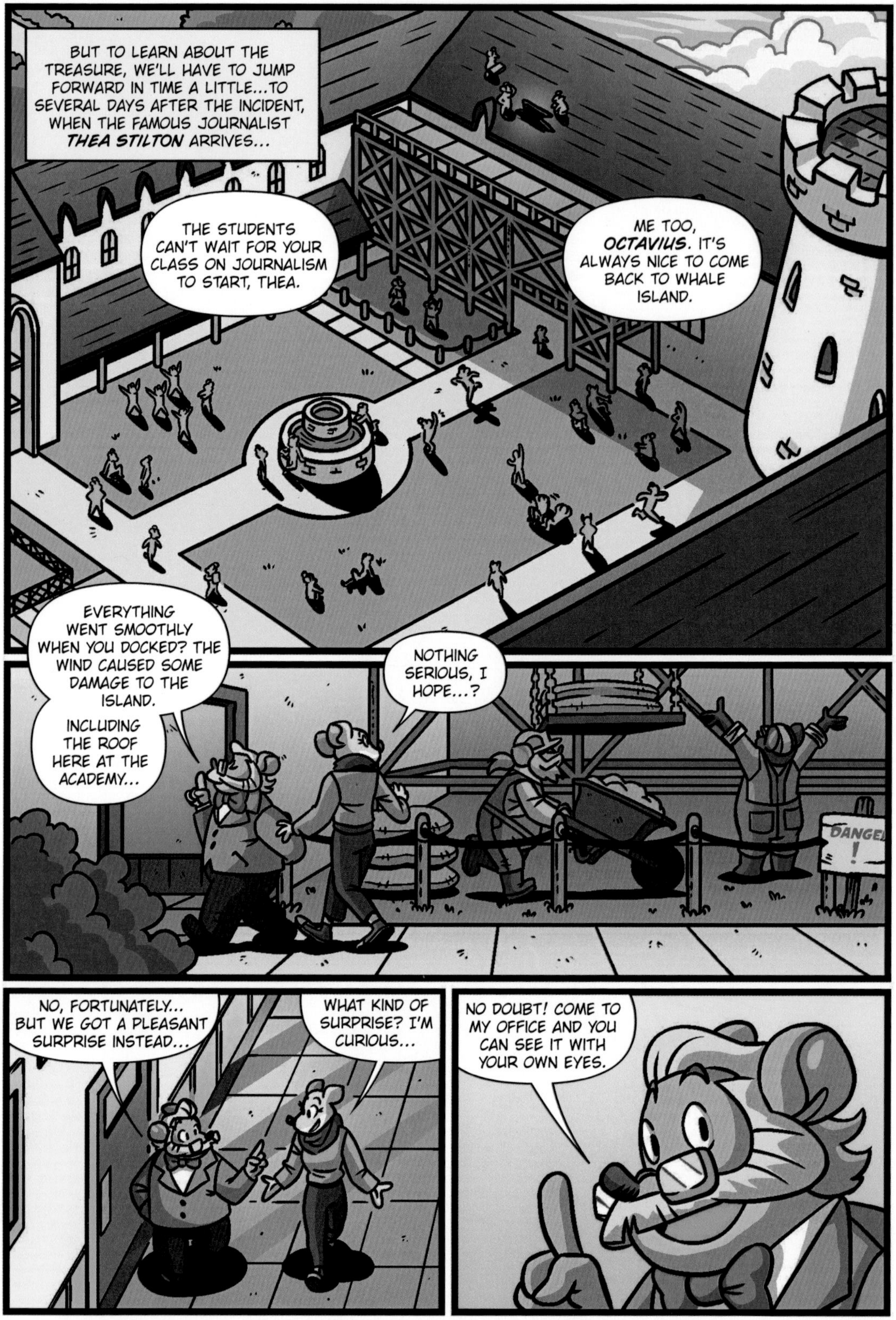
BUT TO LEARN ABOUT THE TREASURE, WE'LL HAVE TO JUMP FORWARD IN TIME A LITTLE...TO SEVERAL DAYS AFTER THE INCIDENT, WHEN THE FAMOUS JOURNALIST THEA STILTON ARRIVES...
THE STUDENTS CAN'T WAIT FOR YOUR CLASS ON JOURNALISM TO START, THEA.
ME TOO, OCTAVIUS. IT'S ALWAYS NICE TO COME BACK TO WHALE ISLAND.
EVERYTHING WENT SMOOTHLY WHEN YOU DOCKED? THE WIND CAUSED SOME DAMAGE TO THE ISLAND.
INCLUDING THE ROOF HERE AT THE ACADEMY...
NOTHING SERIOUS, I HOPE...?
DANGE
!
NO, FORTUNATELY... BUT WE GOT A PLEASANT SURPRISE INSTEAD...
WHAT KIND OF SURPRISE? I'M CURIOUS...
NO DOUBT! COME TO MY OFFICE AND YOU CAN SEE IT WITH YOUR OWN EYES.

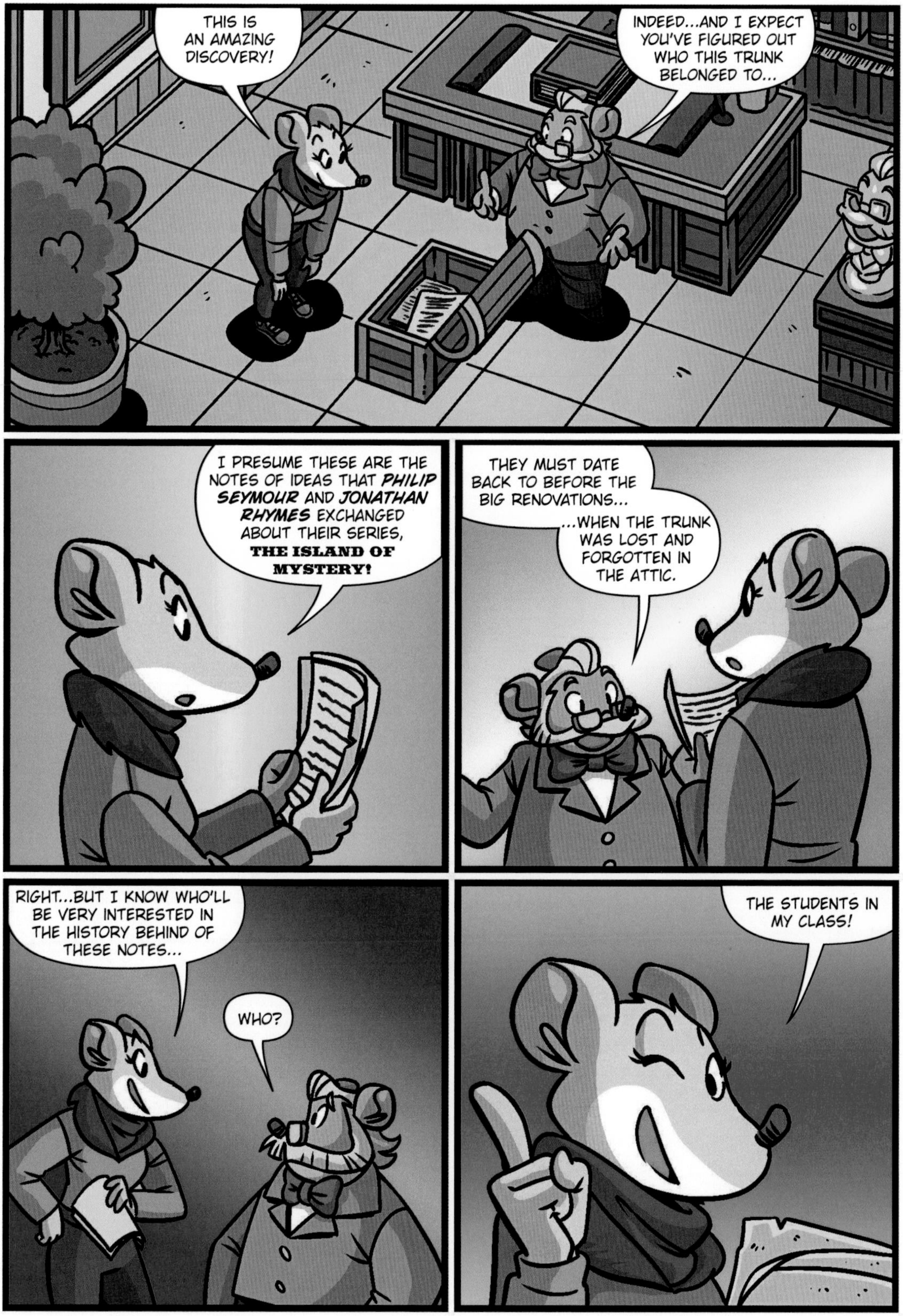
THIS IS AN AMAZING DISCOVERY!
INDEED...AND I EXPECT YOU'VE FIGURED OUT WHO THIS TRUNK BELONGED TO...
I PRESUME THESE ARE THE NOTES OF IDEAS THAT PHILIP SEYMOUR AND JONATHAN RHYMES EXCHANGED ABOUT THEIR SERIES, THE ISLAND OF MYSTERY!
THEY MUST DATE BACK TO BEFORE THE BIG RENOVATIONS...
...WHEN THE TRUNK WAS LOST AND FORGOTTEN IN THE ATTIC.
RIGHT...BUT I KNOW WHO'LL BE VERY INTERESTED IN THE HISTORY BEHIND OF THESE NOTES...
WHO?
THE STUDENTS IN MY CLASS!

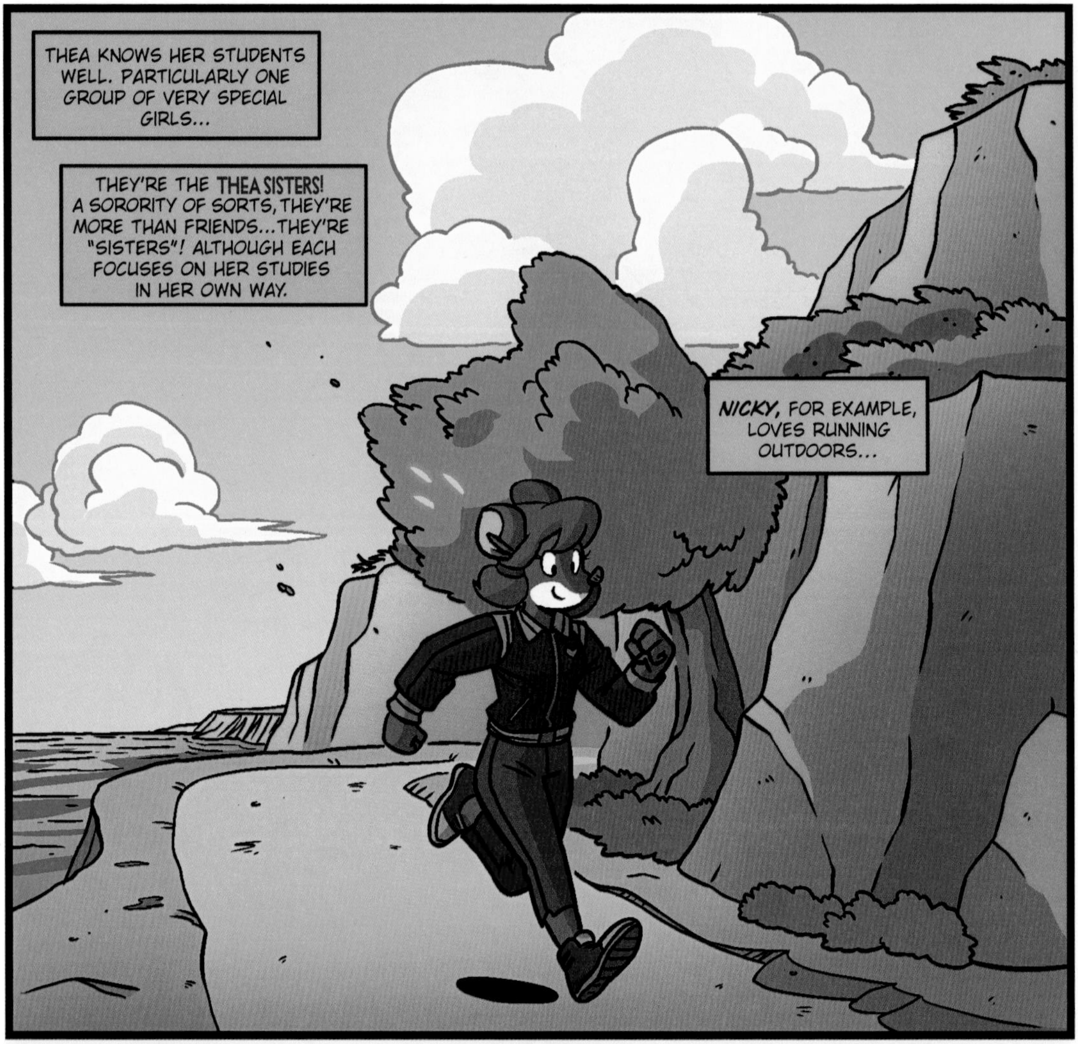

THEA KNOWS HER STUDENTS WELL. PARTICULARLY ONE GROUP OF VERY SPECIAL GIRLS...
THEY'RE THE THEA SISTERS! A SORORITY OF SORTS, THEY'RE MORE THAN FRIENDS...THEY'RE "SISTERS"! ALTHOUGH EACH FOCUSES ON HER STUDIES IN HER OWN WAY.
NICKY, FOR EXAMPLE, LOVES RUNNING OUTDOORS...

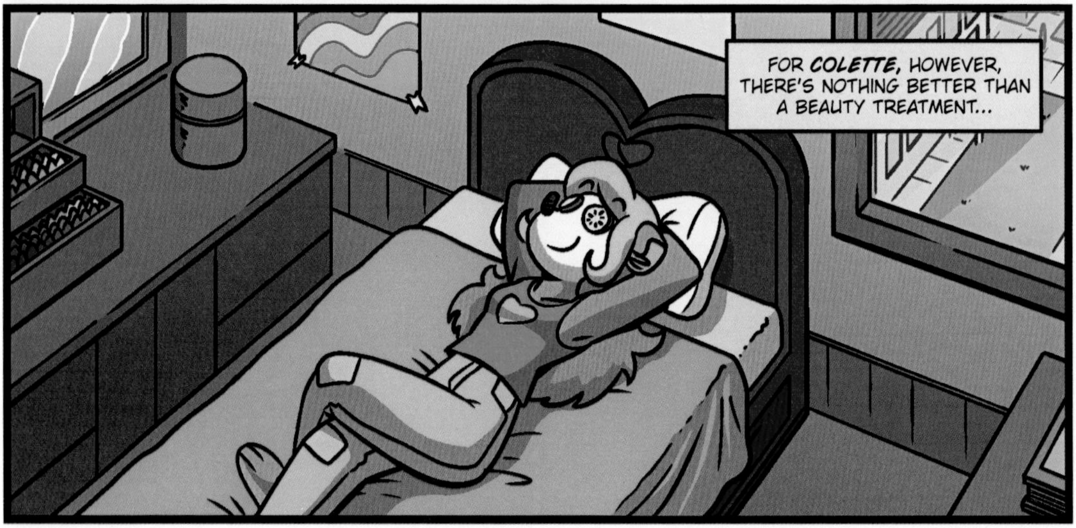

FOR COLETTE, HOWEVER, THERE'S NOTHING BETTER THAN A BEAUTY TREATMENT...

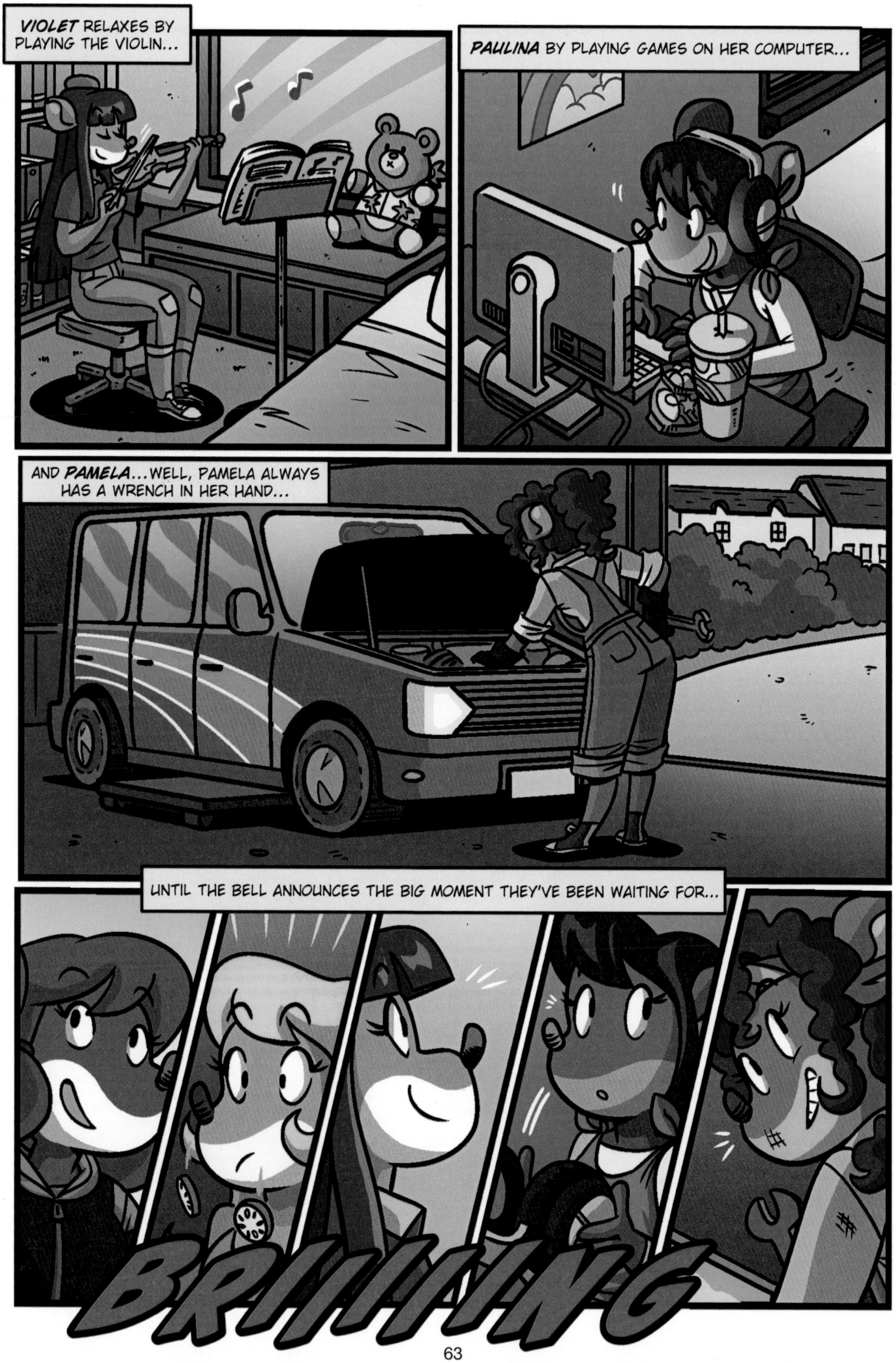
VIOLET RELAXES BY PLAYING THE VIOLIN...
PAULINA BY PLAYING GAMES ON HER COMPUTER...
AND PAMELA...WELL, PAMELA ALWAYS HAS A WRENCH IN HER HAND...
UNTIL THE BELL ANNOUNCES THE BIG MOMENT THEY'VE BEEN WAITING FOR...
BRIIIING

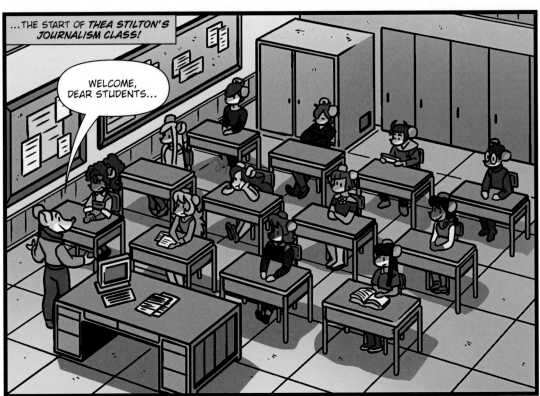

...THE START OF *THEA STILTON'S JOURNALISM CLASS!*

WELCOME, DEAR STUDENTS...

IT'S ALWAYS A PLEASURE TO BE HERE AT MOUSEFORD ACADEMY WITH YOU!

ZOE, I BET THIS WILL BE ANOTHER **BORING** CLASS!

THINK SO, *VANILLA?* HEE! HEE!

SHHH!

64

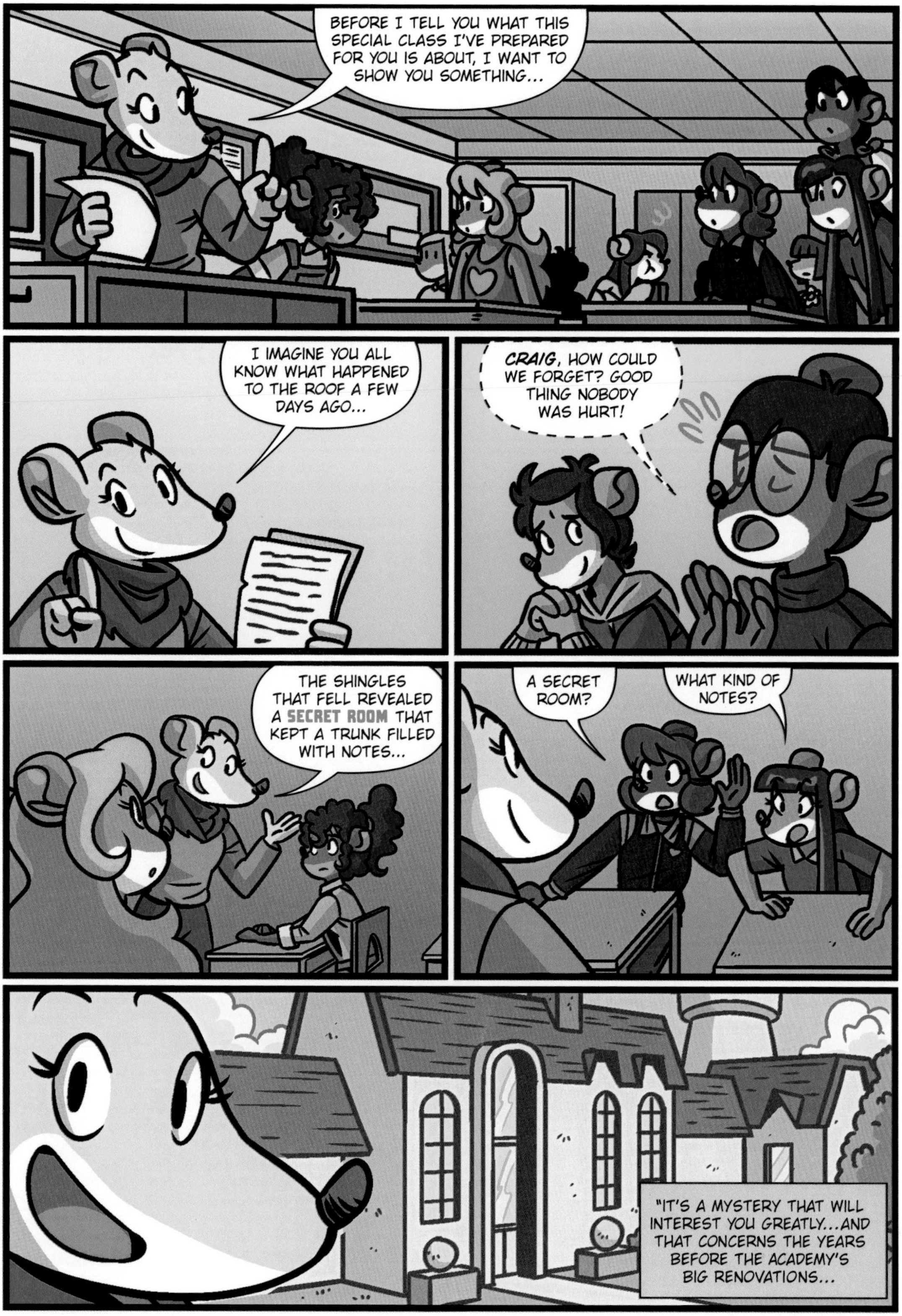
BEFORE I TELL YOU WHAT THIS SPECIAL CLASS I'VE PREPARED FOR YOU IS ABOUT, I WANT TO SHOW YOU SOMETHING...
I IMAGINE YOU ALL KNOW WHAT HAPPENED TO THE ROOF A FEW DAYS AGO...
CRAIG, HOW COULD WE FORGET? GOOD THING NOBODY WAS HURT!
THE SHINGLES THAT FELL REVEALED A SECRET ROOM THAT KEPT A TRUNK FILLED WITH NOTES...
A SECRET ROOM?
WHAT KIND OF NOTES?
"IT'S A MYSTERY THAT WILL INTEREST YOU GREATLY...AND THAT CONCERNS THE YEARS BEFORE THE ACADEMY'S BIG RENOVATIONS...

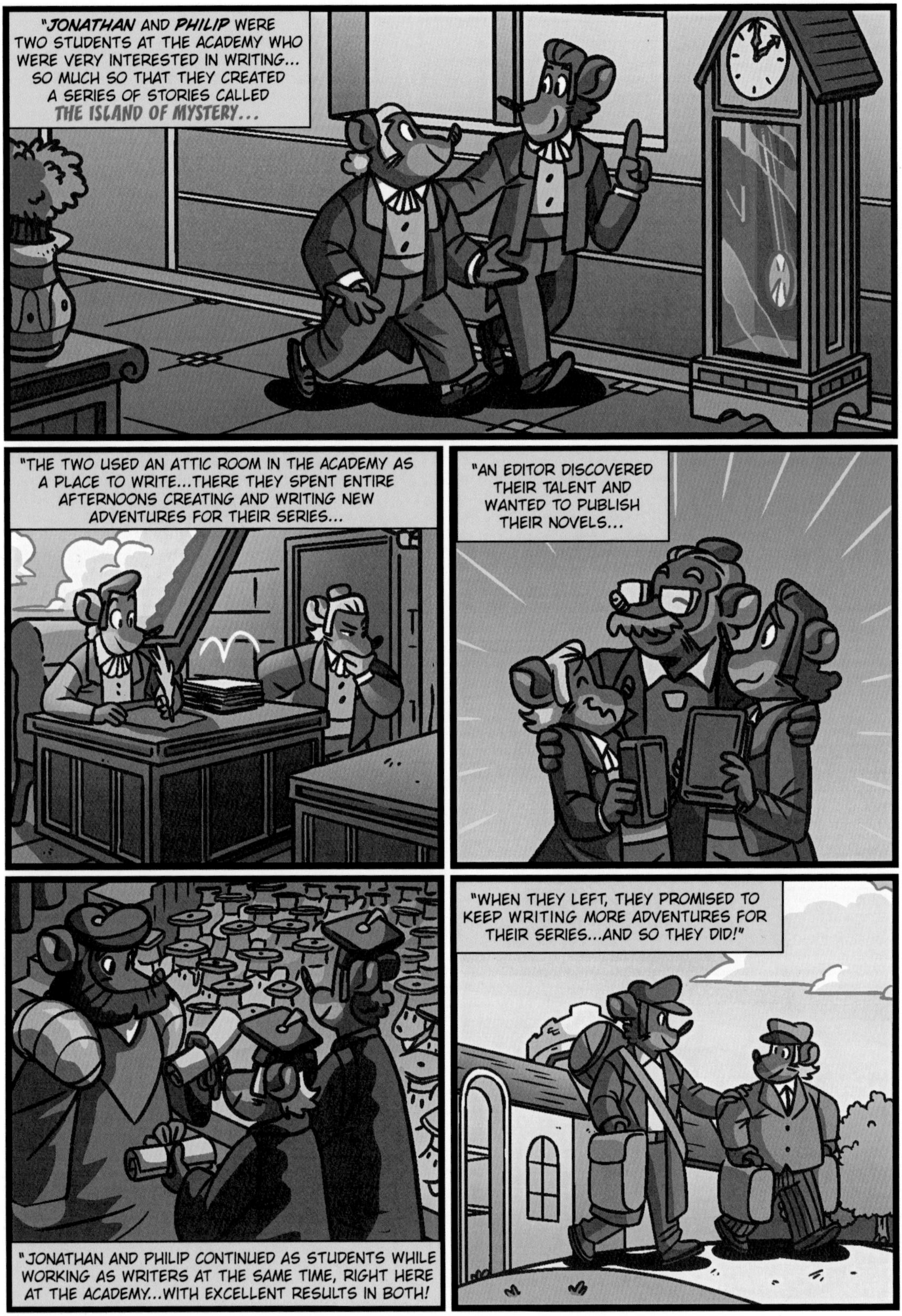
"JONATHAN AND PHILIP WERE TWO STUDENTS AT THE ACADEMY WHO WERE VERY INTERESTED IN WRITING... SO MUCH SO THAT THEY CREATED A SERIES OF STORIES CALLED THE ISLAND OF MYSTERY...
"THE TWO USED AN ATTIC ROOM IN THE ACADEMY AS A PLACE TO WRITE...THERE THEY SPENT ENTIRE AFTERNOONS CREATING AND WRITING NEW ADVENTURES FOR THEIR SERIES...
"AN EDITOR DISCOVERED THEIR TALENT AND WANTED TO PUBLISH THEIR NOVELS...
"JONATHAN AND PHILIP CONTINUED AS STUDENTS WHILE WORKING AS WRITERS AT THE SAME TIME, RIGHT HERE AT THE ACADEMY...WITH EXCELLENT RESULTS IN BOTH!
"WHEN THEY LEFT, THEY PROMISED TO KEEP WRITING MORE ADVENTURES FOR THEIR SERIES...AND SO THEY DID!"

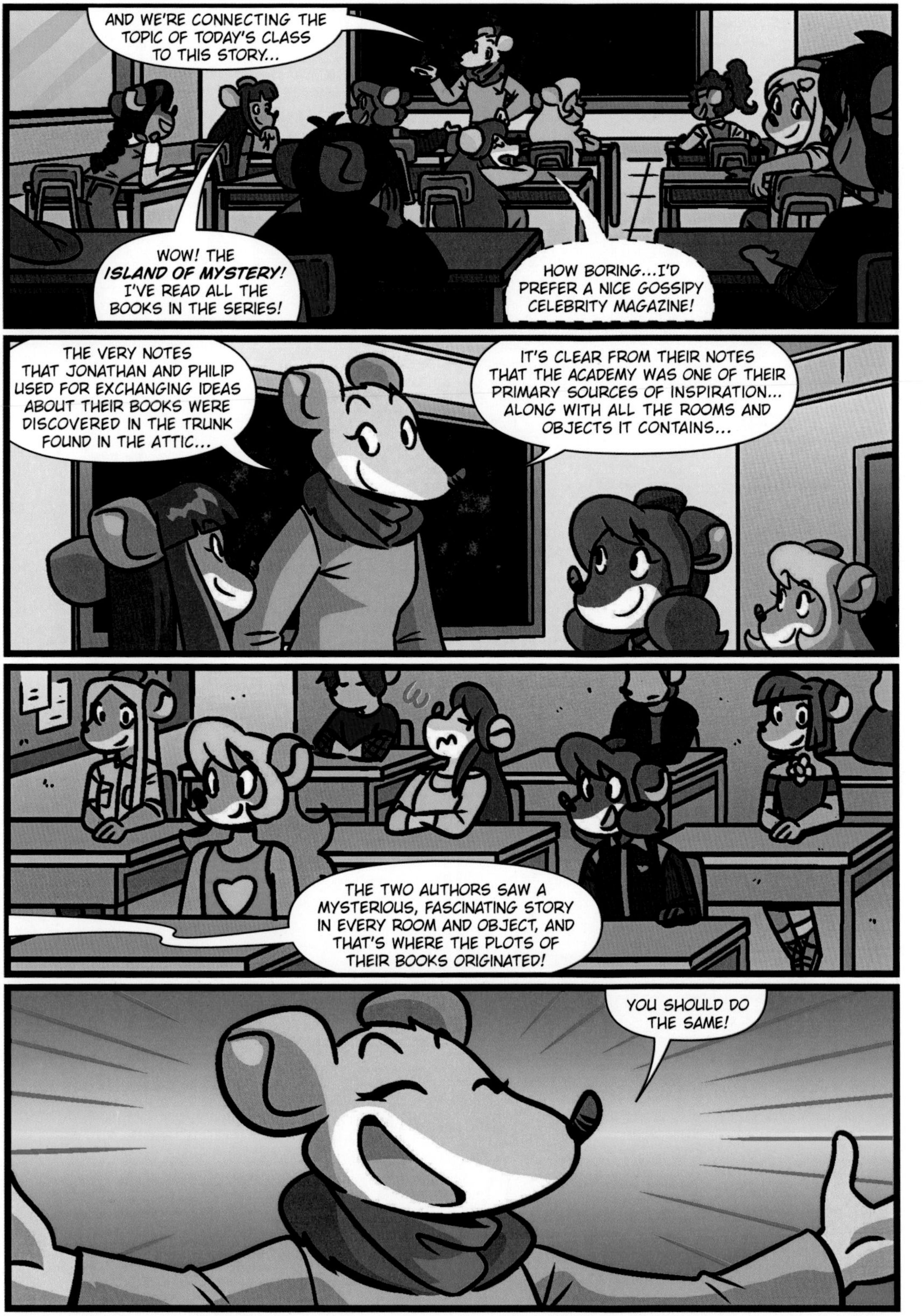
AND WE'RE CONNECTING THE TOPIC OF TODAY'S CLASS TO THIS STORY...
WOW! THE *ISLAND OF MYSTERY!* I'VE READ ALL THE BOOKS IN THE SERIES!
HOW BORING...I'D PREFER A NICE GOSSIPY CELEBRITY MAGAZINE!
THE VERY NOTES THAT JONATHAN AND PHILIP USED FOR EXCHANGING IDEAS ABOUT THEIR BOOKS WERE DISCOVERED IN THE TRUNK FOUND IN THE ATTIC...
IT'S CLEAR FROM THEIR NOTES THAT THE ACADEMY WAS ONE OF THEIR PRIMARY SOURCES OF INSPIRATION... ALONG WITH ALL THE ROOMS AND OBJECTS IT CONTAINS...
THE TWO AUTHORS SAW A MYSTERIOUS, FASCINATING STORY IN EVERY ROOM AND OBJECT, AND THAT'S WHERE THE PLOTS OF THEIR BOOKS ORIGINATED!
YOU SHOULD DO THE SAME!

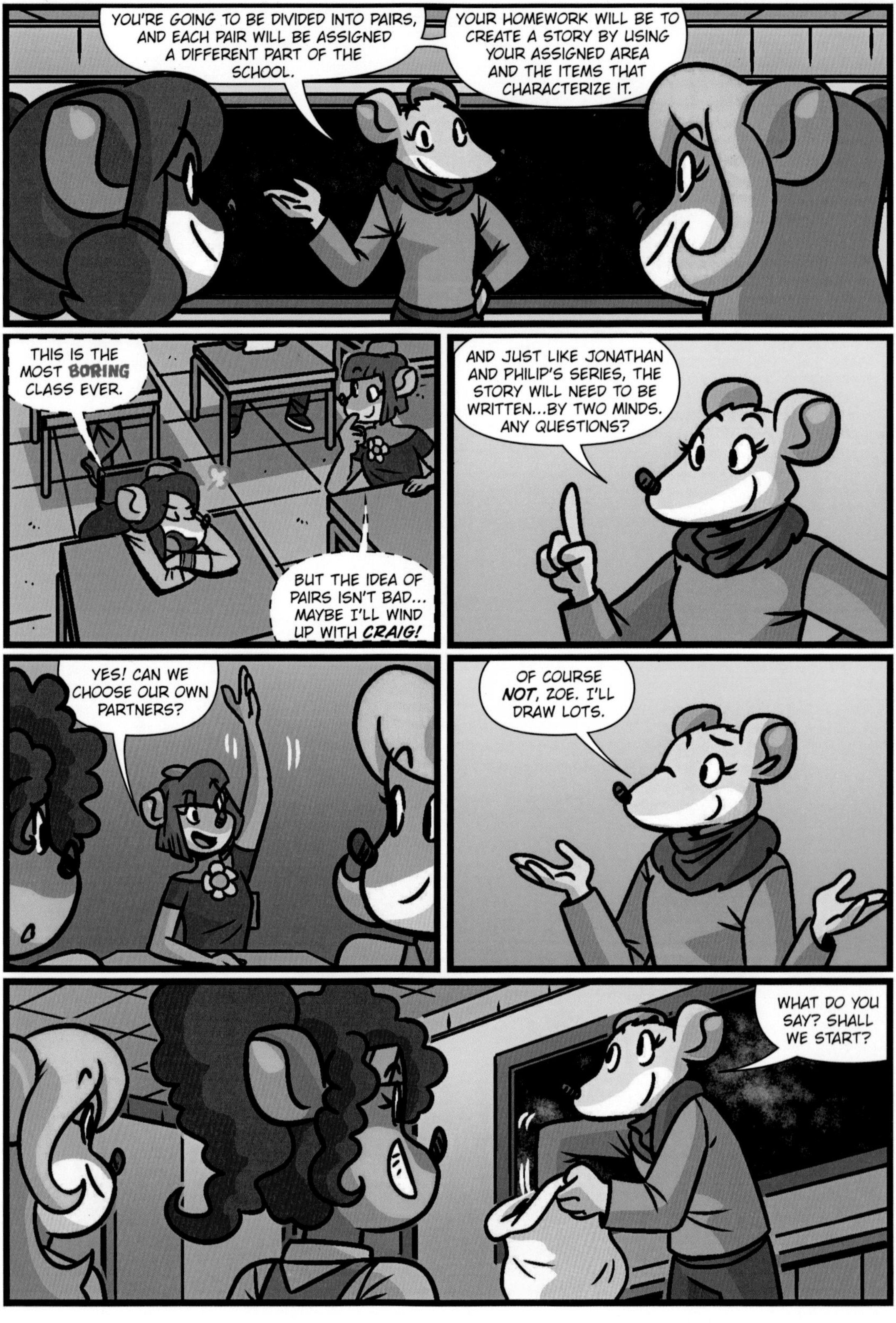
YOU'RE GOING TO BE DIVIDED INTO PAIRS, AND EACH PAIR WILL BE ASSIGNED A DIFFERENT PART OF THE SCHOOL.
YOUR HOMEWORK WILL BE TO CREATE A STORY BY USING YOUR ASSIGNED AREA AND THE ITEMS THAT CHARACTERIZE IT.
THIS IS THE MOST BORING CLASS EVER.
BUT THE IDEA OF PAIRS ISN'T BAD... MAYBE I'LL WIND UP WITH CRAIG!
AND JUST LIKE JONATHAN AND PHILIP'S SERIES, THE STORY WILL NEED TO BE WRITTEN...BY TWO MINDS. ANY QUESTIONS?
YES! CAN WE CHOOSE OUR OWN PARTNERS?
OF COURSE NOT, ZOE. I'LL DRAW LOTS.
WHAT DO YOU SAY? SHALL WE START?

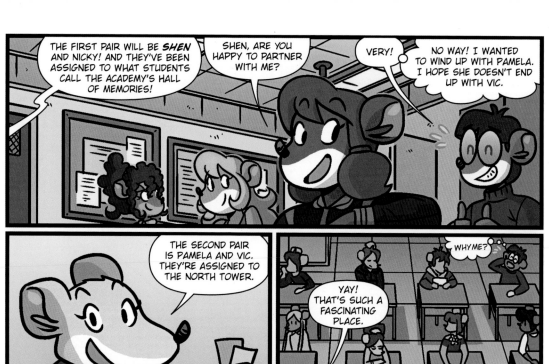

THE FIRST PAIR WILL BE **SHEN** AND NICKY! AND THEY'VE BEEN ASSIGNED TO WHAT STUDENTS CALL THE ACADEMY'S HALL OF MEMORIES!

SHEN, ARE YOU HAPPY TO PARTNER WITH ME?

VERY!

NO WAY! I WANTED TO WIND UP WITH PAMELA. I HOPE SHE DOESN'T END UP WITH VIC.

THE SECOND PAIR IS PAMELA AND VIC. THEY'RE ASSIGNED TO THE NORTH TOWER.

WHY ME?

YAY! THAT'S SUCH A FASCINATING PLACE.

ALICIA AND PAULINA, YOU'RE ASSIGNED TO THE HERB GARDEN.

ZOE, YOU'RE PAIRED WITH CRAIG. YOU'LL BE IN THE MUSIC ROOM.

HURRAY!

CONNIE AND VIOLET, YOU'LL BE IN THE LIBRARY!

OH, NO... THAT JUST LEAVES...

COLETTE AND VANILLA! YOU'RE THE FINAL PAIR! AND YOU'LL GO TO THE GYM!

OH, NO! NOT THE GYM! HOW BORING!

ENJOY YOUR WORK, KIDS!

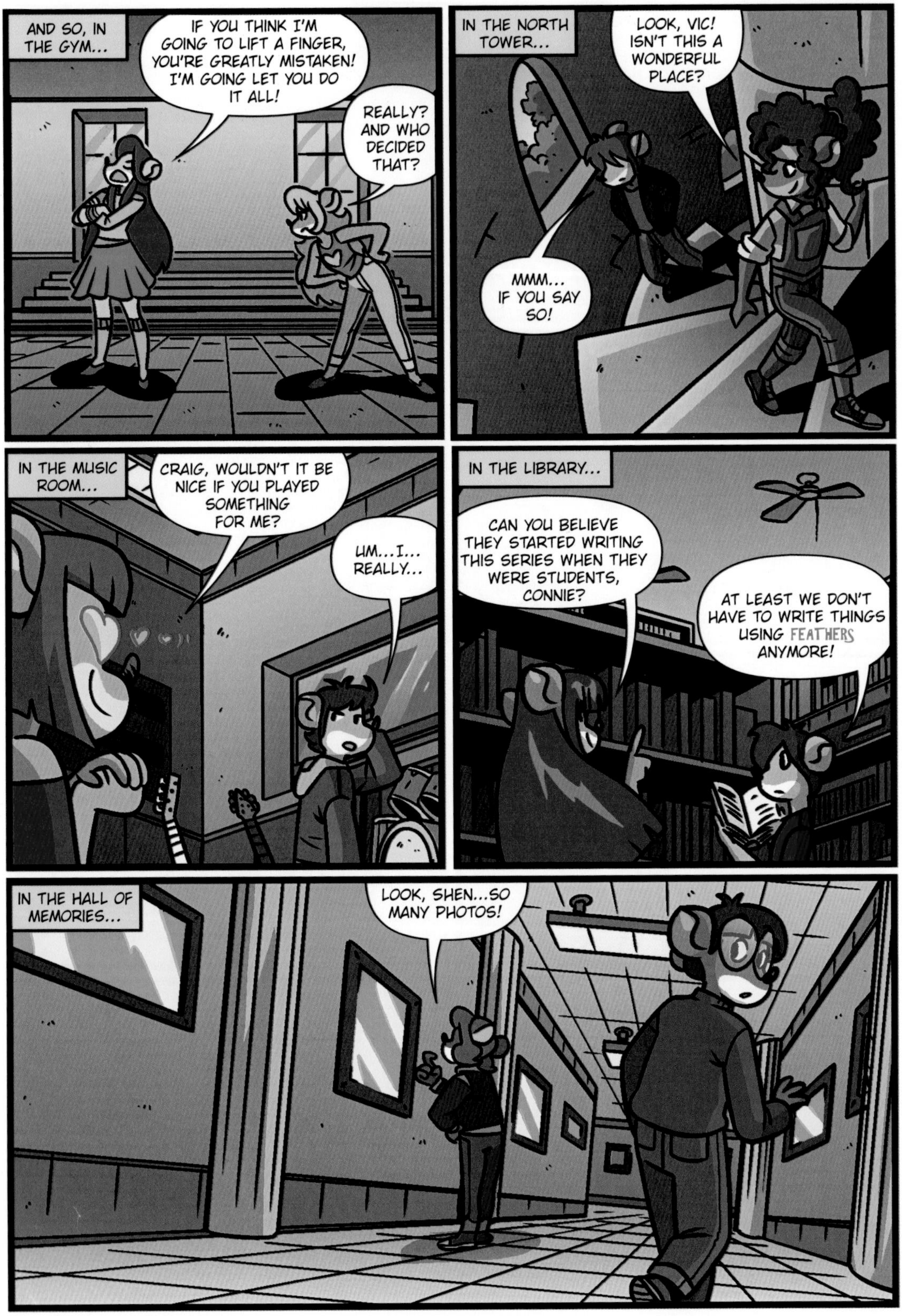
AND SO, IN THE GYM...
IF YOU THINK I'M GOING TO LIFT A FINGER, YOU'RE GREATLY MISTAKEN! I'M GOING LET YOU DO IT ALL!
REALLY? AND WHO DECIDED THAT?
IN THE NORTH TOWER...
LOOK, VIC! ISN'T THIS A WONDERFUL PLACE?
MMM... IF YOU SAY SO!
IN THE MUSIC ROOM...
CRAIG, WOULDN'T IT BE NICE IF YOU PLAYED SOMETHING FOR ME?
UM...I... REALLY...
IN THE LIBRARY...
CAN YOU BELIEVE THEY STARTED WRITING THIS SERIES WHEN THEY WERE STUDENTS, CONNIE?
AT LEAST WE DON'T HAVE TO WRITE THINGS USING FEATHERS ANYMORE!
IN THE HALL OF MEMORIES...
LOOK, SHEN...SO MANY PHOTOS!

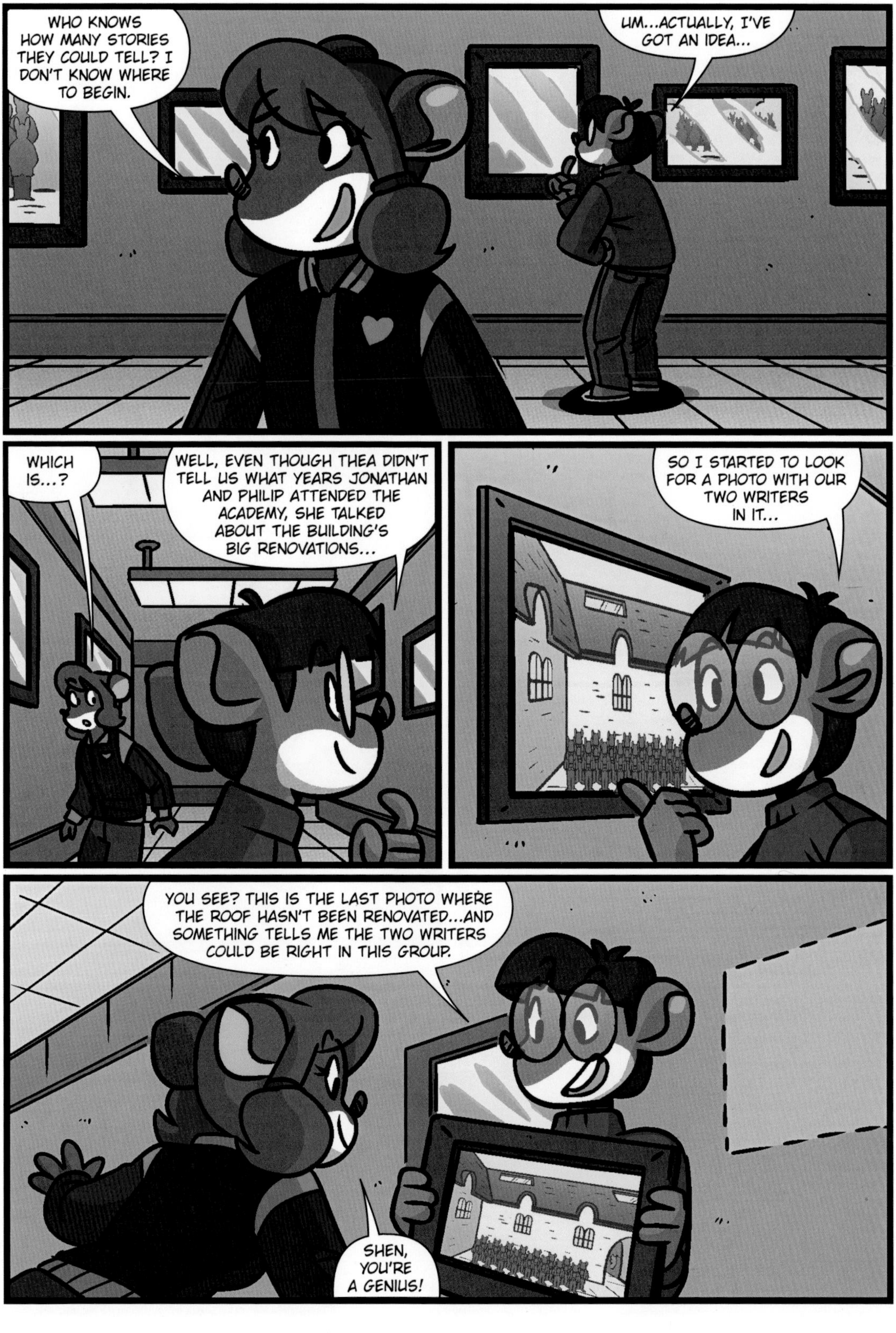
WHO KNOWS HOW MANY STORIES THEY COULD TELL? I DON'T KNOW WHERE TO BEGIN.
UM...ACTUALLY, I'VE GOT AN IDEA...
WHICH IS...?
WELL, EVEN THOUGH THEA DIDN'T TELL US WHAT YEARS JONATHAN AND PHILIP ATTENDED THE ACADEMY, SHE TALKED ABOUT THE BUILDING'S BIG RENOVATIONS...
SO I STARTED TO LOOK FOR A PHOTO WITH OUR TWO WRITERS IN IT...
YOU SEE? THIS IS THE LAST PHOTO WHERE THE ROOF HASN'T BEEN RENOVATED...AND SOMETHING TELLS ME THE TWO WRITERS COULD BE RIGHT IN THIS GROUP.
SHEN, YOU'RE A GENIUS!

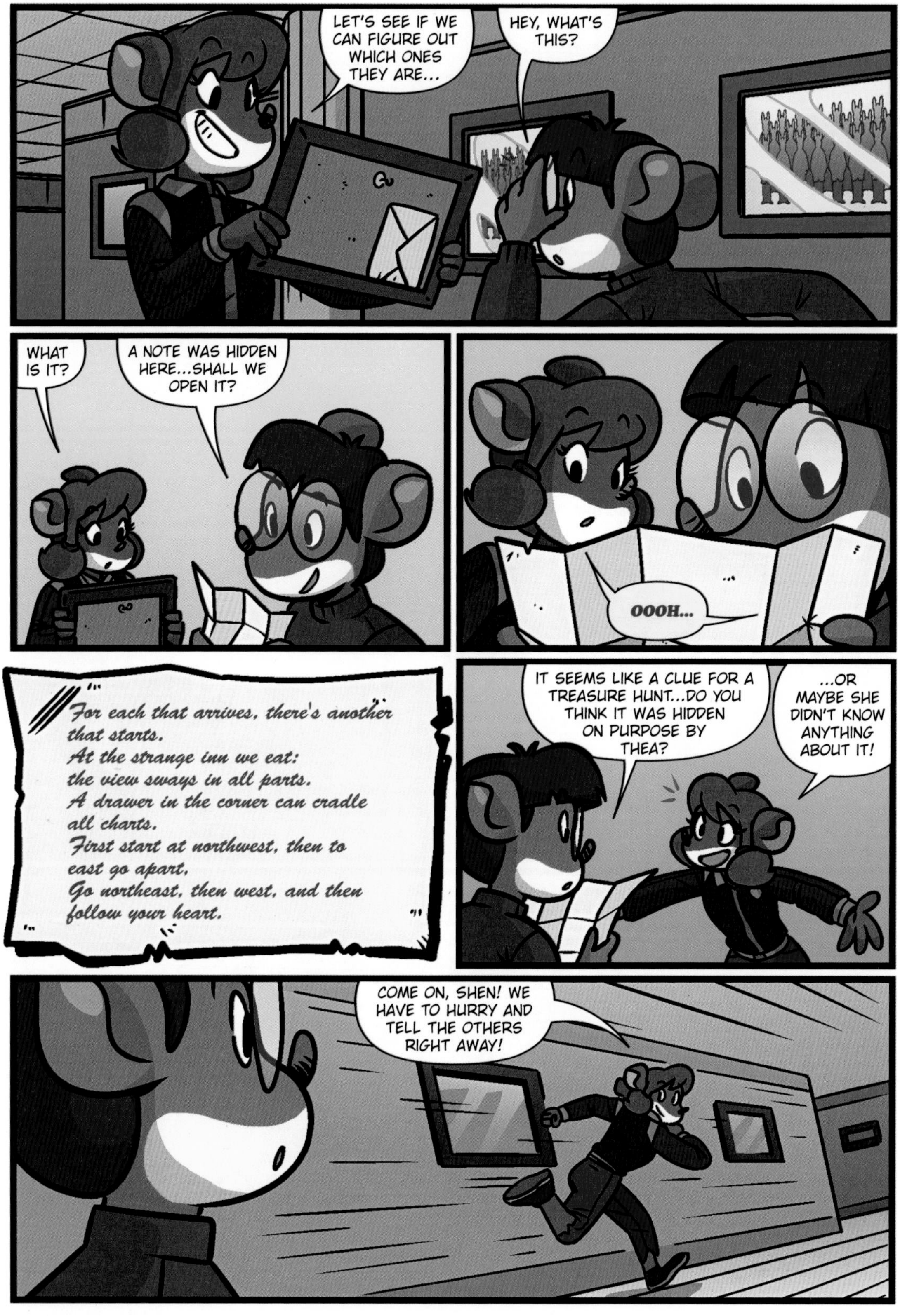

LET'S SEE IF WE CAN FIGURE OUT WHICH ONES THEY ARE...
HEY, WHAT'S THIS?
WHAT IS IT?
A NOTE WAS HIDDEN HERE...SHALL WE OPEN IT?
OOOH...
"For each that arrives, there's another that starts.
At the strange inn we eat:
the view sways in all parts.
A drawer in the corner can cradle all charts.
First start at northwest, then to east go apart,
Go northeast, then west, and then follow your heart."
IT SEEMS LIKE A CLUE FOR A TREASURE HUNT...DO YOU THINK IT WAS HIDDEN ON PURPOSE BY THEA?
...OR MAYBE SHE DIDN'T KNOW ANYTHING ABOUT IT!
COME ON, SHEN! WE HAVE TO HURRY AND TELL THE OTHERS RIGHT AWAY!

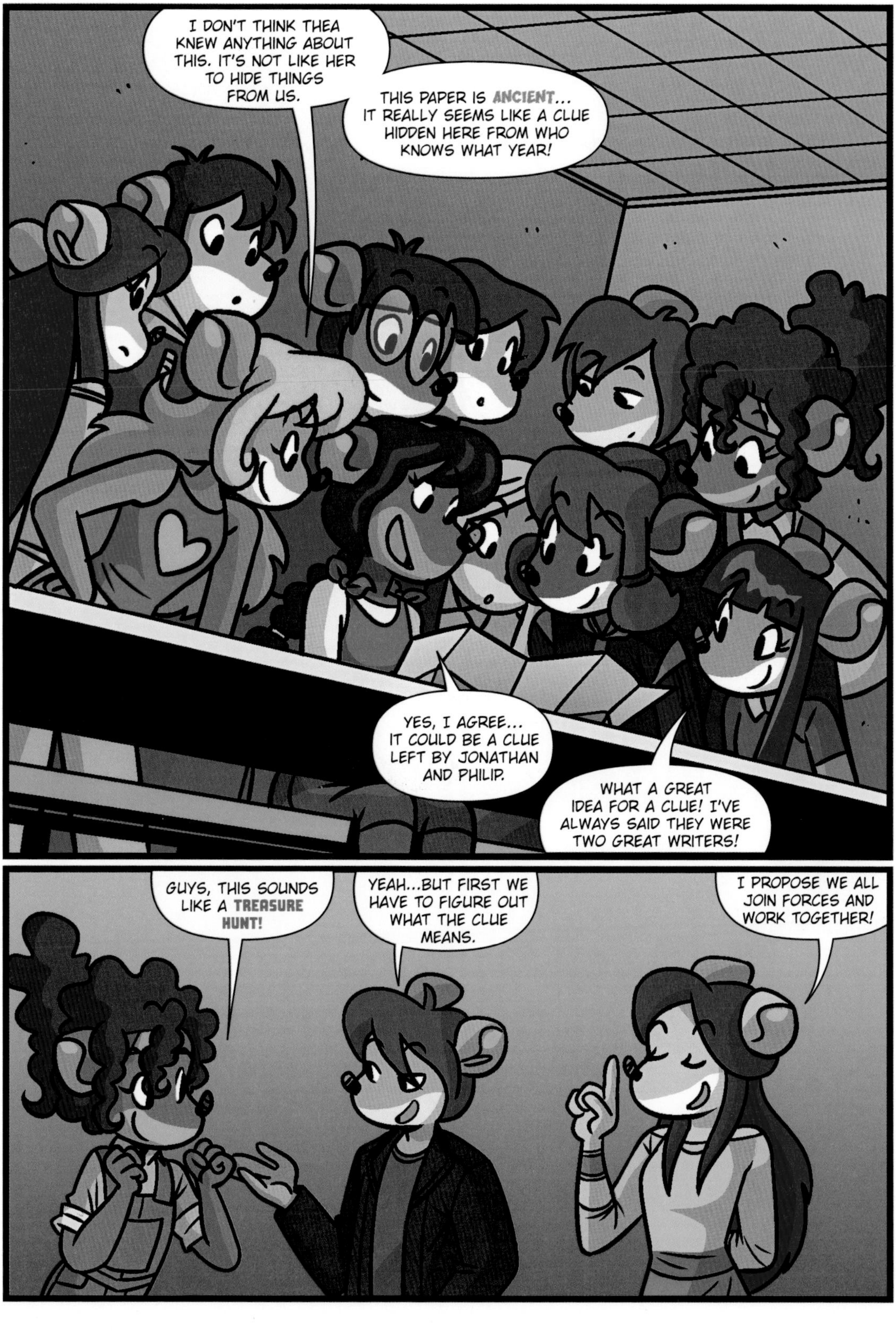
I DON'T THINK THEA KNEW ANYTHING ABOUT THIS. IT'S NOT LIKE HER TO HIDE THINGS FROM US.
THIS PAPER IS ANCIENT... IT REALLY SEEMS LIKE A CLUE HIDDEN HERE FROM WHO KNOWS WHAT YEAR!
YES, I AGREE... IT COULD BE A CLUE LEFT BY JONATHAN AND PHILIP.
WHAT A GREAT IDEA FOR A CLUE! I'VE ALWAYS SAID THEY WERE TWO GREAT WRITERS!
GUYS, THIS SOUNDS LIKE A TREASURE HUNT!
YEAH...BUT FIRST WE HAVE TO FIGURE OUT WHAT THE CLUE MEANS.
I PROPOSE WE ALL JOIN FORCES AND WORK TOGETHER!

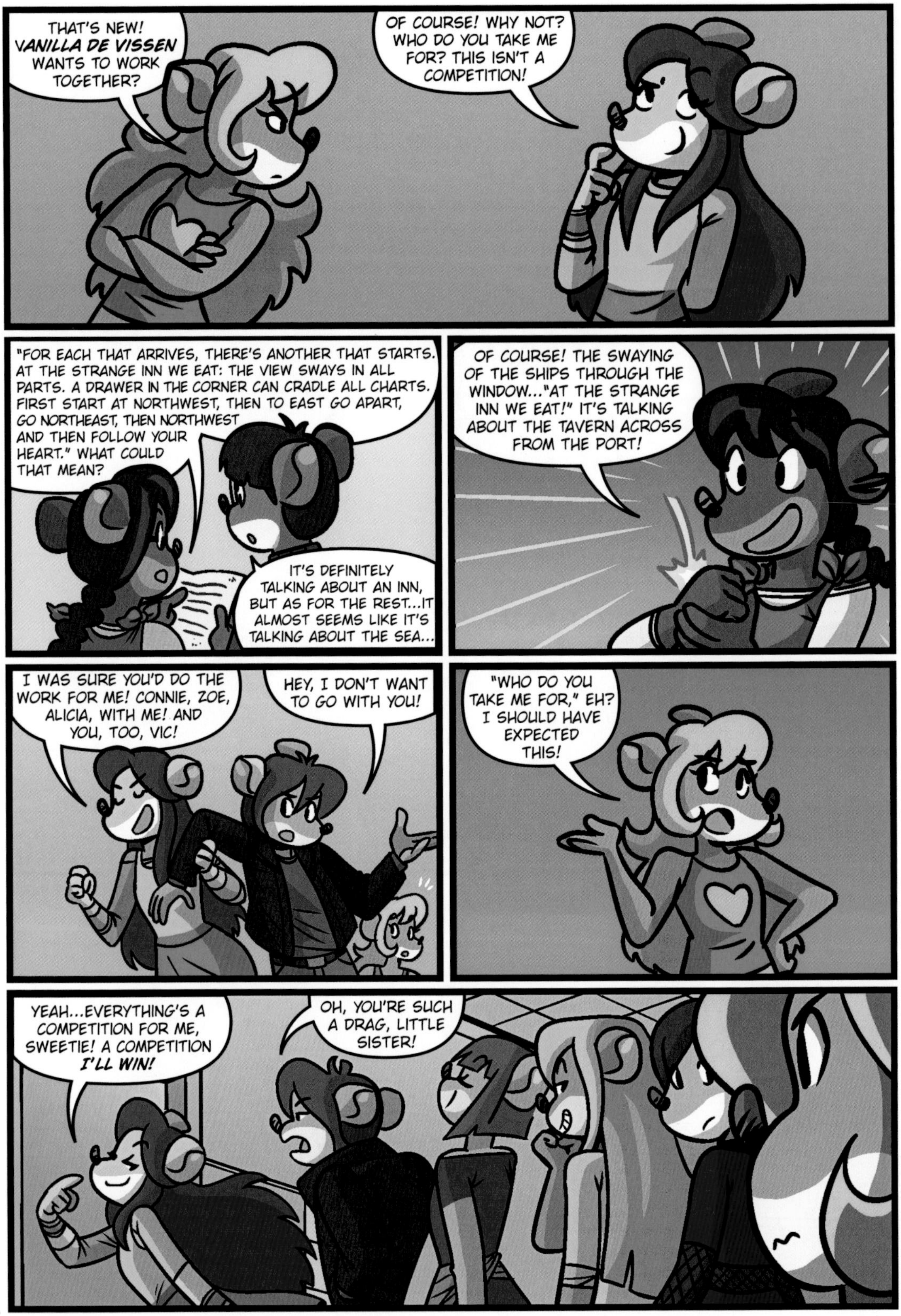

THAT'S NEW! VANILLA DE VISSEN WANTS TO WORK TOGETHER?
OF COURSE! WHY NOT? WHO DO YOU TAKE ME FOR? THIS ISN'T A COMPETITION!
"FOR EACH THAT ARRIVES, THERE'S ANOTHER THAT STARTS. AT THE STRANGE INN WE EAT: THE VIEW SWAYS IN ALL PARTS. A DRAWER IN THE CORNER CAN CRADLE ALL CHARTS. FIRST START AT NORTHWEST, THEN TO EAST GO APART, GO NORTHEAST, THEN NORTHWEST AND THEN FOLLOW YOUR HEART." WHAT COULD THAT MEAN?
IT'S DEFINITELY TALKING ABOUT AN INN, BUT AS FOR THE REST...IT ALMOST SEEMS LIKE IT'S TALKING ABOUT THE SEA...
OF COURSE! THE SWAYING OF THE SHIPS THROUGH THE WINDOW..."AT THE STRANGE INN WE EAT!" IT'S TALKING ABOUT THE TAVERN ACROSS FROM THE PORT!
I WAS SURE YOU'D DO THE WORK FOR ME! CONNIE, ZOE, ALICIA, WITH ME! AND YOU, TOO, VIC!
HEY, I DON'T WANT TO GO WITH YOU!
"WHO DO YOU TAKE ME FOR," EH? I SHOULD HAVE EXPECTED THIS!
YEAH...EVERYTHING'S A COMPETITION FOR ME, SWEETIE! A COMPETITION I'LL WIN!
OH, YOU'RE SUCH A DRAG, LITTLE SISTER!

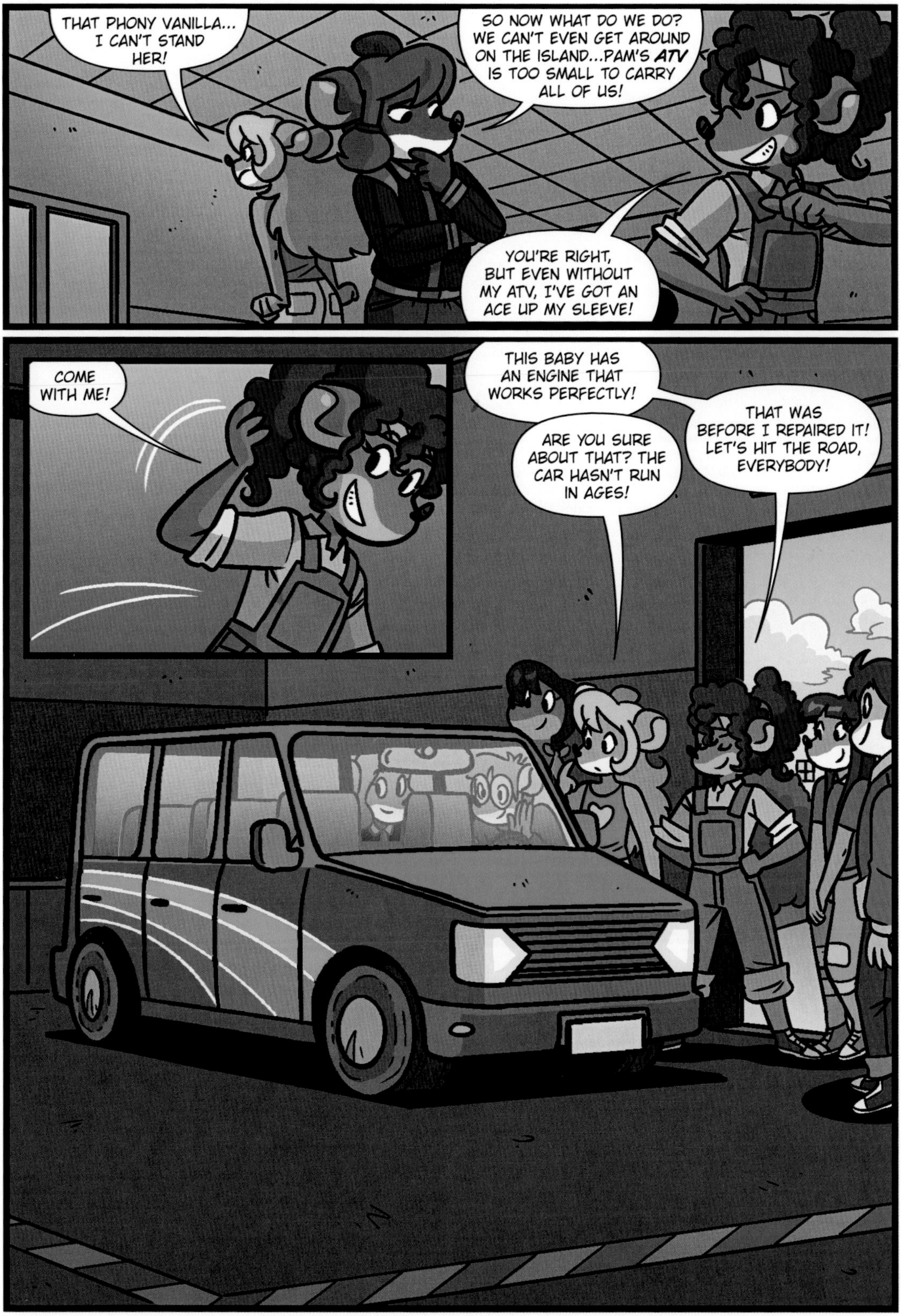
THAT PHONY VANILLA... I CAN'T STAND HER!
SO NOW WHAT DO WE DO? WE CAN'T EVEN GET AROUND ON THE ISLAND...PAM'S ATV IS TOO SMALL TO CARRY ALL OF US!
YOU'RE RIGHT, BUT EVEN WITHOUT MY ATV, I'VE GOT AN ACE UP MY SLEEVE!
COME WITH ME!
THIS BABY HAS AN ENGINE THAT WORKS PERFECTLY!
ARE YOU SURE ABOUT THAT? THE CAR HASN'T RUN IN AGES!
THAT WAS BEFORE I REPAIRED IT! LET'S HIT THE ROAD, EVERYBODY!

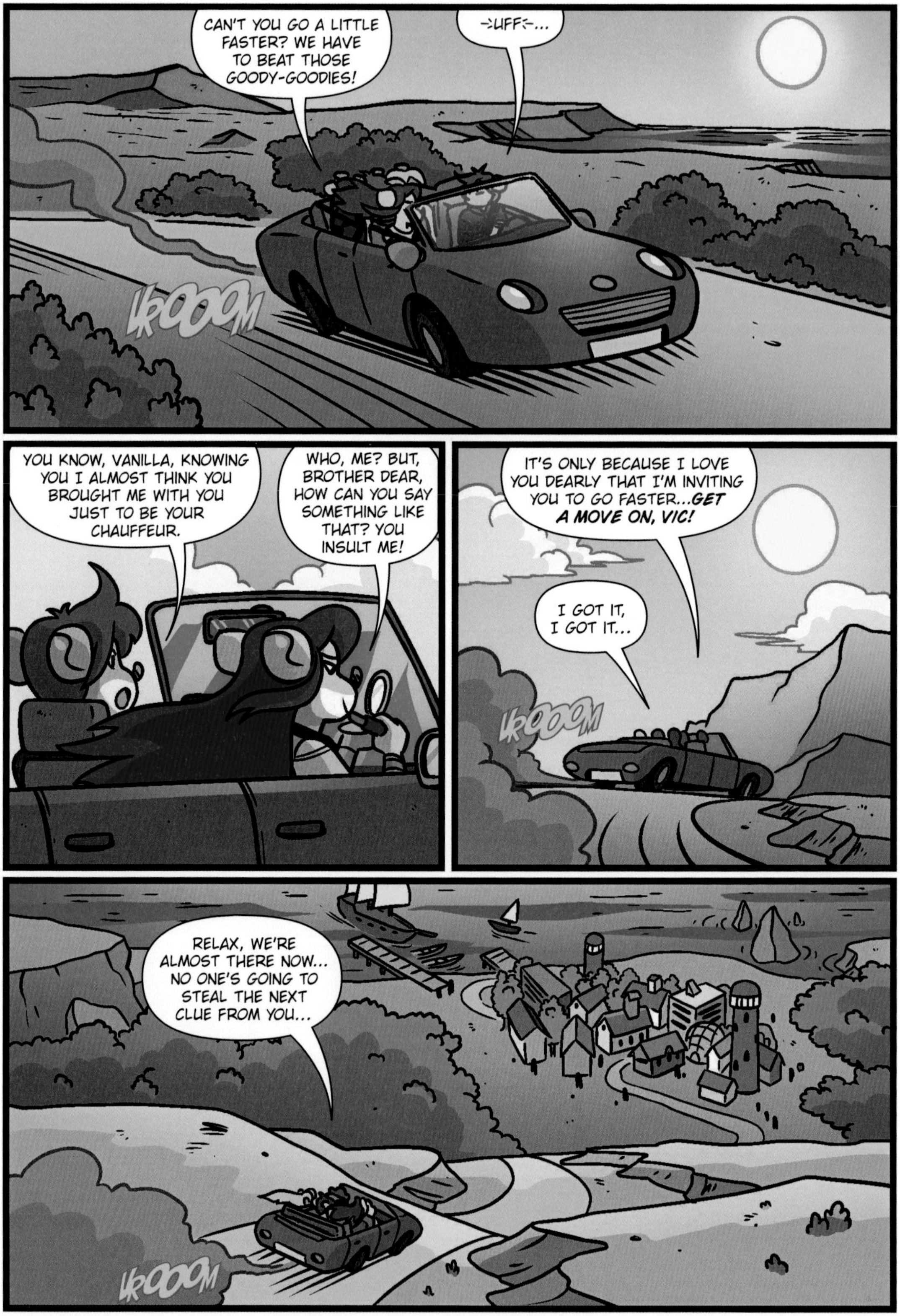
CAN'T YOU GO A LITTLE FASTER? WE HAVE TO BEAT THOSE GOODY-GOODIES!
UFF...
VROOOM
YOU KNOW, VANILLA, KNOWING YOU I ALMOST THINK YOU BROUGHT ME WITH YOU JUST TO BE YOUR CHAUFFEUR.
WHO, ME? BUT, BROTHER DEAR, HOW CAN YOU SAY SOMETHING LIKE THAT? YOU INSULT ME!
IT'S ONLY BECAUSE I LOVE YOU DEARLY THAT I'M INVITING YOU TO GO FASTER...**GET A MOVE ON, VIC!**
I GOT IT, I GOT IT...
VROOOM
RELAX, WE'RE ALMOST THERE NOW... NO ONE'S GOING TO STEAL THE NEXT CLUE FROM YOU...
VROOOM

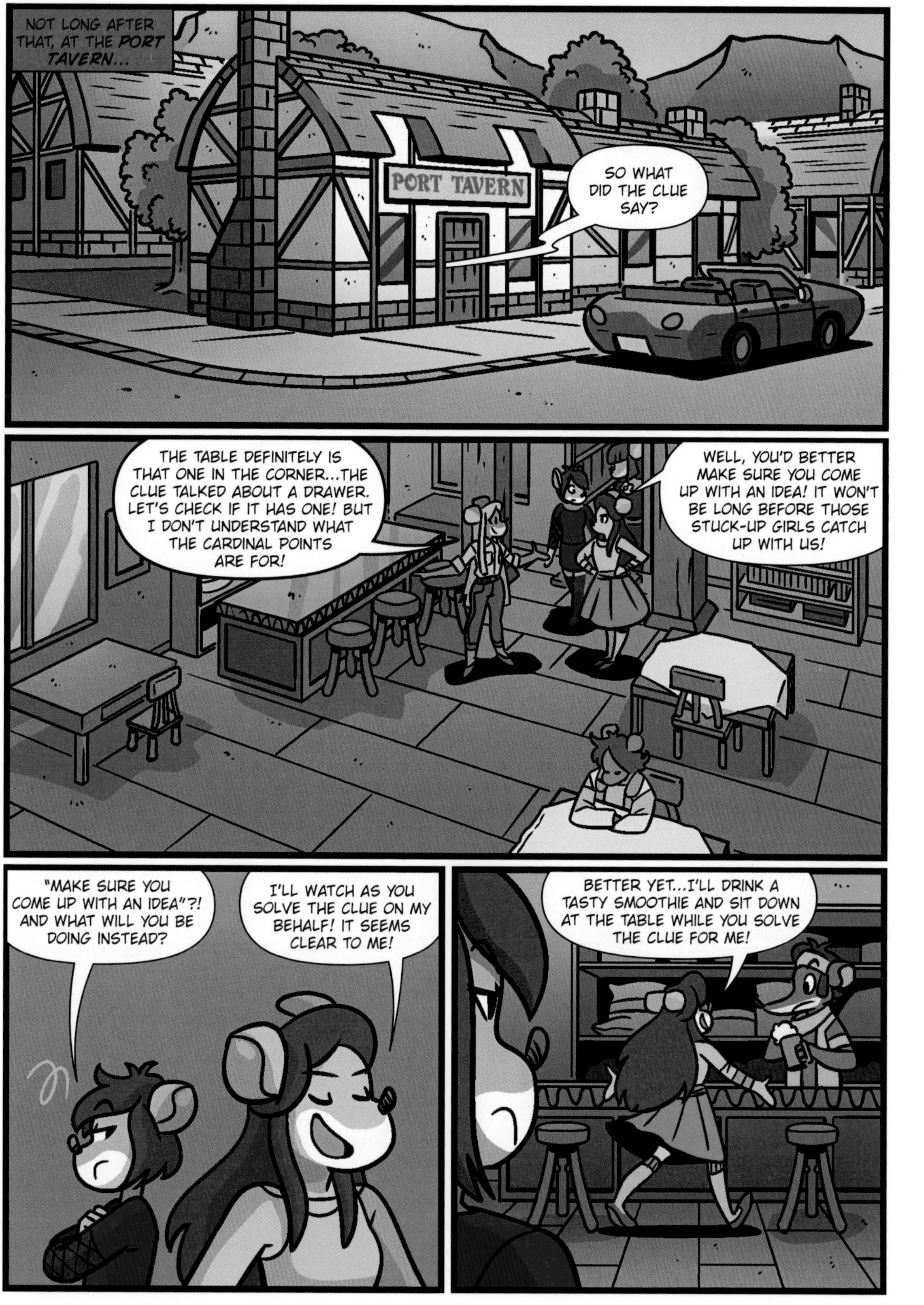
NOT LONG AFTER THAT, AT THE *PORT TAVERN*...
PORT TAVERN
SO WHAT DID THE CLUE SAY?
THE TABLE DEFINITELY IS THAT ONE IN THE CORNER...THE CLUE TALKED ABOUT A DRAWER. LET'S CHECK IF IT HAS ONE! BUT I DON'T UNDERSTAND WHAT THE CARDINAL POINTS ARE FOR!
WELL, YOU'D BETTER MAKE SURE YOU COME UP WITH AN IDEA! IT WON'T BE LONG BEFORE THOSE STUCK-UP GIRLS CATCH UP WITH US!
"MAKE SURE YOU COME UP WITH AN IDEA"?! AND WHAT WILL YOU BE DOING INSTEAD?
I'LL WATCH AS YOU SOLVE THE CLUE ON MY BEHALF! IT SEEMS CLEAR TO ME!
BETTER YET...I'LL DRINK A TASTY SMOOTHIE AND SIT DOWN AT THE TABLE WHILE YOU SOLVE THE CLUE FOR ME!

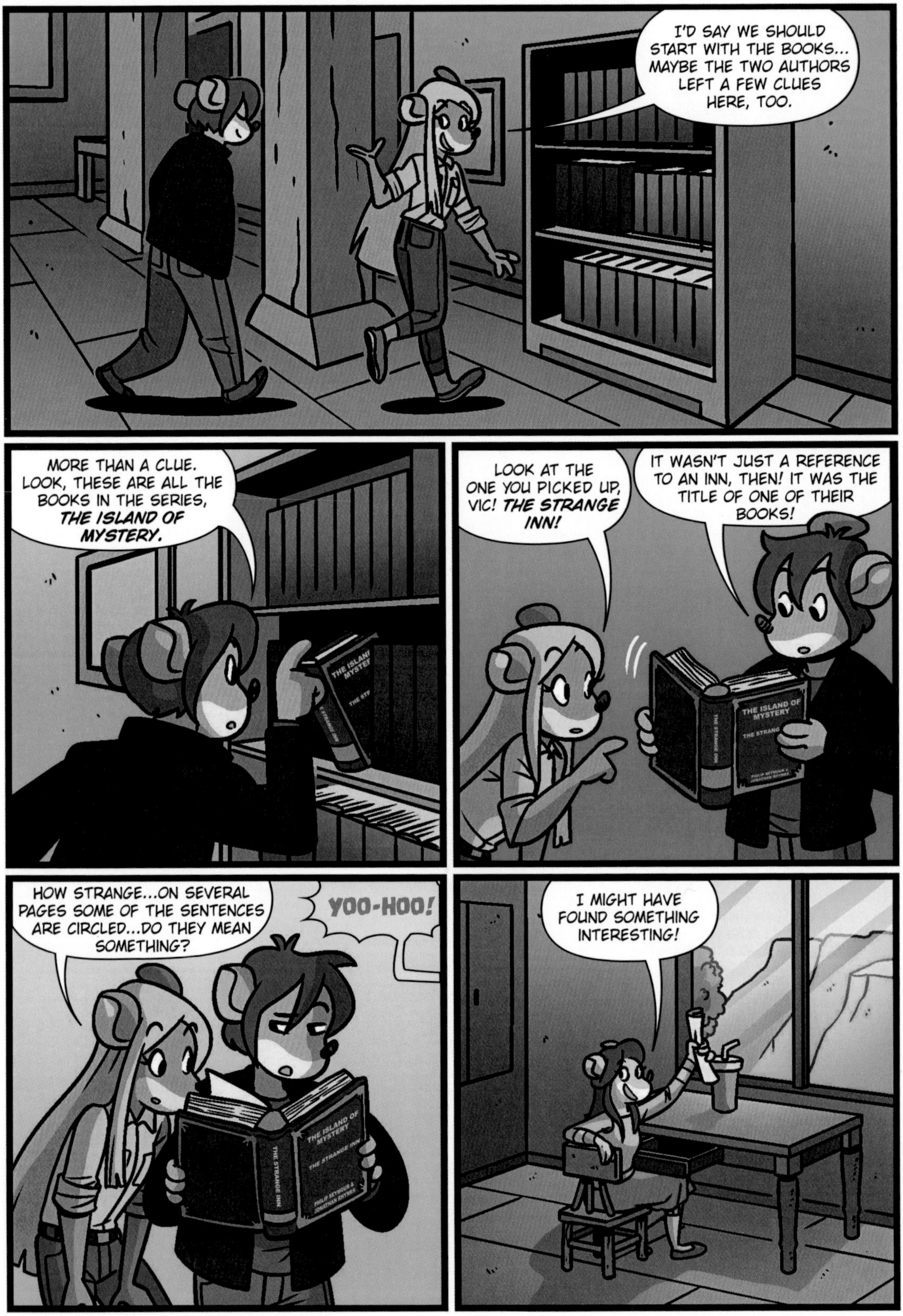
I'D SAY WE SHOULD START WITH THE BOOKS... MAYBE THE TWO AUTHORS LEFT A FEW CLUES HERE, TOO.
MORE THAN A CLUE. LOOK, THESE ARE ALL THE BOOKS IN THE SERIES, THE ISLAND OF MYSTERY.
LOOK AT THE ONE YOU PICKED UP, VIC! THE STRANGE INN!
IT WASN'T JUST A REFERENCE TO AN INN, THEN! IT WAS THE TITLE OF ONE OF THEIR BOOKS!
THE ISLAND OF MYSTERY
THE STRANGE INN
HOW STRANGE...ON SEVERAL PAGES SOME OF THE SENTENCES ARE CIRCLED...DO THEY MEAN SOMETHING?
YOO-HOO!
I MIGHT HAVE FOUND SOMETHING INTERESTING!

THEY'RE NUMBERS! LAID OUT IN THE CARDINAL POINTS, LIKE ON A COMPASS.

ZOE, YOU'RE A GENIUS!

START AT THE NORTHWEST...

6
50
15
123
73
90
104
38

VIC, GO TO PAGE 6!

PAGE 6...

THERE'S SOME TEXT CIRCLED. IT SAYS, *"YOU NEED THE COURAGE OF A LION."*

...o was a beautiful
sorcerous, a closet, an
a beast with a mane. O
was it a man made of r
and one with hay for br
Nevertheless, the young
child protagonist said,
"You need the courage
of a lion!"

6

I FEEL LIKE WE'RE ON THE RIGHT PATH! THE NEXT COORDINATE... "TO EAST GO APART"... PAGE 73!

6
50
23

ANOTHER LINE IS CIRCLED..."TO WATCH A STAR..."

THE ISLAND MYSTERY

THE STRANG

THE STRANG

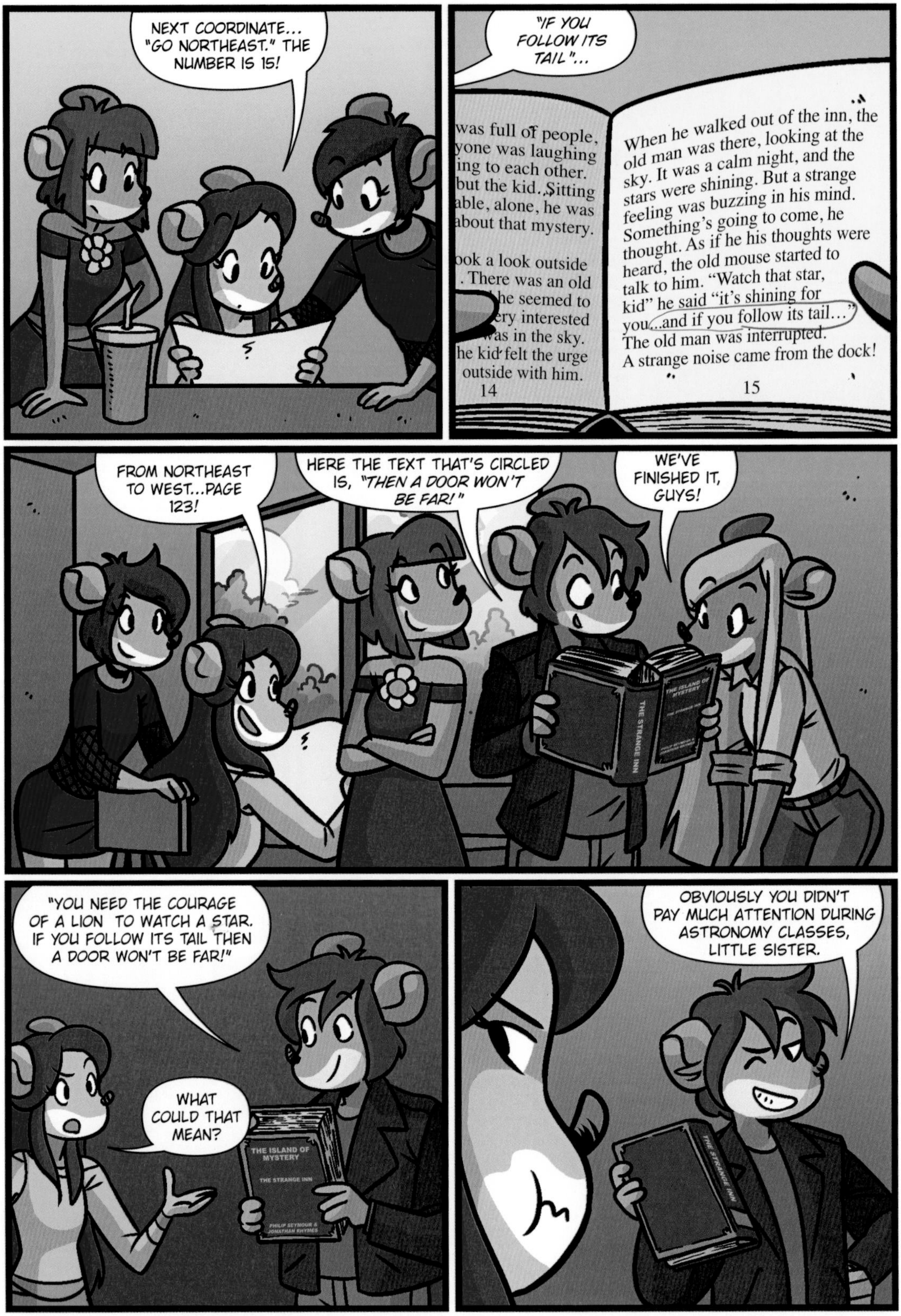
NEXT COORDINATE... "GO NORTHEAST." THE NUMBER IS 15!
"IF YOU FOLLOW ITS TAIL"...
was full of people, yone was laughing ing to each other. but the kid. Sitting able, alone, he was about that mystery.
ook a look outside . There was an old he seemed to ery interested was in the sky. he kid felt the urge outside with him.
14
When he walked out of the inn, the old man was there, looking at the sky. It was a calm night, and the stars were shining. But a strange feeling was buzzing in his mind. Something's going to come, he thought. As if he his thoughts were heard, the old mouse started to talk to him. "Watch that star, kid" he said "it's shining for you...and if you follow its tail..." The old man was interrupted. A strange noise came from the dock!
15
FROM NORTHEAST TO WEST...PAGE 123!
HERE THE TEXT THAT'S CIRCLED IS, "THEN A DOOR WON'T BE FAR!"
WE'VE FINISHED IT, GUYS!
THE ISLAND OF MYSTERY
THE STRANGE INN
"YOU NEED THE COURAGE OF A LION TO WATCH A STAR. IF YOU FOLLOW ITS TAIL THEN A DOOR WON'T BE FAR!"
WHAT COULD THAT MEAN?
THE ISLAND OF MYSTERY
THE STRANGE INN
PHILIP SEYMOUR & JONATHAN RHYMES
OBVIOUSLY YOU DIDN'T PAY MUCH ATTENTION DURING ASTRONOMY CLASSES, LITTLE SISTER.
THE STRANGE INN

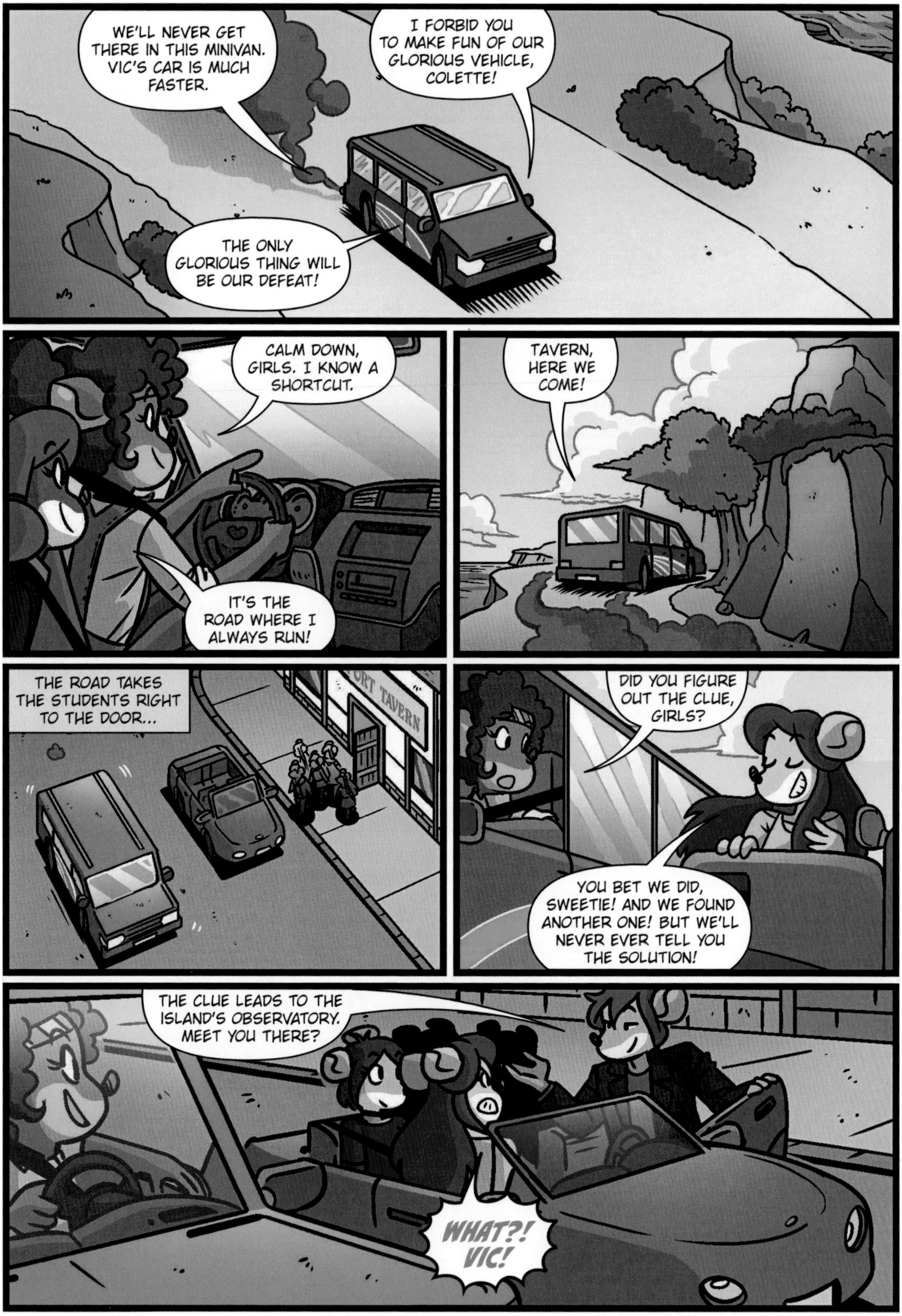
WE'LL NEVER GET THERE IN THIS MINIVAN. VIC'S CAR IS MUCH FASTER.
I FORBID YOU TO MAKE FUN OF OUR GLORIOUS VEHICLE, COLETTE!
THE ONLY GLORIOUS THING WILL BE OUR DEFEAT!
CALM DOWN, GIRLS. I KNOW A SHORTCUT.
IT'S THE ROAD WHERE I ALWAYS RUN!
TAVERN, HERE WE COME!
THE ROAD TAKES THE STUDENTS RIGHT TO THE DOOR...
DID YOU FIGURE OUT THE CLUE, GIRLS?
YOU BET WE DID, SWEETIE! AND WE FOUND ANOTHER ONE! BUT WE'LL NEVER EVER TELL YOU THE SOLUTION!
THE CLUE LEADS TO THE ISLAND'S OBSERVATORY. MEET YOU THERE?
WHAT?! VIC!

WOULD YOU MIND TELLING ME WHAT'S GOING ON IN YOUR HEAD? ARE YOU OR AREN'T YOU A DE VISSEN?!

VROOM

HEH! HEH! VIC'S REALLY GREAT!

DID YOU SAY SOMETHING, PAMELA?

WHO, ME? ABSOLUTELY NOT!

QUICK, TO THE OBSERVATORY!

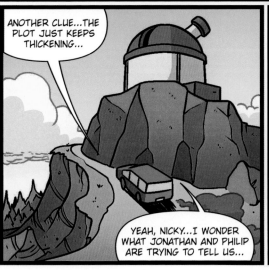

ANOTHER CLUE...THE PLOT JUST KEEPS THICKENING...

YEAH, NICKY...I WONDER WHAT JONATHAN AND PHILIP ARE TRYING TO TELL US...

YES, AS MATTER OF FACT... WE KNOW WE HAVE TO GET TO THE OBSERVATORY, BUT WE DON'T KNOW WHAT THE CLUE SAYS...

CALM DOWN, CRAIG! WE'LL FIND OUT ONCE WE GET THERE!

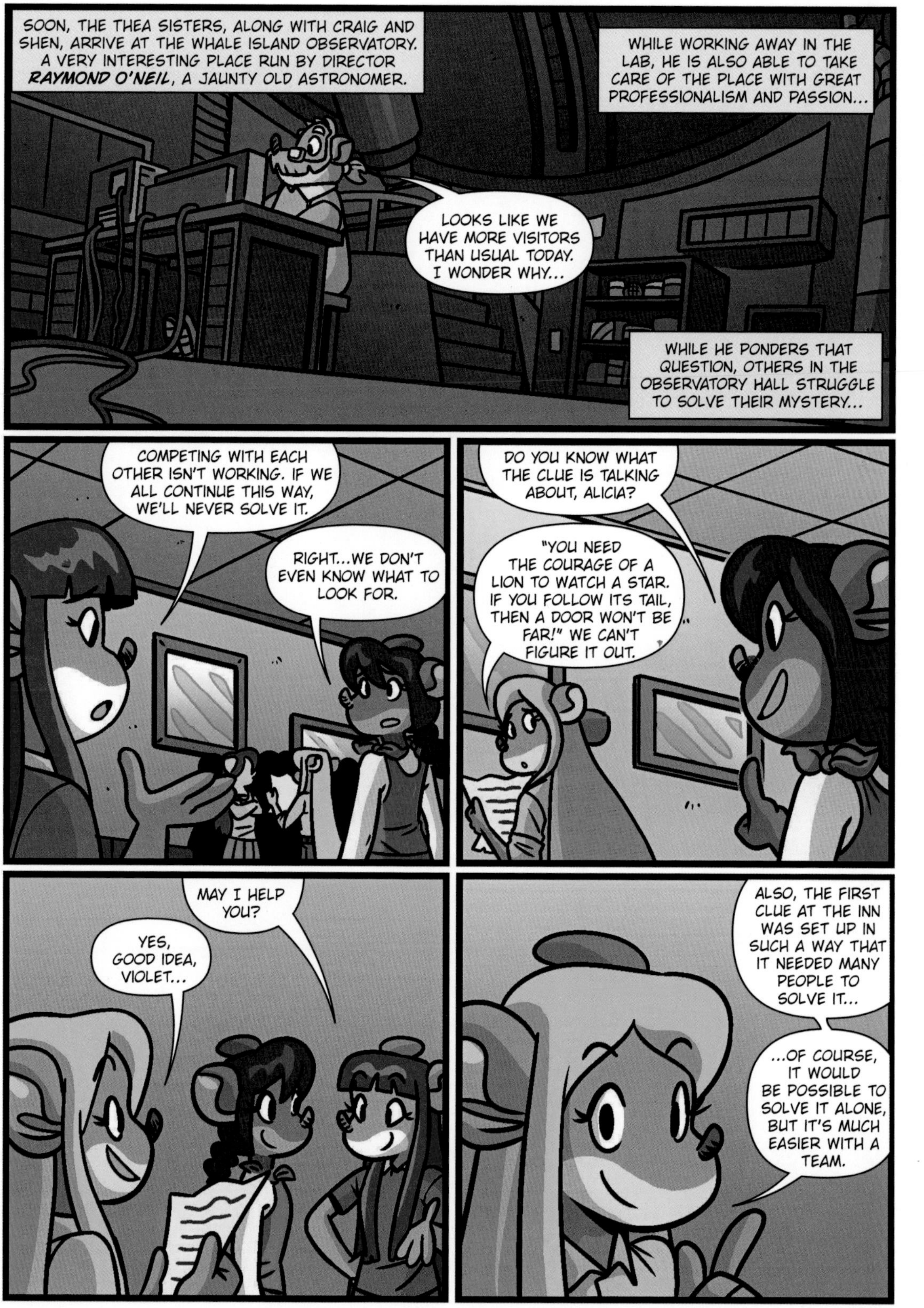
SOON, THE THEA SISTERS, ALONG WITH CRAIG AND SHEN, ARRIVE AT THE WHALE ISLAND OBSERVATORY. A VERY INTERESTING PLACE RUN BY DIRECTOR RAYMOND O'NEIL, A JAUNTY OLD ASTRONOMER.
WHILE WORKING AWAY IN THE LAB, HE IS ALSO ABLE TO TAKE CARE OF THE PLACE WITH GREAT PROFESSIONALISM AND PASSION...
LOOKS LIKE WE HAVE MORE VISITORS THAN USUAL TODAY. I WONDER WHY...
WHILE HE PONDERS THAT QUESTION, OTHERS IN THE OBSERVATORY HALL STRUGGLE TO SOLVE THEIR MYSTERY...
COMPETING WITH EACH OTHER ISN'T WORKING. IF WE ALL CONTINUE THIS WAY, WE'LL NEVER SOLVE IT.
RIGHT...WE DON'T EVEN KNOW WHAT TO LOOK FOR.
DO YOU KNOW WHAT THE CLUE IS TALKING ABOUT, ALICIA?
"YOU NEED THE COURAGE OF A LION TO WATCH A STAR. IF YOU FOLLOW ITS TAIL, THEN A DOOR WON'T BE FAR!" WE CAN'T FIGURE IT OUT.
MAY I HELP YOU?
YES, GOOD IDEA, VIOLET...
ALSO, THE FIRST CLUE AT THE INN WAS SET UP IN SUCH A WAY THAT IT NEEDED MANY PEOPLE TO SOLVE IT...
...OF COURSE, IT WOULD BE POSSIBLE TO SOLVE IT ALONE, BUT IT'S MUCH EASIER WITH A TEAM.

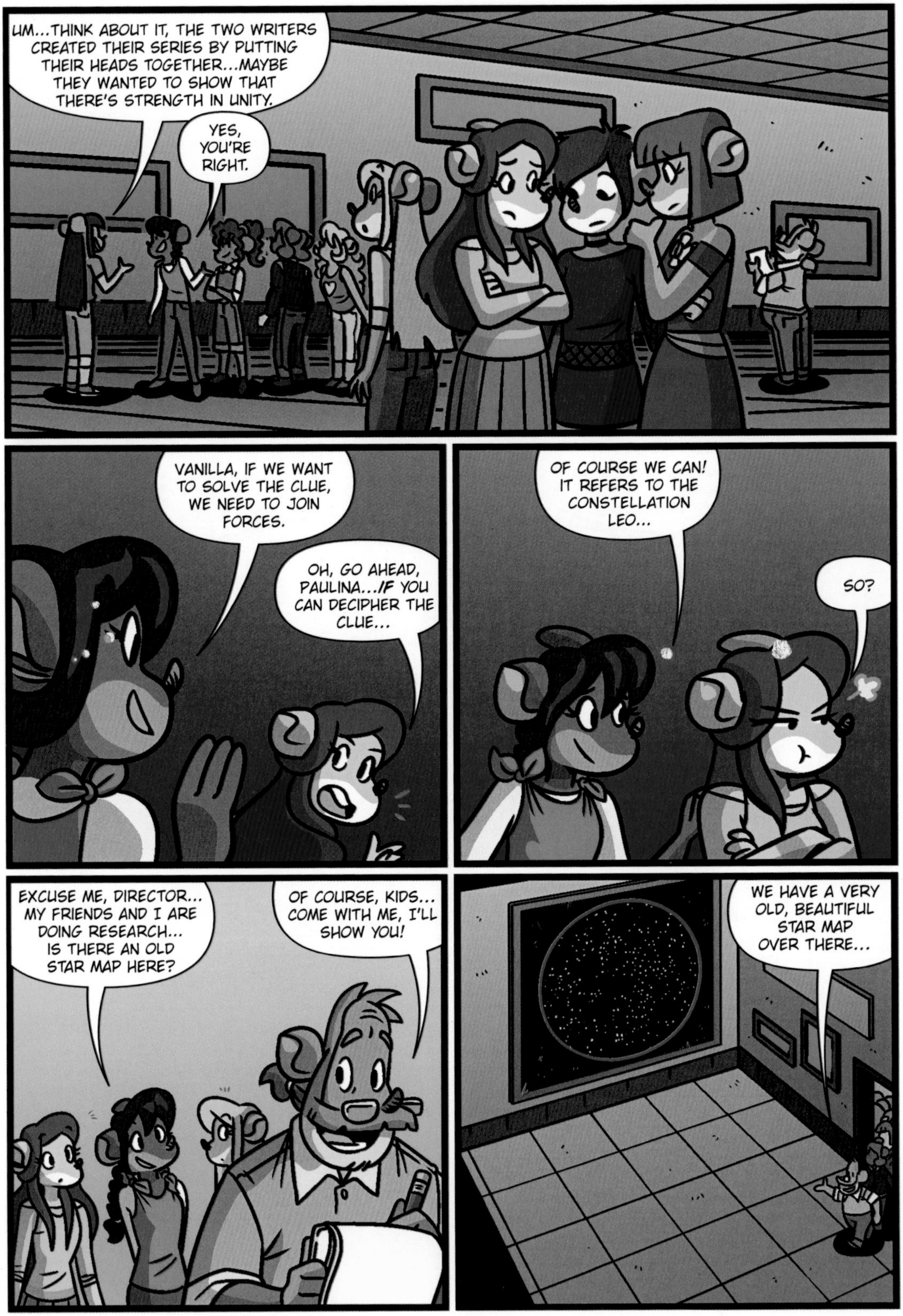
UM...THINK ABOUT IT, THE TWO WRITERS CREATED THEIR SERIES BY PUTTING THEIR HEADS TOGETHER...MAYBE THEY WANTED TO SHOW THAT THERE'S STRENGTH IN UNITY.
YES, YOU'RE RIGHT.
VANILLA, IF WE WANT TO SOLVE THE CLUE, WE NEED TO JOIN FORCES.
OH, GO AHEAD, PAULINA...IF YOU CAN DECIPHER THE CLUE...
OF COURSE WE CAN! IT REFERS TO THE CONSTELLATION LEO...
SO?
EXCUSE ME, DIRECTOR... MY FRIENDS AND I ARE DOING RESEARCH... IS THERE AN OLD STAR MAP HERE?
OF COURSE, KIDS... COME WITH ME, I'LL SHOW YOU!
WE HAVE A VERY OLD, BEAUTIFUL STAR MAP OVER THERE...

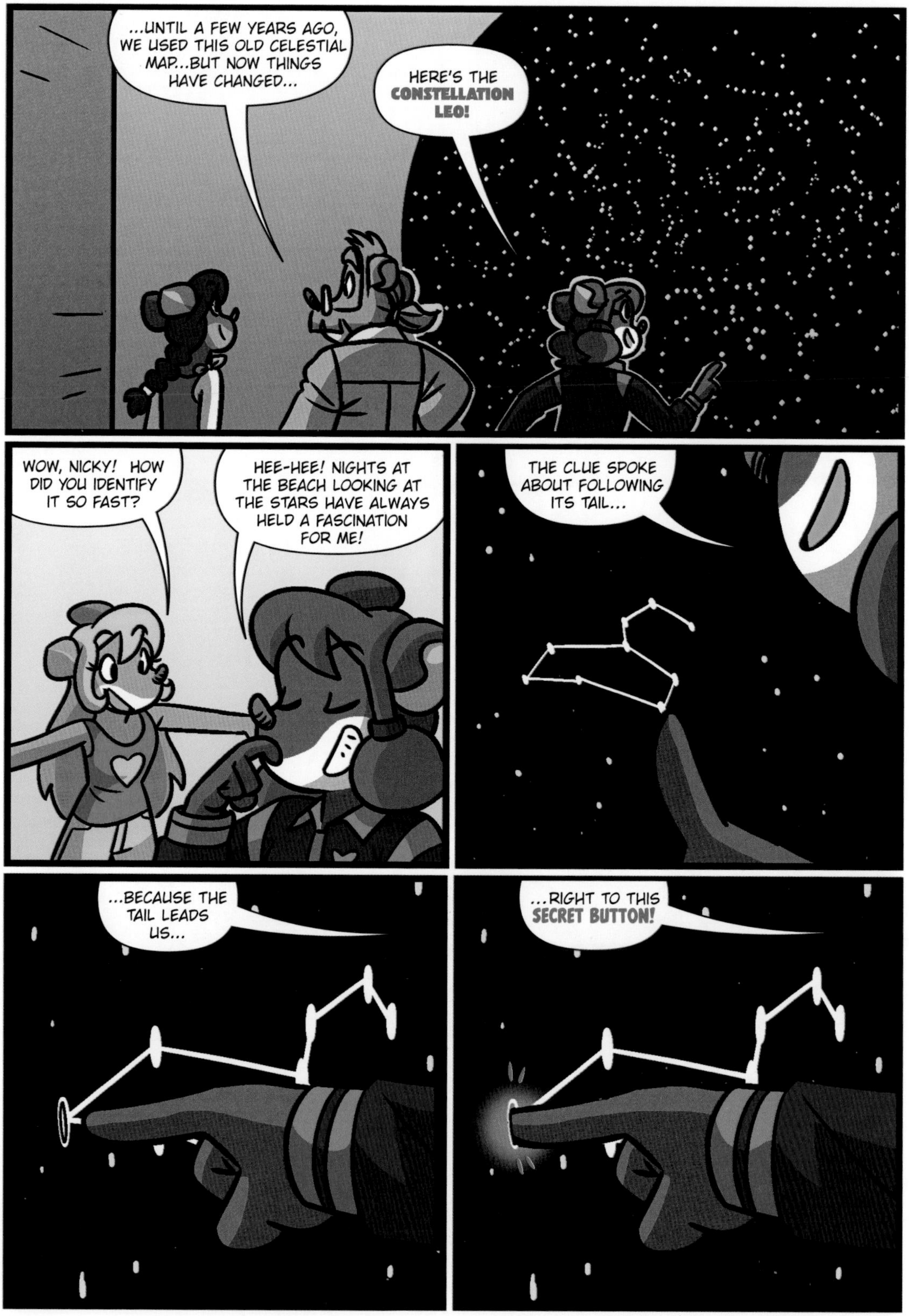
...UNTIL A FEW YEARS AGO, WE USED THIS OLD CELESTIAL MAP...BUT NOW THINGS HAVE CHANGED...
HERE'S THE CONSTELLATION LEO!
WOW, NICKY! HOW DID YOU IDENTIFY IT SO FAST?
HEE-HEE! NIGHTS AT THE BEACH LOOKING AT THE STARS HAVE ALWAYS HELD A FASCINATION FOR ME!
THE CLUE SPOKE ABOUT FOLLOWING ITS TAIL...
...BECAUSE THE TAIL LEADS US...
...RIGHT TO THIS SECRET BUTTON!

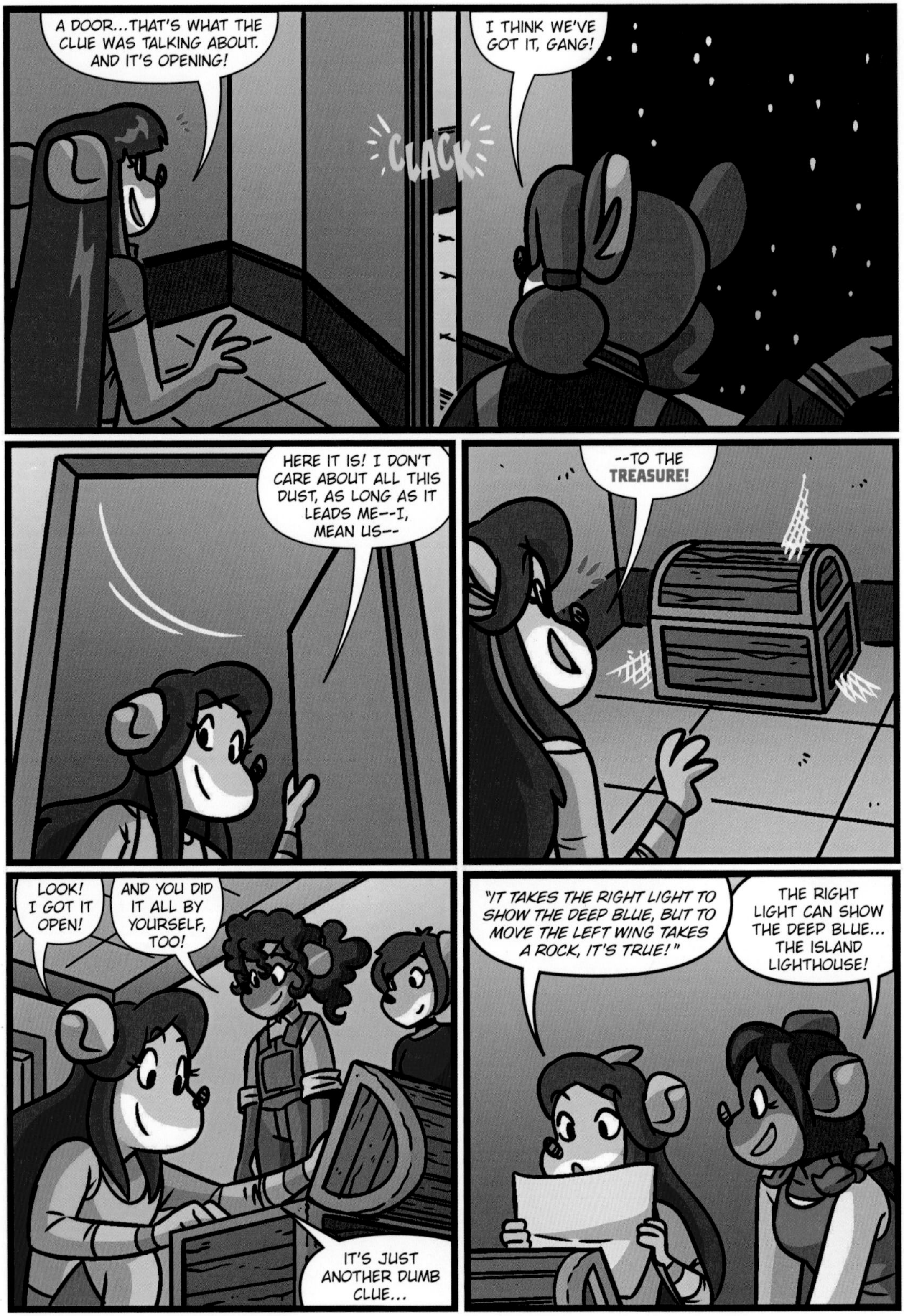
A DOOR...THAT'S WHAT THE CLUE WAS TALKING ABOUT. AND IT'S OPENING!
CLACK
I THINK WE'VE GOT IT, GANG!
HERE IT IS! I DON'T CARE ABOUT ALL THIS DUST, AS LONG AS IT LEADS ME--I, MEAN US--
--TO THE TREASURE!
LOOK! I GOT IT OPEN!
AND YOU DID IT ALL BY YOURSELF, TOO!
IT'S JUST ANOTHER DUMB CLUE...
"IT TAKES THE RIGHT LIGHT TO SHOW THE DEEP BLUE, BUT TO MOVE THE LEFT WING TAKES A ROCK, IT'S TRUE!"
THE RIGHT LIGHT CAN SHOW THE DEEP BLUE... THE ISLAND LIGHTHOUSE!

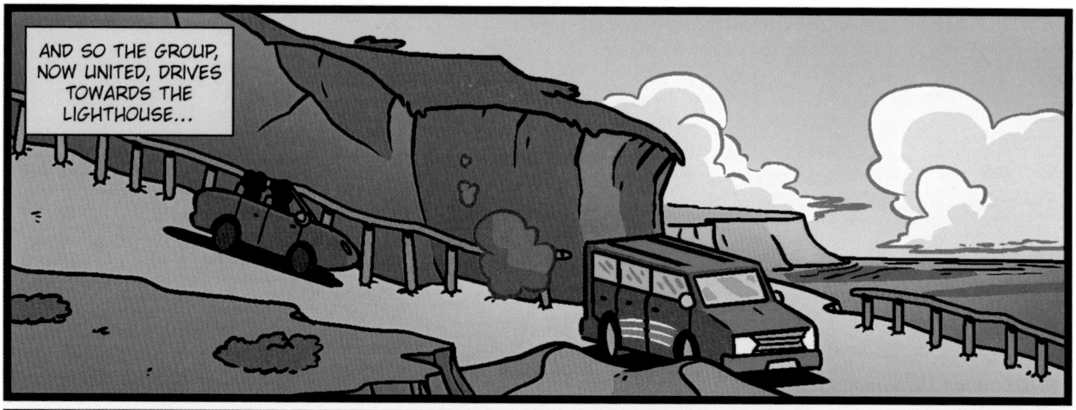
AND SO THE GROUP, NOW UNITED, DRIVES TOWARDS THE LIGHTHOUSE...

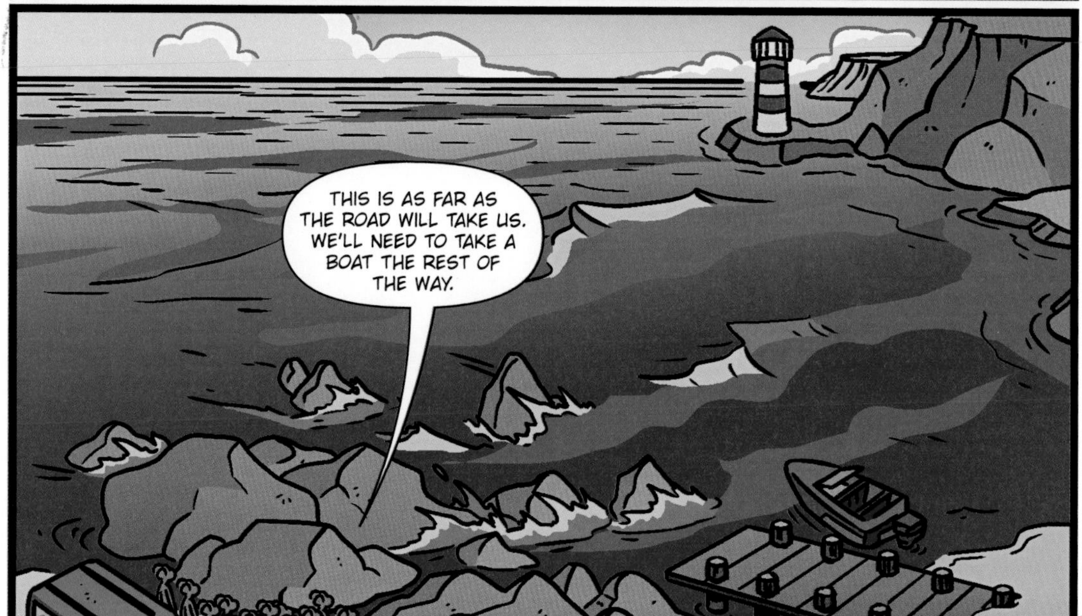
THIS IS AS FAR AS THE ROAD WILL TAKE US. WE'LL NEED TO TAKE A BOAT THE REST OF THE WAY.

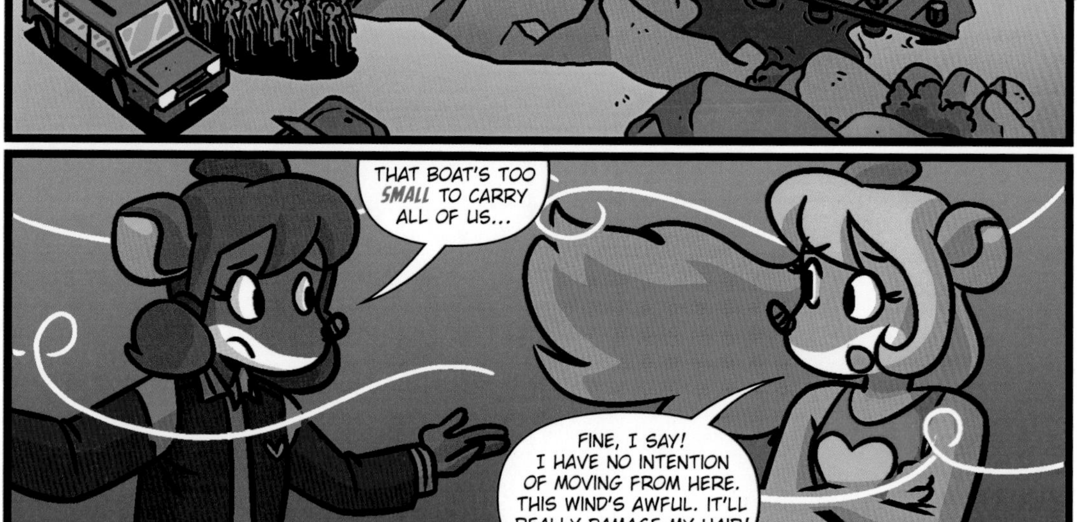
THAT BOAT'S TOO SMALL TO CARRY ALL OF US...
FINE, I SAY! I HAVE NO INTENTION OF MOVING FROM HERE. THIS WIND'S AWFUL. IT'LL REALLY DAMAGE MY HAIR!

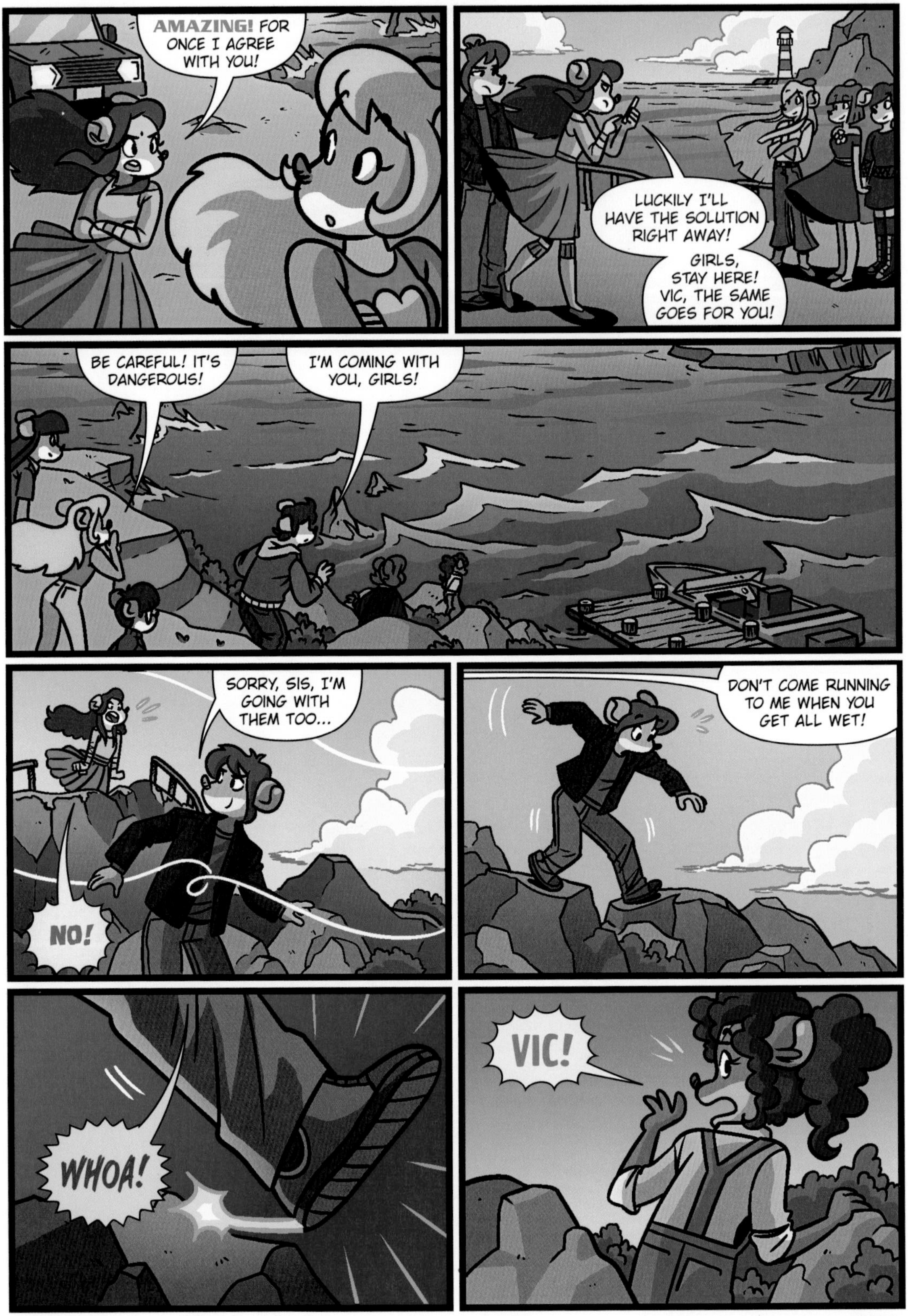
AMAZING! FOR ONCE I AGREE WITH YOU!
LUCKILY I'LL HAVE THE SOLUTION RIGHT AWAY!
GIRLS, STAY HERE! VIC, THE SAME GOES FOR YOU!
BE CAREFUL! IT'S DANGEROUS!
I'M COMING WITH YOU, GIRLS!
SORRY, SIS, I'M GOING WITH THEM TOO...
NO!
DON'T COME RUNNING TO ME WHEN YOU GET ALL WET!
WHOA!
VIC!

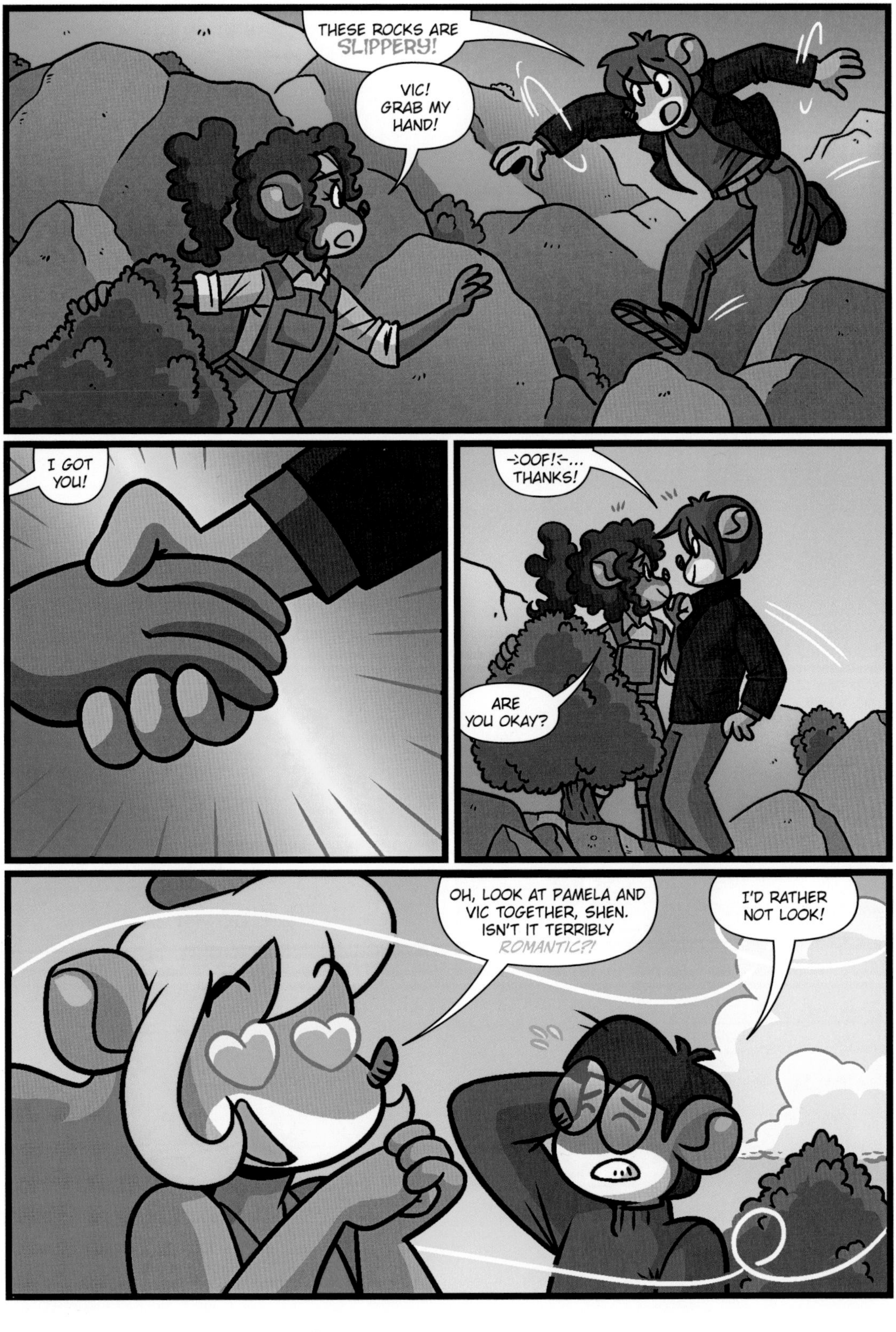

THESE ROCKS ARE SLIPPERY!
VIC! GRAB MY HAND!
I GOT YOU!
-OOF!-... THANKS!
ARE YOU OKAY?
OH, LOOK AT PAMELA AND VIC TOGETHER, SHEN. ISN'T IT TERRIBLY ROMANTIC?!
I'D RATHER NOT LOOK!

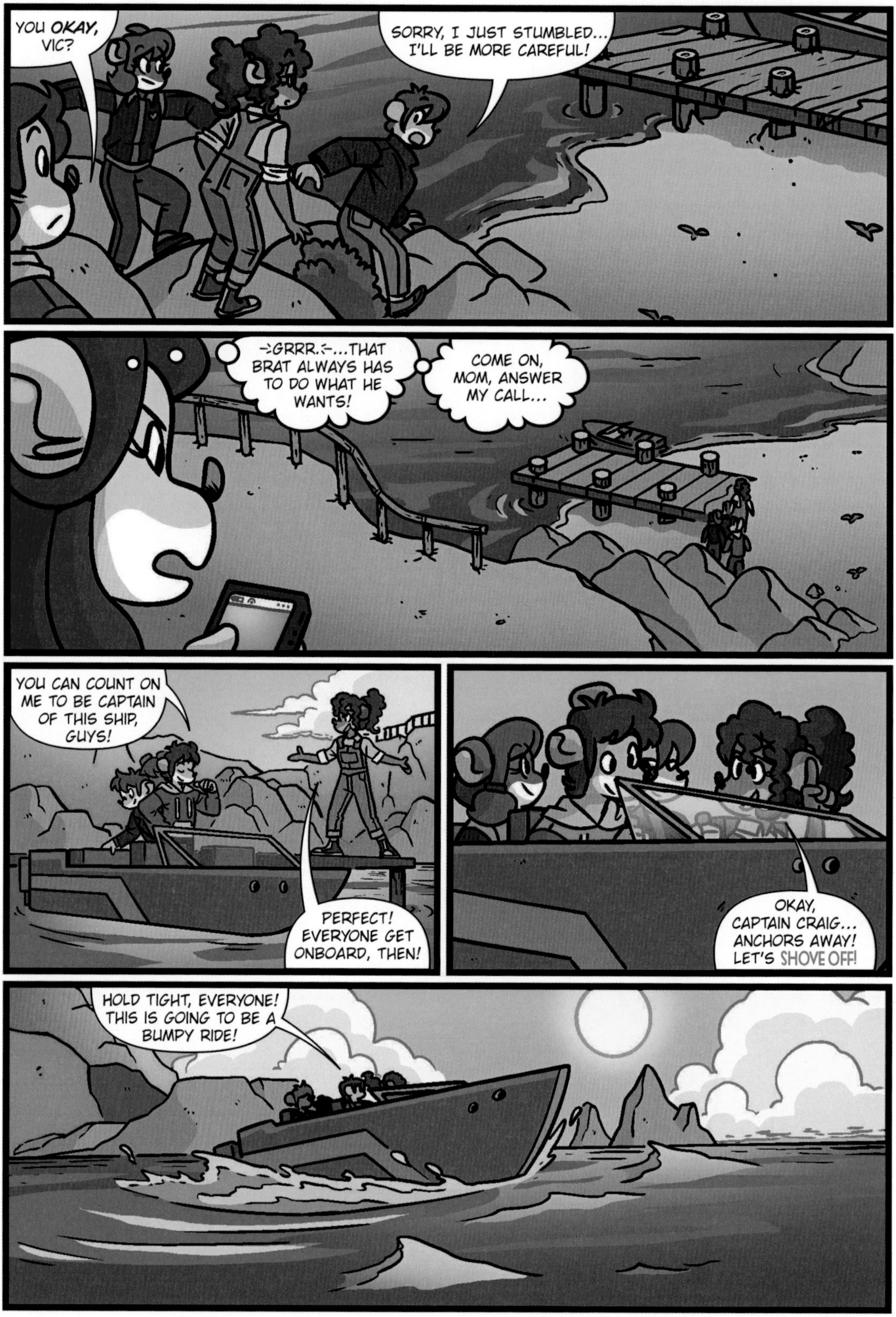

YOU OKAY, VIC?
SORRY, I JUST STUMBLED... I'LL BE MORE CAREFUL!
GRRR. ...THAT BRAT ALWAYS HAS TO DO WHAT HE WANTS!
COME ON, MOM, ANSWER MY CALL...
YOU CAN COUNT ON ME TO BE CAPTAIN OF THIS SHIP, GUYS!
PERFECT! EVERYONE GET ONBOARD, THEN!
OKAY, CAPTAIN CRAIG... ANCHORS AWAY! LET'S SHOVE OFF!
HOLD TIGHT, EVERYONE! THIS IS GOING TO BE A BUMPY RIDE!

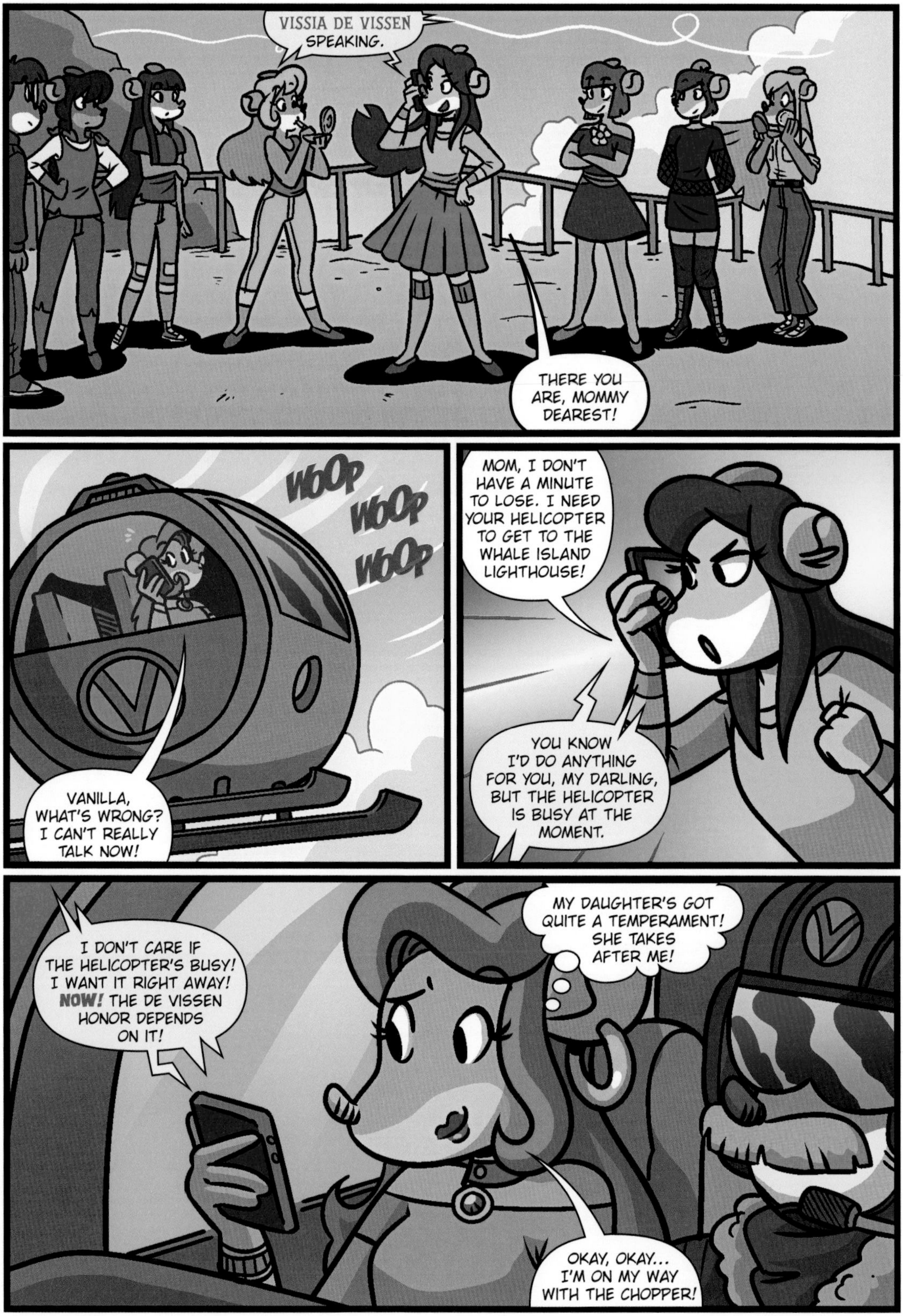
VISSIA DE VISSEN SPEAKING.
THERE YOU ARE, MOMMY DEAREST!
WOOP WOOP WOOP
VANILLA, WHAT'S WRONG? I CAN'T REALLY TALK NOW!
MOM, I DON'T HAVE A MINUTE TO LOSE. I NEED YOUR HELICOPTER TO GET TO THE WHALE ISLAND LIGHTHOUSE!
YOU KNOW I'D DO ANYTHING FOR YOU, MY DARLING, BUT THE HELICOPTER IS BUSY AT THE MOMENT.
I DON'T CARE IF THE HELICOPTER'S BUSY! I WANT IT RIGHT AWAY! NOW! THE DE VISSEN HONOR DEPENDS ON IT!
MY DAUGHTER'S GOT QUITE A TEMPERAMENT! SHE TAKES AFTER ME!
OKAY, OKAY... I'M ON MY WAY WITH THE CHOPPER!

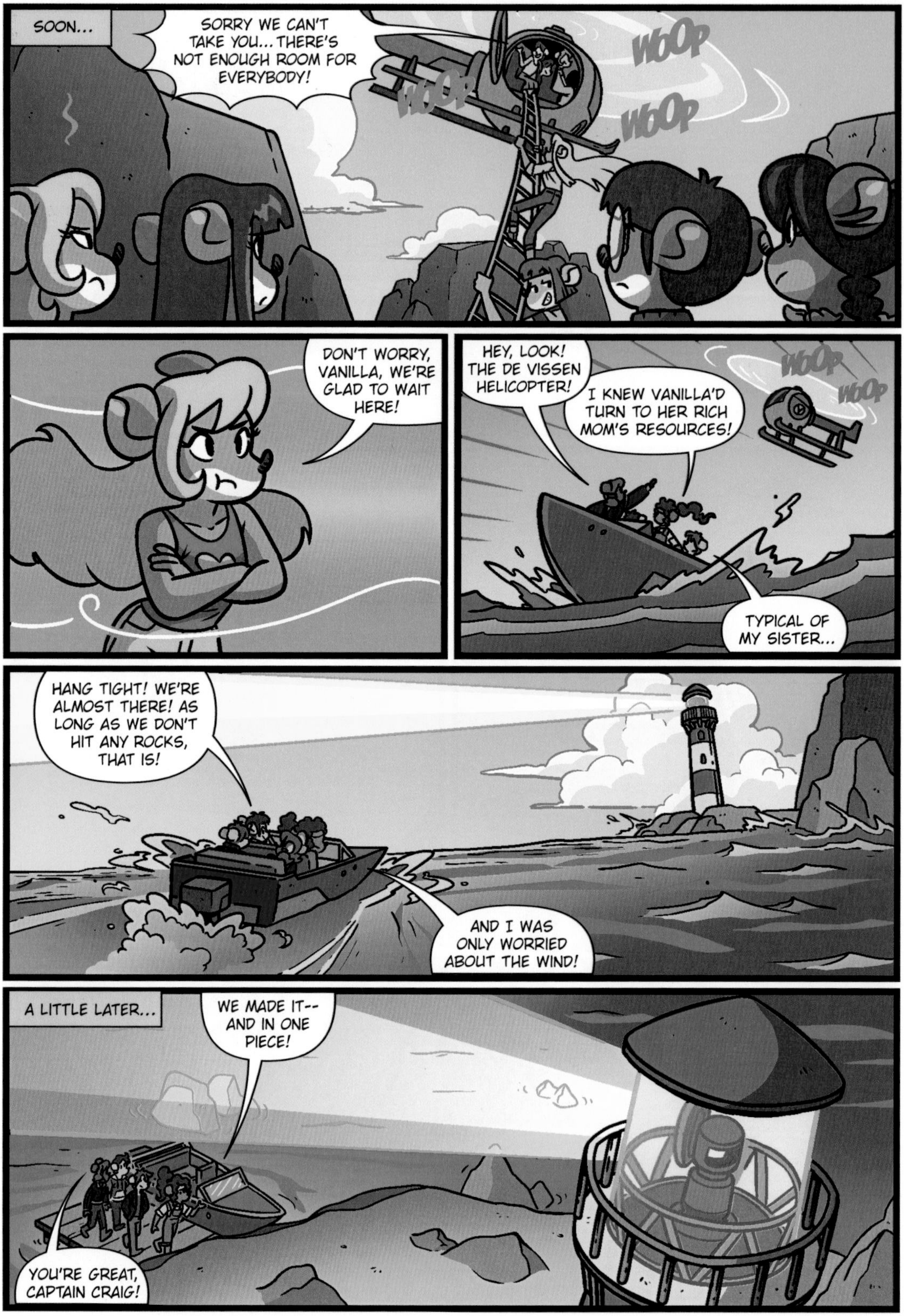
SOON...
SORRY WE CAN'T TAKE YOU... THERE'S NOT ENOUGH ROOM FOR EVERYBODY!
WOOP
WOOP
WOOP
DON'T WORRY, VANILLA, WE'RE GLAD TO WAIT HERE!
HEY, LOOK! THE DE VISSEN HELICOPTER!
I KNEW VANILLA'D TURN TO HER RICH MOM'S RESOURCES!
WOOP
WOOP
TYPICAL OF MY SISTER...
HANG TIGHT! WE'RE ALMOST THERE! AS LONG AS WE DON'T HIT ANY ROCKS, THAT IS!
AND I WAS ONLY WORRIED ABOUT THE WIND!
A LITTLE LATER...
WE MADE IT-- AND IN ONE PIECE!
YOU'RE GREAT, CAPTAIN CRAIG!

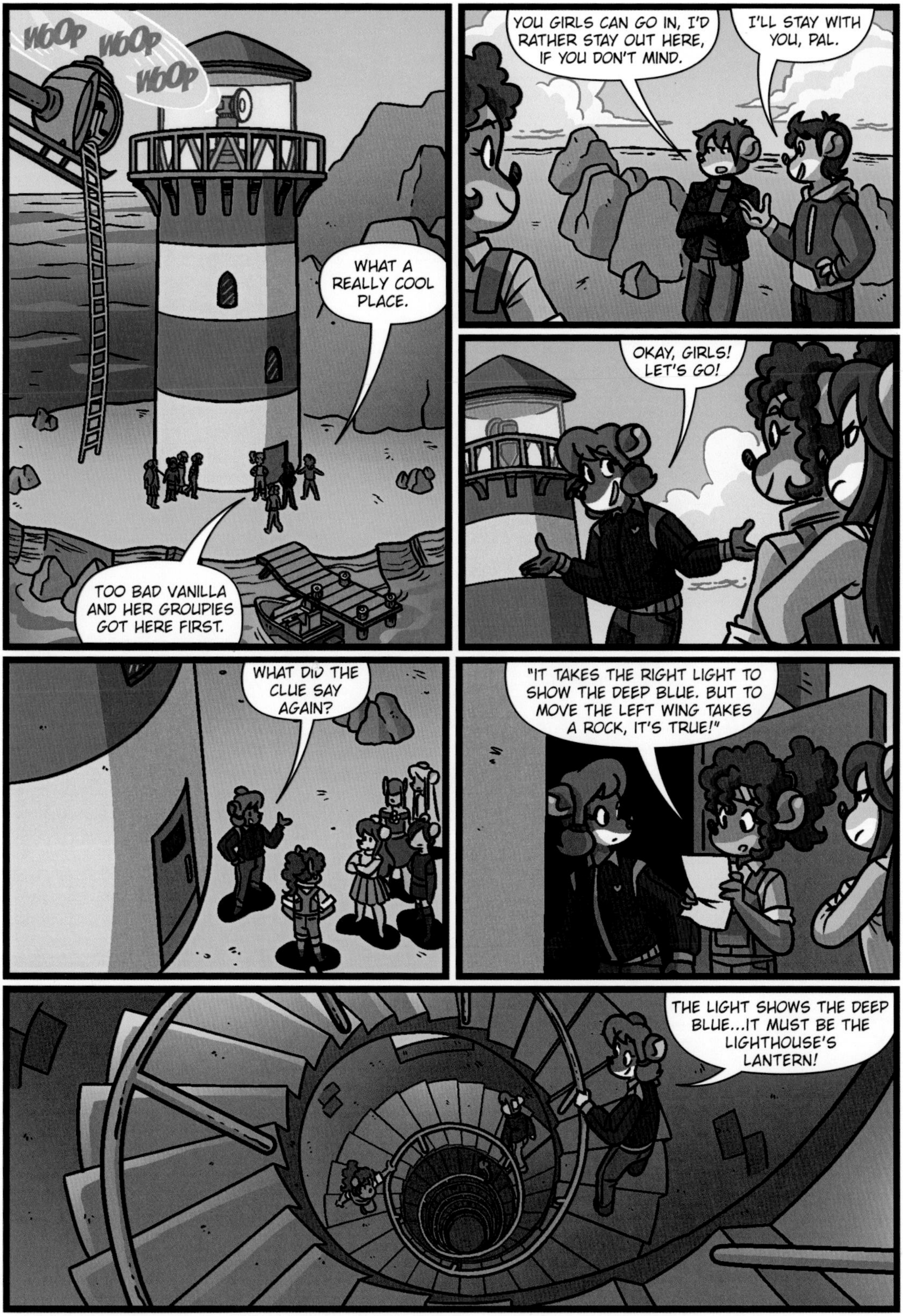
WOOP WOOP WOOP
WHAT A REALLY COOL PLACE.
TOO BAD VANILLA AND HER GROUPIES GOT HERE FIRST.
YOU GIRLS CAN GO IN, I'D RATHER STAY OUT HERE, IF YOU DON'T MIND.
I'LL STAY WITH YOU, PAL.
OKAY, GIRLS! LET'S GO!
WHAT DID THE CLUE SAY AGAIN?
"IT TAKES THE RIGHT LIGHT TO SHOW THE DEEP BLUE. BUT TO MOVE THE LEFT WING TAKES A ROCK, IT'S TRUE!"
THE LIGHT SHOWS THE DEEP BLUE...IT MUST BE THE LIGHTHOUSE'S LANTERN!

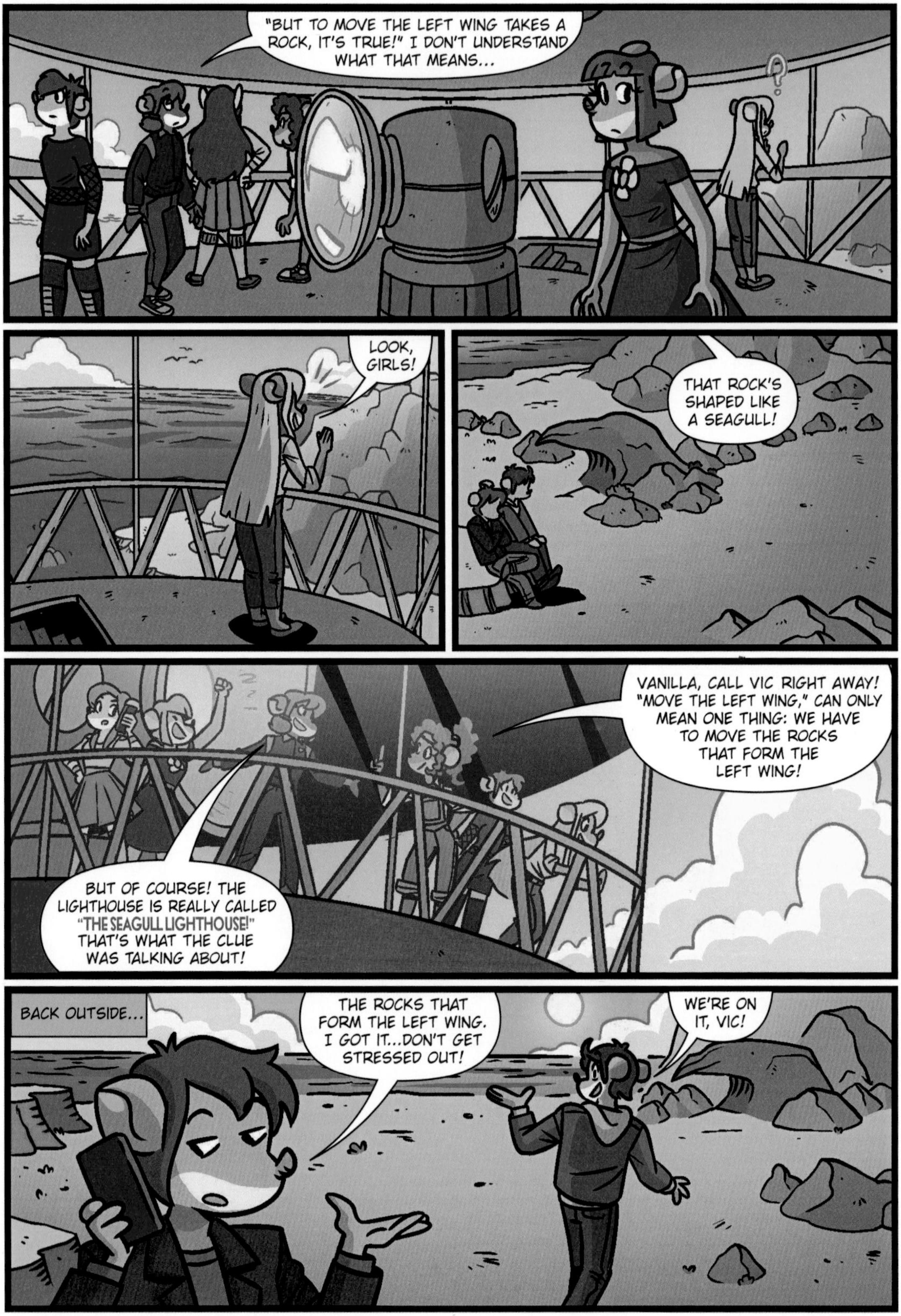
"BUT TO MOVE THE LEFT WING TAKES A ROCK, IT'S TRUE!" I DON'T UNDERSTAND WHAT THAT MEANS...
LOOK, GIRLS!
THAT ROCK'S SHAPED LIKE A SEAGULL!
VANILLA, CALL VIC RIGHT AWAY! "MOVE THE LEFT WING," CAN ONLY MEAN ONE THING: WE HAVE TO MOVE THE ROCKS THAT FORM THE LEFT WING!
BUT OF COURSE! THE LIGHTHOUSE IS REALLY CALLED "THE SEAGULL LIGHTHOUSE!" THAT'S WHAT THE CLUE WAS TALKING ABOUT!
BACK OUTSIDE...
THE ROCKS THAT FORM THE LEFT WING. I GOT IT...DON'T GET STRESSED OUT!
WE'RE ON IT, VIC!

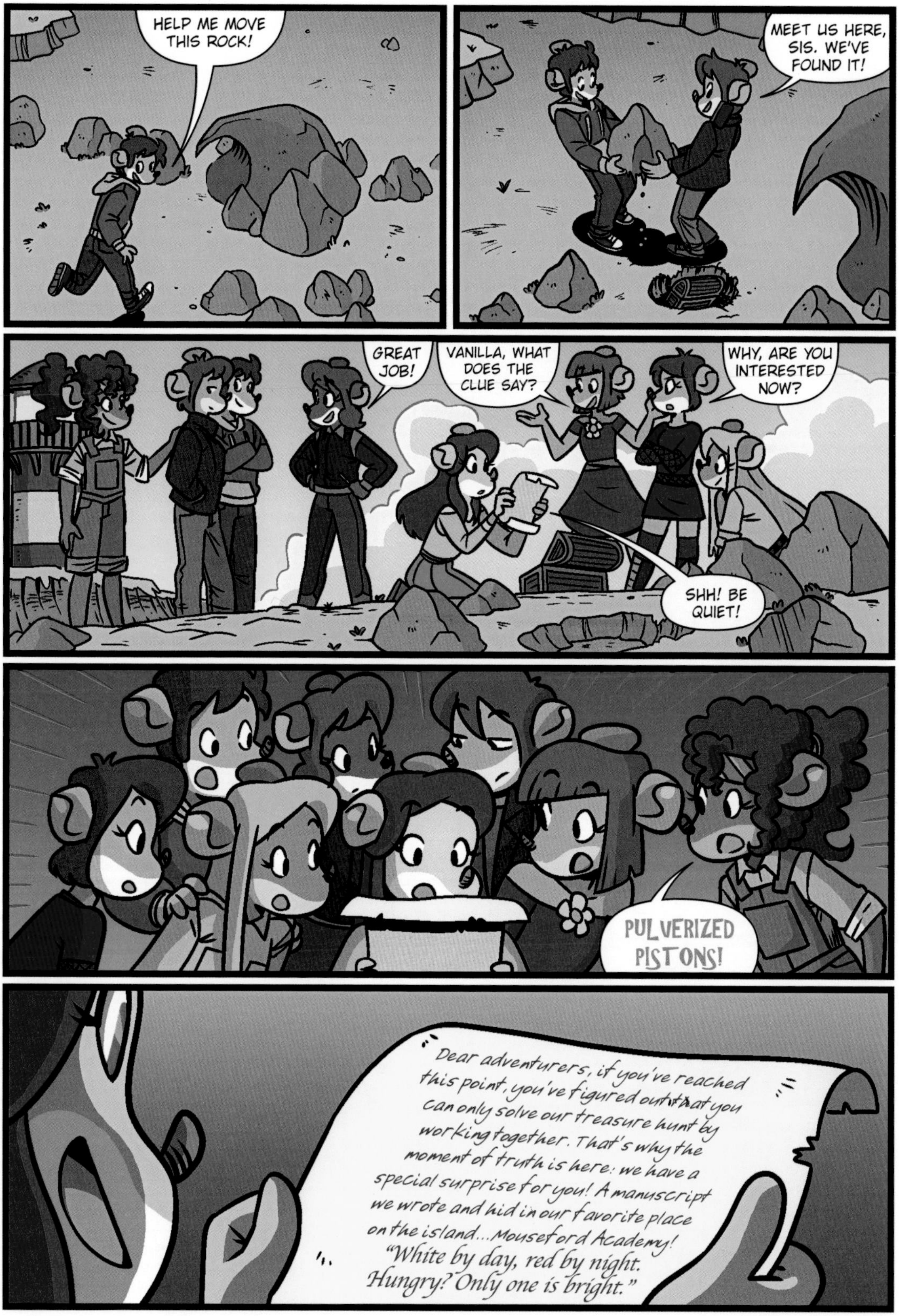
HELP ME MOVE THIS ROCK!
MEET US HERE, SIS. WE'VE FOUND IT!
GREAT JOB!
VANILLA, WHAT DOES THE CLUE SAY?
WHY, ARE YOU INTERESTED NOW?
SHH! BE QUIET!
PULVERIZED PISTONS!
Dear adventurers, if you've reached this point, you've figured out that you can only solve our treasure hunt by working together. That's why the moment of truth is here: we have a special surprise for you! A manuscript we wrote and hid in our favorite place on the island... Mouseford Academy!
"White by day, red by night. Hungry? Only one is bright."

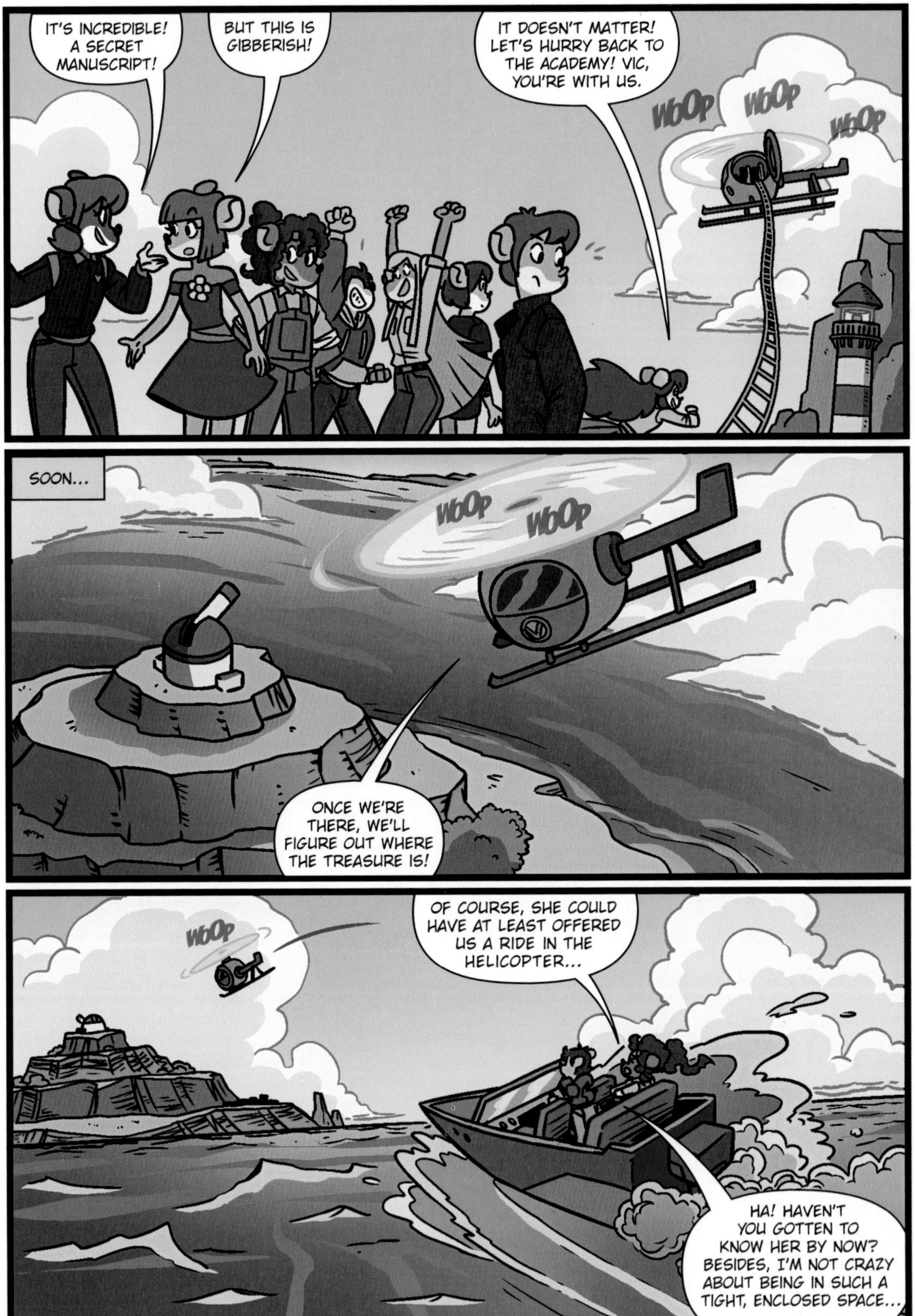
IT'S INCREDIBLE! A SECRET MANUSCRIPT!
BUT THIS IS GIBBERISH!
IT DOESN'T MATTER! LET'S HURRY BACK TO THE ACADEMY! VIC, YOU'RE WITH US.
WOOP WOOP WOOP
SOON...
WOOP WOOP
ONCE WE'RE THERE, WE'LL FIGURE OUT WHERE THE TREASURE IS!
WOOP
OF COURSE, SHE COULD HAVE AT LEAST OFFERED US A RIDE IN THE HELICOPTER...
HA! HAVEN'T YOU GOTTEN TO KNOW HER BY NOW? BESIDES, I'M NOT CRAZY ABOUT BEING IN SUCH A TIGHT, ENCLOSED SPACE...

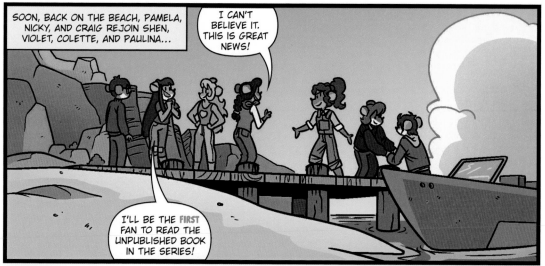

SOON, BACK ON THE BEACH, PAMELA, NICKY, AND CRAIG REJOIN SHEN, VIOLET, COLETTE, AND PAULINA...

I CAN'T BELIEVE IT. THIS IS GREAT NEWS!

I'LL BE THE **FIRST** FAN TO READ THE UNPUBLISHED BOOK IN THE SERIES!

I JUST HOPE VANILLA DOESN'T GET TO THE MANUSCRIPT BEFORE US.

CALM DOWN, COLETTE. THERE'S LITTLE CHANCE SHE'LL BE ABLE TO DECIPHER THE CLUE IF SHE DOESN'T WORK WITH THE TEAM.

ESPECIALLY SINCE SHE DOESN'T HAVE A COOKING EXPERT LIKE PAMELA ON HER TEAM, WHO'D BE ABLE TO FIGURE OUT THE CLUE RIGHT AWAY!

YOU SAID IT, PAULINA! AS SOON AS I HEARD, "HUNGRY," I WANTED TO BAKE A CAKE RIGHT AWAY!

HA! HA! HA!

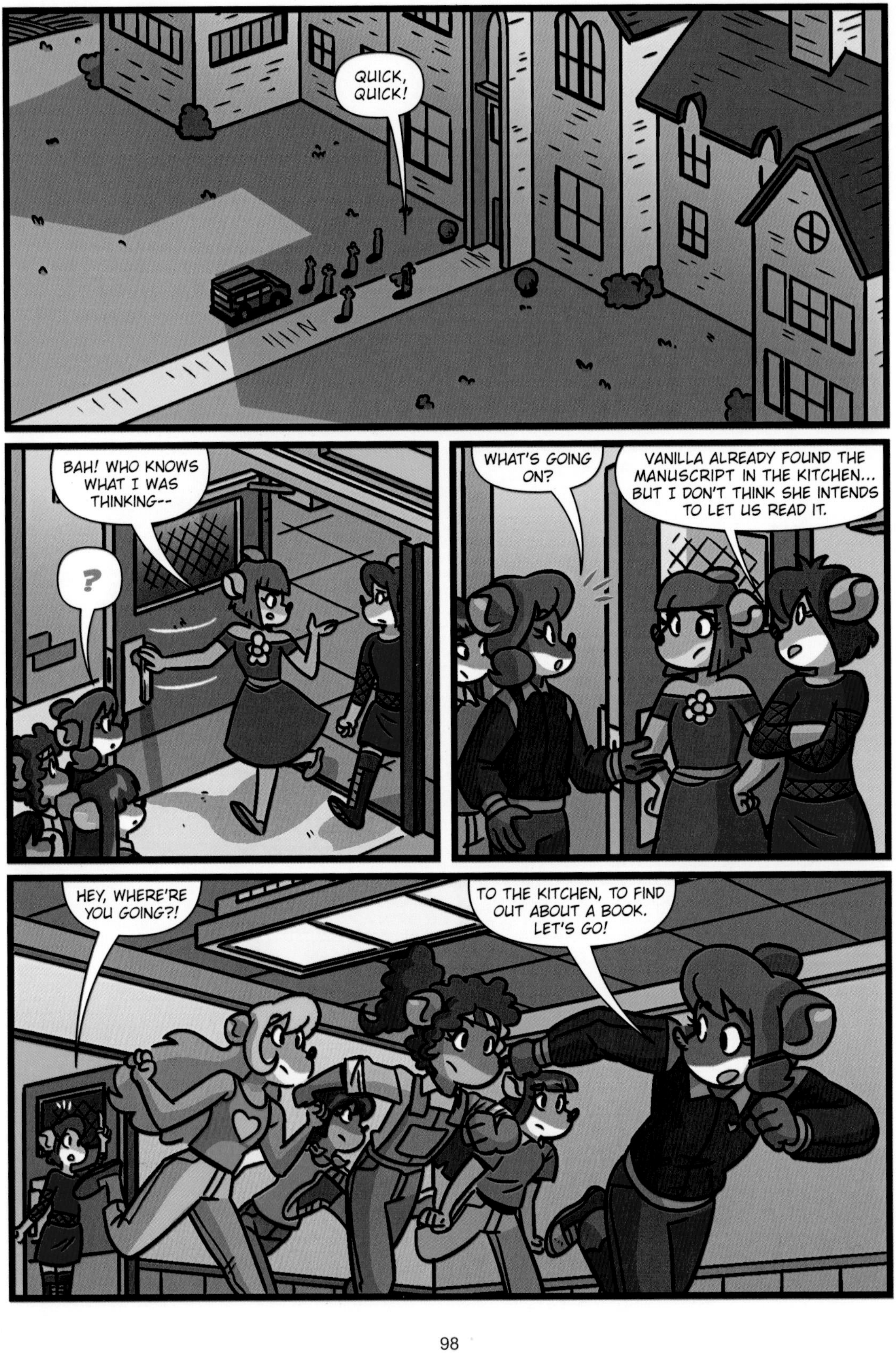
QUICK, QUICK!
BAH! WHO KNOWS WHAT I WAS THINKING--
?
WHAT'S GOING ON?
VANILLA ALREADY FOUND THE MANUSCRIPT IN THE KITCHEN... BUT I DON'T THINK SHE INTENDS TO LET US READ IT.
HEY, WHERE'RE YOU GOING?!
TO THE KITCHEN, TO FIND OUT ABOUT A BOOK. LET'S GO!

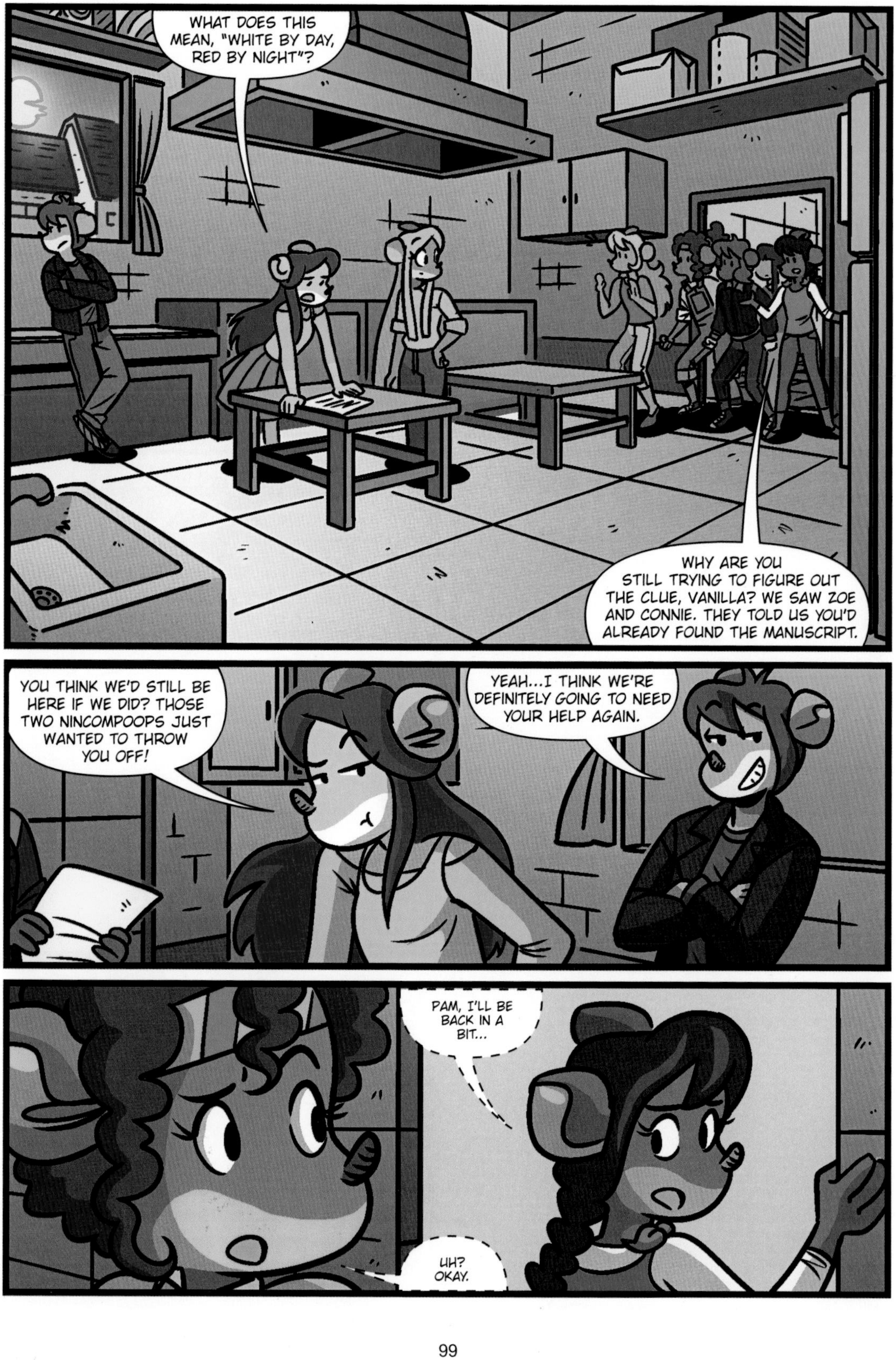
WHAT DOES THIS MEAN, "WHITE BY DAY, RED BY NIGHT"?
WHY ARE YOU STILL TRYING TO FIGURE OUT THE CLUE, VANILLA? WE SAW ZOE AND CONNIE. THEY TOLD US YOU'D ALREADY FOUND THE MANUSCRIPT.
YOU THINK WE'D STILL BE HERE IF WE DID? THOSE TWO NINCOMPOOPS JUST WANTED TO THROW YOU OFF!
YEAH...I THINK WE'RE DEFINITELY GOING TO NEED YOUR HELP AGAIN.
PAM, I'LL BE BACK IN A BIT...
UH? OKAY.

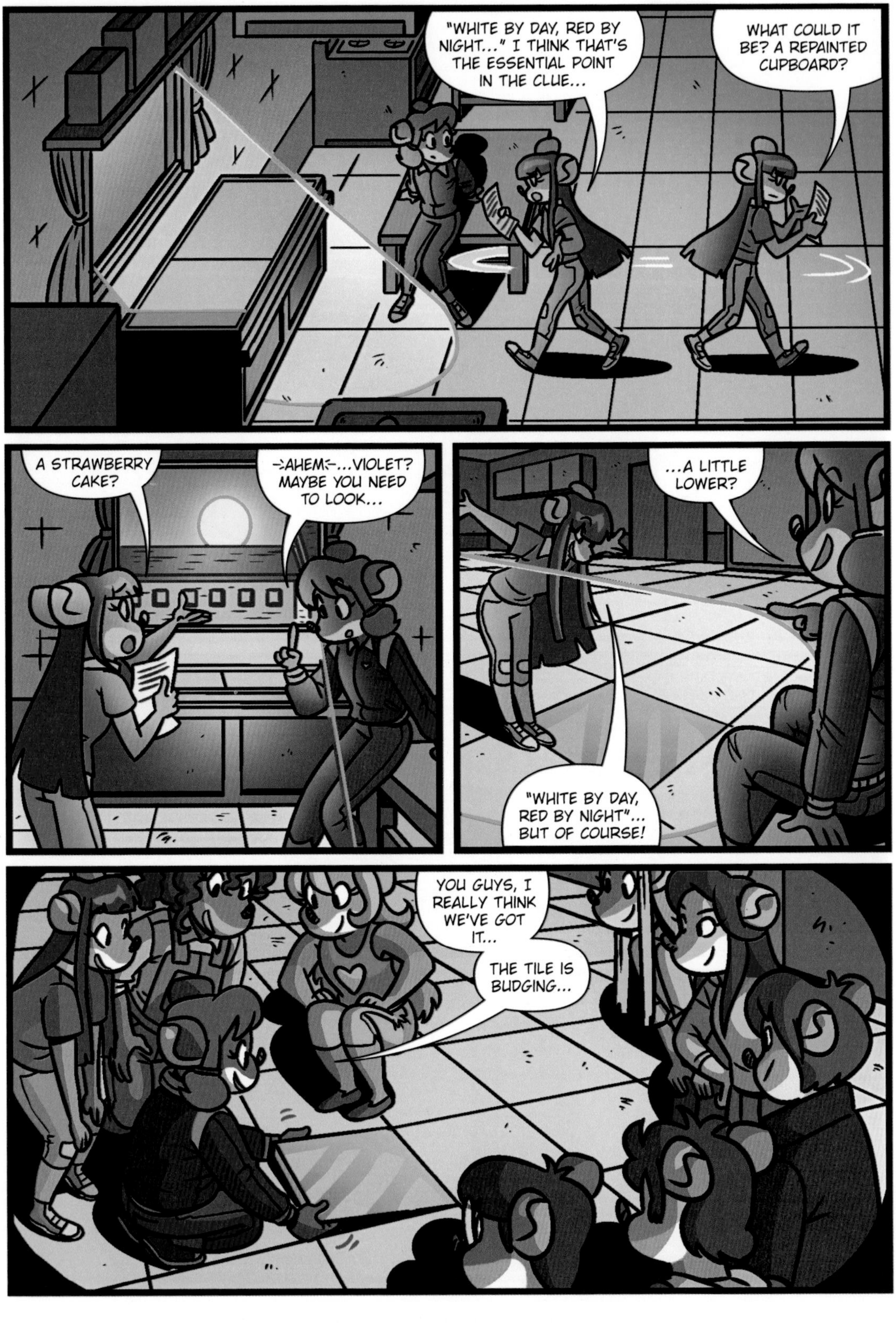
"WHITE BY DAY, RED BY NIGHT..." I THINK THAT'S THE ESSENTIAL POINT IN THE CLUE...
WHAT COULD IT BE? A REPAINTED CUPBOARD?
A STRAWBERRY CAKE?
-AHEM-...VIOLET? MAYBE YOU NEED TO LOOK...
...A LITTLE LOWER?
"WHITE BY DAY, RED BY NIGHT"... BUT OF COURSE!
YOU GUYS, I REALLY THINK WE'VE GOT IT...
THE TILE IS BUDGING...

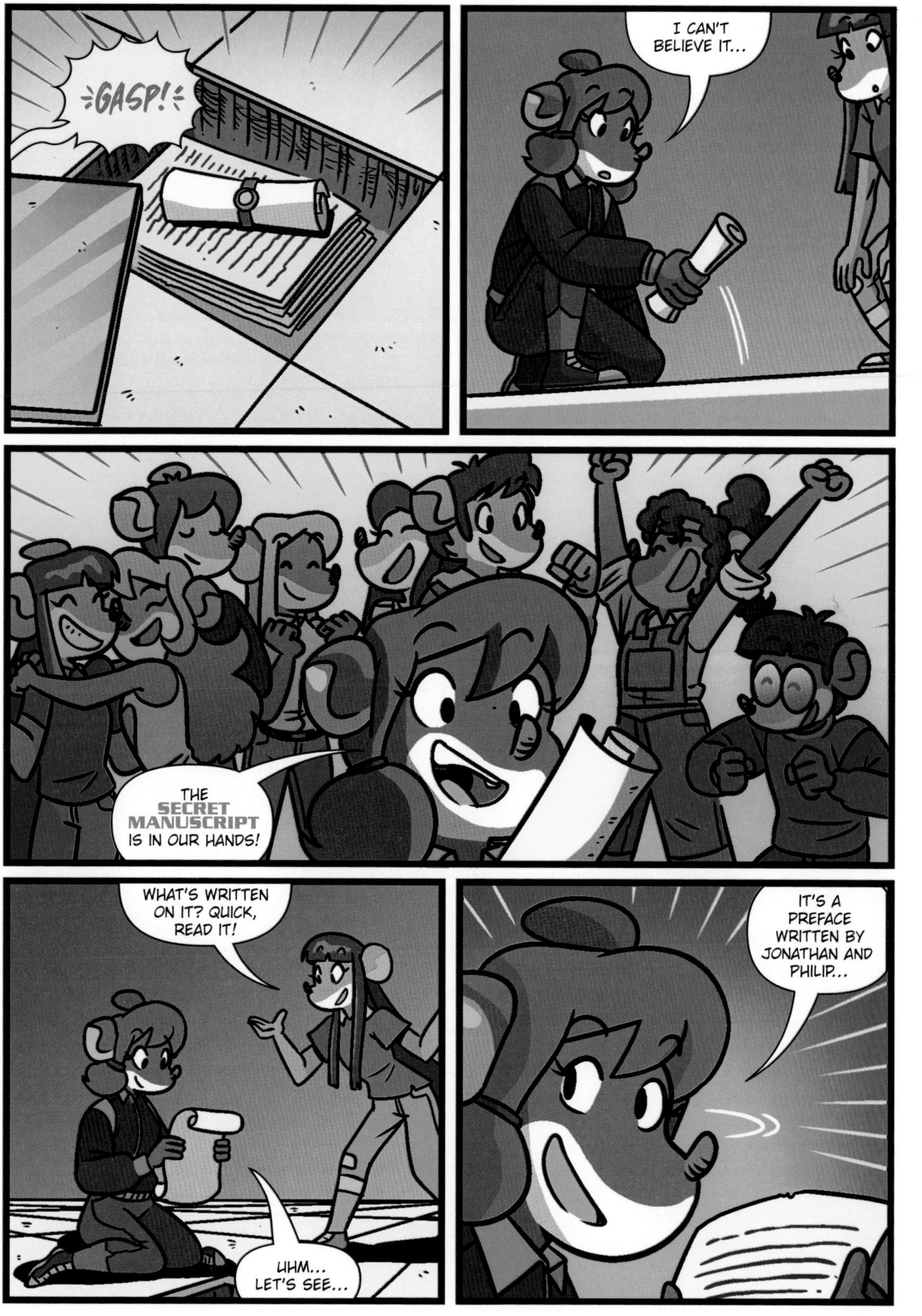
GASP!
I CAN'T BELIEVE IT...
THE SECRET MANUSCRIPT IS IN OUR HANDS!
WHAT'S WRITTEN ON IT? QUICK, READ IT!
UHM... LET'S SEE...
IT'S A PREFACE WRITTEN BY JONATHAN AND PHILIP...

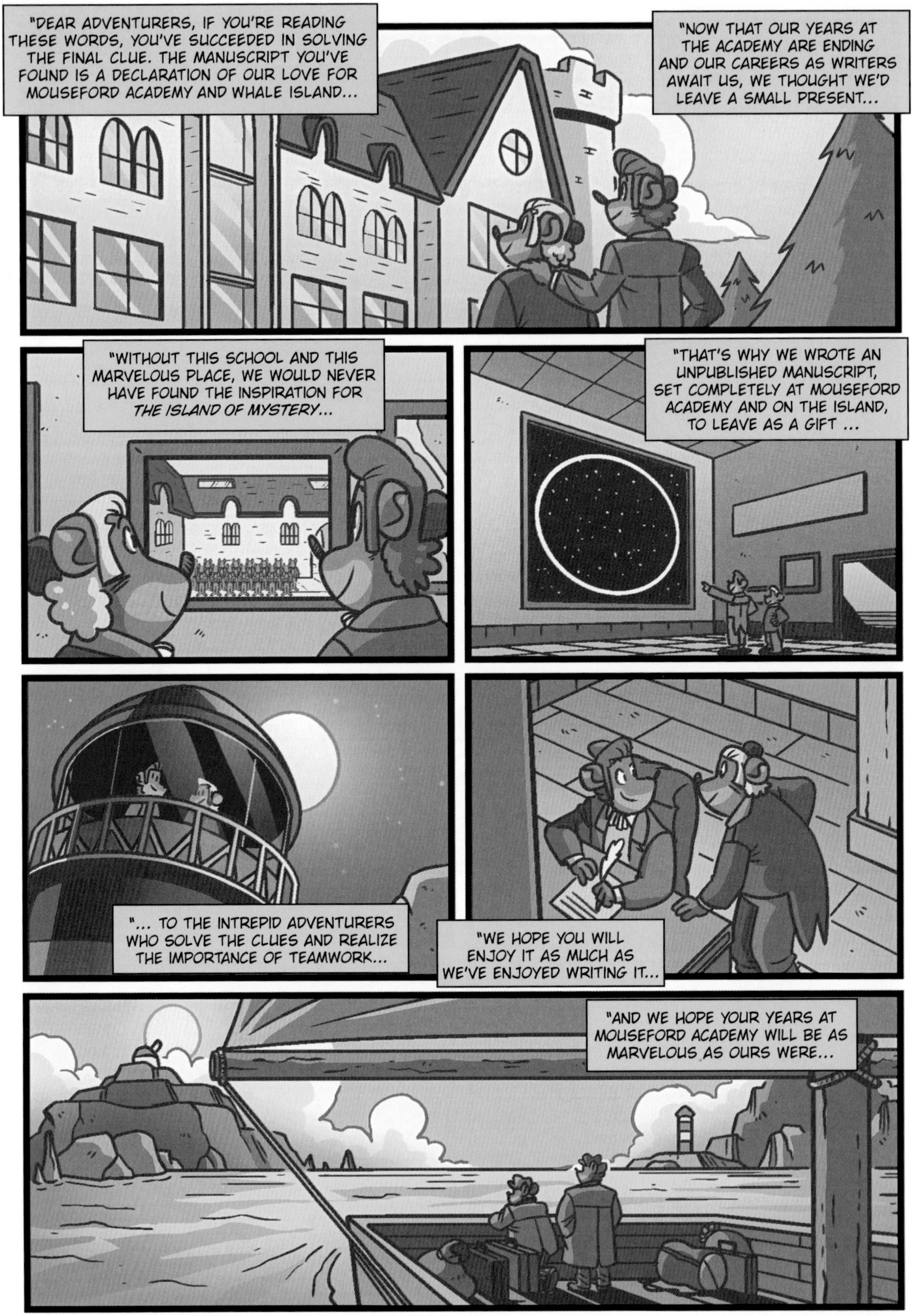
"DEAR ADVENTURERS, IF YOU'RE READING THESE WORDS, YOU'VE SUCCEEDED IN SOLVING THE FINAL CLUE. THE MANUSCRIPT YOU'VE FOUND IS A DECLARATION OF OUR LOVE FOR MOUSEFORD ACADEMY AND WHALE ISLAND...
"NOW THAT OUR YEARS AT THE ACADEMY ARE ENDING AND OUR CAREERS AS WRITERS AWAIT US, WE THOUGHT WE'D LEAVE A SMALL PRESENT...
"WITHOUT THIS SCHOOL AND THIS MARVELOUS PLACE, WE WOULD NEVER HAVE FOUND THE INSPIRATION FOR *THE ISLAND OF MYSTERY*...
"THAT'S WHY WE WROTE AN UNPUBLISHED MANUSCRIPT, SET COMPLETELY AT MOUSEFORD ACADEMY AND ON THE ISLAND, TO LEAVE AS A GIFT ...
"... TO THE INTREPID ADVENTURERS WHO SOLVE THE CLUES AND REALIZE THE IMPORTANCE OF TEAMWORK...
"WE HOPE YOU WILL ENJOY IT AS MUCH AS WE'VE ENJOYED WRITING IT...
"AND WE HOPE YOUR YEARS AT MOUSEFORD ACADEMY WILL BE AS MARVELOUS AS OURS WERE...

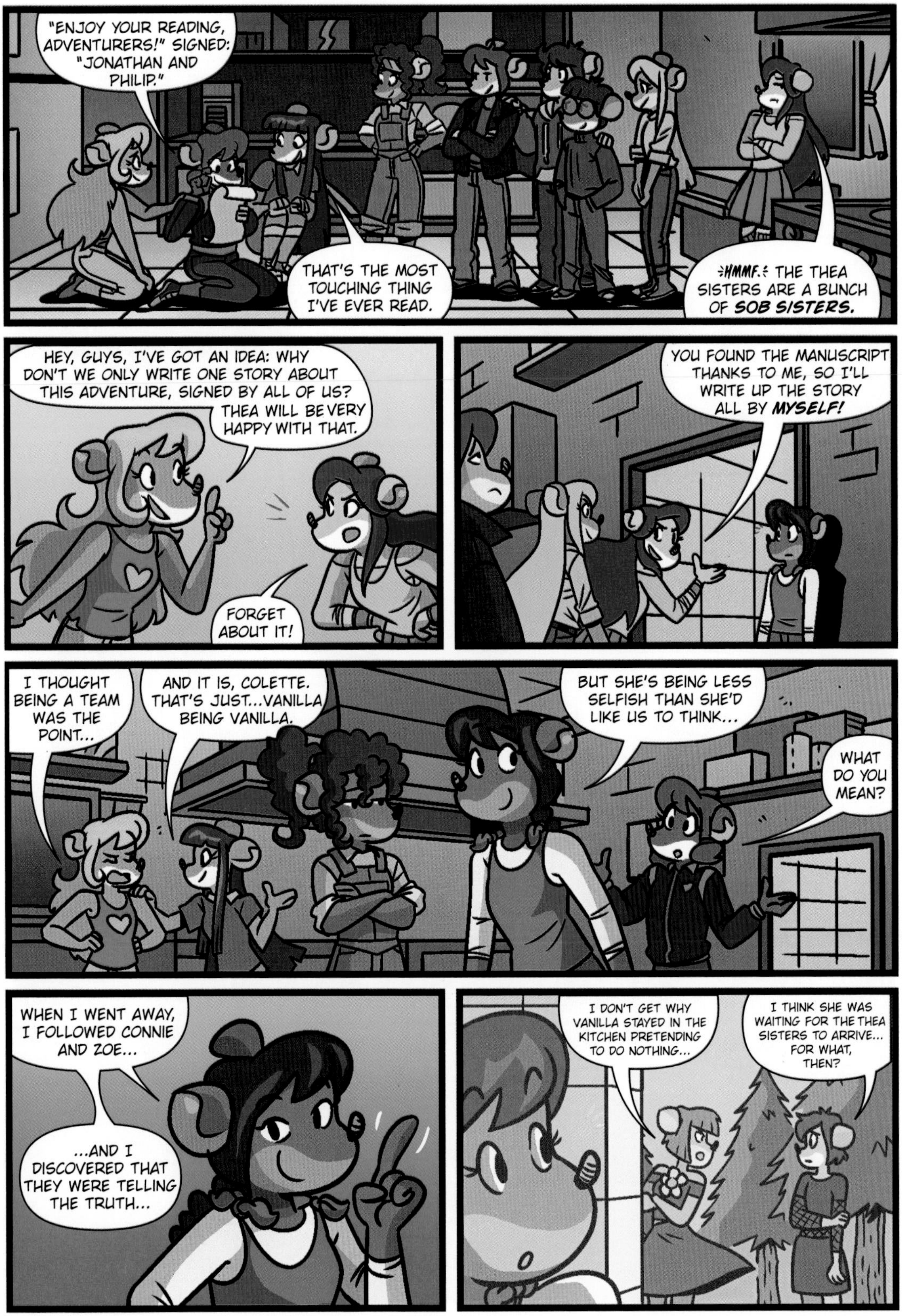

"ENJOY YOUR READING, ADVENTURERS!" SIGNED: "JONATHAN AND PHILIP."
THAT'S THE MOST TOUCHING THING I'VE EVER READ.
HMMF. THE THEA SISTERS ARE A BUNCH OF SOB SISTERS.
HEY, GUYS, I'VE GOT AN IDEA: WHY DON'T WE ONLY WRITE ONE STORY ABOUT THIS ADVENTURE, SIGNED BY ALL OF US?
THEA WILL BE VERY HAPPY WITH THAT.
FORGET ABOUT IT!
YOU FOUND THE MANUSCRIPT THANKS TO ME, SO I'LL WRITE UP THE STORY ALL BY MYSELF!
I THOUGHT BEING A TEAM WAS THE POINT...
AND IT IS, COLETTE. THAT'S JUST...VANILLA BEING VANILLA.
BUT SHE'S BEING LESS SELFISH THAN SHE'D LIKE US TO THINK...
WHAT DO YOU MEAN?
WHEN I WENT AWAY, I FOLLOWED CONNIE AND ZOE...
...AND I DISCOVERED THAT THEY WERE TELLING THE TRUTH...
I DON'T GET WHY VANILLA STAYED IN THE KITCHEN PRETENDING TO DO NOTHING...
I THINK SHE WAS WAITING FOR THE THEA SISTERS TO ARRIVE... FOR WHAT, THEN?

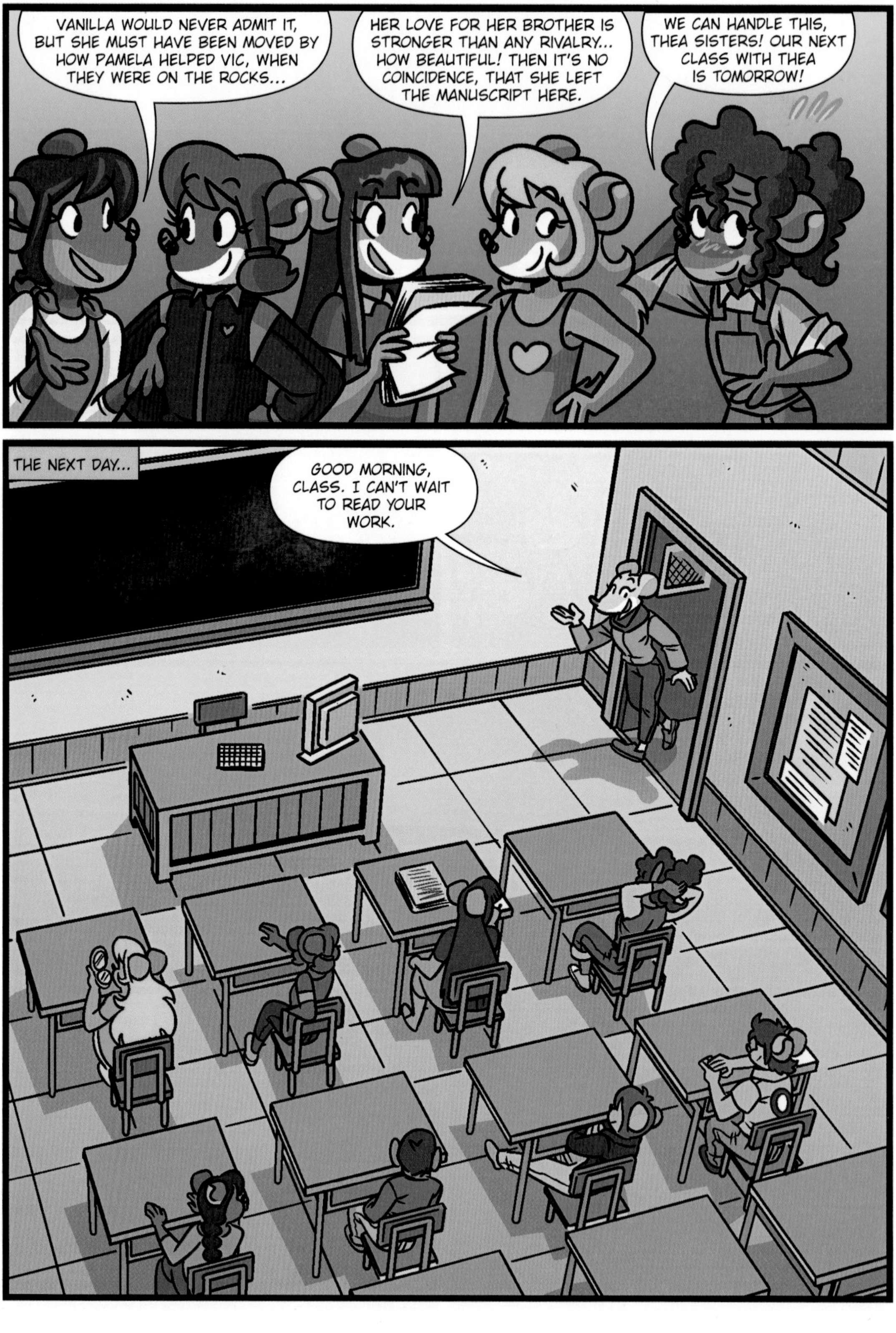
VANILLA WOULD NEVER ADMIT IT, BUT SHE MUST HAVE BEEN MOVED BY HOW PAMELA HELPED VIC, WHEN THEY WERE ON THE ROCKS...
HER LOVE FOR HER BROTHER IS STRONGER THAN ANY RIVALRY... HOW BEAUTIFUL! THEN IT'S NO COINCIDENCE, THAT SHE LEFT THE MANUSCRIPT HERE.
WE CAN HANDLE THIS, THEA SISTERS! OUR NEXT CLASS WITH THEA IS TOMORROW!
THE NEXT DAY...
GOOD MORNING, CLASS. I CAN'T WAIT TO READ YOUR WORK.

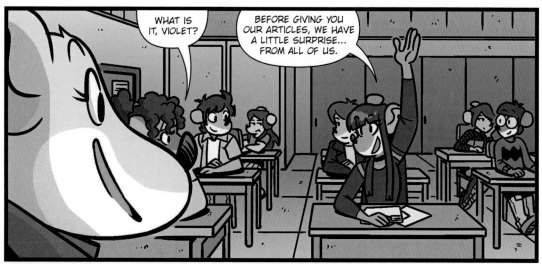

WHAT IS IT, VIOLET?

BEFORE GIVING YOU OUR ARTICLES, WE HAVE A LITTLE SURPRISE... FROM ALL OF US.

A SURPRISE? WHAT'S IT ABOUT?

BUT...BUT THIS IS BY... JONATHAN AND PHILIP? WHAT DOES THIS MEAN?

IT MEANS THAT YOUR HOMEWORK ASSIGNMENT LEAD US ON A FANTASTIC TREASURE HUNT!

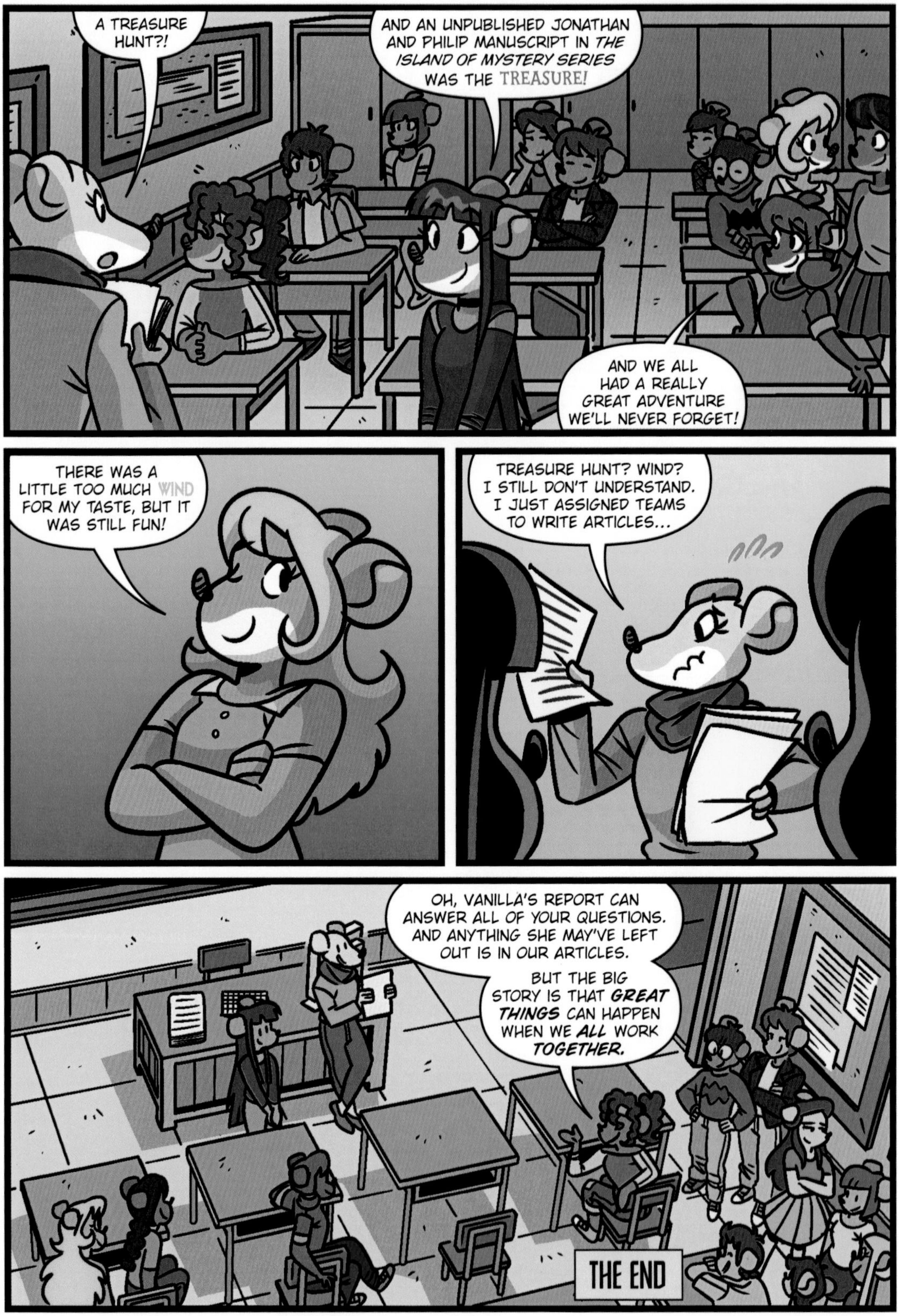
A TREASURE HUNT?!
AND AN UNPUBLISHED JONATHAN AND PHILIP MANUSCRIPT IN *THE ISLAND OF MYSTERY SERIES* WAS THE TREASURE!
AND WE ALL HAD A REALLY GREAT ADVENTURE WE'LL NEVER FORGET!
THERE WAS A LITTLE TOO MUCH WIND FOR MY TASTE, BUT IT WAS STILL FUN!
TREASURE HUNT? WIND? I STILL DON'T UNDERSTAND. I JUST ASSIGNED TEAMS TO WRITE ARTICLES...
OH, VANILLA'S REPORT CAN ANSWER ALL OF YOUR QUESTIONS. AND ANYTHING SHE MAY'VE LEFT OUT IS IN OUR ARTICLES.
BUT THE BIG STORY IS THAT ***GREAT THINGS*** CAN HAPPEN WHEN WE ***ALL*** WORK ***TOGETHER.***
THE END

WATCH OUT FOR PAPERCUTZ

Welcome to the fabulous follow-up to THEA STILTON 3 IN 1—the first and final THEA STILTON 2 IN 1 graphic novel, reported by Thea Stilton, from Papercutz, that thrifty bunch dedicated to publishing great graphic novels for all ages. Originally, we published eight separate volumes of THEA STILTON, and we recently decided to collect the first six volumes in two volumes of THEA STILTON 3 IN 1s, and the final two volumes in this collection. I'm *Salicrup, Jim Salicrup* the Editor-in-Chief and Compulsive Explainer of Things, here to, well, explain a few things...

While this may be the last THEA STILTON graphic novel, the good news is that you can still follow the adventures of Thea Stilton in the GERONIMO STILTON REPORTER graphic novel series, which adapts the animated adventures of Geronimo Stilton which can be seen on Netflix and Amazon Prime.

Still can't get enough of Thea Stilton? Then check out many of the original GERONIMO STILTON graphic novels or GERONIMO STILTON 3 IN 1 collections—Thea is in many of those, battling side-by-side with her brother, saving the future, by protecting the past!

In the GERONIMO STILTON graphic novels—not to be confused with the GERONIMO STILTON REPORTER graphic novels—Geronimo, often along with Thea, Benjamin, Bugsy Wugsy, Trap, and few others, would answer Professor Von Volt's call and travel back in time in the Speedrat to prevent the Pirate Cats from pulling off their crazy schemes. Who are the Pirate Cats? Allow me to explain... Catardone III of Catonia, his daughter, Tersilla, and their assistant, Bonzo Felix, work together to make Catardone's dream of becoming the richest and most famouse cat of all time, usually by taking the Catjet back through time to twist history to their advantage.

Gee, speaking of the Pirate Cats, there are so many cats featured in Papercutz graphic novels, that it's often suggested that we change our name to *Papercatz*. Don't believe me? Well, here's a mini cat-alogue of just some of the other cats you'll find at Papercutz...

Azrael – This naughty kitty belongs to the Smurfs's archfoe, Gargamel. Azrael would love nothing better than to eat a Smurf! You can find Azrael in THE SMURFS graphic novels by Peyo (writer/artist).

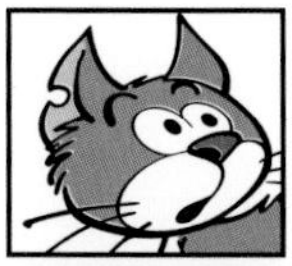

Brina – A two-year-old city cat, named Brina, takes a summer vacation in the country with her owners. Here she meets a group of stray cats who call themselves "The Gang of the Feline Sun," who convince her to run away with them and live life as a free cat. While Brina enjoys her newfound freedom and all the new delectable bugs the countryside has to offer, her young owners are distraught over losing her, someone they consider a member of their family. Brina is terribly conflicted and must choose to return to her owners or to continue to live free in the wild. BRINA THE CAT #1 is by Georgio Salati, writer, and Christian Cornia, artist.

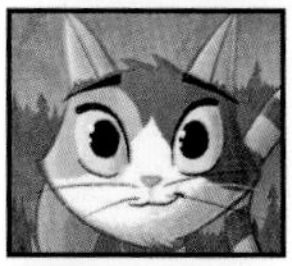

Cartoon – Is a pretty happy cat, and he lives with Chloe and her family. CHLOE, by Greg Tessier (writer) and Amandine (artist) is published by Charmz, a Papercutz imprint focused on young love. Even though Cartoon is a minor character in CHLOE, he's proven so popular that he'll soon co-star with Chloe in CHLOE & CARTOON #1.

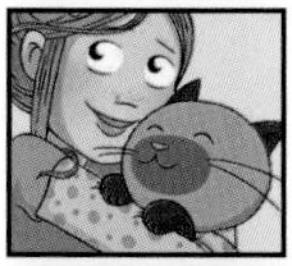

Cliff – Is the pet cat of the Loud family and is just one of the many occupants of THE LOUD HOUSE. There's Lincoln Loud, his ten sisters (Lori, Leni, Luna, Luan, Lynn, Lucy, Lisa, Lola, Lana, and Lily), his parents (Rita and Lynn Sr.), and the other pets, Charles (a dog), El Diablo (a snake), Hops (a frog), Walt (a bird), and Geo (a hamster). Cliff may not be the star of THE LOUD HOUSE, but the fact is that the Nickelodeon animated series is a big hit, as are the Papercutz graphic novels, so who's to say he's not a part of what's making THE LOUD HOUSE so successful?

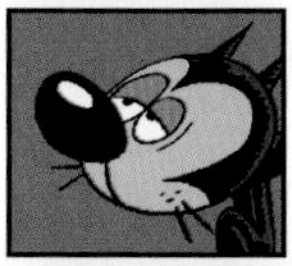

Hubble – Is the snarky pet cat of the Monroe family, and the unofficial mascot of the GEEKY F@B 5. Hubble has watched sisters Lucy and Marina Monroe, start up the Geeky F@b 5 with their friends, Zara, A.J., and Sofia, and tackle all sorts of problems, including finding homes for pets when the local animal shelter suffers major damage from a tornado. Even Hubble must admit that when girls stick together, anything is possible! Written by mother/daughter writing team, Liz & Lucy Lareau, and drawn by artist Ryan Jampole.

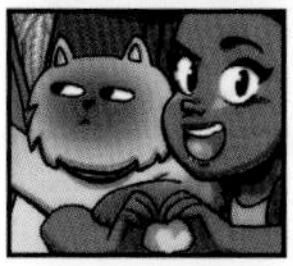

Sybil – Is the cute cat owned by fourteen-year-old (soon to be fifteen) Amy Von Brandt. Amy's life is never dull, and you can find out all about her and Sybil in AMY'S DIARY by Véronique Grisseaux (writer) and Laëtitia Ayné(artist), based on the novels by India Desjardins, and published by Charmz.

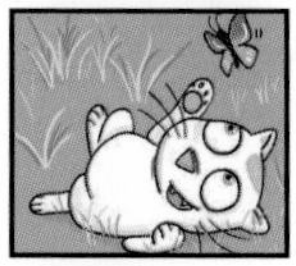

Sushi – Life was quiet for Cat (short for Catherine) and her dad until they adopt a cat named Sushi... then things get a bit too exciting! Between turning everything into either a personal scratching post or litter box, and the constant cat and mouse game of "love me/leave me alone," Cat and her dad have a lot to learn. CAT & CAT is a hilarious chronicle by writers Christophe Cazenove and Hervé Richez and artist Yrgane Ramon, of daily life of a single parent, a little girl named Cat, and their cat.

We could go on and on, but you get the point!

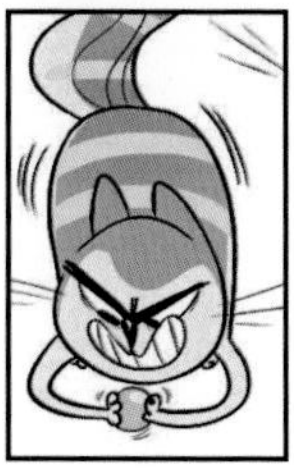

While this volume features the final stories featuring the Thea Sisters, we do have another charming graphic novel series featuring five fun females attending school together and having awesome adventures. But they're not mice, they're not even cats! They're flying unicorns known as Melowies. We invite you to peek at MELOWY #1 "The Test of Magic," in the special super-short preview on the following pages. And if the art seems a little familiar, it's by Ryan Jampole, colored by Laurie E. Smith, and lettered by Wilson Ramos Jr.—the same folks that brought you THEA STILTON! It's not written by Thea Stilton, but by Cortney Powell, based on characters created by Danielle Star. So, as we sadly say good-bye to Whale Island and those five Mouseford Academy students, let's all say hello to the five new students at Destiny—coming your way in MELOWY #1! Be sure to go to papercutz.com for more MELOWY news!

Thanks, Jim

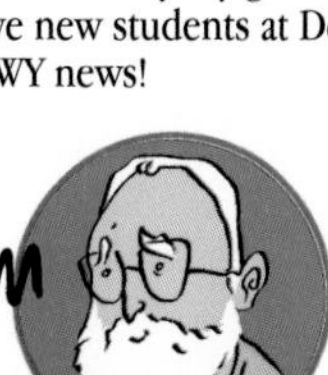

STAY IN TOUCH!

EMAIL:	salicrup@papercutz.com
WEB:	papercutz.com
TWITTER:	@papercutzgn
INSTAGRAM:	@papercutzgn
FACEBOOK:	PAPERCUTZGRAPHICNOVELS
FAN MAIL:	Papercutz, 160 Broadway, Suite 700, East Wing, New York, NY 10038

Special Preview of MELOWY #1...

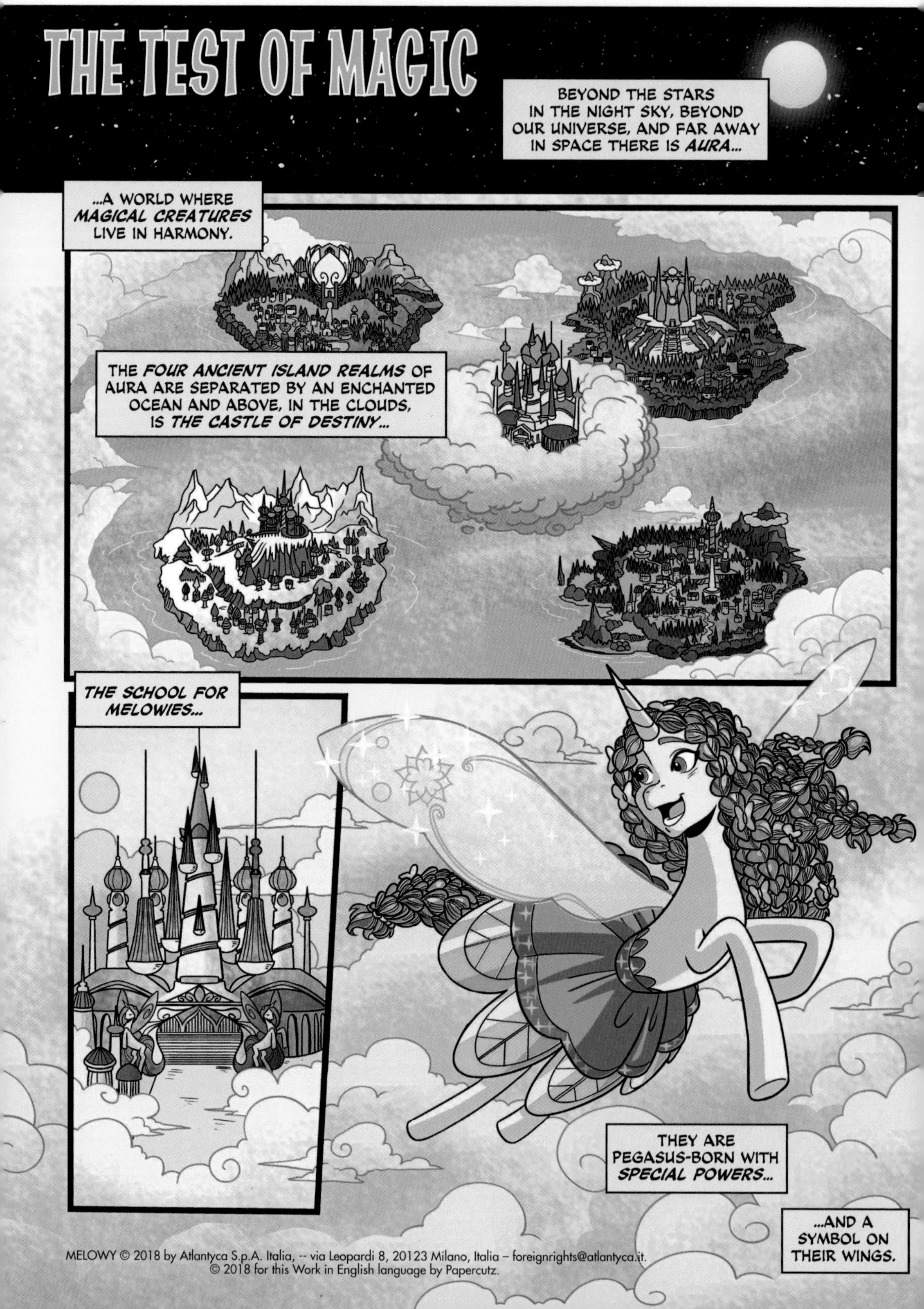

THE TEST OF MAGIC
BEYOND THE STARS IN THE NIGHT SKY, BEYOND OUR UNIVERSE, AND FAR AWAY IN SPACE THERE IS *AURA*...
...A WORLD WHERE *MAGICAL CREATURES* LIVE IN HARMONY.
THE *FOUR ANCIENT ISLAND REALMS* OF AURA ARE SEPARATED BY AN ENCHANTED OCEAN AND ABOVE, IN THE CLOUDS, IS *THE CASTLE OF DESTINY*...
THE SCHOOL FOR MELOWIES...
THEY ARE PEGASUS-BORN WITH *SPECIAL POWERS*...
...AND A SYMBOL ON THEIR WINGS.

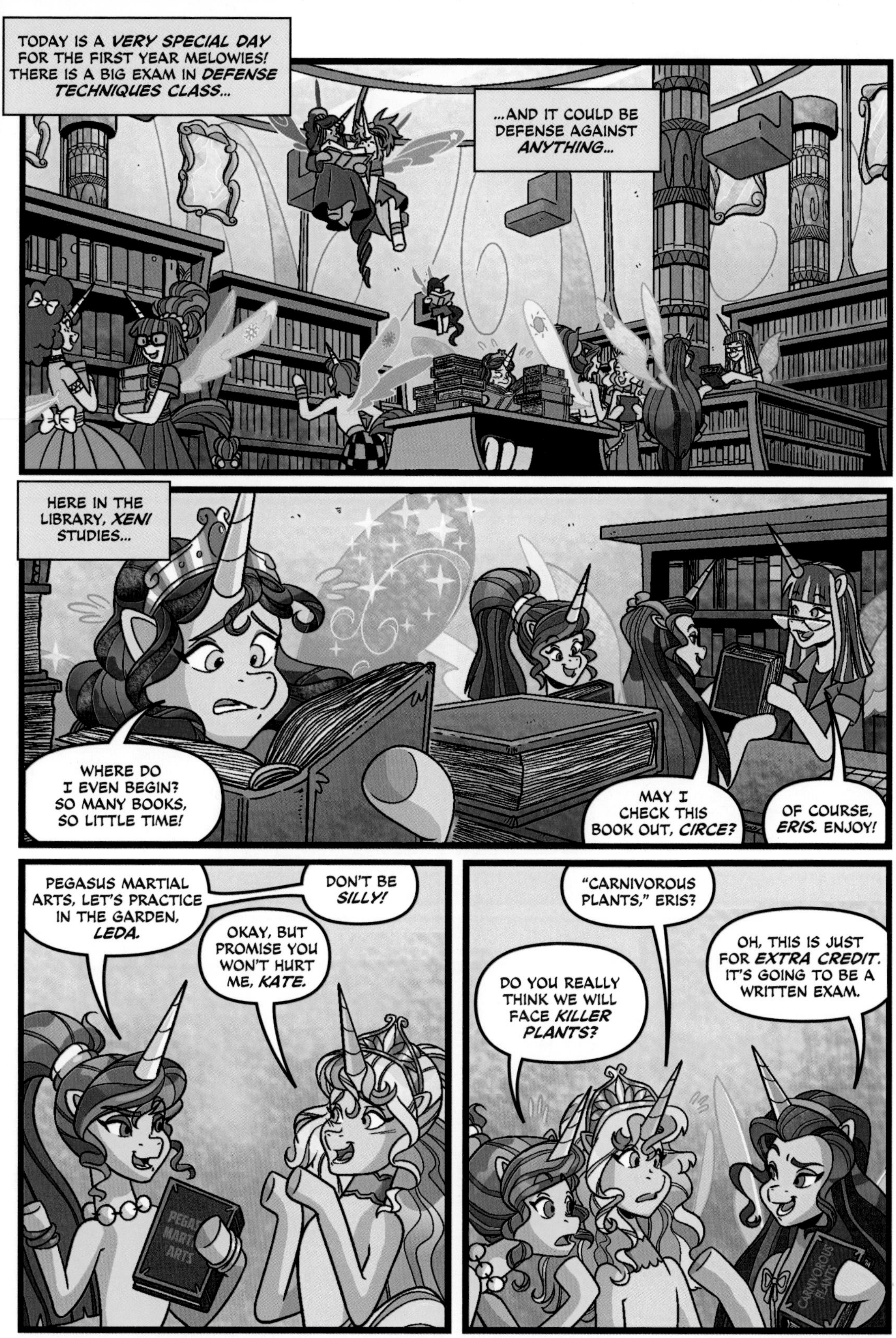
TODAY IS A VERY SPECIAL DAY FOR THE FIRST YEAR MELOWIES! THERE IS A BIG EXAM IN DEFENSE TECHNIQUES CLASS...
...AND IT COULD BE DEFENSE AGAINST ANYTHING...
HERE IN THE LIBRARY, XENI STUDIES...
WHERE DO I EVEN BEGIN? SO MANY BOOKS, SO LITTLE TIME!
MAY I CHECK THIS BOOK OUT, CIRCE?
OF COURSE, ERIS. ENJOY!
PEGASUS MARTIAL ARTS, LET'S PRACTICE IN THE GARDEN, LEDA.
DON'T BE SILLY!
OKAY, BUT PROMISE YOU WON'T HURT ME, KATE.
"CARNIVOROUS PLANTS," ERIS?
DO YOU REALLY THINK WE WILL FACE KILLER PLANTS?
OH, THIS IS JUST FOR EXTRA CREDIT. IT'S GOING TO BE A WRITTEN EXAM.
CARNIVOROUS PLANTS

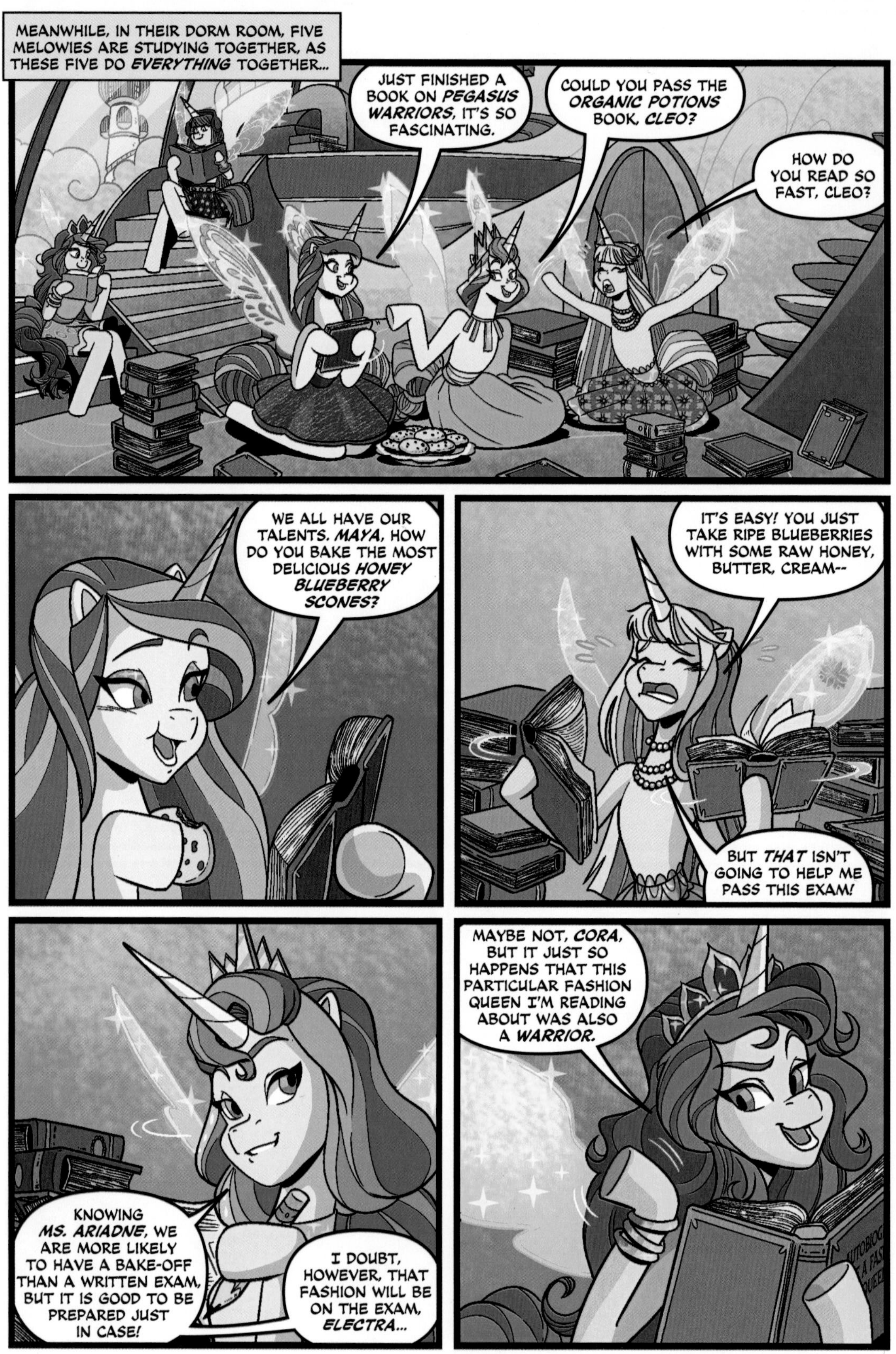
MEANWHILE, IN THEIR DORM ROOM, FIVE MELOWIES ARE STUDYING TOGETHER, AS THESE FIVE DO *EVERYTHING* TOGETHER...
JUST FINISHED A BOOK ON *PEGASUS WARRIORS*, IT'S SO FASCINATING.
COULD YOU PASS THE *ORGANIC POTIONS* BOOK, *CLEO*?
HOW DO YOU READ SO FAST, CLEO?
WE ALL HAVE OUR TALENTS. *MAYA*, HOW DO YOU BAKE THE MOST DELICIOUS *HONEY BLUEBERRY SCONES*?
IT'S EASY! YOU JUST TAKE RIPE BLUEBERRIES WITH SOME RAW HONEY, BUTTER, CREAM--
BUT *THAT* ISN'T GOING TO HELP ME PASS THIS EXAM!
KNOWING *MS. ARIADNE*, WE ARE MORE LIKELY TO HAVE A BAKE-OFF THAN A WRITTEN EXAM, BUT IT IS GOOD TO BE PREPARED JUST IN CASE!
I DOUBT, HOWEVER, THAT FASHION WILL BE ON THE EXAM, *ELECTRA*...
MAYBE NOT, *CORA*, BUT IT JUST SO HAPPENS THAT THIS PARTICULAR FASHION QUEEN I'M READING ABOUT WAS ALSO A *WARRIOR*.

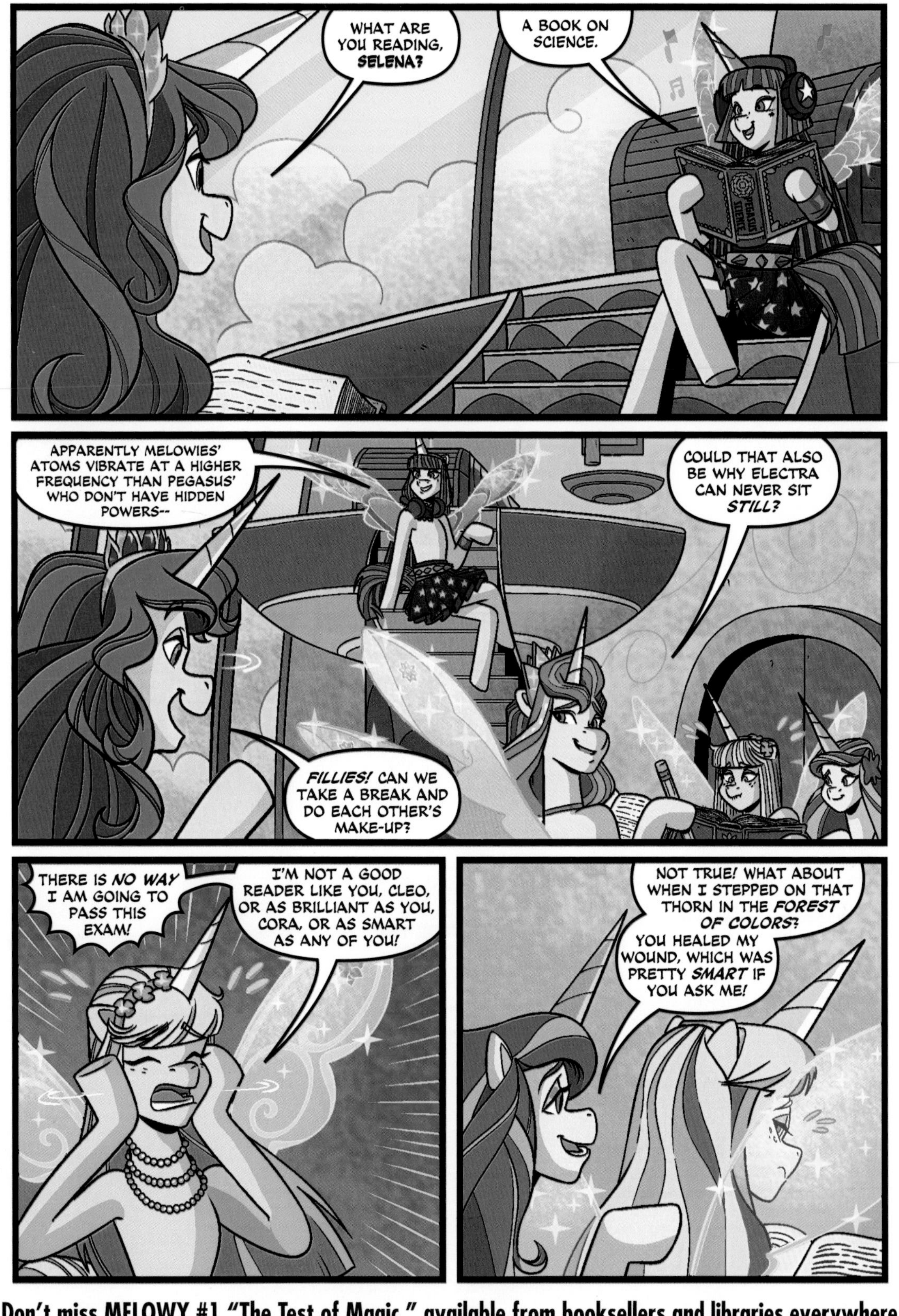

WHAT ARE YOU READING, SELENA?
A BOOK ON SCIENCE.
PEGASUS SCIENCE
APPARENTLY MELOWIES' ATOMS VIBRATE AT A HIGHER FREQUENCY THAN PEGASUS' WHO DON'T HAVE HIDDEN POWERS--
COULD THAT ALSO BE WHY ELECTRA CAN NEVER SIT STILL?
FILLIES! CAN WE TAKE A BREAK AND DO EACH OTHER'S MAKE-UP?
THERE IS NO WAY I AM GOING TO PASS THIS EXAM!
I'M NOT A GOOD READER LIKE YOU, CLEO, OR AS BRILLIANT AS YOU, CORA, OR AS SMART AS ANY OF YOU!
NOT TRUE! WHAT ABOUT WHEN I STEPPED ON THAT THORN IN THE FOREST OF COLORS?
YOU HEALED MY WOUND, WHICH WAS PRETTY SMART IF YOU ASK ME!

Geronimo Stilton

GRAPHIC NOVELS AVAILABLE FROM PAPERCUTZ

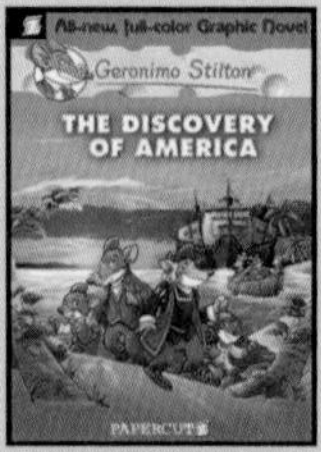
All-new, full-color Graphic Novel
Geronimo Stilton
THE DISCOVERY OF AMERICA
PAPERCUTZ

#1
"The Discovery of America"

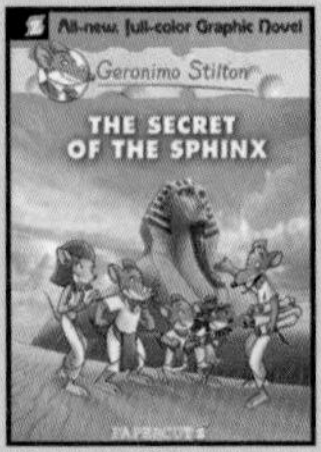
All-new, full-color Graphic Novel
Geronimo Stilton
THE SECRET OF THE SPHINX

#2
"The Secret of the Sphinx"

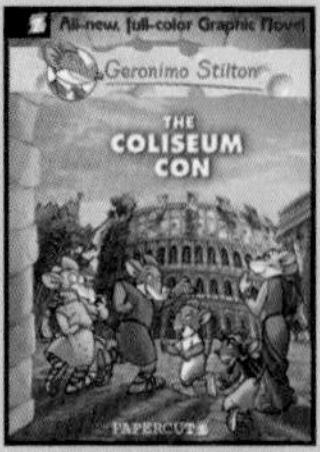
All-new, full-color Graphic Novel
Geronimo Stilton
THE COLISEUM CON

#3
"The Coliseum Con"

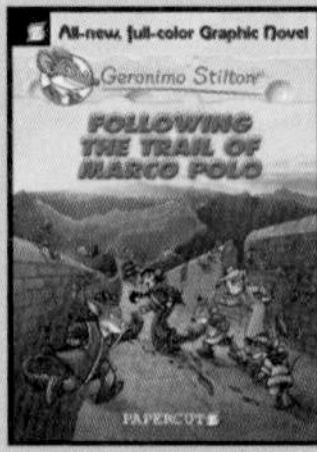
All-new, full-color Graphic Novel
Geronimo Stilton
FOLLOWING THE TRAIL OF MARCO POLO

#4
"Following the Trail of Marco Polo"

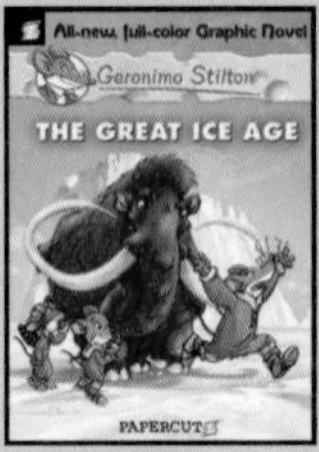
All-new, full-color Graphic Novel
Geronimo Stilton
THE GREAT ICE AGE

#5
"The Great Ice Age"

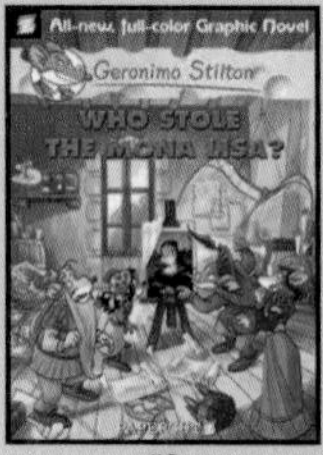
All-new, full-color Graphic Novel
Geronimo Stilton
WHO STOLE THE MONA LISA?

#6
"Who Stole The Mona Lisa?"

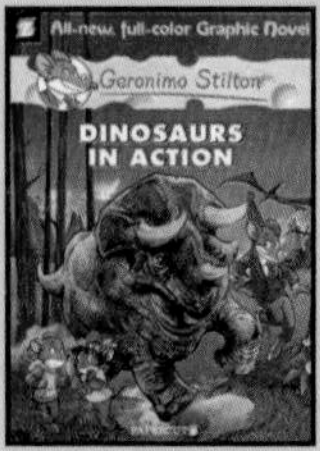
All-new, full-color Graphic Novel
Geronimo Stilton
DINOSAURS IN ACTION

#7
"Dinosaurs in Action"

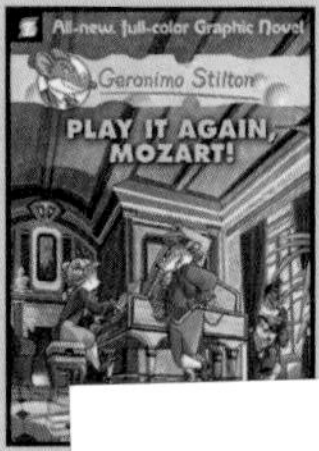
All-new, full-color Graphic Novel
Geronimo Stilton
PLAY IT AGAIN, MOZART!

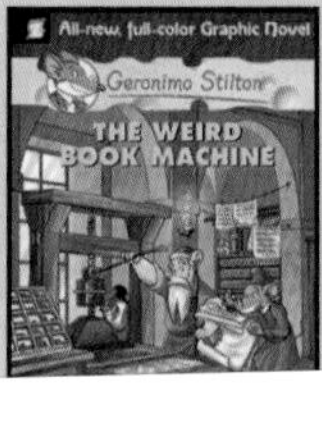
All-new, full-color Graphic Novel
Geronimo Stilton
THE WEIRD BOOK MACHINE

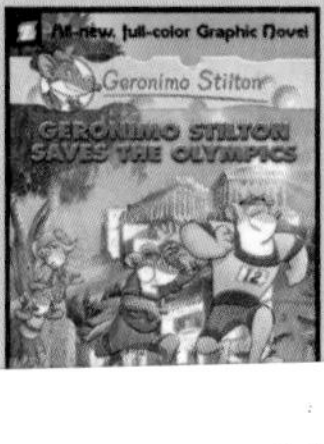
All-new, full-color Graphic Novel
Geronimo Stilton
GERONIMO STILTON SAVES THE OLYMPICS

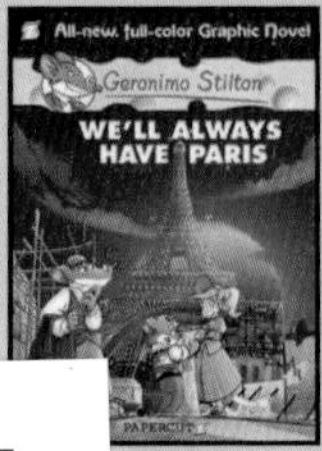
All-new, full-color Graphic Novel
Geronimo Stilton
WE'LL ALWAYS HAVE PARIS

#11
"We'll Always Have Paris"

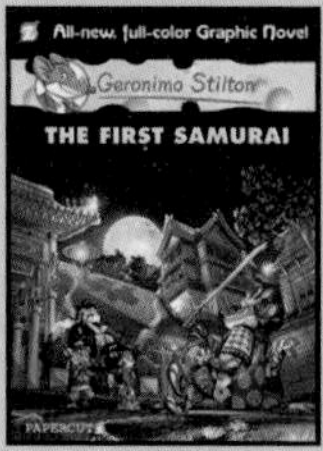
All-new, full-color Graphic Novel
Geronimo Stilton
THE FIRST SAMURAI

#12
"The First Samurai"

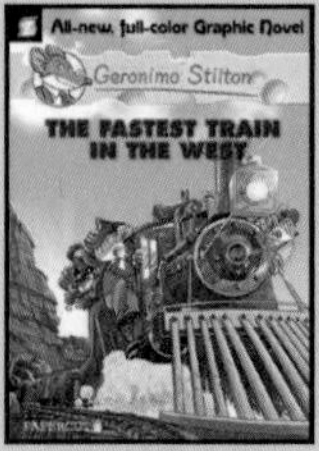
All-new, full-color Graphic Novel
Geronimo Stilton
THE FASTEST TRAIN IN THE WEST

#13
"The Fastest Train in the West"

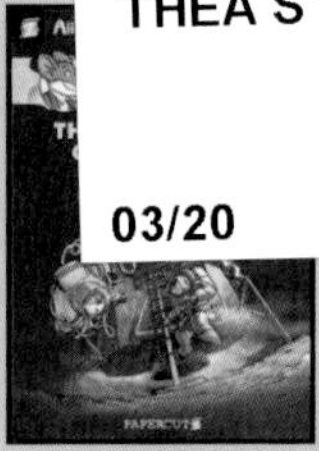

#14
"The First Mouse on the Moon"

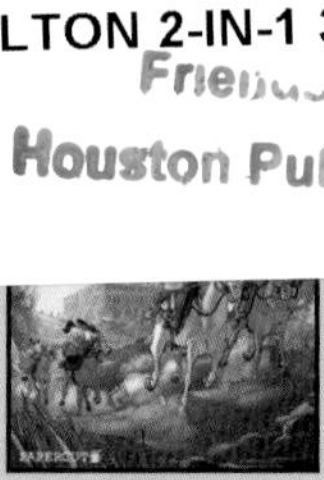

#15
"All for Stilton, Stilton for All!"

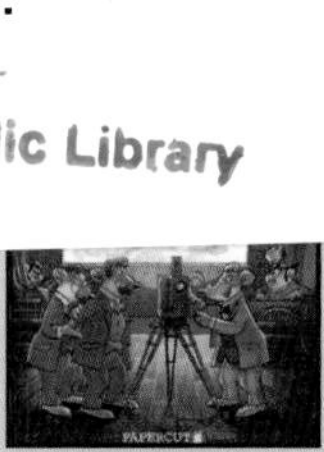

#16
"Lights, Camera, Stilton!"

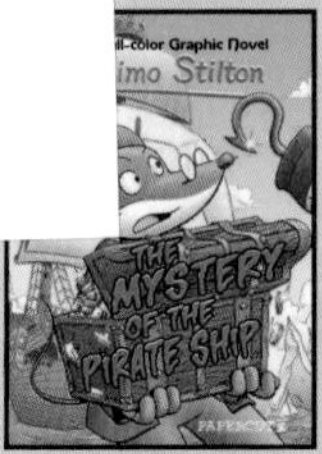
THE MYSTERY OF THE PIRATE SHIP

#17
"The Mystery of the Pirate Ship"

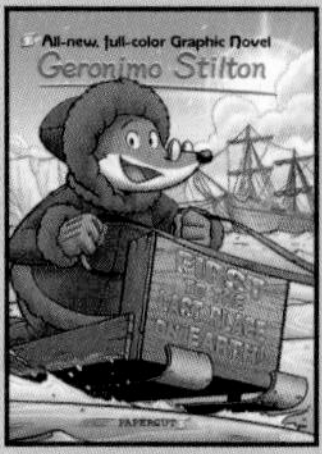
All-new, full-color Graphic Novel
Geronimo Stilton

#18
"First to the Last Place on Earth"

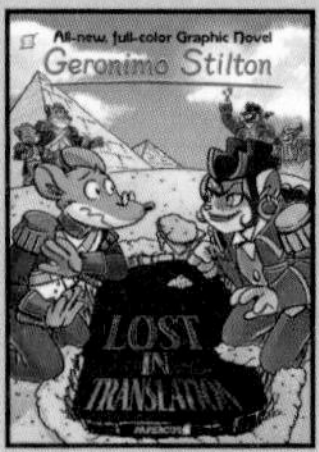
All-new, full-color Graphic Novel
Geronimo Stilton
LOST IN TRANSLATION

#19
"Lost in Translation"

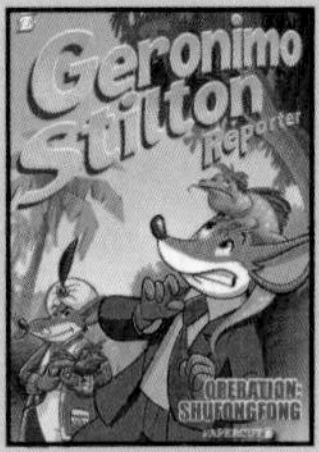
Geronimo Stilton Reporter
OPERATION: SHUFONGFONG

GERONIMO STILTON REPORTER #1
"Operation Shufongfong"

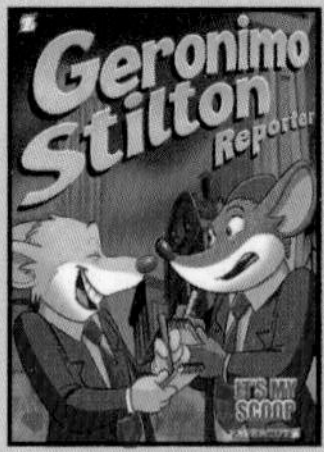
Geronimo Stilton Reporter
IT'S MY SCOOP

GERONIMO STILTON REPORTER #2
"It's My Scoop"

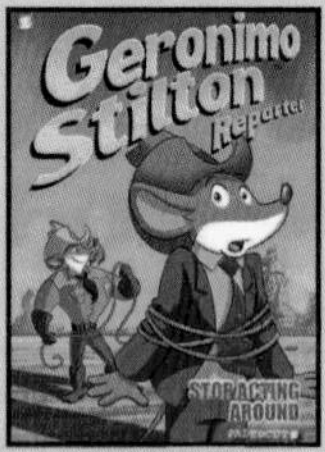
Geronimo Stilton Reporter
STOP ACTING AROUND

GERONIMO STILTON REPORTER #3
"Stop Acting Around"

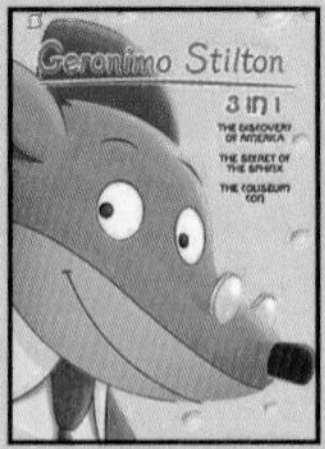
Geronimo Stilton
3 IN 1

GERONIMO STILTON 3 in 1 #1

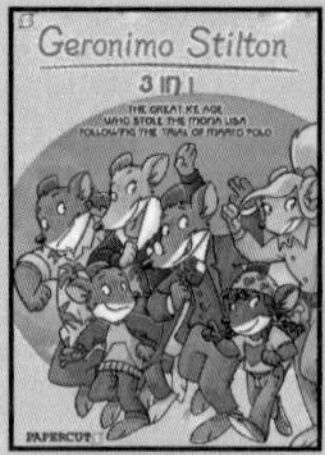
Geronimo Stilton
3 IN 1

GERONIMO STILTON 3 in 1 #2

...ALSO AVAILABLE WHEREVER E-BOOKS ARE SOLD!

GERONIMO STILTON and GERONIMO STILTON REPORTER graphic novels are available for $9.99 each, only in hardcover. GERONIMO STILTON 3 IN 1 graphic novels are available for $14.99 each, only in paperback. Available from booksellers everywhere. You can also order online from papercutz.com. Or call 1-800-886-1223, Monday through Friday, 9 – 5 EST. MC, Visa, and AmEx accepted. To order by mail, please add $5.00 for postage and handling for first book ordered, $1.00 for each additional book and make check payable to NBM Publishing. Send to: Papercutz, 160 Broadway, Suite 700, East Wing, New York, NY 10038.

See more at papercutz.com

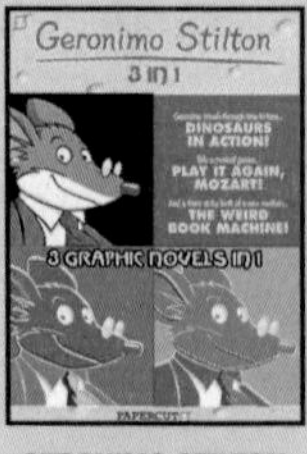
Geronimo Stilton
3 IN 1
DINOSAURS IN ACTION!
PLAY IT AGAIN, MOZART!
THE WEIRD BOOK MACHINE!
3 GRAPHIC NOVELS IN 1

GERONIMO STILTON 3 in 1 #3